DEAD END

"Don't move, Solo," came a voice from the past.

Han froze.

The High Priest had a blaster rifle in his hand, and his eyes held a mad glitter that told Han there was no way to talk his way out of this one.

"Hands raised," the Priest directed. Han, Chewie, and Bria all put their hands up. Han glanced at the others, trying frantically to think of a way to get out of this.

"I shall enjoy this," the Priest said.

"Hey," Han said, "Jabba's a friend of mine. You kill me, he won't take it kindly."

The Priest laughed wheezily. "Hutts do not have friends," he said. "Farewell, Solo."

Pointing the blaster at Han, the Priest's small, stubby finger began to tighten on the trigger.

Han shut his eyes. He heard the sound of the blaster's whine—

—and he felt nothing. No pain. No searing heat.

After a prolonged moment, Han heard the sound of a body fall with a loud *thud*.

STAR WARS.

Rebel Dawn

A. C. Crispin

SPECTRA ™

BANTAM BOOKS
NEW YORK • TORONTO • LONDON • SYDNEY • AUCKLAND

REBEL DAWN

A Bantam Spectra Book / March 1998

SPECTRA and the portrayal of a boxed "s" are trademarks of Bantam
Books, a division of Random House, Inc.

®, TM & © 1998 by Lucasfilm Ltd. Used under authorization.
Cover art by Drew Struzan. Cover art copyright © 1998 by
Lucasfilm Ltd.

ISBN 0-553-57417-5

Published simultaneously in the United States and Canada

Bantam Books are published by Bantam Books, a division of Random
House, Inc. Its trademark, consisting of the words "Bantam Books"
and the portrayal of a rooster, is Registered in U.S. Patent and
Trademark Office and in other countries. Marca Registrada. Bantam
Books, 1540 Broadway, New York, New York 10036.

PRINTED IN THE UNITED STATES OF AMERICA

OPM   19   18   17   16   15   14   13   12   11

This book is dedicated to the memory of Brian Daley.

Acknowledgments

Just about two years age now, Bantam asked me to write the story of Han Solo's life in the ten years before *Star Wars: A New Hope*. I felt so honored, and a bit intimidated by the scope of the task that lay before me.

And now . . . it's behind me. I can hardly believe it. For two years, I've "lived" in the *Star Wars* universe, watching the films over and over, reading the reference books, the other novels, and talking to *Star Wars* fans at conventions, in online chat rooms, and at book signings. *Star Wars* has, quite literally, been my life.

It feels funny to say good-bye to all of that, at least for the immediate future. I'm looking forward to getting back to my big fantasy trilogy for Avon, a project I interrupted (Thank you, John and both Jennifers!) to do these Han Solo novels. There's sadness, too, in leaving behind this universe that I've enjoyed so much. But I've made so many new friends that I'm sure they'll keep me up on Mr. Lucas's universe.

The list of people who helped me with these books continues to grow. *Rebel Dawn* was a tough book to write. I felt as though I had a responsibility to "set the stage" for Han's role in the *Star Wars* films—and that's a tall order. I couldn't have produced this novel without the help of many people. I tried hard to avoid any mistakes in *Star Wars* continuity, but if they exist, they're my own. Many grateful thanks to the following folks:

First and foremost, my dear friend and crackerjack military expert, Steve Osmanski. Steve and his wife Mary have been my staunchest supporters and I could not have done it without you both.

Michael Capobianco, sweetheart, friend, partner. As always, Michael kept me on track, and spotted about a zillion plot holes before they became problems. I suspect at this point we've become two of the world's foremost authorities on Hutts. A distinction to be proud of, truly!

Rich Handley, Craig Robert Carey (godfather of Wookiees!), Mike Beidler, and Pablo Hidalgo, for vital information regarding the *Star Wars* universe. Thanks, guys.

Peter, Paul, Eric, and Tim of West End Games.

Rob Brown and Curtis Saxton for information regarding the *Millennium Falcon*, "the fastest hunk of junk in the galaxy."

R. Lee Brown of Echo Station and Peet Janes of Dark Horse Comics.

My editor, Pat LoBrutto, who is one in a million, and to whom I owe a homemade lasagna dinner with all the trimmings. Also, Tom Dupree, for choosing me to work on the project in the first place. And Evelyn Cainto, who keeps the *Star Wars* editorial department running, and who is always a sympathetic ear.

Sue Rostoni of the Lucasfilm Licensing department, who helped immeasurably, keeping me consistent with the rest of the *Star Wars* universe.

My fellow *Star Wars* novelists, who created material I "borrowed" for *Rebel Dawn*: L. Neil Smith, Brian Daley, Kevin J. Anderson, Kristine Kathryn Rusch, Steve Perry, Mike Stackpole, Timothy Zahn, Rebecca Moesta, and Michael P. Kube-McDowell.

The Star Ladies and all my on-line friends, who made suggestions and took such a keen interest in Han Solo's further adventures. You all know who you are.

Cathy Cathers, Chris Petescia, Roseann Caputo, Glenn Thibert, Linda Jean Weldon, Tim, and Aaron.

Drew Struzan, who designed and painted the great book covers. I loved every one!

And, of course, George Lucas, who started it all. Thank you, Mr. Lucas. It has truly been an honor.

May the Force be with you all . . .

Chapter One:
Winners and Losers

Han Solo leaned forward in the pilot's seat of the *Wayward Girl*. "Entering atmosphere, Captain," he said. He watched the system's big, pale sun slip into the great curve of ruddy light at the world's edge and disappear behind the planet's limb. Bespin's huge, dark nightside loomed up to blot out the stars. Han checked his sensors. "They say Bespin's got some big flyin'—or should I say, floatin'—creatures in its atmosphere, so keep those forward shields at maximum strength."

One-handed, his co-pilot made an adjustment. "What's our ETA to Cloud City, Han?" she asked, a hint of strain in her voice.

"Not long now," Han replied reassuringly, as the *Girl* sliced into the upper atmosphere, swooping over the planet's dark pole, lightning far below making a flickering fog of dim light. "ETA twenty-six minutes. We ought to be in Cloud City in time to catch a late dinner."

"The sooner the better," she commented, grimacing as she flexed her right arm in its pressure-sling. "This thing itches like fury."

"Just hang on, Jadonna," Han said. "We'll get you straight to the med-facility."

She nodded. "Hey, Han, no complaints from me. You've done great. I'll just be glad to get this arm into bacta."

Han shook his head. "Ripped cartilage and ligaments . . . that's gotta hurt," he said. "But Cloud City's sure to have adequate meds."

She nodded. "Oh, they do. It's quite a place, Han. You'll see."

Jadonna Veloz was a short, stocky, dark-skinned woman with long, straight black hair. Han had met her two days ago, after she'd advertised from Alderaan on the spacer-nets for a pilot to fly her ship to Bespin. Veloz's arm had been injured when it was struck by a malfunctioning anti-grav loader, but, determined to meet her tight shipping deadline, she'd postponed real treatment until she delivered her cargo.

After paying Han's passage from Corellia on a fast shuttle to Alderaan, he'd taken over as pilot, and brought them to Bespin right on schedule.

The *Wayward Girl* was through the wispy exosphere now, and plunging deeper, moving toward the evening twilight, blue sky building above them. Han altered course, heading southwest, toward where the setting sun must be. As they streaked along, the tops of the piled, puffy masses of clouds far below began taking on colors, deep crimson and coral, then yellow-orange.

Han Solo had his own reasons for needing a ride to Bespin. If it hadn't been for Jadonna's ad on the nets, he'd have had to dip into his rapidly dwindling stash of credits to buy passage for himself on a commercial vessel.

Veloz's accident couldn't have come at a better time, far as Han was concerned. With the credits she'd promised him, he'd be able to afford a cheap room and a few meals during the big sabacc tournament. The buy-in alone was a staggering ten thousand credits. Han had barely managed to scrape those credits together by fencing the small golden palador figurine he'd stolen from the Ylesian High Priest Teroenza, plus the dragon pearl he'd discovered in Admiral Greelanx's office.

The Corellian wished for a moment that Chewie was here with him, but he'd had to leave the Wookiee behind in their little flat on Nar Shaddaa because he couldn't afford to buy his passage.

They were deep into the atmosphere now, and Han could actually see Bespin's sun, a squashed looking orange ball just clearing a massive bank of clouds. The *Girl* was surrounded by a golden glory of heaped clouds—as golden as Han Solo's dreams of wealth.

Han was staking everything on this big gamble . . . and he'd always been lucky at sabacc. But would luck be enough to let him win? He'd be playing against professional gamblers like Lando.

The Corellian swallowed, then resolutely concentrated on his piloting. This was no time to get an attack of nerves. Han made another adjustment to the *Girl's* approach vector, thinking that he ought to be within range of Cloud City traffic control any time now.

As if in answer to his thoughts, a voice spoke up from his comm. "Incoming vessel, please identify yourself."

Jadonna Veloz reached left-handed to activate their comm. "Cloud City traffic control, this is the *Wayward Girl* out of Alderaan. Our approach vector is . . ." she glanced at Han's instruments and reeled off a string of numbers.

"*Wayward Girl,* we confirm your vector. Cloud City is your destination?"

"That's an affirmative, traffic control," Jadonna said. Han grinned. From what he'd heard, Cloud City was about all there was to Bespin. There were the mining facilities, of course, and gas refining, storage and shipping facilities, but more than half of all incoming traffic was probably bound for the luxurious resort hotels. In the past few years, bored tourists had made the city in the clouds one of their favorite vacation playgrounds.

"Traffic control," Jadonna continued, "we have a priority shipment for the Yarith Bespin kitchens. Nerf tenderloins in stasis. Request a landing vector."

"Permission granted, *Wayward Girl,*" came the voice of the traffic controller. The controller's voice took on a more informal note. "Nerf steaks, eh? I'll have to take my wife out this week. She's been wanting something fancy, and that's a treat we don't get too often."

"These are prime cuts, traffic control," Veloz said. "Hope the chef at the Yarith Bespin appreciates them."

"Oh, he's good," the voice said, then the controller reverted to his official tones. "*Wayward Girl,* I have you slotted in at Level 65, Docking Bay 7A. Repeat. Level 65, 7A. Do you copy?"

"We copy, Cloud City Controller."

"And your assigned landing vector is . . ." the voice hesitated, then gave them more coordinates.

Han punched them into the navicomputer, then they settled back to enjoy the ride. He found himself looking forward to seeing the fabled Cloud City. Bespin itself had already been famous, even before the resort was built. They mined tibanna gas here, which was used in starship engines, and in powering blasters.

Han wasn't sure how they actually mined the gas, but he knew that tibanna gas was very valuable, so the miners must be doing well. Before it was discovered in Bespin's atmosphere, tibanna gas had usually been found in stellar chromospheres and nebular clusters—which made harvesting it hazardous, to say the least. Then somebody had stumbled across the fact that Bespin's atmosphere was loaded with it.

Picking up a sudden burst of electrical activity on his sensors, Han hastily changed course. "Hey—what's *that*?" He pointed at the viewscreen. To their right now, was a monstrous, half-seen shape, drifting amid those incredible aurulent clouds. The thing was so large that it would have dwarfed many small Corellian cities.

Jadonna leaned forward. "That's a beldon!" she exclaimed. "They're really rare. In all the years I've been flying through these clouds, I've never seen one."

Han squinted at the mammoth creature as the *Girl* streaked by it. The beldon resembled some of the gelatinous ocean creatures he'd seen on some worlds, with a huge, dome-like top, and many small feeding tentacles hanging down beneath it.

Han checked his landing vector. "Right on the credits, Captain," he said. Behind them, the leviathan faded into the distance. Han saw another, smaller shape ahead of them that almost resembled an upside-down beldon, and realized it was Cloud City.

It hung in the clouds like some kind of exotic wineglass, topped with a jeweled crown of rounded towers, domed buildings, communication spires, and refinery stacks. In the last wash of sunset, it glowed like a corusca gem.

Staying on their approach vector, Han sent them skimming over the domed buildings of the cityscape in the clouds. Moments later, he brought the *Girl* down in a perfect landing on their assigned spot.

After receiving his pay, and saying farewell to Captain Veloz, Han went looking for a robo-hack to take him to the posh Yarith Bespin hotel, where the sabacc tournament was being held.

Moments later he was punching in his destination on a keypad, sending the little robo-hack zipping through the city streets, up and down levels, traveling at a pace that would have made most humans dizzy—especially when the little vehicle "hopped" low-lying buildings, giving Han a glimpse of the clouds surrounding them and the yawning depths below them. It was almost full night now, and the city sparkled like a lady's open jewel box.

Minutes later the robo-hack pulled up before the Yarith Bespin. Han waved the luggage droid aside and walked through the massive entrance. He'd been in posh hotels before, while touring with his magician friend, Xaverri, so the opulent interior with its spidery, crisscrossing glidewalks that spanned the stories-high atrium didn't phase him. He saw a sign reading "Tournament Registration" in at least 20 languages, and followed the arrow up the glide-lift to the mezzanine.

When he stepped off the floating walkway, he headed purposefully toward the large tables. The place was thronged with gamblers of all species, sizes and descriptions. Han registered, checked his blaster (all weapons had to be checked), received an ID badge, and a voucher that he'd cash in as he needed betting chips. The first game would start tomorrow at midday.

Just as he turned away from the registration area, chip voucher tucked securely into a pocket inside his shirt, next to his skin, Han heard a familiar voice.

"Han! Hey, Han! Over here!"

He turned and saw Lando Calrissian waving to him from across the mezzanine. Waving to show he'd heard, Han jogged over to the glidewalk and hopped aboard, even as Lando leaped aboard the one coming toward Han's side of the enormous room.

When he'd last seen Lando, the gambler was heading off for action in the Oseon system. But he'd been talking about this tournament for months, so Han had been expecting to run into him here.

"Hey, Han!" Lando's dark features broke into a wide grin as their respective glidewalks brought them face-to-face. "Long time no see, you old rascal!"

Han leaped nimbly across open air from his glidewalk to the one Lando was standing on. He'd barely landed before Calrissian grabbed him in a hug that would have done Chewbacca credit. "Good to see you, Lando!" he gasped, as Calrissian thumped him on the back one final time.

The friends stepped off the glidewalk back at the registration area, and stood there a moment, eyeing each other. Han studied his friend, realizing that Lando looked very prosperous—the gambling tables out in the Oseon must be loaded with easy marks. The gambler was wearing an expensive outfit made from Askajian fabric, the best in the galaxy. A new black and silver cape swung behind him, draped in the latest fashion.

Han smiled. The last time he'd seen Lando, the gambler had barely begun growing a mustache. Now his facial adornment was mature, though trimmed. It lent his features a rather piratical air. Han pointed at it. "I see you decided to keep the lip-fur."

Lando stroked the mustache proudly. "Every woman I've met has been *most* complimentary," he said. "I should have done it long ago."

"Some people need all the help they can get," Han

teased. "It's a shame you don't have my way with the ladies, old pal."

Lando snorted derisively.

Han looked around. "So . . . where's your little red-eyed droid buddy? Don't tell me you went and lost Vuffi Raa in a sabacc game?"

Lando shook his head. "Han, it's a long story. To tell it properly, I need a tall glass of something refreshing in front of me."

"Well, what's the short version, then?" Han asked. "Don't tell me the little guy got tired of calling you 'Master' and decided he could do better selling his Class Two abilities somewhere else?"

Lando shook his head, his expression suddenly serious. "Han, you're not going to believe this, but Vuffi Raa decided to go back to his people and grow up. Fulfill his destiny."

Han grimaced. "Huh? He's a *droid*. What do you mean, *destiny*?"

"Vuffi Raa is . . . was . . . a baby starship. I know it sounds crazy, but it's true. He comes from a . . . unique . . . species. Gigantic droid-ships that roam the stars. Sentient, but not biological, life-forms."

Han stared at his friend. "Lando, you been sniffing ryll? You sound like you spent the whole day in the bar."

Lando held up a hand. "It's the truth, Han. You see, there was this evil sorcerer named Rokur Gepta, who turned out to be a Croke, and these vacuumbreathers, and a big fight in this huge Star Cave, and—"

"Cheater!" A deep, raspy voice shouted, startling the friends. "Get him! Don't let him play! That's Han Solo, and he cheats at sabacc!"

Han wheeled around to find an enraged Barabel female bearing down on him. The alien limped slightly from a stiff knee, but she was closing at a respectable clip, massive teeth bared. Barabels were huge, black reptiloids, and Han had only met a few of them in his travels. And only one female.

This female, as a matter of fact.

Han gulped and his hand went down to his blaster, only to slap impotently against his thigh. *Damnation!* He began backing up, holding up his hands placatingly. "Now, Shallamar . . ." he began.

Lando, always quick on the uptake, made sure he was nowhere near the Barabel's approach vector. "Security!" he shouted. "We need security here! Somebody call security!"

The Barabel sputtered and hissed with rage. "He uses skifters! Cheats! Arrest him!"

Han backed up until he bumped into one of the registration tables, then, one-handed, he vaulted it. The Barabel's teeth flashed. "Coward! Come out from behind there! Arrest him!"

"Now, Shallamar," Han said. "I beat you fair and square that time. Holding grudges isn't very sportsmanlike. . . ."

With a bellow, she rushed him—

—only to stop and fall heavily to the floor as a tanglefield encased her feet. Shallamar thrashed, slapping the carpet with her tail, cursing and bellowing.

Han looked over at the hotel security forces, and drew a long breath of relief.

Ten minutes later, with the Barabel still under restraints, Han, Lando and Shallamar were in the security offices, facing the security chief. Shallamar was sulking, because the chief had sensor-scanned Han from the tips of his toes to the top of his head, and the Corellian had proved to be absolutely free of any cheating devices.

Now the Barabel hunkered uncomfortably, her feet still restrained in the tangle-field, as the security chief warned her that any further displays would get her ejected from the competition. ". . . and I think you owe Solo here an apology," the chief concluded.

Shallamar snarled . . . but softly. "I will not molest him further. You have my honor-word."

"But—" the security chief started.

Han waved a hand at him. "Let's not push it, sir. If Shallamar leaves me alone, that's fine with me. I'm just glad to prove that I'm an honest player."

The chief shrugged. "Whatever you say, Solo. Okay, you two are free to go." He glanced at Han and Lando. "I'll release the tangle-field and turn her loose in a couple of minutes." He turned back to the Barabel. "And you, my lady, will be under surveillance. Please keep that in mind. We're running a tournament here, not a free-for-all. Is that clear?"

"Clear," she rasped.

Han and Lando left the office. Han didn't say anything, but he knew Lando too well to think that his friend would let this pass. Sure enough, when they stepped onto the glidewalk leading to the cafe, Lando grinned broadly. "Han, Han . . . yet another old flame, eh? You're so right . . . you certainly have a way with the ladies, you old rogue!"

Han bared his teeth in a snarl nearly as fearsome as Shallamar's. "Shut *up*, Lando. Just . . . shut up."

By then, Lando was laughing too hard to speak anyway . . .

It took the two friends several hours to catch up on events. Han heard the whole story of Lando's adventures in the Oseon system. He discovered that since he'd last seen his friend, Lando had won and lost several fortunes, most recently a cargo of gemstones. "You should have seen them, Han," Lando said, mournfully. "They were gorgeous. Filled half the *Falcon*'s cargo bay. If only I'd hung onto them, instead of using most of them to buy half of that dratted berubian mine!"

Han looked at his friend with mingled sympathy and exasperation. "Salted, right? Proved to be worthless."

"You got it. How did you know?"

"I knew somebody once who ran that scam. Only it was a duralloy asteroid." Han neglected to mention that he'd once lost out on a half-million-credit uranium mine that he'd won in a sabacc game. The mine had been genuine, but the books had been so cooked that he'd been lucky to escape prosecution when the stockholders began their investigation. . . .

But all that was in the past, and Han Solo made it a policy never to indulge in regrets over failed ventures.

"Speaking of the *Falcon*," he said, "where've you got her docked?"

"Oh, she's not here," Lando said. "I left her back at the lot on Nar Shaddaa. Half the trick to winning big at the tables is being able to psych your opponents out, presenting yourself as someone who can afford to play big, win big and lose big. Makes bluffing much more effective. . . ."

"I'll remember that," Han said, filing away the advice. "So, how'd you get here?"

"I came in on one of those big luxury liners, the *Queen of Empire*," Lando said. "Arrived in style. Not to mention that the ship's casino is one of the finest I've encountered. The *Queen* and I go way back."

Han smiled slyly. "I ran into Blue a few weeks ago, and she told me that you were traveling in style aboard that new ship of Drea Renthal's. *Renthal's Vigilance*, that *Carrack*-class picket ship she salvaged after the Battle of Nar Shaddaa."

Lando cleared his throat. "Drea's a great lady," he said. "For a pirate, she's surprisingly . . . refined."

Han snickered. "Whoa, Lando! Isn't she a little old for you? She's gotta be at least forty! How'd you like bein' a pirate queen's favorite plaything?"

Lando bristled. "I wasn't . . . She's not . . ."

Han laughed. "Almost old enough to be your mother, huh?"

Lando's teeth flashed beneath his mustache. "Hardly. And Han . . . my mother was *nothing* like Drea. Trust me."

"So why'd you break up?" Han wanted to know.

"Life aboard a pirate vessel is . . . interesting," Lando said. "But a little too . . . coarse . . . for my taste."

Han, eyeing his friend's dandified clothes, nodded. "I'll bet."

Lando sobered. "But, hey . . . Drea and I parted friends," he added. "These last few months I needed . . . I was . . ." he shrugged, obviously uncomfortable. "Well, Drea came along at a good time. I was . . . Well, it was nice having the company."

Han eyed his friend. "You mean you missed Vuffi Raa?"

"Well . . . how can you miss a droid? But . . . you know, Han, he was really a companion. There were times I didn't even think of him as mechanical. I'd gotten used to having the little guy around, you know? So when the little vacuum cleaner went off with his kinfolk, I did find myself actually . . . missing him."

Han thought about what it would be like to lose Chewie, and could only nod in silent agreement.

The two sat quietly for a moment, sipping their drinks, enjoying the companionship. Finally Han fought back a yawn, and stood up. "Gotta get some sleep," he said. "Tomorrow's going to be a big day."

"See you at the tables," Lando said, and they parted.

Sabacc is an ancient game, dating back to the early days of the Old Republic. Of all the games of chance, sabacc is the most complex, the most unpredictable, the most thrilling—and the most heartbreaking.

The game is played with a deck of seventy-six card-chips. The value of any card-chip can alter throughout the game at random intervals, via electronic impulses transmitted by the "randomizer." In less than a second, a winning hand can change to a "bomb out."

There are four suits in the deck: sabers, staves, flasks and coins. Numbered cards range from positive one to positive eleven, and there are four cards of "rank:" the Commander, the Mistress, the Master and the Ace, with numerical values of positive twelve to fifteen.

Sixteen face cards complete the deck, two of each type, with assorted zero or negative values: the Idiot, the Queen of Air and Darkness, Endurance, Balance, Demise, Moderation, the Evil One and the Star.

There are two different pots. The first, the *hand pot*, is awarded to the winner of each hand. In order to win the hand pot, a player must have the highest card total that is less than or equal to twenty-three—either positive or negative. In case of a tie, positive card value beat negative card value.

The other pot, the *sabacc pot*, is the "game" pot, and can only be won in two ways—with a *pure sabacc*—that is, card-chips totaling exactly twenty-three, or an *idiot's array*, consisting of one of the Idiot face cards, plus a two, and a three—literally, 23—of any suit.

In the center of the table is an *interference field*. As

the rounds of bluffing and betting proceed, sabacc players can "freeze" the value of a card by placing it into the interference field.

The Cloud City Sabacc Tournament had attracted over one hundred high-rollers from worlds all over the galaxy. Rodians, Twi'leks, Sullustans, Bothans, Devaronians, humans . . . all these and more were represented at the gaming tables. The tournament would last for four intensive days of play. Each day, roughly half of the players would be eliminated. The number of tables would dwindle, until only one table remained, where the best of the best would compete during that last hand.

Stakes were high. Winners stood a good chance of walking away with two or three times the ten-thousand-credit buy-in—or even more.

Sabacc was not traditionally a spectator sport the way mag-ball or null-gee polo was, but, since only players were allowed in the tournament hall, the hotel had arranged a huge holo-projection lounge for those who wished to watch the tournament. Companions of players, hangers-on, eliminated players and other interested sentients wandered in and out of the lounge, keeping an eye on the tournament, silently rooting for his, her or its favorite to win.

There was a ranking list displayed beside the holo, IDing the players, and showing the progress of the play. On this, the second day of the tournament, about fifty players clustered around ten tables. The ranking beside their names showed that Han Solo had made it through the first day of play on luck and by the skin of his teeth. He'd lost the sabacc pot, but had won enough hand pots so that he was still a contender.

One of the onlookers in the lounge was rooting for Han to win, though the Corellian had no idea she was

anywhere within parsecs of Bespin—and, if Bria
Tharen had anything to say about it, he wouldn't find
out. In her years of working with the Corellian resistance, Bria had become an expert at disguise. Now her
long, red-gold hair was hidden beneath a short black
wig, her blue-green eyes covered by bio-lenses that
turned them as dark as her hair. Carefully inserted
padding in her elegant business outfit made her look
voluptuous and muscled instead of slender and wiry.
The only thing she couldn't disguise was her height—
and there were many tall human women.

She stood at the back of the lounge, watching the
holo intently, hoping for another close-up of Han.
Silently, she rejoiced that he'd made it this far. *If only
he'd win,* she thought. *Han deserves a big break. If he
had a lot of credits, he wouldn't have to risk his life as a
smuggler. . . .*

For a moment, the holo showed a close-up of Han's
table. Bria saw that his opponents today were a Sullustan, a Twi'lek, a Bothan and two humans, one male and
one female. The woman was evidently from a heavy-gee
planet, judging from the thick, corded muscles in her
neck, and her short, stocky build.

Bria knew little about sabacc, but she knew Han
Solo—even after being separated from him for seven
years now, she knew him. She knew every line of his
face, the way his eyes crinkled at the corners when he
smiled, or narrowed when he was angry or suspicious.
The shaggy tufts of his hair, perennially overdue for
a haircut. She could still recall the shape of his hands,
the fine hairs on the backs of them. . . .

Bria knew Han Solo so well that she realized she
could still tell when he was bluffing . . . as he was at the
moment.

Smiling confidently, Han leaned across the table to

push another heap of chips into the center. Seeing the size of his bet, the Sullustan hesitated, then threw in her hand. The two humans also folded, but the Bothan was made of sterner stuff. He met Han's bet, and then, ostentatiously, raised it by a goodly amount.

Bria's expression didn't change, but her hands curled into fists at her sides. *Will he fold, or play the hand through and hope his bluff will work?*

The Twi'lek pushed another card-chip into the interference field, and matched the bet.

All eyes turned to Han.

The Corellian grinned as though he hadn't a care in the world. Bria could see his lips move as he issued some verbal challenge or wisecrack, then he pushed forward another stack of credit-chips . . . such a huge bet that Bria bit her lip. If he lost his hand, he'd bomb out. There was no way he could cover it!

The Bothan glanced from side to side, for the first time seeming uncertain. Finally, he tossed in his hand. The Twi'lek's head-tails twitched with frustration and nerves.

Finally, slowly, the Twi'lek laid his hand down. Han's grin broadened, and he reached forward to scoop up yet another hand pot. *Did he genuinely have a winning hand,* Bria wondered, *or was I right? Was it all a bluff?*

The Sullustan, her droopy jowls working, made a sudden grab for Han's card-chips, but the dealer spoke up, clearly warning her against such an action. By now the dealer would have signaled for a change in the card-chip values, anyway.

Bria nodded emphatically at the holo. *Great! Keep it up, Han! Beat them! Win!*

Beside her, someone snarled, then spoke in raspy, hissing tones, "May all the Blights of Barabel curse that villain Solo! He wins again! He *must* be cheating!"

Bria glanced out of the corner of her eye and saw a huge Barabel female, obviously a very *irritated* Barabel. The corners of her mouth twitched. *Han has such a way with people . . . what do you suppose he did to make her so mad?*

Something rustled on Bria's other side, and she turned to find her aide, a Corellian named Jace Paol, beside her. The man lowered his voice until even Bria could barely hear him, though his mouth was barely a handspan from her ear. "Commander, the representatives from Alderaan have arrived. They are on their way to the meeting site."

Bria nodded. "I'll be right up, Jace."

As her aide left the lounge, Bria checked her expensive datapad (a dummy, she committed as little as possible of her real business to any readable form), smiled vaguely at the Barabel, and left the lounge. Time to get on with her mission here in Cloud City.

When she'd discovered that Cloud City would be hosting the big sabacc tournament, Bria had realized that this was the ideal location for a top-secret meeting between representatives of several of the rebellions. Resistance groups were growing by leaps and bounds on many Imperial worlds, and it was essential to establish links between them. But such meetings had to be kept clandestine. The Imps had spies everywhere.

Any intelligence operative knew that the easiest place to hide was in a crowd. And Cloud City was pretty far from the Imperial Core, so the Imps didn't pay it much attention. A big tournament provided perfect cover. With so many ships coming and going, both alien and human, a few humans, a Sullustan and a Duros meeting in a hotel conference room on Cloud City would arouse little interest from anyone.

Bria wouldn't admit even to herself that part of her

reason for selecting Cloud City during the tournament was that she'd hoped to catch a glimpse of Han Solo. She couldn't be sure he'd attend, of course, but knowing Han, when there was the chance of winning big, he was there, ready and eager.

As she rode the glidewalk to the nearest turbolift, Bria imagined removing her disguise, then going to Han's room late that night. He would still have vivid memories of the last time he'd seen her, when she'd been posing as Moff Sarn Shild's mistress, but surely he'd believe her when she explained—that she'd been spying for the Corellian resistance, and that there had been nothing between her and Shild.

So after she'd told him the truth about their last encounter, they would talk. Perhaps they'd sip some wine. After a while, they'd hold hands. And then . . .

The Rebel operative closed her eyes as the turbolift swept her upward amid the crystalline and pastel splendor of the Yarith Bespin's fifty-story atrium. Perhaps, when she'd explained everything, Han would want to join the resistance, help his fellow Corellians as they plotted to free their planet from that tyrant Emperor who held so many worlds in a death-grip.

Perhaps. . . . Bria envisioned the two of them, doing battle shoulder to shoulder on land or in space, fighting bravely, covering each other's backs during the battles, winning victories over the Imperial forces . . . then holding each other close when the day's fighting was over. . . .

Bria couldn't imagine anything better than that.

Feeling the turbolift decelerate, she sighed and opened her eyes. Fantasies were all very well . . . sometimes they were all that kept her going. But she couldn't allow them to interfere with her mission.

As the turbolift doors slid open, she was ready. Moving with confident strides, she exited the lift and headed down the carpeted corridor.

When she reached the meeting room, she tapped out her coded signal, and was admitted. She glanced at Jace, and his nod confirmed that he'd checked the room for surveillance devices and found it safe. Only then did Bria turn to greet the other members of the conference.

The first representative to step forward was a typically mournful-faced, blue-skinned Duros, Jennsar So-Billes. He had come alone, as had Sian Tevv from Sullust. Bria greeted the two aliens warmly, thanking them and their respective groups for allowing them to make the dangerous journey—and it *was* dangerous. Just last month one of the high-ranking Rebel leaders from Tibrin had been captured while on his way to such a conference. The Ishi Tib was forced to suicide in order to avoid the Imp mind-probes.

Alderaan had sent three representatives, two human and one Caamasi. The senior member of the delegation was a middle-aged man with grizzled hair and beard, one Hric Dalhney, Deputy Minister of Security, and a trusted member of Viceroy Bail Organa's cabinet. Accompanying him was a young girl, not even out of her teens, with long, crystal-white hair. Dalhney introduced her as "Winter," commenting that they were posing as father and daughter as their "cover" during this trip. The non-human member of the delegation was a Caamasi. Bria was intrigued by him, never having met one before. Their species was now somewhat rare in the galaxy.

Caamas had been essentially destroyed after the Clone Wars, thanks to the efforts of the Emperor's minion, Darth Vader, but it was a little-known fact that many of its people had managed to flee to Alderaan and lived there, mostly in seclusion.

The Caamasi's name was Ylenic It'kla, and he introduced himself as an advisor to the Viceroy of Alderaan. Tall, even taller than Bria, the Caamasi wore a single kilt-like garment and jewelry. Generally humanoid in appearance, Ylenic was covered in golden down, with purple stripes marking his face. His eyes were large, dark and held a faint air of calm sadness that touched Bria, knowing what sufferings this being must have witnessed.

Ylenic said little as the delegates exchanged greetings, but something about him impressed Bria. She resolved to seek out his opinions if he did not offer them. The Caamasi had an air of quiet power, of confidence, that told the Rebel Commander that this was a being to be reckoned with.

After a few minutes of chitchat, Bria seated herself at the long table, and formally brought the meeting to order. "Fellow Rebels," she said, speaking with the quiet authority of someone who had done this many times before, "I thank you for risking your lives in our cause. We of the Corellian Rebel movement are contacting other underground groups like our own, urging all the various Rebel groups to unite. Only as a strong, cohesive group can we have any hope of confronting the Empire that is strangling our worlds, and killing the spirit of our peoples."

Bria took a deep breath. "I know what a daunting and dangerous proposal this is, believe me. But only if we can unite, form an alliance, can the Rebel groups have any hope of eventual victory. As long as we remain fragmented, planet-bound groups, we are doomed to failure."

She paused. "The Corellian movement has long considered this proposal. We are fully aware what a radical change this would entail—and how difficult such an alliance would be. As long as we are individual groups, the Empire cannot wipe us all at one blow. If we were to unite, they might conceivably be able to destroy all of us in one battle. We also know how taxing it can be for different species to work together. Disparate ethical and moral systems, ideologies, religions—not to mention equipment and weapon design differences—all of these things can present problems."

Bria faced her onlookers steadily. "But, my friends, unite we must. Somehow we must find ways to work around our differences. Surely we can do that . . . and that's the subject of this conference."

The Duros representative tapped his fingers on the table. "Your words are stirring, Commander. In spirit, I agree with them. But let us face facts here. In asking the non-human worlds to ally with you, you are asking us to put ourselves at far greater risk. Everyone knows the Emperor's disdain for non-humans. If an alliance challenged Palpatine's forces, and lost, the Emperor's wrath would be mostly directed at the non-human worlds. He might well destroy us as a lesson to the human Rebels."

Bria nodded. "Your point is well taken, Jennsar." She glanced around the table. "Minister Dalhney, what are your thoughts?"

"We of Alderaan have supported the Rebel movement from the beginning," the man said. "We have provided intelligence, funding, and technical expertise. But this talk of battles is anathema to us. Alderaanian culture is built on the absence of weapons and violence. We are a peaceful world, and the way of the warrior is abhorrent to us. Count on us to support your efforts— but I cannot imagine that we would ever be able to join you as combatants."

Bria gazed at Dahlney somberly. "It is possible, Minister," she said, "that Alderaan may not have the option to refrain from violence." She turned to the little Sullustan. "Sian Tevv, what are your initial thoughts?"

"Commander, my people are so crushed beneath the heel of the Empire that few of them have the wherewithal to plot any kind of rebellion." The little alien's jowls quivered, and his dark, liquid eyes were sorrowful. "Though many complain about the Imperial troops under their breaths, only a handful of my people have ever dared to openly resist. Our caves are places of fear. The Soro Suub Corporation essentially controls my world, and their biggest client is the Empire. If we were to join a Rebel Alliance, it would cause civil war!"

Bria sighed. *It's going to be a long conference,* she thought bleakly. "I recognize that all of you have valid concerns," she said, keeping her voice level and neutral. "But it won't hurt anything, or commit you to anything, simply to discuss these issues, right?"

After a moment, the delegates from the three worlds agreed to talk. Taking a deep breath, Bria started in. . . .

I can't believe I've made it this far, Han thought wearily, as he eased himself into the seat at the one remaining sabacc table. It was night on the fourth day of the tournament, and only the finalists were left. *If only my luck holds out a little longer . . .*

Slowly he stretched the kinks out of his back, wishing he could sleep for about twenty hours. The past few days had been grueling . . . hours of unending play, with only a few breaks for meals or sleep.

The other finalists had also taken their places around the table. A diminutive Chadra-Fan, a Bothan male, and a Rodian female. Han wasn't sure whether the

Chadra-Fan was a male or a female. Both sexes wore the same long robes.

As Han glanced around at his fellow players, the last player, another human, sat down opposite Han in the last empty chair. Han groaned inwardly. *Somehow I knew this would happen. What chance can I have against a professional like Lando?*

Han was very conscious of the fact that he was probably the only "amateur" player at the table. It was a fair bet that the others, like Lando, made their primary living by winning at sabacc.

For a moment he was tempted to just call it quits, walk away. To lose now, after all these days of play . . .

Lando nodded tightly to his friend. Han nodded back.

The dealer approached. In most games of sabacc, the dealer actually played for credits, but in tournament games, the dealer only dealt the card-chips and monitored the game . . . he or she was prohibited from playing.

The dealer was a Bith. The alien's large, five fingered hands featured both an opposable thumb and little finger, giving the dealer considerable dexterity as he dealt. The lights of the monstrous chandelier in the ballroom gleamed on the alien's large, bare, cranium.

The dealer ostentatiously opened a fresh pack of card-chips and riffled them, then triggered the randomizer several times, thus demonstrating that nobody could predict the order the card-chips would be dealt. After this initial demonstration, the randomizer itself altered the values of the card-chips at random intervals.

Han looked over at Lando, and was cheered to note that his friend was showing signs of strain. Lando's natty outfit was creased, and there were dark circles beneath his eyes. His hair looked as though it hadn't been combed all day.

Han knew he was no prize himself. He rubbed his hand blearily across his face, and only then realized he'd forgotten to shave. Stubble rasped his fingernails.

Forcing himself to sit up straight, Han picked up his first hand of card-chips. . . .

Three and a half hours later, the Bothan and the Rodian had been eliminated. They'd left without a backward glance. The Bothan male had "bombed out"—bet his entire trove of credit-chips on the game. When Lando took that hand, the alien had stalked away without a farewell. The Rodian female had folded, but she hadn't bombed. Han figured that she'd decided to cut her losses and get out while she still had a profit. The stakes were getting very high. The sabacc pot alone contained nearly twenty thousand credits.

Han's luck had held. He had enough credit-chips to cover any of the bets he'd seen tonight. Mentally, he added them up. If he folded now, he'd leave Bespin with twenty thousand credits, give or take a couple hundred. His eyesight was getting blurry, and the card-chips were hard to count when they were in stacks.

The Corellian considered. Twenty thousand was a lot of money. Almost enough to buy a ship of his own. Should he fold? Or should he stay in?

The Chadra-Fan raised the bet another five thousand. Han covered it. So did Lando, but it took nearly all his credit-chips.

Han assessed his hand. He had the card-chip for Endurance, which had the value of negative eight. *Appropriate*, Han thought. *This battle is becoming one of endurance.* . . . He also had the Ace of Staves, with a value of positive fifteen. And the six of flasks. Value, positive six.

Thirteen. He needed to take another card, and hope that he didn't get a ranked card, which would put him out of the game. "I'll take a card," Han said.

The dealer tossed one down on the table. Han picked it up, saw with a sinking feeling that it was Demise, which was negative thirteen. *Great! I'm farther away than ever!*

And then the cards rippled and changed before his eyes. . . .

Han now had the Queen of Air and Darkness, with a value of negative two, plus the five of coins, the six of staves, and the Master of coins, with a value of fourteen. Total value . . . twenty-three. His heart leaped. *Pure sabacc!*

With this hand, he could take both the hand pot and the sabacc pot . . . to win the tournament.

There was only one hand that could beat him, and that was an idiot's array.

Han took a deep breath, then pushed forward all but one of his stacks of credit-chips. For a moment he considered tossing all his cards into the interference field, but then his opponents would know for sure he wasn't bluffing. He needed them to cover his bet if he was going to clean up.

Hold steady, he thought to his card-chips, willing the randomizer not to change the patterns. Honest randomizers truly *were* random. Sometimes they changed card-chip patterns multiple times per game. Other times, they did so only once or twice. Han figured the odds for his card-chips changing within the next three minutes—the average time for a round of betting with this many players—were about 50-50.

Han kept his features composed, his body relaxed, with an effort of will that was nearly painful. He had to make them think he might be bluffing!

On Han's right, the little Chadra-Fan's huge ears flickered rapidly back and forth, then he (Han had learned that he was male during the hours of play) uttered the faintest of squeaks. Deliberately, precisely, the alien folded his card-chips and placed them on the table, then got up and walked away.

Han stared at his card-chips. *Hold . . . hold!* His pulse was hammering, and he hoped Lando couldn't see it.

The professional gambler hesitated for a long second, then requested a card. Han's blood rushed in his ears as, slowly and deliberately, Calrissian extended a hand, and placed a card-chip facedown into the interference field.

Han stiffened. He'd caught just a glimpse of the primary color of the card-chip reflected against the faint ionization of the field. Violet. If Han's bleary eyes weren't playing tricks on him, that meant the card-chip was the Idiot. The most vital card in the Idiot's Array.

Han tried to swallow, but his mouth was too dry. *Lando is an expert at this,* he thought. *He could have put that card down in just that manner, knowing I'd see its telltale color, and guess that he's holding the Idiot. But why? To bluff me? Scare me into folding? Or am I imagining things?*

Han looked back up at his opponent. Lando was holding two cards in his hand now. The professional gambler smiled at his friend, then, quickly punching a notation onto a data-card, he pushed it and his few remaining credit-chips toward Han. "My marker," he said, in his smoothest, most mellow tones. "Good for any ship on my lot. Your choice of my stock."

The Bith turned to Han. "Is that acceptable to you, Solo?"

Han's mouth was so dry he didn't dare speak, but he nodded.

The Bith turned back to Lando. "Your marker is good."

Lando was holding two cards plus the Idiot, which was safely in the interference field. Han fought the impulse to wipe his hand across his eyes. Could Lando see him sweating? *Have to stay calm, think,* Han ordered himself. *Does he have the Idiot's Array . . . or . . . is he bluffing?*

There was only one way to find out.

Hold, hold, he ordered his hand, and slowly, deliberately, he pushed forward his last stack of chips. "I call," he said. His voice emerged as a strained croak.

Lando stared at him across the table for an endless second, then the gambler smiled slightly. "Very well." Slowly, he reached over and turned up the card in the Interference field.

The Idiot stared up at Han.

Moving deliberately, Lando took his next card-chip, and laid it down beside the Idiot, face up. The Two of Staves.

Han couldn't breathe. *I'm dead . . . I've lost everything. . . .*

Lando turned over the last of his cards.

The Seven of Flasks.

Han stared unbelievingly at the losing hand, then, slowly, he raised his eyes to regard his friend. Lando smiled wryly and shrugged. "Gotta hand it to you, buddy," the gambler said. "I thought I could bluff you."

Lando was bluffing! The Corellian's head whirled as it sank in. *I won! I can't believe it, but I won!*

Slowly, deliberately, he laid down his card-chips. "Pure sabacc," he said. "The sabacc pot is mine, too."

The Bith nodded. "Captain Solo is our tournament winner, gentlebeings," he said, speaking into the tiny amplifier attached to his collar. "Congratulations, Captain Solo!"

Dizzily, Han nodded at the Bith, then he noticed that Lando was leaning across the table, his hand out. Excitedly, Han reached over and wrung his friend's hand. "I can't believe it," he said. "What a game!"

"You're a better player than I ever gave you credit for being, old man," Lando said genially. Han wondered how Lando could be so composed when he'd just lost so much, then he reflected that the gambler had probably won and lost fortunes before.

Han picked up the data-card that was Lando's marker, and studied it. "So, what ship are you going to claim?" Lando asked. "I've got an almost new YT-2400 Corelli-systems light stock freighter that would be your best bet. Wait'll you—"

"I'm taking the *Falcon*," Han said, in a rush.

Lando's eyebrows went up. "The *Millennium Falcon*?" he said, obviously dismayed. "Oh, no. Han, that's my own personal vessel. That was never part of the deal."

"You said any ship on your lot," Han reminded him, levelly. Their eyes locked. "You said any of your stock. The *Falcon's* sitting on your lot. I claim her."

"But—" Lando's mouth tightened, and his eyes flashed.

"Yeah, buddy?" Han said, letting an edge creep into his voice. "You gonna honor this marker, or what?"

Slowly, deliberately, Lando nodded. "Nobody can say I don't honor my markers." He drew a long breath, then let it out in an angry hiss. "All right then . . . the *Falcon's* yours."

Han grinned, then threw both arms up into the air and whirled around in an impromptu dance, giddy with joy. *Wait'll I tell Chewie! The* Millennium Falcon *is mine! At last! A ship of our own!*

Bria Tharen stood alone in the deserted holo-lounge, watching Han Solo as he rejoiced in his victory, wishing she could be there to hug him, kiss him, celebrate with him. *This is wonderful!* she thought exultantly. *Oh, Han, you deserved to win! You played like a champion!*

She wondered what the dark-skinned gambler had given the Corellian as a marker. Something valuable, obviously. Han was clutching the data-card as though it were the key to the most wonderful treasure in the universe.

It was late on the night of the fourth day, and the Corellian Commander's meetings with the Duros, the Sullustan and the Alderaanians would be concluded tomorrow morning. They'd made progress in reaching some agreements, and all of them had learned a great deal about each other's culture, but nothing major had been decided. None of the three other Rebel groups had been willing to commit to Corellia's proposed Rebel alliance.

Bria sighed. She'd done her best, but it was obvious that there was still a long way to go. She supposed she shouldn't blame the other groups for their caution, but she couldn't help it. The situation with the Empire was only going to get worse, and the others were blind if they couldn't see that for themselves.

Hearing the sound of footsteps, Bria turned, to find the Alderaanian girl, Winter, coming toward her. She was a lovely young woman with her crystal-colored hair and pale green eyes. Her simple, modestly cut green dress revealed a slender, regal figure. She was tall, though not as tall as Bria.

The Corellian Commander nodded, and the two of them watched the action from the tournament ball-room for a few minutes. Han was in the midst of other players now, mingling, being congratulated. Food and drink were circulating, and tournament officials, deal-ers, and hotel staff were now part of the crowd. A party atmosphere reigned.

"It looks like they're having more fun than we are in our meetings," Bria said dryly. "I envy them. Not a care in the world."

"Oh, I'm sure they have cares," Winter said. "But at the moment they've thrown them aside so they can exist only in the present."

Bria nodded. "Quite the philosopher, aren't you?"

The girl laughed a little, a musical, pleasant laugh. "Oh, we Alderaanians have a long tradition of debating philosophy, ethics, and morality. There are cafes in Aldera where citizens sit and argue philosophy all day long. It's a planetary tradition."

Bria chuckled a little. "Corellians have more of a reputation for being hot-headed doers, who get things accomplished, but love taking risks."

"Perhaps our two worlds need each other as a balance," Winter observed.

Bria gave her a thoughtful glance. "Winter, would you like to go over to the bar and get a cup of vine-coffeine?"

"I'd like that," the girl said, nodding. Her crystalline hair rippled over her shoulders with each movement. Bria had heard that adult Alderaanians didn't cut their hair. Winter's cascaded down her back like a glacier.

When they were comfortably seated, with cups of the steaming, fragrant brew before them, Bria discreetly pressed a button on her golden bracelet, and aimed the corusca jewels that studded it outward into the room, then she turned her wrist upward, all the while studying the jewels. When no light flashed amidst them, she relaxed. *No spy devices. Not that I expected any, but better to be safe than sorry. . . .*

"So, Winter, tell me about yourself," Bria said. "How did you happen to come on this mission?"

"The Viceroy has been like a father to me," the girl said, quietly. "He raised me with his own daughter, Leia. I've been the princess's companion ever since we were little children." She smiled faintly, and Bria was struck once again by how poised, how mature, she was for her age. "There have been times when I've actually been mistaken for the princess. But I'm glad I'm not royal. It's hard being in the public eye all the time, the way the Viceroy and Leia are. Constant pressures, being hounded by the press . . . your life isn't your own."

Bria nodded. "I suspect it's worse than being a vid-star, being royalty." She took a sip of her vine-coffeine.

"So Bail Organa raised you . . . and yet he allowed you to come on this mission, knowing there could be danger, if we were discovered?" Bria raised her eyebrows. "I'm surprised. You seem a little young to have to endure such risks."

Winter smiled. "I'm a year and a few months older than the princess. I just turned seventeen. That's the age of responsibility on Alderaan."

"Same as Corellia," Bria said. "Too young. When I was seventeen, I didn't have a bit of sense." She grinned ruefully. "That's so long ago . . . it seems like a million years, instead of nine."

"You seem older than that," Winter observed, "even if you don't look it. Twenty-six and a Commander? You must have started young." She stirred traladon milk into her vine-coffeine.

"I did," Bria agreed, lightly. "And if I seem older than my age, well . . . a year as a slave on Ylesia will do that to a girl. Those spice factories take a lot out of you."

"You were a slave?" Winter seemed surprised.

"Yes. I was rescued from Ylesia by a . . . friend. But physically getting off the planet was the easy part," Bria admitted. "Long after my body was free, my mind and spirit were still enslaved. I had to learn to free myself, and it was the hardest thing I've ever done."

Winter nodded, her gaze sympathetic. Bria was a bit surprised at herself for opening up to the girl this way, but the Alderaanian teenager was amazingly easy to talk to. It was obvious that she wasn't just making conversation, she really *cared* about what Bria was saying. The commander shrugged slightly. "It cost me everything that was important to me, basically. Love, family . . . security. But it was worth it, to be myself. And it brought me a new purpose in life."

"Fighting the Empire."

The older woman nodded. "Fighting the Empire that condones and encourages slavery. The filthiest, most degrading practice ever developed by supposedly civilized sentients."

"I've heard about Ylesia," Winter said. "The Viceroy ordered an investigation of the place a few years ago, when a few unpleasant rumors surfaced. Since that time, he's kept up a public information campaign to let Alderaanians know the truth about the place—about the spice factories, the forced labor."

"That's the worst thing about it," Bria said, bitterly. "They *don't* force you. People work themselves to death there, and they do it willingly. It's horrible. If only I had the soldiers and weapons, I'd head for Ylesia tomorrow with a couple of squadrons. We'd shut that stinking mudhole down for good."

"It would take a lot of troops."

"Yes, it would. They have eight or nine colonies there, now. Thousands of slaves." Bria cautiously sipped the hot beverage. "So . . . are you looking forward to tomorrow's session?"

Winter sighed. "Not really."

"I don't blame you," Bria said. "It must be pretty boring, hearing us wrangle all day over whether or not a Rebel Alliance is the right course of action. You ought to skip tomorrow's session, and go have some fun. Cloud City has tours to go watch the beldon herds, and there are aerial rodeos where thranta riders do stunts. I've heard it's an amazing thing to watch."

"I have to be at the conference tomorrow," Winter said. "Minister Dahlney needs me."

"Why?" Bria was puzzled. "For moral support?"

The girl smiled faintly. "No. I am his recorder. He needs me to help him prepare his report for the Viceroy."

"Recorder?"

"Yes. Everything I see, or experience, or hear, I remember," Winter said. "I cannot forget, though sometimes I wish I could." Her lovely features grew sad, as though she was recalling some unpleasant scene from the past.

"Really?" Bria was thinking how handy that would be, to have someone like that on staff. She herself had taken lessons and hypno-conditioning to improve her own recall, because so little of what she did could be entrusted to datafiles or flimsies. "You're right, that would make you invaluable."

"The reason that I said I wasn't looking forward to tomorrow's session," Winter said, leaning forward across the table, "wasn't that I was bored, Commander. What I meant was that it's hard for me to listen to Hric Dahlney stubbornly insist that Alderaanian ethics are more important than defeating the Empire."

Bria cocked her head. "Oh . . . now, *that's* interesting. What makes you say that?"

"Twice, when I accompanied Leia and the Viceroy to diplomatic functions on Coruscant—" she stopped herself, then smiled ruefully, "I mean, to Imperial Center— I saw the Emperor. One of those times, Emperor Palpatine stopped and spoke to me, just a perfunctory greeting, but . . ." She hesitated, biting her lip, and for the first time, Bria saw her maturity slip, and a frightened child in those youthful features.

"Bria, I looked into his eyes. I cannot forget them, no matter how I try. Emperor Palpatine is *evil*. Unnatural, in some strange way. . . ." The girl shuddered, despite the cozy warmth of the bar. "He frightened me. He was . . . malevolent. That's the only word that fits."

"I've heard stories," Bria said. "Though I've never met him. I've seen him from a distance, but that's all."

"You don't want to meet him," Winter said. "Those eyes of his . . . they fasten on you, and you feel as though they will drink up your spirit, all that makes you what you are."

Bria sighed. "That's why we must resist him," she said. "That's what he wants, to engulf us all . . . planets, sentients . . . everything. Palpatine is determined to become the most absolute despot in history. We have to fight him, or we'll all be ground to dust."

"I agree," Winter said. "And that's why I'm going to go back to Alderaan and tell the Viceroy that we of Alderaan must arm ourselves and learn to fight."

Bria blinked, startled. "Really? But that's not the way Minister Dahlney thinks."

"I know," the girl said. "And I know that the Viceroy is opposed to taking up arms. But your words over the past few days have convinced me that if Alderaan doesn't fight, we'll be destroyed. We'll know no true peace as long as the Emperor rules."

"Do you think Bail Organa will listen to you?" Bria said, feeling a spark of hope. *At least I reached one person these past few days . . . it wasn't a complete waste. . . .*

"I don't know," Winter replied. "Perhaps. He is a good man, and respects those who can make their points well, even if they are young. He does believe in resisting the Empire. He has already arranged for me and his daughter to be given special training in intelligence-gathering techniques. He's aware that two young, innocent-seeming girls may be able to go places and do things where seasoned diplomats would fail."

Bria nodded. "I've found that out myself," she said. "It's a sad but unfortunate fact that a pretty face and a sweet smile can provide a passport to places inside the Imperial bureaucracy and the High Command . . . where other efforts would be doomed to fail."

The attractive Commander smiled wryly as she poured another cup of vine-coffeine. "As you've no doubt noticed, the Empire is a male-dominated, human-dominated organization. And human males can be . . . manipulated . . . by woman, sometimes all too easily. I don't like it, and it doesn't make it right, but it's the results that count. I've learned that, over the years."

"Even if Viceroy Organa won't listen to me," Winter said, "I'm sure Leia will. She insisted that our Intelligence training include lessons in how to use weapons effectively. Both of us have learned to shoot, and to hit what we aim at. The Viceroy didn't like the idea, at first, but when he thought it over, he agreed, and even chose a Weapons Master for Leia. He's an intelligent man, and he could see that there might be situations where we'd need to know how to defend ourselves."

"What good will convincing the princess do?" Bria asked. "I know she's supposed to be well-loved, but she's still just a young girl."

"The Viceroy is considering appointing her Alderaan's representative to the Imperial Senate next year," Winter said. "Don't underestimate Leia's strength of purpose or influence."

"I won't," Bria said. She smiled at Winter. "I'm so glad we had this talk. I was feeling so discouraged, and you've lifted my spirits. I'm very grateful."

"I'm grateful to *you*, Commander," Winter said. "For speaking the truth in my hearing. The Corellian resistance is right. Our best hope is a Rebel Alliance. I only hope it can happen one day. . . ."

• • •

As the post-tournament party began to wind down, Han found himself beside Lando. He gestured at the door. "C'mon, I'll buy you a drink."

Lando smiled wryly. "You'd better be buying, old buddy. You've got all my credits."

Han grinned. "I'm buying. Hey . . . Lando, need a loan? And do you want to book passage back to Nar Shaddaa on that liner that's leaving tomorrow?"

Lando hesitated. "Yes . . . and no. I'd like to borrow a thousand, and I'm good for it. But I've decided to stay here on Bespin for a while. Some of the sentients who didn't make it to the finals of the tournament are bound to be hitting the casinos here on Cloud City, trying to recoup some of what they lost. I should do all right."

Han nodded, and counted out credit vouchers equaling fifteen hundred credits, then handed them to Lando. "Take your time, buddy. No hurry."

Lando gave his friend a grin as they approached the bar. "Thanks, Han."

"Hey . . . that sabacc pot added to my other winnings . . . well, I can afford it." The Corellian felt physically tired, but so exhilarated that he knew he couldn't sleep—not yet. He had to savor his victory, his ownership of the *Falcon*, just a little bit longer.

"Well, I'm headin' back tomorrow. No reason to stick around, and Chewie'll be wondering how I am."

Lando glanced across the bar and raised an eyebrow. "Oh, I see at least two reasons to stick around."

Han followed his friend's glance, saw the two women who were leaving the bar through the lobby exit. One was tall and full-bodied, with short black hair, the other was little more than a girl, slender, with long white hair. He shook his head. "Lando, you never quit. That tall one could put you on your rear, she's built like a null-gee wrestler, and the other is an invitation to a nice jail cell for corrupting a minor."

Lando shrugged. "Well, if not those two, then there are plenty of other lovely ladies here in Cloud City. And I want to check out the business opportunities here. I kind of like the place."

Han grinned smugly at his friend. "Suit yourself. Myself, I can't wait to get home and take *my* ship out for a spin." He signaled the robo-bartender. "What's your pleasure, my friend?"

Lando rolled his eyes. "Polanis red for me, and a nice shot of poison for you."

Han laughed.

"So . . . where are you going first in your new ship?" Lando asked.

"I'm gonna keep a promise I made to Chewie almost three years ago and take him to see his family on Kashyyyk," Han said. "With the *Falcon* I ought to be able to slip past those Imp patrols, no sweat."

"How long has it been since he was on Kashyyyk?"

"Almost fifty-three years," Han said. "A lot could have happened in that time. He left a father, some cousins, and a lovely young Wookiee female behind. 'Bout time he went home and checked up on 'em."

"Fifty years?" Lando shook his head. "I can't think of any human woman that would wait fifty years for me. . . ."

"I know," Han said. "And apparently Chewie never did have an understanding with Mallatobuck. I warned him he'd better expect to find her married and a grandmother."

Lando nodded, and, when the drinks arrived, raised his in a toast. Han lifted his glass of Alderaanian ale. "To the *Millennium Falcon*," Lando said. "The fastest hunk of junk in the galaxy. You take care of her, now."

"To the *Falcon*," Han echoed. "My ship. May she fly fast and free, and outrun every Imp vessel in existence."

Solemnly, they clinked their glasses, then together, they drank.

It was a sultry day on Nal Hutta, but, then, almost every day was sultry there. Sultry, rainy, damp and polluted . . . that was Nal Hutta. But the Hutts liked it that way; they loved their adopted homeworld. "Nal Hutta" meant "Glorious Jewel" in Huttese.

But one Hutt was too intent on his holo-cast unit to even notice the weather. Durga, the new leader of the Besadii clan since his parent Aruk's untimely death six months ago, had eyes and attention only for the full-sized holo-image projected into his office.

Two months after Aruk's death, Durga had hired a team of the best forensic examiners in the Empire to journey to Nal Hutta and conduct a rigorous autopsy on his parent's bloated corpse. He'd had Aruk frozen, then placed in a stasis field, because Durga was convinced that his parent had not died from natural causes.

When the examiners had arrived, they'd spent several weeks taking samples of every kind of tissue to be found in the Hutt leader's massive corpse, and running tests on them. Their early results had turned up nothing, but Durga insisted that they keep on looking—and he was the one paying, so the forensic specialists did as ordered.

Now Durga stared at the coalescing holo-image of the leader of the team of forensic specialists, Myk Bidlor. He was human, a light-skinned, slightly built male with pale hair. He wore a lab coat over his rumpled clothing. As Bidlor saw Durga's image forming before him, he bowed slightly to the Hutt Lord. "Your Excellency. We have received the results from the latest round of tests on the tissue samples we brought back to Coruscant . . . I mean, to Imperial Center."

Durga waved a small, impatient hand at Bidlor, and addressed the man in Basic. "You are late. I was expecting your report two days ago. What have you learned?"

"I regret, your Excellency, that the test results were somewhat delayed," Bidlor apologized. "However, this time, unlike our other rounds of tests, we have discovered something I believe you will find very interesting. Unexpected, and unprecedented. We had to contact specialists on Wyveral and they are currently checking to see if they can discover where it was manufactured. The morbidity factor has been difficult to test, since we have no pure quantities, but we are persisting, and when we tested the PSA count of the specimen's—"

Durga slammed his small hand down on a nearby table, sending it crashing over. "Get to the point, Bidlor! Was my parent murdered?"

The scientist drew a deep breath. "I cannot say for certain, Your Excellency. What I can tell you is that we have discovered a very rare substance concentrated in the tissues of Lord Aruk's brain. The substance is not natural. None of my team has ever encountered it before. We are running tests even now to discover its properties."

Durga's birthmarked face grew even uglier as his scowl deepened. "I knew it," he said.

Myk Bidlor raised a cautioning hand. "Lord Durga, please . . . allow us to finish our tests. We will continue our work, and we will report back as soon as we have something definitive to report."

Durga waved a dismissive hand at the forensics expert. "Very well. See that you report to me instantly when you discover what we are dealing with here."

The man bowed. "You have my assurance, Lord Durga."

With a muttered curse, the Hutt Lord broke the connection.

Durga was not the only unhappy Hutt on Nal Hutta. Jabba Desilijic Tiure, second-in-command of the powerful Desilijic clan, was both depressed and displeased.

Jabba had spent the entire morning with his aunt, Jiliac, the leader of Desilijic, trying to finish the final report on the losses to Desilijic that had resulted from the Imperial attempt to raze Nar Shaddaa and subjugate Nal Hutta. The Empire's attack had failed, mostly due to Jabba and Jiliac's successful bribe of the Imperial Admiral, but it would be a long time before business on Nar Shaddaa was back to normal.

Nar Shaddaa was a large moon that orbited Nal Hutta. The other name for Nar Shaddaa was "the Smuggler's Moon," and it was apt, for most of its denizens lived there because they were connected with the illegal trade that moved through Nar Shaddaa every day. Running spice, running guns, fencing stolen treasures and antiquities . . . Nar Shaddaa saw all of that and more.

"Shipping is down forty-four percent, aunt," Jabba said, his comparatively small, delicate fingers touching the data-pad expertly. "We lost so many ships, so many captains and crews when that thrice-cursed Sarn Shild mounted that attack. Our spice customers have been complaining that we can't move our product the way we used to. Even Han Solo lost his ship, and he's our best pilot."

Jiliac glanced at her nephew. "He has been flying our ships ever since the attack, Nephew."

"I know, but most of our ships are older models,

aunt. Slower. And, in our business, time equals credits." Jabba did another calculation, then made an exasperated sound. "Aunt, our profits this year will be the lowest we've experienced in ten years."

Jiliac replied with a mighty belch. Jabba looked up and saw that she was eating again, some high-sustenance goop she smeared on the backs of her swamp-wrigglers before stuffing them into her enormous mouth. Ever since becoming pregnant last year, Jiliac had been undergoing one of the typical Hutt growth spurts most adult Hutts experienced several times in their adult lives.

In the space of a year, Jiliac was nearly a third again the size she had been before her pregnancy.

"You'd better be careful," Jabba warned. "Those wrigglers gave you terrible indigestion the other day. Remember?"

Jiliac belched again. "You're right. I should cut back . . . but the baby needs the nourishment."

Jabba sighed. Jiliac's infant was still spending much of its time inside its mother's pouch. Baby Hutts depended upon their mothers for all their nourishment for the first year of their lives.

"Here is a message from Ephant Mon," Jabba said, seeing that his "message" indicator was blinking on his comlink. Quickly the Hutt Lord scanned the communiqué. "He says I should return to Tatooine. He is running my business interests as ably as he can, I am sure, but the Lady Valarian is taking full advantage of my prolonged absence to try and move in on my territory."

Jiliac turned her bulbous eyes on her nephew. "If you must go, Nephew, go. But see that it is a quick trip. I will need you to handle the conference with the Desilijic representatives from the Core Worlds in ten days."

"But, Aunt, it would do you good to handle it yourself. You have gotten rather out of touch with those reps," Jabba pointed out.

Jiliac burped delicately, then yawned. "Oh, I shall plan to attend, Nephew. But the baby is so demanding. . . . I will need you to be there and handle things when I must rest."

Jabba started to protest, then forced back the words. What good would it do? Jiliac simply wasn't interested in the affairs of Desilijic the way she had been before motherhood. It was probably hormonal. . . .

For months now, Jabba had been working to recoup the losses the Desilijic kajidic suffered in the Battle of Nar Shaddaa. He was getting tired of shouldering—speaking figuratively, of course, for Hutts did not really have shoulders—the burden of running Desilijic.

"Here is a note that should interest you, Aunt," Jabba said, examining another message. "Repairs to your yacht have been completed. The *Dragon Pearl* is fully operational again."

In the old days, Jiliac's first question would have been "how much?" but she did not ask it. The bottom line was no longer her primary interest in life. . . .

Jiliac's yacht had been hijacked by some of the defenders of Nar Shaddaa, and had suffered considerable damage in the battle. For a long time Jabba and his aunt had thought the ship lost altogether, then a Hutt smuggler had spotted the vessel drifting among the abandoned hulks that were scattered in orbit surrounding the Smuggler's Moon.

Jabba had ordered the *Pearl* towed into spacedock, and had spent a goodly sum in bribes, but he'd never been able to discover which of the smugglers had hijacked the vessel and used it in the battle.

In the old days, Jabba reflected sadly, news of her precious ship would have been of major concern to his aunt. But the *Dragon Pearl* had been damaged because Jiliac had forgotten to have the ship brought safely to Nal Hutta before the battle. "The stress of motherhood," as she'd put it.

Well, the "stress of motherhood" had cost Desilijic well over fifty thousand credits in repairs. Just because Jiliac had been careless.

Jabba sighed, and absently reached for a wriggler from his aunt's snackquarium. He heard a snort, then a buzzing nasal rumble, and turned to see that Jiliac's massive eyes were closed, and her mouth was half-open as she snored.

Jabba sighed again, and went back to work. . . .

That same night, Durga the Hutt was eating his evening repast with his cousin, Zier. Durga did not like Zier, and he knew that the other Hutt lord was his chief rival for the leadership of Besadii, but he tolerated him because Zier knew better than to oppose Durga in any overt fashion. Remembering Aruk's advice to "keep your friends close . . . and your enemies even closer," Durga had informally made Zier his lieutenant, entrusting him with matters pertaining to the administration of Besadii clan's vast Nal Hutta enterprises.

Durga kept Zier on a very short leash, however, and trusted him not at all. The two Hutt lords fenced back and forth verbally as they ate, each watching the other as a predator regards prey.

Just as Durga was lifting a particularly succulent morsel to his mouth, his majordomo, a servile, pale Chevin humanoid, appeared. "Master, there has been a message sent. You are to expect an important holotransmission from Coruscant within a few minutes. Do you wish to take it here?"

Durga gave Zier a quick glance. "No. I'll take it in my office."

He undulated after the Chevin, Osman, until he reached his office. The "connection" light was just beginning to flash. *Is it Myk Bidlor with news about the substance found in my parent's brain tissues?* the Hutt wondered. He had clearly gained the impression from the human that it would be some time, perhaps months, before they would complete their investigation.

Waving the bowing Chevin humanoid out of the room, Durga activated the security locks, keyed on the "shielded frequency" field, and then accepted the communication.

A blond human female suddenly stood before him, nearly life-sized. Durga wasn't very familiar with human standards of attractiveness, but he recognized that she appeared fit and limber. "Lord Durga," she said. "I am Guri, aide to Prince Xizor. The prince would like to speak with you personally."

Oh, no! If Durga had been human, he would have broken out in a sweat. But Hutts did not sweat, though their pores did secrete an oily substance that kept their skin comfortably moist and slick.

Aruk the Hutt had not raised a fool, however, so none of Durga's unease showed. Instead he inclined his head, the closest a Hutt could come to a humanoid bow. "The prince honors me."

Before Durga's eyes, the figure of Guri stepped to one side of the transmission field, and was almost instantly replaced by the tall, imposing form of the Falleen prince, Xizor, the leader of the huge criminal empire known as Black Sun.

Xizor's people, the Falleen, had evolved from a reptilian species, though the prince was very humanoid in appearance. His skin had a definite greenish cast, and

his eyes were flat and expressionless. His body was muscled and lithe, and might have been in his mid-thirties
(though Durga knew his age was closer to one hundred). Xizor's skull was bare save for a topknot of long
black hair that fell to his shoulders. He wore an expensive surcoat over a one-piece garment that resembled a
pilot's jumpsuit.

As Durga gazed at Xizor, the leader of Black Sun inclined his head in a faint nod. "Greetings, Lord Durga.
It has been several months since I have heard from you,
so I thought it best to see for myself that you are well.
How is Besadii doing in the wake of your esteemed parent's untimely death?"

"Besadii is doing well, Your Highness," Durga said.
"Your help was most appreciated, I assure you."

When Durga had first succeeded to the leadership of
Besadii, he'd faced so much opposition from other leaders in the clan—mostly due to the young Hutt's unfortunate facial birthmark, which Hutt lore held to be an
extremely bad omen—that he'd had to ask Prince Xizor
for help. Within a week after his request, Durga's three
main opponents and detractors had died in "unrelated"
accidents. Opposition had grown far quieter after
that. . . .

Durga had paid Xizor for his help, but the prince's fee
had been so modest, so much less than the young Hutt
lord was expecting, that Aruk's heir knew he hadn't seen
the last of Black Sun.

"I was only too glad to provide whatever assistance
you needed, Lord Durga," Xizor said, spreading his
hands apart in a gesture that conveyed sincerity. Durga
didn't have any trouble believing the Falleen Prince *was*
sincere. The Besadii Lord had known for a long time that
Black Sun would be only too happy to gain a foothold in

Hutt space. "And I must say, it is my most humble wish that we will have cause to work together again."

"Perhaps we will, Your Highness," Durga said. "At the moment, all my time is taken up with running the affairs of my clan, and I have little time for anything outside Nal Hutta."

"Ah, but surely you have time for Besadii's Ylesian interests," Xizor said, as if doing nothing more than musing aloud. "Such an impressive operation, such efficiency, all of it achieved in such a comparatively short span of time. Most impressive."

Durga felt his stomach contract around his supper. *So that is what Xizor wants,* he thought. *Ylesia. He wants a share of the Ylesian profits.*

"Of course, Your Highness," Durga said. "Ylesia is essential to Besadii's business interests. I take my duties toward our Ylesian enterprise most seriously."

"That does not surprise me at all, Lord Durga," the Falleen Prince said. "I would have expected no less. Your people are akin to mine in their efficiency in running their business affairs. So much better than many of the other species that pride themselves on their business acumen, frankly . . . like the humans, for instance. All their dealings colored by emotion, rather than remaining rational and analytical."

"Indeed, Your Highness, you are entirely correct," Durga said.

"However, both our peoples have regard for family ties," Xizor said, after a moment's pause.

What in the name of all the denizens of space is he getting at? Durga wondered. The Hutt Lord was completely in the dark, and that irritated him greatly. "Yes, that is also true, Your Highness," Durga agreed after a moment, keeping his voice neutral.

"My sources reveal that you may need some assistance in discovering the truth behind your parent's death, Lord Durga," Xizor said. "Apparently some . . . irregularities have surfaced."

How did he learn about the forensic report so quickly? Durga wondered, then he mentally shook himself. This was *Black Sun* he was talking to, the greatest criminal organization in the entire galaxy. It was possible that not even the Emperor himself had better spy networks.

"My people are conducting investigations," Durga said, neutrally. "I will let you know if I require assistance, Your Highness. But I am gratified by your wish to help me in my bereavement."

Xizor inclined his head respectfully. "Family must be honored, debts must be paid, and, when necessary, vengeance must be swift, Lord Durga. I am sure my sources could be of considerable assistance to you." He looked Durga square in the eye. "Lord Durga, let me be frank. Black Sun's interests in the Outer Rim are not being served as capably as they could be. It seems to me that we would do well to ally ourselves with the natural masters of that region of space—the Hutts. And it is very evident to me that *you*, Lord Durga, are Nal Hutta's rising star."

Durga was not flattered by Xizor's words, nor reassured. Instead he flashed back to a conversation with his parent. Prince Xizor had contacted Aruk several times in the past two decades, and had made the Besadii lord several similar offers. Aruk had always refused as gracefully as possible. The Besadii Lord knew better than to anger Xizor, but he did not want to become one of the Falleen prince's lieutenants, or, as Xizor termed them, "Vigos."

"The power of Black Sun is seductive, my child," Aruk had said. "But beware it, for there is no turning back as long as Prince Xizor is alive. Easier in some way to say no to the Emperor himself. Give Black Sun a kilometer, and they will take a parsec. Remember this, Durga."

I remember, Durga thought, and faced the holo-image squarely. "I will think upon your words, Prince Xizor," Durga said. "But at the moment, Hutt custom demands that I pursue my investigations and possible vengeance as a sacred . . . and solo . . . trust."

Xizor inclined his head again. "I quite understand, Lord Durga. I shall look forward to hearing from you when you have had the time to ponder my proposal."

"Thank you, Your Highness," Durga said. "Your concern honors me, and your friendship pleases me."

For the first time, Xizor smiled faintly, then he reached out and broke the connection.

The moment the prince's holo-image vanished, Durga let himself slump. He felt exhausted after fencing with the Falleen prince, but congratulated himself that he'd held up rather well.

Ylesia. He wants a share in Ylesia, he thought. Well, Xizor could want all he pleased, but wanting wasn't the same thing as getting, as every sentient child soon discovers.

If Xizor knew that I had authorized another colony on Ylesia, and sent survey teams to Nyrvona to begin choosing the best spot for a new Pilgrim planet, he'd be twice as eager, he thought. Good thing he'd been very close-mouthed about his ambitions for the new Besadii expansion.

Durga had a sudden, vivid vision of a whole handful of Ylesias, worlds where raw spice was turned into pure profit by contented, happy Pilgrims. *Perhaps I could even expand into the Core Worlds,* he thought. *Palpatine would not stop me, he values the slaves I sell his minions. . . .*

The Hutt lord smiled, and went gliding back to his interrupted dinner, appetite fully restored.

Far away, on Imperial Center, Prince Xizor turned away from his comm unit. "Not just a crafty Hutt, but an eloquent one, it seems," he commented to his human-replica assassin droid, Guri. "Durga is proving more of a challenge than I expected."

The HRD—who bore the seeming of a surpassingly beautiful human woman—made a very subtle movement of one hand. Yet the meaning—and menace—in her gesture were unmistakable. "Why not eliminate him, then, my prince. Easy enough to do. . . ."

Xizor nodded. "For you, Guri, not even a Hutt's thick skin would prove a challenge, I know," he said. "But killing a potential opponent is not nearly so efficient and effective as making him a dedicated subordinate."

"The young Besadii lord's control of his clan and his kajidic is still tenuous, by all report, my prince," Guri said. "It is possible that Jabba the Hutt might prove a better candidate?"

Xizor shook his head. "Jabba has been of use to me in the past," he said. "We have traded information—almost all of which I already knew—and I have done him some favors. I would rather have him beholden to me, so that when I choose to have him return these favors, he will do so with . . . enthusiasm. Jabba respects Black Sun. Fears it, too, though he would never admit it."

Guri nodded. Most beings in the galaxy who had any sense—and any knowledge of Black Sun, which the vast majority of sentients did not—were afraid of Black Sun.

"Also, Jabba is too . . . independent, too used to having his own way," Xizor continued, thoughtfully. "On the other hand, Durga is equally intelligent, and, unlike

Jabba, he is still young enough to be effectively . . . molded . . . into what I wish him to be. He would make a valuable addition to Black Sun. Hutts are ruthless and venal. In short, ideal."

"Understood, my prince," she replied, composedly. Guri was always composed. She was, after all, an artificial creation—though she was as far above most of the clanking, clumsy droids most people thought of when they thought of droids as Prince Xizor was above one of the slithering creatures that were his distant evolutionary cousins.

Xizor walked over to his form-chair and dropped into it, stretching almost lazily while the chair hastily conformed to his every move. Thoughtfully, he stroked one sharp-nailed finger down his cheek, the talon barely grazing his greenish skin. "Black Sun needs a foothold in Hutt space, and Durga is my best chance of gaining it. Also . . . Besadii controls Ylesia, and that operation, though small in scale compared to most of Black Sun's enterprises, impresses me. Lord Aruk was a most cunning old Hutt. He would never work for me . . . but his son may be a different matter."

"What is your plan, my prince?" Guri asked.

"I shall give Durga time to realize just how much he needs Black Sun," Xizor replied. "Guri, have Durga's investigations into Aruk's death closely monitored. I want our operatives to *stay ahead* of Durga's own knowledge of the forensics team's findings. I wish to know how Aruk died before the Besadii lord does."

She nodded. "As you wish, my prince."

"And if the discoveries of Durga's forensics team provide links back to Aruk's murderer—most likely Jiliac or Jabba—then I want that link eliminated in the most subtle way. I do not want Durga to realize that he is being deliberately thwarted in his search for his father's killer . . . is that clear?"

"It is, my prince. It shall be as you wish."

"Good." Xizor looked pleased. "Let Durga play detective if he wishes for a few months . . . even a year. Let him chase his own slimy tail. The frustration will build, until he is only too happy to throw in his lot—and a goodly percentage of Ylesia—with Black Sun."

Han Solo arrived back at his shabby flat on Nar Shaddaa in the early hours of the morning to find the assorted denizens of his motley household still fast asleep. That didn't last long, though. "Hey, everyone!" the Corellian bellowed. "Chewie! Jarik! Wake *up*! I *won*! Lookit this!" He ran through the apartment, yelling and waving a stack of credit vouchers thick enough to choke a bantha.

Han and Chewie shared their dilapidated flat with his young friend Jarik and an ancient droid named ZeeZee Han had "won" off Mako Spince in a recent friendly game of sabacc. After spending a month or two in ZeeZee's company, however, Han was pretty sure that Mako, an experienced card sharp, had "cooked" that deck to make sure he *lost*.

As a house-droid, ZeeZee had proved a twittery, stammering nuisance rather than a help. Han had gotten so annoyed with the droid's efforts to clean up the place that several times he'd considered junking the blasted antique, but somehow he'd never gotten around to it. Finally, in disgust, Han had ordered ZeeZee to "leave everything the way it is!"

Jarik "Solo" was a street kid from the depths of Nar Shaddaa. About a year ago he'd introduced himself to Han as a distant relative. He'd obviously been in awe of

Han, who was known far and wide as one of the hottest pilots around. Jarik was a brash, good-looking kid, and he reminded Han a little of himself when he'd been in his late teens. The Corellian had had Jarik's claim investigated, and turned up the truth—Jarik had no more right to the name "Solo" than Chewie did. But by the time Han knew for sure they weren't related, that Jarik was lying, he'd gotten kind of attached to the boy. So he'd let him hang around, even fly with them, and Jarik had turned into a pretty fair gunner.

Despite the youth's fears, he'd proven himself at the Battle of Nar Shaddaa, shooting down several TIE fighters, and helping Han, Lando and Salla Zend turn the tide of the engagement. So Han had never told the youth that he knew the truth. It was important for Jarik to have a sense of identity, even if it was a false one. And Han was willing to let the kid "borrow" his last name.

Now, as he raced around his apartment, Han was bouncing off the walls with excitement as his groggy friends gathered around. "C'mon, wake up!" Han shouted. "I *won*, guys! And I won the *Falcon* from Lando!"

Hearing the exciting news, Chewbacca roared, Jarik cheered, and poor ZeeZee was so confused by the excitement that the elderly droid short-circuited and had to be reset. After a round of back-slapping and congratulations, Han, Chewie and Jarik headed immediately for Lando's used-spaceship lot, with Lando's marker in hand.

After the formalities of ownership exchange had been processed, Han stood back, just looking at the *Millennium Falcon*. "Mine . . ." he said, and grinned until his face hurt.

The Corellian's mind filled with plans for fixing up the *Falcon*. There were so many things he wanted to do, to modify her into being the ship of his dreams. And, thanks to the sabacc tournament . . . he had the credits to do them!

For one thing, he intended to get Shug and Salla to help him salvage the military armor plating off the Imperial derelict *Liquidator*, a bulk cruiser that had become a casualty of the Battle of Nar Shaddaa. The airless hulk was still drifting amidst the space junk orbiting the Smuggler's Moon. Better armor plating would be a priority. Han didn't want what had happened to the *Bria* happening to the *Falcon*.

Another thing, he wanted a getaway blaster he could lower from the ship's belly. Smuggling could get risky, sometimes, and a quick exit was required. A quick exit with cover fire was even better. . . .

Yes, and he was going to overhaul the *Falcon*'s hyperdrive, and install a light blaster cannon under the nose. Concussion missile launchers, definitely. And maybe he'd move the quad laser turrets so they'd be one on top of the other, instead of on top and on the ship's right side. Perhaps stronger shielding, too?

Han stood there with his friends, contemplating his ship, dreaming of what he could do to her and with her . . . modifying the YT-1300 into the perfect ship. His ultimate smuggling ship.

"Fake compartments," he muttered.

"What?" Jarik turned to him. "What did you say, Han?"

"I said I'm gonna build some fake compartments under the decking, kid," Han said, throwing an arm around the youth's shoulders. He grinned up at Chewbacca. "And guess who gets to help me?"

Jarik grinned back at him. "Great! What's your first cargo going to be?"

Han thought for a moment. "Our first port of call is gonna be Kashyyyk. I'd say a nice load of bowcaster explosive quarrels would probably do well, there, what do you think, Chewie?"

Chewbacca voiced his agreement, long and loud. Now that the Wookiee knew that he'd be going home, he was more excited at the prospect than Han had ever seen him before.

Two days later, with the *Falcon*'s new below-decks compartments crammed with contraband, Han Solo flew his ship out of Shug Ninx's spacebarn and headed straight up, exulting in the *Millennium Falcon*'s quick acceleration. Chewie was in the copilot's seat, and Jarik was riding along as gunner. Han hoped to avoid Imperial patrols, but he intended to be prepared for a fight if one erupted.

Kashyyyk was an Imperial "protectorate" (translation: slave) world. The Imperials had managed to pacify the inhabitants, though they kept their forays into Wookiee cities and homes to a minimum, and they always went heavily armed, and in numbers. Wookiees were known to have quick tempers and to act impulsively.

Han managed to dodge the Imp patrols and to stay out of range of any sensor satellites as he approached the verdant sphere that was Kashyyyk. The Wookiee homeworld was mostly forest, covered with monstrous wroshyr trees, with four continents divided by bands of ocean. Archipelagoes of islands dotted the gleaming coastal seas like emeralds scattered across blue satin. There were only a few desert regions, mostly on the rain-shadow side of the equatorial mountain ranges.

When they were within communication range, Chewbacca took over the comm station, setting a coded frequency, then speaking into the comm in a series of grunts, growls, houfs, barks, and hrnnn's that, to the untrained human ear, sounded exactly like his usual speech—but wasn't.

Han frowned, realizing that, although many of the words sounded familiar, he basically hadn't understood a word that his friend had said. When Chewie stopped speaking into the comm, a voice came back, giving a series of what were obviously directives.

Han, who had been watching the sensors sharply, made a quick course correction. There was an Imperial ship taking off, just past the limb of the planet.

"Jarik, look sharp, kid," he said, keying the ship's intercom. "I don't think we've been spotted, but let's be ready."

Several tense seconds later, Han heaved a sigh of relief as the instruments indicated that the Imp vessel was proceeding serenely on its way, unaware of them.

When Han turned back to Chewie, the Wookiee launched into a series of directives and coordinates that his contact had given him. Han was to fly low, actually within the boundaries of the tallest wroshyr treetops, and to be prepared to make precise course changes the instant Chewbacca told him to.

"Okay, pal," the Corellian said. "It's your world, and you're the boss. But . . . what was that lingo you were talkin'? Some kinda Wook code?"

Chewbacca chuckled, then explained to his human friend that the Imperials were so stupid that most of them didn't even realize that all Wookiees were not the same. There were several related, but somewhat different, Wookiee sub-species. Han already knew that Chewbacca was a *rwook*, and bore the typical brown, red and chestnut hair of that people. He also knew that the language that he had learned to understand, but not speak, was called *Shyriiwook*, which, loosely translated, meant, "tongue of the tree-people."

Chewie went on to explain that the language Han had just heard him speak, *xaczik*, was a traditional tribal language spoken by the Wookiees indigenous to the Wartaki island and several outlying coastal regions. It was seldom heard, since *Shyriiwook* was the common language of trade and travel. So, when the Imperials had taken over Kashyyyk, the Wookiee underground had adopted *xaczik* as their "code" language. They used it whenever they had to give directives or pass along information that they didn't want the Imperials finding out about.

Han nodded. "Okay, pal. You just tell me how to fly, and where, and I'll take us where your buddies in the underground tell me."

Flying low, skimming barely above, and, at times, between the tip-top branches of the wroshyr trees, Han sent the *Falcon* blasting along in the precise course and speed Chewie specified. Every minute or so, the Wookiee conferred with his underground contact.

Finally, as they neared Chewie's hometown, Rwookrrorro, a kilometer-wide city set on platforms made by crisscrossing branches of the wroshyrs, Han's copilot made him shear off in a dangerous swoop and take them straight *down* between the branches for a thirty-second plunge. Han's heart was in his mouth as the *Falcon* dived like its namesake into the green forest, but Chewie's coordinates were right on the credits.

Even though it looked through the viewport as though they were going to be engulfed and smashed to flinders, nothing touched the ship. Chewie barked an order, and Han shouted, "Hard to port . . . now!"

He sent the *Falcon* into a screaming left turn, then, before him, saw something that the Corellian at first took to be a huge cave, a vast black hole waiting to swallow them up.

But as he neared it, Han realized that what it was in actuality was a massive wroshyr branch, balanced across other equally huge branches. Either by accident or design, the branch had split off from the main tree, and been hollowed out, to form a "cave" the size of a small Imperial docking bay.

"You want me to land in *there*?" Han hollered at the Wookiee. "What if we don't fit?"

Chewie's snarled comment assured Han that *of course* they would fit.

Han fired his braking thrusters hard as he neared the "cave" opening. They passed through it, and suddenly the muted sunlight was gone, and the space before them was revealed only by the *Falcon*'s infrared sensors and the beams of the landing lights.

Han killed the last of their forward motion, then lowered them onto their landing struts, using his repulsors.

Moments after they touched down, Jarik appeared in the doorway of the cockpit. The youth's hair was practically standing on end. "Han, you're crazier than I thought! That landing—!"

"Shut up, kid," Han snapped. Chewie was howling at him insistently, demanding that Han immediately turn off all power in the *Falcon* except for the batteries to power the airlocks, and to do it *now*!

"Okay, okay," Han muttered, doing as he was told. "Keep your fur on. . . ." Quickly he killed all the power, save for the batteries. The interior of the ship was now lit only by the weak, red-tinted emergency lights.

"So, want to tell me just what is going on?" the Corellian grumbled. "Fly here, turn there, land here, turn off the power . . . good thing I'm a sweet-natured guy who learned to take orders while I was in the Navy. So what gives?"

Chewbacca urgently beckoned the humans to follow

him. The Wookiee seemed nearly beside himself with excitement. He roared his pleasure and his eagerness to breathe the air of his homeworld.

Outside, something clanged against the *Falcon*'s new armor-plating. "Hey!" Han yelled, jumping up and elbowing his hairy friend out of the way, "watch it, that's my hull!"

Hitting the "open ramp" release, Han raced down the ramp, then stopped in wonder. When he'd first flown into the "cave" it had seemed a tight fit, but now he realized the place was so big it had echoes.

Back at the entrance, a hydraulic lift whined as it raised a huge "curtain" of some kind of camouflage net over the entrance. Teams of Wookiees were busily draping the *Falcon* in more netting.

Chewie came up behind him, and growled a soft apology for not warning his friend better about what was going to happen. "Let me guess," Han said, surveying the "nets." "Those things contain either jamming nodes or they send out some kind of camouflage frequency, so the Imps can't trace us here."

Chewbacca confirmed Han's guess. Local Wookiees used this landing site to receive smuggled goods, and they knew the drill.

"Wow," Jarik muttered. The young man was staring around the "cave" in openmouthed wonder as the lights came up. The inside of the "cave" was a well-stocked, completely functional docking site and repair facility. "Wow! This is something!"

Han still couldn't believe they were standing inside a *tree*. No, not a *tree*, but a *tree branch*. If one branch of a wroshyr was this big, the idea of the whole tree was mind-boggling. He shook his head. "I gotta admit, Chewie, your people have got a slick operation here."

After carefully locking the *Falcon*, Han and Jarik followed Chewie out toward the front of the "cave." There they were introduced to a crowd of Wookiees. Han had some trouble following the conversation, because he wasn't used to hearing seven Wookiees talking rapidly all at the same time. Chewbacca was howled at, hugged, thumped, shaken, thumped some more and generally exclaimed over with great joy.

When Chewie introduced Han as his "honor brother" to whom he owed a life debt for freeing him from slavery, Han in turn was in grave danger of being similarly thumped, shaken, etc., but, thankfully, Chewbacca intervened and provided more conventional introductions. Not all of the Wookiees understood Basic, so a lot of translating was necessary.

Three of the Wookiees Han met were relatives of Chewie's . . . the Wookiee with the whorls of auburn hair turned out to be his sister, Kallabow. Jowdrrl, a smaller, chestnut colored female (Han was surprised to note that he could actually see a family resemblance!) was a cousin, and Dryanta, a darker brown male, was another cousin. The other four were members of the Wookiee underground resistance movement, who had come in especially to meet Han and negotiate for his cargo.

Motamba was an older Wookiee, a munitions expert whose blue eyes lit up when Han revealed how many boxes of explosive quarrels he had to sell. Katarra was a young Wookiee, younger than Chewbacca, and she was the underground resistance's leader, as near as Han could tell. The Wookiees listened to her with a great deal of respect. She consulted regularly with her father, Tarkazza, a burly male who was the first Wookiee with black fur Han had ever seen. He had a stripe of silver-colored fur running down his back, which was evidently a family trait, for Katarra had one, too, though her fur was brown and tan.

After several minutes of confusion, Chewbacca roared an order to his friends. Han caught most of it. Something about, "fetch the quulaars."

What are quulaars? Han wondered.

He soon found out. Two long bag-like pieces of woven fabric—or was it woven hair?—were produced. Chewbacca turned to Han, and pointed from the Corellian to the quulaar. Han stared at his friend, incredulous, and shook his head. *"Get inside?* You want me and Jarik to crawl into those things? So you can carry us up the trees? No way, pal! I can climb, just as good as you can."

Chewbacca looked at his friend and shook his head. Then he grabbed Han's arm, and hustled the Corellian over to the entrance to the cave, and, lifting the camouflage hanging, gestured Han to step outside, onto the lip of the cave.

Jarik had followed them outside, as had the other Wookiees. The youth was confused, having understood almost nothing of what had been said. "Han? What do they want?"

"They want us to crawl into these sacks, kid, so they can haul us up the tree trunks until we can catch the lift for Rwookrrorro. I just told Chewie no way, that I can climb just as good as he can."

Jarik walked over to the lip and cautiously leaned over to look down. Then he walked back to Han, gave him a long, silent look. Without speaking, he began climbing into his quulaar.

Out of curiosity, Han walked over to look down, too.

He'd known it intellectually, of course, but it was one thing to know it with his brain, another to know it in his gut. He was *kilometers* high in the air. Below him the forest went on . . . and on . . . and on. . . .

The tree trunks stretched down, past the point where Han's excellent eyesight could distinguish them from each other. Despite all his piloting experience and his outstanding sense of balance, the sight made Han's head swim for a moment. He walked back to Chewbacca, who was helpfully holding out the quulaar. When Han hesitated, the Wookiee flexed his powerful hands and made his claws pop out. They were very sharp, and, coupled with Chewie's great strength, would enable him to dig deep into a tree trunk when climbing.

"I'm gonna regret this. . . ." Han muttered, and climbed into the sack.

Chewbacca wanted to carry Han, but his relatives convinced him that, since it had been a long time since he'd done any forest-traversing, it would be better if he had only himself to worry about.

So Motamba carried Jarik, and Tarkazza carried Han, both humans stuffed inside their respective quulaars. Han wanted to look out, but Tarkazza was firm, pushing the human's head down into the sack, warning him to keep his arms inside, too, and to stay still, so he wouldn't disturb his carrier's balance.

Inside the quulaar, Han felt the bag sway as Tarkazza walked to the edge of the platform lip. Then, with a grunt and a powerful leap, the Wookiee launched himself. They were falling, falling!

Han barely managed to hold back a yell, and he heard Jarik let out a short, bitten-off cry.

Seconds later Tarkazza smacked into a hard surface, clung, then began climbing rapidly upward. Leaves swished against the quulaar. Han had just started to relax, when suddenly they leaped again!

The next few minutes, all Han could do was try not to move, and to keep concentrating on not being sick. The sack swung and jerked and spun and slapped against the tree trunks, despite Tarkazza's best efforts.

Swing, scramble, climb.

Leap, grip, swing.

Grab, grunt, swing-climb. . . .

Han finally had to close his eyes, not that he could see much anyway, and just try to hang on. It seemed as though the nightmare journey took hours, but Han realized when he checked his chrono later, that it had taken only about fifteen minutes.

Finally, with a last swing and grunt of effort, the movement stopped, and Han found himself lying on the ground, still inside the quulaar. When the world around him stopped spinning (which took a moment) the Corellian began clawing his way out of the sack.

Moments later, he was standing, legs braced wide apart for balance, on the great platform where the great, mostly enclosed city of Rwookrrorro was located. It was a massive, flattened ovoid, with homes studding the outskirts and scattered all over the platform. Branches grew straight up along the avenues, through the material making up the streets, adding touches of green.

The world steadied around Han, and he drew a deep breath. The city before him was beautiful, in a way that was hard to describe. Not as pastel as Cloud City, Rwookrrorro had some of the same openness and airiness. Perhaps because it was, like Cloud City, so high up?

Some of the buildings were several stories tall, yet they harmonized, somehow, with the treetops. All around them the vivid green topmost branches of the wroshyr trees swayed in the breeze. The sky overhead was blue, with a hint of green. Thick, flattened masses of sparkling white clouds drifted by.

Hearing a strangled gurgle, Han looked over and saw Jarik, bent over, clutching his middle, obviously in distress. He went over and touched the youth's shoulder. "Hey, kid, you okay?"

Jarik shook his head, then looked as though he'd regretted doing that. "I'm gonna be okay," he mumbled. "Jus' tryin' not to upchuck. . . ."

"There's a trick to that," Han said mock-seriously. "Just don't think about traladon and tuber stew."

Jarik gave Han a quick, betrayed glance, then, hand over his mouth, bolted for the edge of the platform. The Corellian shrugged, then turned to find Chewie there. "Poor guy. Hey, Chewie, what a way to travel. Good thing your people brought those sacks along. What do you usually carry in them? Luggage?"

Chewbacca's lip curled, then he gave a brief, amused translation of the word "quulaar."

Han bristled. *"Baby-sack?"* You haul Wook babies around in 'em?"

Chewbacca began to laugh, and the madder his human friend got, the more the Wookiee cracked up. Han was rescued by a roar from a party of Wookiees coming their way from the city. There were at least ten of them, all ages. Han noted a somewhat stooped, short, graying Wookiee, and just then Chewbacca took off, racing toward the newcomers with roars of joy.

Watching Chewie thump and pound and hug the old Wookiee, Han turned to Kallabow, who, thankfully, understood Basic. "Attichitcuk?" he guessed, naming Chewbacca's father.

Chewbacca's sister confirmed that, yes indeed, that was their father, Attichitcuk, who had talked of nothing else since discovering that his son would soon be home.

"There's someone else that Chewie's looking forward to seeing," Han said. "Mallatobuck. She still live here in Rwookrrorro?"

Kallabow's formidable teeth flashed in a Wookiee grin and she nodded, human-style.

"She married?" Han asked, dreading the answer. He

had some idea of how much that question meant to his best friend.

Kallabow's grin widened, as slowly, deliberately, she shook her head, *no*.

Han grinned back. "Whoo-hoo! That's something to celebrate, I guess!"

Han felt a touch on his shoulder, and turned to find Katarra standing there, with yet another male Wookiee. To Han's profound astonishment, the tall Wookiee opened his mouth and said, in amazingly understandable Wookiee, [Greetings, Captain Solo. I am Ralrracheen. Please call me Ralrra. We are honored, Hansolo, that you have come to Kashyyyk.]

Han's mouth dropped open with surprise. It had taken him years to learn to understand Wookiee speech, and he couldn't pronounce it even after many efforts. And yet this Wookiee spoke in a fashion that Han could understand very easily—and could even have reproduced. "Hey!" Han blurted. "How do you do that?"

[A speech impediment,] the Wookiee said. [Unfortunate for me when conversing with my own people, but, when humans visit Kashyyyk, it is useful.]

"It sure is . . . ." Han muttered, still amazed.

With Ralrra's help, Han and Katarra were able to begin negotiations over the cargo of explosive quarrels. [We need them desperately,] Ralrra said. [But we are not asking for charity. We have something to trade for them, Captain.]

"And what's that?" Han wondered.

[Armor from Imperial stormtroopers,] Ralrra said. [My people began collecting it from soldiers who had no further use for it, first as trophies, then because we learned it was valuable. We have many suits and helmets.]

Han thought about that. Stormtrooper armor was indeed made from valuable materials, and could be recycled as other kinds of body armor. It also could be chemically melted and then recast. "Like to take a look at it," he said, "but we may have ourselves a trade there." He shrugged. "Course . . . used armor ain't worth much. . . ."

Which wasn't true. A suit of stormtrooper armor in good shape was worth well over two thousand credits, depending on the market. *But hey,* Han thought. *They've got no use for it, and I gotta make a profit on this trip. . . . I ain't in the handout business. . . .*

Katarra hrrrrnnnnned vehemently, than spoke to the interpreter in rapid, accented *Shyriiwook* that Han had trouble following. Something about a dawn-haired human?

Ralrra turned back to Han. [Katarra says that she knows that the armor is valuable. She knows because the female from your world of Corellia, with hair the color of sunrise, told her so.]

Han's attention was suddenly focused completely on the underground leader. "Corellian?" he said, sharply. "A Corellian woman? Fair-haired?"

Ralrra conferred briefly with Katarra. [Yes. She came here just after our most recent Life Day—about a standard year, Captain—and she met with the leaders of the Underground, advising us on organization, codes, tactics, and so forth. She was a member of the resistance movement on your homeworld.]

Han stared at Katarra. "Her name. What was her *name*?"

Ralrra turned to the underground leader, spoke rapidly, then turned back. [Katarra says that she did not know her name, which is standard procedure, in case of interrogation. During her visit, we called her 'Quarrr-tellerrra' which means 'sun-haired warrior.']

Han took a deep breath. "What did she look like?"

he asked. "I may know this Corellian. She may be . . ." He hesitated. "She may be my . . . mate. We were separated long ago, by the Empire."

Which was true, strictly speaking. Bria had left when Han was preparing to go into the Imperial Academy, saying she didn't want to hold him back. He still had the flimsy she'd written him. It was stupid, keeping it, and every time he ran across it, he resolved to throw it away, but, somehow, he never had. . . .

Katarra's wary expression visibly softened upon hearing this. She put out a paw-hand and laid it on Han's arm, expressing sympathy. The Empire was evil, had torn apart so many families. . . .

Ralrra made a gesture in the air on the level of Han's nose. [This tall,] he said. [Long hair, the color of the sunset . . . golden-red. Eyes the color of our sky. Not wide.] His hands described a slender form. [She was the leader of the team, a person of rank. She said she had been asked to come to Kashyyyk because she understood what it was like to live as a slave. She told us she had been a slave, on the planet Ylesia, and she would give her life to free Kashyyyk and any other world enslaved by the Empire. She spoke with much passion.]

Ralrra's voice changed slightly, took on a more personal note. [I, too, was a slave until my friends freed me from the Empire. Quarrr-tellerrra spoke truth about having been enslaved. I could tell. She knew what it was like. We talked much of how much we hate the Empire.]

Han's mouth was dry. He managed to nod, and mumble, "Thanks for telling me. . . ."

Bria, he thought, numbly. *Bria, a member of the Corellian rebellion? How in the galaxy did that happen?*

Chapter Three:

MALLATOBUCK

It was wonderful to be back on his own world. Chewbacca was taken from home to home, and his father, Attichitcuk, proudly showed off his son, the adventurer, the former slave, and his human friends. All of the Wookiees made much of Han and Jarik.

Of course, Kashyyyk was a world occupied by Imperial forces, so care had to be exercised to conceal Han's real purpose in coming there. For the duration of his stay, Han donned clothing more befitting one of the human traders who lived in Rwookrrorro. He and Jarik posed as brothers who'd come to trade trinkets and household items with the Wookiees. This fiction was strengthened by the fact that both humans had brown hair and eyes, and Jarik was only a little shorter than Han.

The Imperial presence of Kashyyyk was mostly confined to the posts scattered around the planet. Troopers were sent out in squads, since single troopers had a disturbing tendency to vanish without a trace.

Han and Jarik were careful to avoid any contact with the Imperial squads that occasionally patrolled Rwookrrorro. And, with the *Millennium Falcon* concealed in the special "smuggler's dock," protected by the camouflaged and jamming devices, there was nothing to link them with any illegal activity.

Han spent time with the Wookiee techs down in the spacedock, tinkering with his new baby. Several of the Wookiees were experienced techs, and they spent hours with the Corellian, checking out every system, overhauling every bit of equipment. The *Falcon* was far from a new ship, but, under the ministrations of the Wookiee techs, it was now in better shape than it had been for a long time.

Chewbacca hadn't realized how much he'd missed his home and family. Seeing them all again made him tempted to come home for good—but that was not possible. Chewie owed a life debt, and his place was by Han Solo's side.

Still, he enjoyed his time on Kashyyyk. He visited with all his cousins, with his sister and her family. Since Chewie had last been home, Kallabow had married a fine male named Mahraccor.

Chewie loved playing with his nephew. The little Wookiee was smart and fun to be with, with a lively curiosity about the universe. He spent hours getting his uncle to talk about his adventures out in the spacelanes.

In addition to Chewbacca's family, he saw old friends . . . Freyrr, his second cousin, the best tracker in the family, Kriyystak, and Shoran. It was a source of sorrow that Salporin, Chewie's best Wookiee friend, was not there. He had been captured and enslaved by the Empire, and there was no news of his fate—no one even knew if he was alive or dead.

Chewbacca mourned his friend, wondering if he'd ever see him again.

But he didn't have time to mourn very much. Life on Kashyyyk was too busy. In addition to all his friends and family, there was . . . Mallatobuck.

The Wookiee female was even lovelier than Chewie had remembered, and her shy blue glance was even more intriguing. He saw her their first night at home, and was pleased to discover that she'd journeyed from a neighboring village, where she had been working as a teacher and caregiver in a Nursery Ring. Malla had many friends in Rwookrrorro, and it didn't take much urging from Chewie to convince her to extend her visit there.

The two spent long hours wandering the bough-trails, looking up at the nighttime sky, hearing the soft sounds of the arboreal dwellers. They did not talk much, but their silence was filled with unspoken things. . . .

On his third day on Kashyyyk, Chewbacca decided it was time to go hunting. Han was busy haggling with Katarra, Kichiir and Motamba about the cargo of explosive quarrels. His friend would be occupied for hours. The Corellian had taken a sudden, unaccustomed interest in the resistance here on Kashyyyk, something that Chewie would have found puzzling, and a bit disturbing, if he'd noticed it. Usually Han was nothing but scornful toward sentients who risked their necks (or whatever equivalent body part) for causes other than their own well-being.

But Chewie was too distracted to notice Han's odd

behavior. He was concentrating on bagging himself a quillarat. Quillarats are smallish creatures, standing only half a meter high. They are reclusive little animals, hard to find, because they were a mottled brownish-green in color, and tended to simply melt into the surrounding brush.

The most distinctive feature of the quillarat was the long, needle-sharp quills that studded most of its body. Capturing and killing a quillarat was something of a challenge, because the beasts could actually hurl their quills at a hunter. Wookiee males (and only males hunted quillarats) had to approach the creature with some kind of shield to collect the barrage of quills until the quillarat's supply of "throwable" quills was exhausted.

To complicate matters, tradition declared that the quillarat must be hunted bare-handed, and killed by blows delivered by a Wookiee's own strength, as opposed to quarrels or any other kind of projectile.

Chewbacca did not tell anyone about his quest. He simply waited until late in the day, when darkness would be deepening in the lower levels, then left Rwookrrorro and began his long climb downward.

Even Wookiees never went down all the way to Kashyyyk's surface. There were rumored to be night-crawlers down there that feasted on the blood and spirits of their victims. It was said that the spirits of those who had not honored their debts sank down to the surface, and prowled there, ready and waiting to trap and kill anyone foolish enough to come near them.

There were reputedly seven levels of distinct ecology on Kashyyyk, with the seventh level being the topmost tree branches. Normally, not even the bravest Wookiees ever descended below the fourth level, and even Wookiee legend did not speculate on what lay below that. No one that Chewbacca had ever known had walked on the actual surface of his world. The bottommost levels of Kashyyyk were a mystery . . . and would likely remain so.

To bag his quillarat, Chewie had to travel down below the fifth level. Life was different here, for the forest in the late afternoon was almost completely dark. Animals down at this level had large eyes to facilitate their living at such dim light levels. There were dangerous predators . . . the kkekkrrg rro, or Shadow Keepers, that had ventured up a level to hunt, and the katarn. Chewbacca kept a sharp eye out, his every sense alert.

Old habits came back to him as he traveled the forest trails, seeing bridal-veil suckers, broad-leafed mock shyr, and kshyy vines in profusion. Things were not really green down here, but pale and washed-out looking. There was not enough sunlight to support the green growth from above.

Chewbacca walked the broad trails, feeling the rough bark of the wroshyr boughs beneath his feet. His eyes moved constantly, searching for quillarat spoor. His nostrils twitched, filtering and identifying the scents he had not whiffed in more than fifty years.

The Wookiee's gaze was caught and held by a tiny scrape of the wroshyr bark, and a small rip in the tracery of the bridal veil plant next to it. The height was correct . . . yes, a quillarat's quills had done this, and . . . Chewie dropped to one knee to examine the spoor . . . not long ago.

The animal had been heading off, on this far smaller, secondary bough. Chewbacca walked warily down a bough-trail not much more than two meters across. On either side of him yawned the green-brown-gray gulfs of the forest.

The Wookiee kept every sense alert, eyes scanning,

ears listening for the faintest rustle, nostrils twitching. Quillarats had a distinctive, and, to a Wookiee, enticing odor.

His "shield," made from woven strips of bark on a lashed-together frame, was held ready on his left forearm.

Chewie's steps slowed . . . then the Wookiee stopped, every muscle poised. *There! Amid those leaves!*

The quillarat froze, sensing danger. Chewie leaped, shield held out.

Suddenly the air before him was filled with a rain of quills. They thudded into the shield, for the most part, though a few embedded themselves in the Wookiee's shoulders and chest. Chewbacca's right hand went out, grabbed the quillarat by the quilled tail, moving his hand in a particular twist that made the quills lie flat beneath his flesh.

The terrified animal squawked, turned to bite, but it was too late. Chewie heaved it up, and sent it thudding hard against the bough beneath his feet. Stunned, the animal went limp, and another quick swing dispatched it altogether.

Only then did Chewbacca take a moment to pull the quills from his chest and shoulders, and spread a salve on the tiny, burning wounds. His right hand had one small puncture, which he also treated.

Then, wrapping the quillarat in the woven bag he'd brought, the Wookiee began a triumphant journey back to Rwookrrorro.

It took him quite a while to find Mallatobuck. He didn't want to ask anyone where she was, since any of his friends and family would be bound to identify the scent of the quillarat in his bag. Chewie wasn't in the mood for advice or jokes.

But, finally, he located her, wandering along a little-used trail. By now two of Kashyyyk's three tiny moons had risen, and moonlight silvered her fur as she wandered along, not at first noticing that anyone was approaching her.

She had been picking *kolvissh* blossoms and weaving their stems into a headpiece. As Chewie watched her, she placed the flowers on her head, tucking their fragile white beauty behind her left ear.

Chewbacca halted on the trail and stood there, lost in wonder at her beauty. His stillness attracted her attention as his movement had not, and she stopped, looked up, and saw him.

[Chewbacca,] she said softly. [I did not see you. . . .]

[Malla,] Chewie said. [I have something for you. A gift that I hope you will accept. . . .]

She froze, eyes wide with either consternation or hope, as he walked toward her, bag in hand. *Let it be hope she feels,* Chewie thought fervently. *By my honor, let it be hope. . . .*

As he stopped before her, Chewbacca, in one fluid motion, knelt and removed the quillarat from its bag. Careful of the quills, he balanced the animal across his palms and held it up to Mallatobuck. His heart was pounding as though he'd climbed all the way from ground level.

[Mallatobuck. . .] Chewie tried to get the rest of it out, but his voice failed him. He was overcome with fear, as he had never been in battle. What if she refused him? What if she took his traditional proposal-offering and tossed it off the trail, sending the dead quillarat, and his hope of happiness, plummeting into the depths?

Malla stared at him for a long moment. [Chewbacca . . . you have been long away from your people.

Do you remember our customs? Do you know what you are offering?]

Relief flooded Chewie, for her tone was bantering, flirtatious.

[I know,] he replied. [My memory is good. In all the years I was gone, I never for a moment forgot your face, your strength, your eyes, Mallatobuck. I dreamed of the day that we could be married. Will you? Will you take me for your husband?]

She replied in the traditional manner by cautiously picking up the stiffening quillarat and taking a big bite out of its soft underbelly.

Chewie's heart was flooded with joy. *She accepts me! We are betrothed!* Getting up off his knees, he followed Malla to a sheltered niche behind a screen of leaves. There they sat down close together and shared the quillarat, nibbling delicately on its tasty entrails, savoring its liver, feeding each other choice bits of this greatest of Wookiee delicacies.

[I had proposals, you know,] Mallatobuck said. [People told me I was foolish for waiting so long. They said you were dead, that you would never return to Kashyyyk. But I knew, somehow . . . I knew that was not so. I waited, and now my joy fills the world.]

Tenderly, Chewbacca licked blood and tissue off her face, washing her, as she returned the favor. Her fur was silky on his tongue.

[Malla . . . you know about the life debt I have pledged to Han Solo?] Chewie asked, as, sated, they sat back, arms around each other.

Malla's voice quivered just a tiny bit. [I know. I cherish your honor as my own, my husband-to-be. But let us be married quickly, so we may have as much time together as possible before you and Captain Solo must depart.]

[Nothing would please me more,] Chewie said.

[How quickly can you be ready? How long will it take to prepare your wedding veil?]

She chuckled, a rich, throaty sound in the darkness. [It has been ready for fifty years, Chewbacca. Ready and waiting.]

Chewbacca's heart was full of love and pride. [Tomorrow, then, Malla.]

[Tomorrow, Chewbacca. . . .]

Teroenza, High Priest of Ylesia, lounged back in his resting sling, watching Kibbick, Ylesia's figurehead Hutt overlord, trying to go over last month's accounts and make sense of them. The huge, four-legged t'landa Til groaned inwardly. He'd long since ceased to be amused by Kibbick's troubles comprehending even the most rudimentary record-keeping. Kibbick was an idiot, and it was Teroenza's unfortunate task to bring him up to speed on the running of Ylesia.

As though Besadii doesn't realize that if Kibbick actually managed to master the skills necessary to keep the spice factories running smoothly, I would be out of a job, the High Priest thought disgustedly. *But the chances of that are vanishingly small. . . .*

When Teroenza, with the help of the Desilijic leader, Jiliac, had plotted Aruk the Hutt's murder, he'd hoped that the aging Hutt Lord's only offspring, Durga, would never be declared the head of Besadii clan. After all, Durga had that hideous birthmark, and that should, by rights, have disqualified him from any leadership position.

But Durga had proven stronger and more able than Teroenza had realized. He'd managed (some said with the help of Black Sun) to eliminate his most vocal detractors in a most summary fashion. There was still talk against him, but it was more of a cautious murmur these days than a protesting shout.

Teroenza had pinned his hopes on Zier the Hutt, hoping that the senior Besadii member would be strong enough and clever enough to outwit Durga and take over both the Besadii clan, and the kajidic, its criminal arm, that was part of it.

But no. Durga had emerged (at least for the moment) with a shaky victory, and had promptly announced that Teroenza must adhere to all of Aruk's directives.

Including teaching Kibbick, Durga's idiot cousin, how to manage a top-level credit-making enterprise.

Here on Ylesia, religious "Pilgrims" were recruited by t'landa Til missionaries during traveling revival shows. Anyone unfortunate enough to fall prey to the addictive Exultation would follow the Ylesian missionaries to the steaming jungle planet. There the malnourished, brainwashed and addicted Pilgrims became willing slaves in the Ylesian spice factories, toiling from sunup to sundown for their Ylesian masters.

Teroenza's people were distant cousins of the Hutts, though they were far smaller and more mobile. With their huge bodies balanced on trunklike legs, the t'landa Til had a broad face that rather resembled a Hutt's countenance, but with the addition of a single long horn just above their nostrils. A long, whip-like tail was carried curled over their backs. Their arms and hands were tiny and weak compared to the rest of them.

The most interesting feature of the t'landa Til males, however, was not physical. They possessed the ability to project empathic "feel-good" emotions at most humans. These empathic projections, coupled with a soothing vibration produced in the males' throat sacs, was like a jolt of a powerful drug to the Pilgrims. They quickly became addicted to their daily "fix" and believed that the Priests were divinely gifted.

Nothing was further from the truth, however. The t'landa Til's ability was simply an adaptation of a male mating display, evolutionarily developed to attract t'landa Til females.

"Teroenza," Kibbick said fretfully, "I don't understand this. It says that we spent thousands of credits for a fertility-inhibitor that's placed in the slaves' gruel. Why can't we eliminate most of that? Can't we just let them breed? It would save credits, wouldn't it?"

Teroenza rolled his bulbous eyes, but Kibbick fortunately wasn't looking. "Your Excellency," the High Priest said, "if the Pilgrims are allowed to breed, that cuts into the energy they have to work. Their production declines. That would mean less spice processed and ready for market."

"Perhaps," Kibbick said. "But, Teroenza, surely there must be some way to manage this without expensive drugs. Perhaps we could encourage them to mate, then use their larvae and eggs for foodstuffs."

"Your Excellency," Teroenza said, hanging on to his patience by a thread, "most humanoids don't lay eggs or produce larvae. They have live births. They also have a very strong abhorrence for eating their own young."

It was true that, every so often, a couple of slaves would emerge from the Exultation-induced haze enough to feel lust for each other. It was rare, but human children had actually been born here on Ylesia. Teroenza had contemplated simply killing them out of hand, but, in the end, had decided that with a modicum of care, these children could be raised to become guards and administrative assistants. So he'd ordered them to be cared for in the slave barracks.

And, nowadays, fertility-inhibiting drugs were automatically added to the food served the slaves. It had been at least five years since the last accidental birth.

"Oh," Kibbick said. "Live births. I understand." He went back to his records with a grimace.

Idiot, thought Teroenza. *Idiot, idiot, idiot . . . how many years have you been here, and you never troubled to find out the most rudimentary facts about the Pilgrims. . . ?*

"Teroenza," said Kibbick presently, "I've found something else I don't understand."

Teroenza took a deep breath, then counted to twenty.

"Yes, Your Excellency?"

"Why do we have to spend extra credits on weapons and shields on these ships? They're only carrying slaves, after all, shipping them to the spice mines and the pleasure palaces after we have gotten the best work out of them. Who cares if raiders take them?"

Kibbick was referring to a raid a month ago by a group of human Rebels on a slave ship preparing to leave the Ylesian system. It wasn't the first such raid. Teroenza didn't know who was responsible, but he couldn't stop thinking that it had to be Bria Tharen, that wretched Corellian traitor and renegade.

Besadii had placed a sizable bounty on her head, but so far, no one had claimed it. *Perhaps it's time to talk to Durga about increasing the bounty on Bria Tharen*, Teroenza thought.

Aloud he said, with exaggerated patience, "Your Excellency, while it's true we don't care about the slaves once they leave here, they're still worth credits to us. And ships are expensive. Having big holes blown in them tends to render them unusable—or, at least, very expensive to repair."

"Oh," said Kibbick, his brow furrowing. "Yes, I guess that would be correct. Very well."

Idiot!

"Which brings to mind something I wanted to say to you, Your Excellency," Teroenza said. "Something that I hope you will mention to your cousin. We must have greater protection here on Ylesia. It is only a matter of time until we here on the planet are attacked again. These space-raids are bad enough, but if this Rebel group were to attack one of the colonies, you and I might conceivably be in danger."

Kibbick was staring at the High Priest, obviously alarmed by the suggestion. "Do you think they'd dare?" he asked, his voice a trifle unsteady.

"They did before, Your Excellency," Teroenza reminded him. "Bria Tharen, that ex-slave, led them. Remember?"

"Oh, yes, that's true," Kibbick said. "But that was over a year ago. Surely they've learned the futility of trying to attack this world by now. They did lose a ship in our atmosphere."

Ylesia's turbulent atmosphere was one of its best defenses.

"True," Teroenza agreed. "But I would rather be safe than sorry, Your Excellency."

"Safe than sorry . . ." Kibbick repeated, as though Teroenza had said something startlingly original and clever. "Yes, well . . . perhaps you have a point. We must be protected here. I will speak to my cousin about that today. Safe than sorry . . . yes, indeed, we must be safe. . . ."

Still mumbling, Kibbick went back to his records. Teroenza relaxed back into his sling, and allowed himself the luxury of another roll of his bulbous eyes.

Chapter Four:

Domestic Bliss and Other Complications

Chewbacca and Mallatobuck's wedding day dawned bright with promise and hope. Han, who had been told about the wedding only that morning, was glad that his friend was happy, but saddened at the prospect of losing him. They'd had a good couple of years together, though, and he figured that after a few years of marital joy, Chewie might be willing to come back and make occasional smuggling runs with him. Being a happy married guy was one thing, but being married didn't mean you were *dead*, right?

He and Chewie barely had a moment to speak together before the bustle of the wedding plans took his friend off on other duties. Apparently Wookiees did not have "best men" companions the way humans did, but Chewie, in deference to Han, asked the Corellian to stand beside him. Han had grinned. "Okay, I get to be 'best human,' eh?"

Chewbacca roared with amusement, and told Han that was as good a term for it as any.

As he sat in a corner in Attichitcuk's home, staying out from underfoot, Han thought about the only time he'd ever asked a woman to marry him. That had been Bria, when he was nineteen, and she was eighteen, and he'd been a lovestruck, moony-eyed kid, too young and dumb to know any better. Good thing for him that Bria had left him. . . .

Han opened the inner pocket of his vest and took out a much folded, aging piece of flimsy. Opening it, he read the first line:

Dearest Han,
    You don't deserve for this to happen, and all I can say is, I'm sorry. I love you, but I can't stay. . . .

Han's mouth twisted, then he folded the flimsy again and shoved it back into his pocket. Until last year, just before the Battle of Nar Shaddaa, he'd thought that Bria must have gone crawling back to the Ylesians, unable to live without the Exultation.

And then he'd encountered her, gorgeously gowned and coiffed, in Moff Sarn Shild's fancy penthouse on Coruscant. She'd called Shild "darling" and there had been every indication that she'd been the Moff's concubine. Han had done his best to despise her ever since. The idea that Bria might have actually loved the Moff never entered his head . . . he *knew* who she still loved. When she'd first seen him she'd gone pale, and it was still there, in her eyes, though she'd tried to disguise it. . . .

Moff Shild had committed suicide shortly after the Battle of Nar Shaddaa. The news-vids had been full of it. Vids of his memorial service (and Han had watched them deliberately) had shown no glimpse of Bria, though.

And now . . . to find out that she's some kind of Rebel agent for Corellia. . . Han thought. The more he thought about it, the more he wondered whether that was what Bria had been doing in Moff Shild's household. Had she been a Rebel intelligence operative, assigned to spy on the Moff, and, through him, the Empire?

It made sense. Han didn't like it, but he found that he had more respect for Bria if she'd been sleeping with the Moff to gain information, than if she'd just been what she appeared to be—a spoiled, gorgeous plaything.

He wondered what she was doing, now that the Moff was dead. Visiting planets and helping their underground Rebel movements get organized, obviously.

Also . . . Han had heard that a year or so ago, a group of human Rebels had hit Ylesia, attacking Colony Three and rescuing about a hundred slaves. Could Bria have been involved with that?

The way Katarra and the other Wookiees talked about her, she was some kind of warrior saint, risking her life to bring them arms and ammo from the Corellian rebels. And Kashyyyk was an Imperial slave world.

Han remembered how betrayed she'd been when she'd realized that the Ylesian religion was a hokey bunch of fake mumbo-jumbo. She'd been furious and bitter. She'd hated the fact that, in the space of a second, she'd been altered from *Pilgrim* to *slave*. In the years since that horrifying realization, had she taken that fury and translated it into action against the Ylesians and the Empire's slavers?

Han Solo hadn't lacked for female company since Bria, by any means. Back on Nar Shaddaa, Han and Salla Zend had been an item for more than two years now. Salla was a spirited, exciting woman, an expert tech and mechanic as well as a skilled pilot and smuggler. She and Han had so many things in common—and one of the foremost things that characterized their affair was that neither of them was interested in anything but having a good time—while it lasted.

Han's relationship with Salla was something that he could count on, without it getting in the way. They'd never made any promises to each other about anything, and that was the way they both liked it.

Han had often wondered whether he really loved Salla—or she him. He knew he cared for her, would do almost anything for her, but love? It was safe to say that he'd never felt about her or any woman the way he'd felt about Bria.

But I was a kid then, he reminded himself. *Just a reckless kid, who didn't know any better than to fall like a ton of neutronium. Now I'm a lot smarter. . . .*

As he sat musing in his corner, Kallabow, Chewbacca's sister, who had been rushing back and forth with platters for the coming wedding feast, suddenly stopped, hands on hips, and glared at him. Then she beckoned to him, exclaiming indignantly. Han got to his feet. "Hey, of course I ain't hiding," he said, in response. "I was just tryin' to stay outta the way. Is everything ready?"

Kallabow agreed emphatically that everything was ready, and Han should come *now*.

Han followed Chewie's sister out into the sunlight amid the rustling treetops. As he walked, Jarik fell into step with him. The kid had stayed pretty close by Han's side, since he didn't understand Wookiee, and, unless Han was around, could only speak to Ralrra. "So, this is it?" he asked Han.

"This is apparently it, kid," Han said. "Chewie's moments of freedom are numbered."

Kallabow, catching Han's words, gave the human males a scathing glance and an indignant, "Huuuuum-mmmpppppphhhhhhh!" that needed no translation. Han chuckled. "We better be careful, kid. She could break us both in two without half tryin'."

The Wookiee female led them down one of the bough-roads that was as wide as a street on some worlds. They were headed away from the city, deeper into the treetop area where many Wookiees had built homes. Malla's house, Han had gathered, was one of the tree-house-type places, since she lived where she could be close to her work.

Within minutes, they branched off onto another trail, then another. "Wonder where we're going?" Jarik said, uneasily. "I'm lost. If she left us out here, I wouldn't have a clue as to how to get back to Rwookrrorro. Would you?"

Han nodded. "Remind me to brush you up on your navigation skills, kid," he said. "But if Kallabow walks us much farther, I'm gonna be too tired to party."

The little party turned onto yet another, smaller trail, and ahead of them, Han and Jarik could see many Wookiees gathered. They walked, then the trail came to an abrupt end.

The wroshyr branch that they were standing on had been sheared off in some manner, and plunged down to rest atop lower branches. With the massive branch weighing the nearby treetops down, the effect was like looking out across a vast green valley—breathtaking.

Rounded green hills rose in soft swells to the west. The yellow sun shone down, bright as a beacon, and everywhere there were birds wheeling through the air.

"Hey . . ." Han said to Kallabow. "Nice view."

She nodded, and explained that this was a sacred place to Wookiees. Here, with this vista before them, they could truly appreciate the grandeur of their world.

The ceremony was ready to begin. There was no priest to officiate; Wookiee couples married themselves. Han walked up to stand beside Chewbacca, then gave his friend, who appeared more than a bit nervous, a reassuring grin, and reached up to ruffle the Wookiee's head-fur. "C'mon, relax," he said. "You're gettin' a great girl, pal."

Chewie replied that he knew that quite well . . . he just hoped he could remember his lines!

As they stood at the end of the trail, with a crowd of Wookiees between them and the pathway leading back to Rwookrrorro, the crowd suddenly parted in the middle. Mallatobuck paced down the trail toward them.

She was covered from head to foot in a sheer veil of silvery gray. The veil was so light, so translucent, it almost appeared that she was clothed in some glimmering energy field. But as she came up beside Chewie, Han could tell that the veil was actually some kind of knit or woven fabric, almost completely transparent. Han could see Malla's blue eyes clearly through her bridal veil.

Han listened intently as Chewie and Malla exchanged vows. Yes, they loved each other beyond all other beings. Yes, each other's honor was as dear to them as their own, Yes, they promised to be faithful to each other. Yes, death could part them, but could not end their love.

The life-power was with them, they said. The life-power would make their union strong, and they would be complete . . . together. The life-power would be with them . . . always.

Han felt a wave of unaccustomed solemnity wash over him. For a moment, he almost envied Chewie. He could see love shining in Mallatobuck's eyes, and felt a pang. Nobody had ever loved *him* that much. *Except maybe Dewlanna*, he thought, remembering the Wookiee widow who had raised him.

Bria . . . he'd used to think she loved him that much. But she sure had a funny way of showing it. . . .

Now Chewie was raising Malla's veil, and clutching her to him. They rubbed their cheeks together tenderly. Then, with a huge, triumphant roar, Chewie picked her up and swung her around as though she were child-sized instead of a grown Wookiee only a little shorter than he was.

The crowd of Wookiees broke into a chorus of hoots, roars and howls of appreciation.

"Well," said Han to Jarik, "guess that's it!"

But the wedding celebration was far from over. The honored couple was escorted to tables in the treetops that groaned with every kind of Wookiee delicacy. Han and Jarik moved among the tables, sampling cautiously, for Wookiees tended to serve most meats raw. Some were cooked, but even there humans had to be cautious. Wookiees enjoyed highly seasoned foods—and some were spicy and hot enough to damage a human gullet.

Han examined the tables and introduced Jarik to many "safe" Wookiee delicacies: Xachibik broth, a thick meat, herb and spice combination . . . Vrortik "cocktail," a layered dish that combined various meats and layers of wroshyr leaves that had been soaked in potent grakkyn nectar for weeks . . . Factryn meat pie, frozen Gormar, chyntuck rings, and fried Klak. . . .

There were also salads and flatbreads, plus forest-honey cakes and assorted chilled fruit delicacies.

Han advised Jarik against partaking of the various types of spirits being passed around. The Corellian knew from painful experience how potent Wookiee liquor could be. There were many kinds: accarragm, cortyg, garrmorl, grakkyn and Thikkiian brandy, to name a few.

"Take my advice, kid," Han said. "Wookiees know how to make homebrew that will put a human on the floor in minutes. I'm sticking to gorimn wine and Gralinyn juice."

"But the children drink Gralinyn juice," Jarik protested. "And this other stuff . . ."

"Jaar," Han said. "Sweetened alcoari milk and vineberry extract. It's too sweet for my taste, but you might like it."

Jarik was looking longingly at a huge flask of Thikki-ian brandy. Han shook his head warningly. "Kid . . . don't. I ain't takin' care of you if you wind up sick as a poisoned mulack-pup."

The youth made a face, but then picked up a cup of the gorimn wine. "Okay, I guess you know what you're talkin' about."

Han smiled and they clinked their glasses. "Trust me."

A few minutes later, as Han stood off by himself, holding a plate of barbecued trakkrrrn ribs and a spicy salad garnished with rilllrrnnn seeds, a dark-brown Wookiee who seemed vaguely familiar—though the Corellian was sure he'd never met him before—walked up to him. The Wookiee stood there, studying Han, and then introduced himself.

Han nearly dropped his plate. "You're Dewlannamapia's *son*?" he cried. "Hey!" Putting his plate and cup down hastily, he grabbed the Wookiee male in an excited hug. "Hey, guy, I'm so glad to meet you! What's your name?"

The Wookiee returned Han's embrace, replying that he was called Utchakkaloch. Han stood back, looking at him, and found that his eyes were stinging. Chakk (or so he asked to be called), seemed equally moved, as he told Han that he had hoped to meet him, partly because he hoped the human could tell him how his mother had died.

Han swallowed. "Chakk, your mom died a hero," he said. "I wouldn't be alive today it if wasn't for her. She was one brave Wookiee. She died a warrior's death, fighting. A guy named Garris Shrike shot and killed her, but . . . he's dead, too."

Chakk wanted to know whether Han had killed Shrike in order to avenge his mother's death. "Not exactly," Han said. "Someone else got him first. But I put a good hurtin' on him, before he bought it."

Chakk rumbled his approval. He told Han that he felt Han was an adopted brother, since they had shared the same mother. All of his mother's communications during her days aboard *Trader's Luck* had been full of anecdotes about the little human boy who loved her wastril bread, and who wanted so much to become a pilot.

"Well, Chakk," Han said, "Dewlanna never lived to see it, but I am a pilot today. And my best friend in all the universe is a Wookiee. . . ."

Chakk guffawed, and then told Han that he and Chewbacca were distantly related through a second cousin three times removed who had emigrated to Rwookrrorro and married Chewbacca's great-aunt's niece. Han blinked. "Distant . . . uh, yeah. Well, that's great. Just one big happy family."

Han led Chakk over to the bridegroom and introduced him to Chewie, explaining the situation. Chewbacca roared his welcome of Han's "adopted brother" and thumped Chakk soundly on the back.

The celebration continued far into the night. Wookiees danced, sang, and played wooden instruments that had been handed down in their families for generations. Han and Jarik celebrated with them, until the humans were so exhausted, and so tipsy, that they wound up curling up beneath one of the massive tables and falling asleep.

When Han awoke in the morning, the celebration was over, and Chewie and Malla, he was informed, had gone off into the woods for that time of privacy that was the Wookiee equivalent of a honeymoon. Han was sorry . . . in a couple of days his negotiations with Katarra would be concluded, the *Falcon* would be reloaded with her new cargo, and he'd be leaving Kashyyyk. He wouldn't get to tell Chewie goodbye.

But you couldn't expect a guy to remember his best friend on his wedding night, Han mused, with a hint of regret. Besides, he fully intended to come back to Kashyyyk again, so it wasn't as though he'd said goodbye to Chewie forever. . . .

Safe in the privacy of his office on Nal Hutta, Durga the Hutt wriggled closer to Myk Bidlor's holo-image as it solidified. His bulbous, slit-pupiled eyes protruded even further in his eagerness as he demanded, "You have news about the autopsy results? You have identified the substance?"

"Your Excellency, this substance was so rare that we

could not at first identify it, or be certain as to its effects," the senior forensic specialist looked tired and harried—as though he really had been working night and day, as he claimed. "But our tests on that substance, and our tracing of it, is now conclusive. Yes, the substance is a poison. We have traced its origin to the planet Malkii."

"The Malkite poisoners!" Durga exclaimed. "Of course! Secret assassins who specialize in exotic and almost undetectable poisons . . . who else could come up with a substance that would prove fatal to a Hutt? My people are very difficult to poison. . . ."

"I am aware of that, Your Excellency," Myk Bidlor said. "And this substance—so rare that we have been unable to find a name for it—is one of their crowning achievements in toxins. We call it X-1 for want of a better name."

"And X-1 does not occur in nature anywhere on Nal Hutta," Durga said, wanting to make absolutely sure. "This could not possibly have been an accident."

"No, Your Excellency. X-1 must have been deliberately administered to Lord Aruk."

"Administered? How?"

"We cannot be certain, but ingestion seems the most likely method."

"Someone fed my parent a fatal dose of poison," Durga said, his voice going cold and deadly with rage. "Someone is going to pay . . . and pay . . . and pay."

"Uh . . . not exactly, Your Excellency." The specialist licked his lips nervously. "The scheme was not nearly so . . . obvious . . . as that. It was actually . . . rather ingenious."

If it was that clever, it must certainly have been a Hutt, Durga thought. He glared at the scientist. "What, then?"

"The substance is deadly in large quantities, Lord Durga. But in small quantities, it would not kill. Instead, it would concentrate in the brain tissues, causing the victim to experience a progressive deterioration of the thought processes. And the substance is also highly addictive. Once the victim grew accustomed to ingesting it in high enough doses, the abrupt *withdrawal* of the substance would cause the symptoms you described—wracking pain, convulsions, and death." He took a breath. "And that, Lord Durga, is why your parent died. Not from the X-1 in his system . . . but from its abrupt withdrawal."

"How long," Durga said, gritting the words out, "would this substance have to have been given to my parent for him to become addicted to it?"

"I would suspect a period of a few months, Lord Durga, but I cannot say for certain. Weeks, at minimum. It would take time to build up the dosage until the withdrawal would prove quickly fatal." The specialist hesitated. "Lord Durga, our investigations also revealed that X-1 is very expensive. It is produced from the stamens of a type of plant that grows only on one world in the galaxy—and the location of that world is a sworn secret held by the Malkite Poisoners. So only a person or persons of great wealth could have purchased enough of it to kill your parent."

"I see," Durga said, after a moment. "Continue with any tests that may shed further light on the subject, Bidlor. And send me all of your data. I intend to find out just where that X-1 came from."

Bidlor bobbed in a nervous bow. "Certainly, Your Excellency. But . . . sir . . . these investigations are not . . . inexpensive."

"Price is no object!" Durga snarled. "I must know, and I will pay what it takes to find the truth! I will find the source of that X-1, and I will trace it to whomever fed it to my parent! Besadii's resources are *my* resources! Do you understand, Bidlor?"

The scientist bowed again, more deeply. "Yes, Your Excellency. We will continue to investigate."

"See that you do."

Durga broke the connection and then undulated back and forth across his office, fuming. *Aruk was murdered! I knew it all along! Wealth enough to buy X-1. It has be Desilijic—Jiliac . . . or perhaps Jabba. I will find the one responsible for this, and I will kill him or her with my own hands! I swear it to my dead parent—I will have vengeance. . . .*

Over the next ten days, Durga had all the servants in the palace interrogated ruthlessly—especially the cooks. Though several died during questioning, there was no evidence to indicate that any of them had been tampering with Aruk's meals.

The young Hutt Lord neglected his other duties as he attended each interrogation session. His rival, Zier, came to visit him toward the end of the sessions, and arrived just as droids were bearing away the limp corpse of a t'landa Til female who had served as a minor administrative clerk for Besadii.

The elder Hutt looked disdainfully at the huge, four-legged body as it was borne out by the droids. "How many does that make?" he asked, with more than a touch of sarcasm.

Durga glared at Zier. He'd have loved to have linked the other Besadii to Aruk's death, but Zier had been on Nar Hekka overseeing Besadii interests until a few months ago, when he'd been recalled home after Aruk's death. When he'd first turned up, Durga had had Zier investigated thoroughly, but there was not even the smallest hint of a link between him and Aruk's murder.

For one thing, Zier, though well-off, did not possess

nearly the financial resources to purchase large quantities of X-1. And there had been no unusual withdrawals from his accounts.

"Four," the young Hutt snapped. "They do not have our strength, cousin. It is no wonder the lesser races bow to us . . . they are far inferior physically, as well as mentally."

Zier sighed. "I must say I will miss that Twi'lek chef of yours," he said. "He prepared filets of mulblatt larvae in fregon-blood sauce superbly." He sighed again.

Durga's huge mouth turned down. "Chefs can be replaced," he said shortly.

"Has it occurred to you, my dear cousin, that the forensic specialist you hired might be *wrong* in his conclusions?"

"He and his team are the best to be had," Durga said. "Their references were excellent. They have performed investigations for the Emperor's top military aides . . . even Governor Tarkin."

Zier nodded. "A good recommendation," he admitted. "From what I hear, the governor is not an official to disappoint if one wishes to live."

"That is what they say."

"Still, cousin . . . is it possible that you have demanded of this team that they find evidence of murder, and so they have? Whether or not it is true?"

Durga considered that for a moment. "I do not believe that," he said, finally. "The evidence is there. I have seen the lab reports."

"Lab reports can be faked, cousin. Also . . . in your obsession, you have spent a great many credits. These scientists are earning much from Besadii. It is possible that they do not wish this stream of credits to end."

Durga faced his cousin. "I am certain that the team has reported their findings accurately. As to the cost . . .

Aruk was the head of all Besadii. Isn't it proper to find out what really happened? Lest others think we can be killed with impunity?"

Zier's pointed tongue ran slowly across the lower part of his mouth as he thought. "Perhaps you are right, cousin. However . . . I would suggest that in order for you to not be regarded as a reckless spendthrift, you begin paying for this investigation out of your own personal funds, rather than Besadii operating capital. If you agree to this, no more will be said. If you do not . . . well, there is a clan meeting approaching. As a conscientious clan leader, it is my duty to comment on our financial report."

Durga glared at his cousin.

Zier glared back. "And . . . cousin . . . if any accidents befall me, it will go the worse for you. I have filed copies of the financial reports in places you have no way of discovering. They will be produced should I die—no matter how much it might seem that I perished of natural causes."

The younger Hutt resisted the urge to order his guards to shoot Zier. Hutts were notoriously hard to kill, and another death might well cause all of Besadii to rise up against him.

Durga drew a deep breath. "Perhaps you are right, cousin," he said, finally. "From this day forward, I will personally finance the investigation."

"Good," Zier said. "And . . . Durga. In your parent's absence I feel I must give you the benefit of my experience."

If Durga had possessed teeth, he would have ground them together in rage. "Go on," he said.

"Black Sun, Durga. It is an open secret that you used their resources to consolidate your power. I caution you against doing so again. One cannot just employ Black Sun and then walk away. Their services are . . . expensive."

"They have been fully compensated for their services," Durga said tightly. "I am not such a fool as you think, Zier."

"Good," the other Hutt Lord said. "I am glad to hear that. I was worried about you, dear cousin. Any Hutt who would rid himself of such a chef—on a whim—is suspect."

Seething, Durga undulated off in search of another staff member to interrogate.

Jabba the Hutt and his aunt Jiliac were lounging together in their palatial receiving room in Jiliac's palace on Nal Hutta, watching Jiliac's baby inch its way around the room. The infant Hutt was now old enough to spend almost an hour outside Jiliac's pouch. At this stage of its life, the little creature resembled a huge, chubby grub or insect larva more than a Hutt. Its arms were nothing more than vestigial stubs, and would not develop or grow digits until the baby Hutt had left the maternal pouch for good. The only way in which the baby Hutt resembled the adult members of its species was its pop-eyed, vertical-pupiled stare.

Hutt babies were born almost mindless, and Hutt youngsters did not reach the age of accountability until they were about a century old. Before that, they were looked upon as creatures who needed good care and feeding, and not much else.

As he watched the baby wriggle along the polished stone floor, Jabba wished they were back on Nar Shaddaa, where he could get more done. It was difficult to oversee the Desilijic smuggling empire from Nal Hutta. Jabba had suggested more than once that he and his aunt go back to Nar Shaddaa, but Jiliac adamantly refused, insisting that the polluted atmosphere of Nar Shaddaa would be unhealthy for her baby.

Jabba thus spent much of his time shuttling back and forth between Nal Hutta and Nar Shaddaa. His holdings on Tatooine were suffering by his absence. Ephant Mon, the non-humanoid Chevin, was looking after Jabba's interests, and doing it well, but it just wasn't the same as being there himself.

Jabba had shared many adventures in the past with Mon, and the ugly sentient from Vinsoth was the only being in the universe that Jabba really trusted. For some reason (even Jabba wasn't sure why), Ephant Mon was completely loyal to Jabba, and always had been. Jabba knew that the Chevin had turned down multiple offers to betray him for fabulous profit. Yet . . . Ephant Mon had never turned, no matter how much he was offered.

Jabba appreciated his friend's loyalty and repaid it by keeping only minor tabs on Ephant Mon's actions. He didn't expect Mon to betray him, not after all these years . . . but it was well to be prepared for anything.

"Aunt," Jabba said, "I have read the newest report from our source in the Besadii accounting office, and their profits are impressive. Even the dissension over Durga's leadership has not slowed them. Ylesia continues to produce more processed spice with every month that passes. Shiploads of Pilgrims are arriving nearly every week. It is depressing."

Jiliac turned her massive head to regard her nephew. "Durga has done better than I ever gave him credit for, Jabba. I did not think he could hold onto the leadership. By now I envisioned that Besadii would be ripe for our takeover—but, even though there is muttering and discontent with Durga's leadership, his outspoken opponents are dead, and no one has surfaced to replace them within the clan."

Jabba blinked at his aunt, and a spark of hope awakened. That speech sounded almost like the old, premotherhood Jiliac! "Do you know why they are dead, Aunt?"

"Because Durga was foolish enough to deal with Black Sun," Jiliac said. "The deaths of his opponents were too blatant to be Hutt doing. Only Black Sun has that many resources. Only Prince Xizor would be so coldly daring as to assassinate them all within days of each other."

Jabba was getting excited, now. *Is she coming out of her maternal mental haze?* he wondered.

"Prince Xizor is indeed someone to be reckoned with," he said. "That is why I have done him favors from time to time. I would prefer to stay on his good side . . . just in case I ever need a favor in return. As I did that one time on Tatooine. He helped me then, and asked nothing in return, because I have done him favors in the past."

Jiliac was shaking her head slowly back and forth, a mannerism she'd picked up from humans. "Jabba, you know my thinking on this, I have told you many times. Prince Xizor is not one to be trifled with. Best to stay far away from him, and to have nothing to do with Black Sun. Open the door to them just once, and you risk becoming his vassal."

"I am cautious, Aunt, I assure you. I would never do as Durga has done."

"Good. Durga will soon discover that he has opened a door that cannot easily be closed. If he steps through it . . . he will no longer be his own master."

"So should we hope he does that, Aunt?"

Jiliac's eyes narrowed slightly. "Hardly, Nephew. Xizor is not a foe I wish to contend with. He has evidently set his sights on Besadii, but he would willingly take Desilijic, too, of that I have no doubt."

Jabba silently agreed. Xizor would move in on the whole of Nal Hutta if given the opportunity. "Speaking of Besadii, Aunt," he said, "what of these Ylesian profits I was reporting on? What can we do to stop Besadii? They now have nine colonies on Ylesia. They are preparing to start another colony on Nyrvona, the other habitable world in the system."

Jiliac thought for a moment. "Perhaps it is time to utilize Teroenza again," she said. "Durga apparently has no suspicion that he was responsible for Aruk's death."

"Utilize him how?"

"I don't know yet. . . ." Jiliac said. "Perhaps we can encourage Teroenza to declare his independence from Durga. If they fought, Besadii profits would be bound to plummet. And then . . . we could pick up the pieces."

"Very good, Aunt!" Jabba was happy to hear the old, scheming Jiliac acting like herself again. "Now, if I can just report on these figures here, and get your input on reducing our costs in—"

"Ahhhhhhhh!"

Jabba broke off, interrupted by Jiliac's deep, maternal coo of affection, and saw the baby Hutt wriggling up to its mother, tiny vestigial arms held up, its bulbous eyes fixed on Jiliac's face intently. The baby's mouth opened, and it chirruped inquiringly.

"Look, Nephew!" Jiliac's voice was warm, indulgent. "My little one knows mama, yes, doesn't he, precious?"

Jabba rolled his eyes until they nearly emerged from their sockets and splatted onto the floor. *Witness the demise of one of the greatest criminal minds of this millennium,* he thought, bleakly.

Then, as Jiliac scooped up the baby Hutt and guided

it back into her pouch, Jabba glared at the little creature with an expression very close to outright hatred. . . .

Han spent the next couple of days with the members of the Wookiee underground, finalizing their deal. The time came when he opened up the *Falcon*, and he and Jarik unloaded the explosive quarrels from the secret compartments. Katarra, Kichiir and Motamba clustered around the boxes, exclaiming excitedly over their new toys.

Meanwhile, other Wookiees from the underground movement made a steady stream inside the ship, loading it with stormtrooper armor. Han was able to pack nearly forty complete suits and ten helmets into the *Falcon*. If the armor fetched the market price, he'd doubled his investment on the trip. Not a bad bit of bargaining!

By the time all the armor was stowed away enough so that the *Falcon's* crew could move about, night was falling. Han decided that he wanted to wait for dawn for his tricky exit of the cave and straight-up flight through the trees. He and Jarik said farewell to their hosts and stretched out on the pilot's seats to sleep.

Han was awakened before sunrise the next morning by a loud—and familiar!—Wookiee roar. The Corellian opened his eyes and jumped up, nearly tripping over the sleepy Jarik. Activating the ramp, he raced down it. "Chewie!"

Han was so glad to see the big furball that he didn't even complain when the Wookiee grabbed him, swung him around, and ruffled his hair until it stood on end. All the while, Chewbacca was whining out a steady stream of complaints. What had Han been thinking of, preparing to leave him behind? Didn't he know any better? What could you expect from a human!

When the Wookiee finally released him, Han looked up at Chewie, completely confused. "Huh? Whaddaya mean, I was gonna leave you behind? I'm goin' back to Nar Shaddaa, pal, and, in case it's slipped your attention, Chewie, you're a married guy now. Your place is here, on Kashyyyk, with Malla."

Chewie shook his head, uttering protesting hoots and remonstrations. "Life debt? Pal, I know you've sworn a life debt, but let's be realistic here! You belong with your wife, on your own planet, now! Not dodgin' Imp cruisers with me."

The Wookiee had just started in again when a loud, angry roar from behind Han made him jump and dodge. A large, hairy hand grabbed his shoulder, and Han was swung around as though he weighed no more than a scrap of flimsy. He looked up to see Mallatobuck towering over him. Chewie's wife was furious, teeth bared, blue eyes narrowed. Han put up both hands, and shrank back against his friend's hairy chest. "Hey, Malla! Take it easy, now!"

Mallatobuck roared again, then launched into an angry tirade. Humans! How could they be so ignorant of Wookiee customs and Wookiee honor? How *dare* Han imply that Chewbacca would abandon a life debt? There was no greater insult he could offer a Wookiee! Her husband was possessed of great honor! He was a courageous warrior, a skilled hunter, and when he gave his word, he *kept* it! Especially about a life debt!

Faced with Malla's ire, Han turned both hands up and shrugged, but couldn't get a word in edgewise. He looked up imploringly at his friend. Chewie, taking pity on his Corellian buddy, intervened. He stepped between Malla and Han, and spoke quickly, telling her that of course Han had meant no insult, no offense. His comment had been made out of ignorance, not malice.

Finally, Malla relaxed, and her roars turned to grumbles. Han gave her an apologetic smile. "Hey, no offense, Malla. I know Chewie here better'n almost anyone, and I know he's a terrific guy, brave, smart, all that stuff. I just didn't know that to a Wookiee, a life debt outweighs everything else."

He turned back to his friend. "So, okay, you're comin' with us, and we're gettin' ready to grab some space, pal. So say goodbye to your bride."

Chewbacca and Mallatobuck walked away together, while Han and Jarik conducted the preflight checks. A few minutes later, Han heard the *clang* of the *Falcon's* ramp closing. Moments later, Chewbacca slipped into the copilot's seat. Han looked at him, "Don't worry, pal, I swear to you we'll come back again . . . soon. I did some good dealing with Katarra and her underground. Your people are going to need lots of ammo before they can even hope to take on the Imps and free your world. And I'm gonna help 'em get it."

Jarik's voice came over the intercom from the starboard gunner's turret. "Yeah, at a tidy profit, of course."

Han laughed. "Yeah . . . of course! Chewie . . . stand by! Here . . . we . . . go!"

With great dignity, the *Millennium Falcon* rose upward on her repulsors, then drifted forward until she was out of the tree-branch "cave." Then, with a suddenness that sent everyone sinking back into their seats, Han sent his ship whooshing straight up, through the tunnel of trees. They soared up into the skies, now flushed with the red-gold dawn. As the *Falcon* went higher, sunrise seemed to burst over the world in a shower of gold.

Quarrr-tellerrra, Han thought. The sun-haired warrior, the woman he had known as Bria. . . . *What was she doing now?* he wondered. *Does she ever think about me?*

Moments later, Kashyyyk was only a rapidly dwindling green ball behind them, as they tore through the star-flecked blackness. . . .

Boba Fett sat in a sleazy rented flat on the Outer Rim world of Teth, listening to Bria Tharen meeting with the Tethan Rebel leaders. The most famous bounty hunter in the galaxy had many resources, including a spy network that most planets would have envied. Since he accepted Imperial assignments from time to time, he was often privy to communiqués and other information most Rebel Commands would have loved to see.

Even though she was a Rebel officer, the bounty on Bria Tharen had not been posted by the Empire. No, this was a far larger bounty, the sum of fifty thousand credits for a live, unharmed capture, no disintegrations permitted. Aruk the Hutt, the old leader of Besadii clan, had originally posted the bounty, but his heir, Durga, had continued it after his death, and had promised a bonus for delivery within three months.

Boba Fett had been searching on and off for Bria Tharen for over a year now. The woman kept being sent out on "deep cover" assignments that made her extremely hard to trace. She had severed all ties with her family, probably to lessen the danger to them should she be captured by the Imperials. When she was on her home planet of Corellia, she lived inside a series of secret Rebel command bases, with extensive security and guard mounts.

Such high security was understandable . . . after all,

the Rebels lived in fear of a full-scale attack by Imperial stormtroopers. So they kept the locations of their bases top-secret, and moved them continually. One bounty hunter—no matter how deadly and effective—stood little chance of getting close enough to manage a live capture.

If only Besadii would have been satisfied with having Bria dead, Boba Fett was fairly sure he could have managed to kill her, even within the protection of a Rebel base. But live, unharmed capture was much more difficult. . . .

However, a few days ago, Boba Fett had learned through his spy network that there was a meeting scheduled for the underground Rebel movement on Teth. Taking a calculated risk that Bria would be there, he had flown *Slave I* to Teth two days ago. The risk had paid off; she had shown up yesterday evening.

Two days ago, when he'd first arrived on Teth, Boba Fett had located the current Rebel enclave, which was situated beneath the port city in a series of old storm drains and sub-basements. He'd infiltrated the outskirts of the base, via the ancient storm drains and ventilation shafts, enough to locate the base janitorial supplies. There he'd placed minuscule audio pickups on a number of small robot floor cleaners that roved freely from room to room, sucking up anything their tiny scanners identified as "dirt."

Since that time, he'd been monitoring the pickups, and today his preparations had paid off. Bria Tharen was in a meeting with two top-ranked Tethan Rebels. The tiny floor-cleaner, per its programmed instructions, had scuttled out of their way when they'd entered the room, and was now biding its time in an inconspicuous corner.

Boba Fett had no use for the whole concept of the

various rebellions. He considered the idea of rebellion against any established government criminal. The Empire maintained order, and Boba Fett valued order. The Tethan resistance was no exception . . . a bunch of misguided idealists who were out to create anarchy. . . .

Within the confines of his helmet, Boba Fett's eyes narrowed with disdain as he listened. The Tethan leaders were Commander Winfrid Dagore and her aide, Lieutenant Palob Godalhi. At the moment the Tharen woman was arguing with them about the necessity for the various resistance groups to unite into a Rebel Alliance. There were indications, she said, that the idea of an Alliance was gaining support in high places.

A prestigious Imperial Senator, Mon Mothma of Chandrila, had recently met secretly with Bria's superiors in the Corellian Rebel underground, and talked. The senator agreed that in the wake of the Empire's massacres on planets such as Ghorman, Devaron, Rampa 1 and 2, that the Emperor was either pathologically insane or totally evil, and must be overthrown by sentients of good conscience.

The Tharen woman spoke with misguided passion, her clear alto voice quivering slightly with controlled emotion. It was obvious she really cared about her cause.

When she was finished, Winfrid Dagore cleared her throat. Her voice was rough with age and strain. "Commander Tharen, we sympathize with our brothers and sisters on Corellia, Alderaan and the other worlds. But here on the Outer Rim, we are so far away from the Core Worlds that we could be of little help to you, even if we did ally with your groups. We do things our way out here. The Emperor pays little attention to us. We raid the Imperial shipping, and oppose the Empire in many ways—but we value our independence. We are not likely to join a larger group."

"Commander Dagore, that isolationist policy is an invitation to an Imperial massacre," Tharen said, her tone bleak. "Mark my words, it will happen. Palpatine's forces will not overlook your groups forever."

"Perhaps . . . or perhaps not. Still, I doubt that we could do more than what we are currently doing, Commander Tharen."

Boba Fett heard a chair creak and the rustle of fabric as someone moved. Then Tharen spoke again. "Commander Dagore, you have ships. You have troops. You have weapons. You are one of the closest worlds to the Corporate Sector, though we realize that's a long way off. But still, you could help. You could help with purchasing weapons in the Corporate Sector and funneling them back here to be shipped to other undergrounds. Don't think because you're out here, that your help isn't needed."

"Commander Tharen, weapons cost credits," Lieutenant Godalhi said. "Where will those credits come from?"

"Well, we'd certainly appreciate it if you Tethans managed to come up with a few million to help us out," Bria said dryly, and a sad chuckle ran around the room. "But we're working on it. Financing the resistance is very hard, but there are enough citizens who are being squeezed until they can't see straight that, even if they don't have the ability or the courage to join a Rebel group outright, they're smuggling us spare credits. Some of the Hutt lords have also seen fit to contribute . . . clandestinely, of course."

Interesting . . . , thought Fett. This was news to him, though, now that he thought about it, Hutts were notorious for playing both sides plus their own side in any conflict. If they could look forward to an increase in credits or power, Hutts were usually right there. . . .

"We are not far from Hutt space," Dagore said, a thoughtful note in her voice. "Perhaps we could make contacts with other Hutt lords . . . see if they'd be willing to help."

"Help?" Bria Tharen's voice sputtered with laughter. "Hutts? They may contribute, and some have, but they do it for their own reasons, trust me, and those reasons have nothing to do with our aims. Hutts are devious . . . but sometimes their goals and ours coincide. That's when they hand out their credits. Half the time we can't even guess what benefit they may be getting as a result of their 'donation.' "

"Probably better not to guess," Lieutenant Godalhi said. "Still, Commander Tharen, there may be some merit in our increasing our commitment at this time. Our new Imperial Moff is far less . . . vigilant than Sarn Shild was. We have been getting away with far more lately than we could under Shild's rule."

"That's another thing," Bria Tharen said. "We've been studying this new Moff, Yref Orgege. Most of the new procedures he's put in place here in the Outer Rim are so ill-advised that we're beginning to wonder if he has Gamorrean blood."

Laughter rippled throughout the room.

Bria continued, "Orgege is both arrogant and stupid. He's insisting that he won't make Shild's mistake, and he's going to keep close personal control over his military force. This policy has cut down tremendously on the Imperial threat here in the Outer Rim. The Imp Commanders have to check with Orgege about the smallest things. He is managing them into paralysis, Commander Dagore."

"We're aware of that, Commander," Dagore agreed. "What do you want us to do about it?"

"Increase your raids on Imperial supply vessels and munitions dumps here in the Outer Rim, Commander. We need those weapons. And by the time Orgege can be contacted and give his orders, you and your people will be long gone."

Dagore considered for a moment. "I think we can promise you that much, Commander Tharen. For the rest . . . we'll take it under advisement."

"Talk to your people today," Bria said. "I'll be leaving tomorrow."

Boba Fett strained his ears, silently urging her to reveal her plans. But there was no other sound except the scrapings of chairs as the Rebels got up and left the room.

Fett kept a close survey on all the nearby spaceports, but he was unable to catch even a glimpse of Bria Tharen the next day. She must have been smuggled aboard a Rebel ship by some clandestine means.

The bounty hunter was slightly disappointed at his failure, but the most important trait of any hunter—and Boba Fett lived for the hunt—was *patience*. He resolved to find some way of tipping off the Imperials about Mon Mothma's treachery, and the Rebels' plans, without letting them know who their informant was. Many Imperial officers were openly scornful of bounty hunters, referring to them as "scum"—and worse. Fett wished he had more specific information to offer as a tip. If only the Rebels had revealed plans for an actual operation!

In the meantime, Fett's trip to Teth would not be wasted. He'd checked with the Guild, and there was an open bounty here on their books, a rich, reclusive businessman who had a high-guarded and "secure" estate in the mountains of Teth.

"Secure" that is, insofar as ordinary bounty hunters went, but Boba Fett was in a class by himself. The businessman's activities had been so predictable that planning was laughably easy. The man was a creature of habit. Boba Fett wouldn't even have to go up against his bodyguards, since this was a bounty permitting disintegrations. Only the kill was required.

Boba Fett had found a vantage point in a laakwal tree that would allow him to erect a temporary blind, make the kill, then slip away before the bodyguards or security forces could even pinpoint his location. One shot would be all that he needed. . . .

Chapter Five:

"From One Side of this Galaxy to the Other"

Over the next five months, Han Solo and his Wookiee First Mate rose to the top of the smuggler heap. For a miracle, Han managed to actually hang on to some of the money he'd won long enough to do most of the modifications on the *Millennium Falcon* that he'd envisioned.

His half-alien master technician and starship mechanic, Shug Ninx, let him berth the *Falcon* in his Spacebarn. Shug's Spacebarn was almost a legend in the Corellian section of Nar Shaddaa. Within its cavernous interior, traders, pirates and smugglers tinkered with their ships, modifying them, determined to squeeze the last bit of speed and firepower out of them. After all, the faster a smuggler delivered a cargo, the quicker he, she or it could take off again with another shipment. Time was credits, in the life of a smuggler.

Han, Jarik and Chewbacca did most of the work themselves, with an occasional hand from Salla, who was also an expert technician, and Shug, the acknowledged master.

Once he had the ship's armor-plating the way he wanted it—no lucky Imperial shot was going to take out the *Falcon* the way Han's previous ship, the *Bria*, had been destroyed!—he started on the engines and the armament. He added a light laser cannon under the nose, then moved the quad lasers so the *Falcon* had gun turrets both dorsally and ventrally—top and bottom. Then Han and Salla installed two concussion missile launching tubes between the forward mandibles.

All the while that he was installing weapons and armor, Han, Shug and Chewie worked on the *Falcon's* engines and other systems. The *Falcon* already boasted a military-grade hyperdrive. Together Han and Shug tinkered with both the hyperdrive and sublight engines until they were even more powerful, and the *Falcon* was making faster and faster times on Han's smuggling runs.

They also installed new sensor and jamming systems. The new jamming system had a less than auspicious first trial, however. When Han triggered it, the pulse was so powerful that it also jammed the *Falcon's* own internal communications, disrupting the signals from the cockpit to the ship's systems! The incident happened at the worst possible time—while the *Falcon* was ducking into a planet's gravity well in an attempt to shake off an Imperial frigate. As their ship hurtled down, grazing upper atmosphere, totally out of control, Han and Chewbacca stared at their instruments in dismay. Only the fact that the new jammer was so powerful that it burned out almost immediately saved them from being incinerated in the planet's atmosphere.

The day came when Han looked at the *Falcon* with satisfaction, and threw an arm around Shug Ninx's shoulders. "Shug old pal, you are one master mechanic. I don't think there's anyone better with a hyperdrive in the whole galaxy. She's purring like a Togorian kit-cub, and we've increased her speed another two percent."

The half-alien master mechanic smiled at his friend, but shook his head. "Thanks, Han, but I can't claim that title. I've heard that there's a guy in the Corporate Sector name of 'Doc' who can make a hyperdrive dance a jizz-jig with one hand tied behind his back. If you want her to go even faster, you'll have to hunt him up."

Han listened with some surprise, but filed the information away in his mind as potentially useful. He'd always had a yen to see the Corporate Sector, and now he had a reason to go there.

"Thanks, Shug," he said. "I'll have to consider contacting this guy if I ever get there."

"From what I've heard about Doc, you don't contact him. He'll contact you, if he decides it's a good idea. Ask Arly Bron about him. He's spent time in the Corporate Sector, he might know how you'd go about contacting Doc."

"Thanks for the word," Han said. He knew Arly Bron, as he did most of the smugglers who hung out in the Corellian Sector of Nar Shaddaa. Bron was a stocky, aging smuggler with a genial air and a sharp tongue. He enjoyed needling fools, but he was fast enough on the draw to still be among the living, which said something for his speed and accuracy. He flew a beat up old freighter named *Double Echo*.

Now that Han had the fast and (comparatively) reliable *Millennium Falcon*, he could take on the most challenging jobs. He still worked mostly for Jabba, who was basically running the Desilijic kajidic these days, but he also took jobs for other employers. The Corellian and his Wookiee sidekick became almost a legend on Nar Shaddaa as they broke speed records for the Kessel Run and flew rings around Imperial patrol vessels.

Han had never been happier. He had a fast ship, friends in Chewie, Jarik and Lando, an attractive, savvy lady friend in Salla, and credits in his pocket. True, money had a way of slipping through his fingers, no matter how he tried to hold on to it, but to Han, that was only a minor worry. So what if he liked living high, gambling and expensive flings? He could always make more!

But even though Han's personal life was going splendidly, dark clouds were gathering on the horizon. The Emperor continued to tighten his grip, and his reach was extending even into the Outer Rim these days. There was a massacre on Mantooine in the Atrivis Sector, and the Rebels that had managed to capture an Imperial base there were wiped out practically to the last defender.

There were other massacres as object lessons to inner Imperial worlds. Gunrunners had to be increasingly wary and fast, in order to deliver their cargoes. When Han had first begun making the Kessel Run, it was unusual to even pick up an Imp craft on ship's sensors. Now it was unusual to *not* spot one. To support his fleets and armies, Emperor Palpatine levied taxes that had citizens of the Empire groaning beneath the financial burden. These days, the average citizen of the Empire struggled just to put decent food on the table.

(Han and his friends, naturally, did not pay taxes. No tax collectors came to the Smuggler's Moon—collecting taxes from the motley denizens of Nar Shaddaa was such a daunting task that the moon was simply "over-looked" each tax time.)

In the past, Han had paid little attention to news-vids about the struggle between the Imperials and the underground Rebel groups. But now, knowing that Bria might be involved in those actions, he found himself listening to the news-vids with undivided attention. *Palpatine must be crazy,* Han found himself thinking, on more than one occasion. *He's askin' for a wholesale rebellion with these tactics . . . massacres, murders, citizens hauled out of their homes in the middle of the night, and never seen again. . . . You mess over people bad enough, long enough, you're askin' for revolt. . . .*

Dissent in the Imperial Senate was growing by leaps and bounds. One of the more prominent Senators, Mon Mothma, had been forced to flee not long ago, after the Emperor ordered her arrest on charges of treason. Mon Mothma had been a prestigious member of the Senate, and the Emperor's high-handed move caused demonstrations on Chandrilla, her home planet—demonstrations that resulted in yet another ruthless massacre of Imperial citizens.

The Emperor's attacks on financial well-being and personal freedom had another effect, one that Han found particularly disturbing. More and more down-trodden, poverty-stricken people were chucking their old lives and heading for Ylesia to become Pilgrims—or, as Han knew, *slaves.*

Many of the new Pilgrims came from Sullust, Bothu-wui, and Corellia, worlds that had recently suffered reprisals for civil unrest and anti-taxation demonstrations. Han arrived home one day from a smuggling run to discover that, for the first time, the t'landa Til had held a revival on Nar Shaddaa. As a result, a number of Corellians from the Corellian sector of Nar Shaddaa had packed up and were waiting to board a ship bound for, among other places, Ylesia.

When he heard this, Han grabbed a tube over to the disembarkation point, and raced up to the line of hollow-eyed, weary looking Corellians waiting to board the transport. "What do you think you're *doing*?" he shouted. "Ylesia is a *trap*! Haven't you heard the stories about it? They lure you there, then turn you into *slaves*! You'll wind up dyin' in the mines of Kessel! Don't go!"

One old woman looked at him suspiciously. "Shut up, youngster," she said. "We're going to a better place. The Ylesian priests say they'll take care of us, and we'll have a better life . . . a blessed life. I'm sick of scratchin' here. The cursed Empire is making it too hard these days to earn a dishonest living."

The others muttered similar imprecations at him as he moved up and down the line, expostulating with the Pilgrim-candidates. Han finally stopped and stood there, wanting to howl aloud with rage, like a Wookiee. Chewie *did* howl in frustration.

"Chewie, short of setting my blaster on stun and *shooting* them all, there ain't no way of stoppin' them," the Corellian observed, bitterly.

"Hrrrrrrrrrnnnnnnnnn," Chewie agreed, sadly.

In a last ditch effort, Han tried talking to some of the younger people, even going so far as to offer one or two a job. None would listen to him. He soon gave up in disgust. This had happened to him once before, on Aefao, a remote world at the opposite side of the galaxy from Nar Shaddaa. There had been an Ylesian revival, and Han had tried to warn those who were heading for the ships, but he found he couldn't compete with the Pilgrim-candidates' wide-eyed memories of the Exultation. Only a few of the small, orange-skinned, hu-

manoid Aefans had listened to him. Over a hundred
had boarded the Ylesian missionary ship. . . .

Han watched the line of Corellians shuffling into the
waiting transport, and shook his head. "Some people
are just too dumb to live, Chewie," he said.

Or too desperate, the Wookiee rejoined.

"Yeah, well, just another reminder to me that stickin'
your neck out is a good way to get your head chopped
off," Han said, disgustedly, as he turned his back on the
doomed Corellians and began walking away. "Next time
I think about doin' that, pal, I want you to give me a
Wookiee love-tap that will put me on my butt. You'd
think after all these years I'd learn. . . ."

Chewie promised, and, together, they walked away.

Despite the fact that he had his undersized hands
full running Besadii, Durga the Hutt refused to give up
his search to find his parent's murderer. Six members of
the household staff had died under rigorous interrogation, but there was absolutely no indication that any of
them had been involved.

If the household staff was innocent, then how had
Aruk been poisoned? Durga had another conversation
with Myk Bidlor, who confirmed this time that there
were traces of X-1 in Aruk's digestive tract. The lethal
substance had indeed been eaten.

Durga terminated the communication, and went for
a long undulation, roaming the halls of his palace,
thinking. His expression was so forbidding that his
staff—already highly nervous, and understandably so—
fled before his approach as though he were an evil spirit
from the Outer Darkness.

In his mind, the young Besadii lord was going over
the last months of his parent's life, mentally ticking off

every moment of every day. Everything Aruk had eaten had come from their own kitchens, prepared by the staff of chefs—including the ones now deceased. (He made a mental note to hire two new chefs. . . .)

Durga had had the entire kitchen and the servants' quarters scanned for any trace of X-1. Nothing. The only place that they'd picked up even the smallest hint of the substance had been on the floor in Aruk's office, not far from his usual parking spot for his repulsor sled. And that had been just the barest trace.

Durga frowned, contorting his birthmark-stained features into something resembling a demon-mask. Something was niggling at him. A memory. Niggling . . . wiggling . . . niggling . . .

Wiggling . . . wriggling! The nala-tree frogs!

Suddenly the memory was there, sharp and clear. Aruk, belching as he reached for yet another live nala-tree frog. Up until now, Durga had never considered the possibility that the poison could have been delivered by means of a living creature—after all, it seemed only reasonable that the creature would die from the poison long before it could be ingested.

But what if nala-tree frogs were *immune* to the effects of X-1? What if their tissues had been filled with ever-increasing amounts of X-1, without affecting them?

Aruk had loved his nala-tree frogs. He'd eaten them every day, sometimes as much as a dozen of them every day.

"Osman!" Durga bellowed. "Fetch me the scanner! Bring it straight to Aruk's office!"

The Chevin appeared briefly, acknowledged the order, and then vanished. The sounds of his running feet faded into the distance. Durga began undulating at top speed toward his parent's sanctum.

When he reached there, he was only seconds ahead of the panting servant, who was carrying the scanning device. Durga grabbed it from his hands, then rushed into the office. *Where is it?* he thought, looking wildly around.

Yes, there! he realized, heading for the corner. Standing in the corner, forgotten, was Aruk's old snack-quarium. He'd used it to keep live food fresh, and, the last few months of his life, that live food had mostly been nala-tree frogs!

Thrusting the scanner's probe-tip into the snack-quarium, Durga activated the instrument. Moments later, he had his answer. The mineral deposits on the globe's glassine sides contained sizable amounts of X-1!

Durga let out a bellow of rage that made the furniture rattle, then went berserk, smashing the snackquarium with one mighty blow of his tail, slamming his bulk into furnishings, crushing and destroying everything in his path. Finally, hoarse and panting, he halted in the ruins of Aruk's office.

Teroenza. Teroenza sent the frogs.

Durga's first impulse was to fly to Ylesia and personally smash the t'landa Til to a bloody pulp, but, after a moment's reflection, he realized that it would be beneath him to soil his hands and tail on a lesser being. Besides, he couldn't just do away with the High Priest. Teroenza was a good High Priest, and would be hard to replace. The Besadii lord was uncomfortably aware that if he had Teroenza killed, the t'landa Til on Ylesia might well refuse to continue their charade as priests in the Exultation. Teroenza was well-liked by those who served under him. He was also an able administrator, who had brought Besadii ever-increasing profits from the spice factories.

I'll have to have a trained replacement ready to step in before I act against him, Durga thought.

Also, Durga reflected, the evidence against the High Priest was purely circumstantial. It was remotely possible that Teroenza was innocent. Durga had kept a close eye on Teroenza's expenditures, and no large sums of credits had left his account. He could not have purchased the poison unless he did it in a very clandestine way . . . and he did not have the kind of credits it would take to purchase large amounts of X-1.

Unless he sold that wretched collection of his. . . . Durga thought, but he knew that hadn't happened. He kept close watch over all the shipping manifests going into and out of Ylesia, and Teroenza had, in fact, been *adding* to his collection for the past nine months.

The Besadii lord resolved to begin training a new t'landa Til that very week. He'd continue his investigations, and by the time the new High Priest was ready, he'd hire a bounty hunter to bring him Teroenza's horn. Durga envisioned the horn, mounted on the wall of his office, right next to Aruk's holo-portrait.

Teroenza might not be the only one who deserved to die on Ylesia. Someone had had to capture the nala-tree frogs, put them into shipping containers, and load them onto ships. Durga resolved to investigate the situation from all angles before placing his bounty.

Of course the *real* murderer was the individual who had purchased the X-1 and masterminded the entire operation. Jiliac was his prime suspect. She had the credits, she had the motivation.

Durga had already begun searching for links between Jiliac and the Malkite Poisoners. Now he would also search for links between the Desilijic leader and Teroenza. . . .

Surely he'd find something . . . some record. Shipping records, deposits of credits, withdrawals, records of purchases . . . somewhere there would be evidence that would link both Teroenza and Jiliac to Aruk's death, and he, Durga, was going to find them.

He knew that the search would require both time and credits. His own personal credits, unfortunately. Durga didn't dare jeopardize his admittedly precarious position as leader of Besadii by spending huge amounts of the kajidic's money on what would be called a personal vendetta.

Zier and his other detractors were already watching him, just ready to pounce on unjustified expenses.

No, he'd have to pay for it himself . . . and it would strain his personal resources to do so.

Durga thought for a moment of Black Sun. A word to Prince Xizor, and he'd have all of Black Sun's impressive resources at his command. But that would be opening the door to a Black Sun takeover of Besadii, and possibly all of Nal Hutta.

Durga shook his head. He couldn't risk that. He didn't want to wind up as one of Xizor's vassals. He was a free and independent Hutt, and no Falleen Prince was going to give him his marching orders.

Durga left Aruk's smashed office, and went to his own. He had a long session of work at his datapad before him. He couldn't let his work for Besadii suffer, so most of his search would have to be done at night, while most Hutts were sleeping.

Grimly, Durga reached for his datapad, and began keying in requests for information.

He had found his parent's murderers, he was sure of it. He knew the how, and the why. Now to gain the proof that would allow him to challenge Jiliac and demand personal satisfaction for a blood-debt.

Durga's tiny fingers began racing over his datapad,

and the greenish tip of his tongue protruded from the corner of his mouth as he concentrated. . . .

Teroenza paced slowly down the hallway in the Ylesian Administrative Center to meet with Kibbick. The Hutt "overlord" had requested his presence almost twenty minutes ago, but Teroenza had been busy. In the old days he'd never have dared to keep a Hutt lord waiting, but things on Ylesia were changing, slowly but surely.

He, Teroenza, was taking over. That idiot Kibbick was just too stupid to realize it.

Every day he was making plans, hiring the additional guards Durga had authorized, and fortifying the planet. Instead of hiring mostly Gamorrean guards, strong but even dumber than Kibbick—which was saying something!—Teroenza was carefully choosing toughened mercenary fighters. They cost more, but they'd be worth it in battle.

And Teroenza knew there was going to be a battle. . . . The day would come when he'd have to openly declare his break with Nal Hutta. Besadii would never take such a bid for independence lying down, but Teroenza planned to be ready. He would direct his troops in battle, and victory would be theirs!

The High Priest was already making arrangements to bring the mates of the t'landa Til priests to Ylesia. His own mate, Tilenna, would be one of the first to arrive. Kibbick was such an idiot that he probably wouldn't even notice for some time. The differences between male and female t'landa Til were most readily apparent to t'landa Til. To most other species, except for the male's horn, they appeared virtually identical.

Teroenza was also planning on increasing the defenses,

even if he had to sell off part of his collection to do it. He'd checked the price of a ground-mounted turbo-laser and been horrified, but perhaps Jiliac would help him out with the credits he needed. After all, he, Teroenza, was the only one who could implicate her in Aruk's murder. It made sense that she'd want to stay on his good side.

When Teroenza reached Kibbick's audience chamber, he hesitated before the portal, consciously summoning up enough of a servile air to pass. He didn't want Kibbick to be aware of his contempt. Not yet.

Soon, though. . . .

Soon, Teroenza comforted himself. *Play your part. Listen to him babble. Agree with him. Flatter him. Soon you won't have to do this any more. Only a few more months to put up with his foolishness. Soon.* . . .

One of the first things Han Solo did after getting the *Millennium Falcon* was challenge his girlfriend, Salla Zend, to a race. In the smaller, unreliable *Bria* he'd never had a hope of defeating her swift *Rimrunner*, but now . . .

Whenever the two of them happened to have cargoes bound for the Kessel Run, the two smugglers would race through that dangerous area of space. They frequently ran spice and other contraband to the Stenness System, and the Kessel Run was the fastest way there.

One time Han would win . . . the next, Salla. The two ships were very evenly matched. Neither of the two smugglers liked losing, and their friendly competitions became increasingly fierce. They began taking chances . . . dangerous ones. Especially Salla. An expert pilot, she flew her ship alone and was proud of her skill at getting the last bit of power out of her vessel.

One morning Han and Salla left her apartment together, kissed each other goodbye, and promised to meet on Kamsul, one of the seven inhabited worlds in the Stenness System. Han grinned at Salla. "Loser buys dinner?"

She smiled back at him. "I'm going to order the most expensive thing on the menu just to spite you, Han."

Han laughed, waved, and they parted to go to their respective ships.

The run to Kessel was uneventful. Han managed to beat Salla in by nearly fifteen minutes, but one of the loader droids assigned to his ship developed a malfunction, and slowed the loading process. Salla's *Rimrunner* came swooping down for a reckless landing while he was still loading up, and Han was barely five minutes ahead of her in lifting off.

He was flying with Chewie as copilot and Jarik in the topmost gunner's mount. Imperial patrols in the Kessel region were becoming more and more prevalent these days.

Han keyed his intercom as they went blasting into the Run. "Look sharp, kid," he told Jarik. "I don't want any Imp patrols catching us by surprise."

"Right, Han. Just keep a lookout on those souped-up sensors of yours, and I'll blast 'em before they know what hit 'em."

The first obstacle to be faced once they left Kessel was the Maw—a treacherous, roughly spherical region of space containing black holes, a few neutron stars, and scattered main-sequence stars. From a distance, the Maw appeared in Kessel's nighttime sky to be a rounded, fuzzy, vari-colored glow, much like a nebula. But as a ship drew closer, the spherical shape became clearer. The Maw glowed with the light from the suns within it, the ionized gas and dust trails snaking throughout in bands of color. And, seemingly looking back at Han, were the accretion disks of the black holes.

The accretion disks resembled white, watching eyes against the dimmer regions of the Maw. Depending on their angle relative to the *Falcon*, those eyes were slitted, narrowed, or wide open. In the middle of each "eye" was a pinprick black "pupil" marking each of the black holes that were sucking in the trails of starstuff.

Almost like the jungle on an Ylesian night, Han thought. *Black nights with watching predator eyes. . . .*

Navigating the perimeter of the Maw at normal sublight speeds was a tricky proposition, and racing around it at full throttle was asking for disaster. Han glanced at his sensors, and saw that Salla was gaining on them. He increased speed, pouring it on, until he was going faster than he ever had before on a run.

"She won't catch us now," Han said to Chewie. "I'm gonna hold this lead until we're into the Pit and then we'll be far enough ahead that we'll make our jump to hyperspace at least twenty minutes ahead of *Rimrunner.*"

"The Pit" was a perilous asteroid field encased within a wispy gaseous arm of a nearby nebula. Together, the Maw and the Pit made the Kessel Run the dangerous proposition it was. Hearing Han's boast, Chewie gave an unhappy moan and made a suggestion.

"Whaddaya mean, let her beat us?" Han demanded indignantly, his gloved fingers flying over the controls as they went screaming past the first cluster of black holes. The gas and dust from nearby stars was being pulled into the accretion disks in long, attenuated streamers of blue-white and rose. "You crazy? I ain't buying dinner! I'm gonna win a nerf tenderloin with a broiled ladnek tail, surf and turf special, fair and square!"

Chewie eyed the *Falcon*'s speed indicator nervously, and voiced another suggestion.

"*You'll* buy everyone's dinner if I slow down?" Han gave his copilot an incredulous glance. "Hey pal, marriage must be makin' you soft these days. I can handle this. The *Falcon* can handle it. We're gonna win this one!"

Even as he spoke, his instruments registered a strange sensor signature from the recklessly accelerating *Rimrunner*. Han stared, eyes wide, at his board. "Oh, no . . ." he whispered. "Salla, you crazy? Don't do it!"

Moments later *Rimrunner's* mynock-shaped form elongated, then popped out of real space. Chewie howled. "Salla!" Han yelled, uselessly. "You crazy fool! Tryin' a microjump near the Maw is just asking for trouble!"

Chewie fretted as Han frantically increased speed even more, checking his sensors to try and find the *Rimrunner*. "Where'd she go? Crazy woman! Where'd she *go*?"

Ten minutes passed, then fifteen, as the *Falcon* sped along, hugging the perimeter of the Maw. Han considered trying a microjump himself, but he had no way of discovering what course Salla had followed. The only thing he could be sure of was that she wouldn't have tried jumping straight from one side of the Maw to the other. The deep gravity wells from the black holes and neutron stars would have yanked her out of hyperspace in short order—and probably straight into a black hole's event horizon, the point of no return.

No, she had to have jumped along the perimeter, perhaps to get a straight shot at the Pit. . . .

Chewie whined and stabbed a hairy finger at the sensors. "That's her!" Han said, studying *Rimrunner's* readings. Salla was still moving, but she wasn't headed toward the Pit. She was . . .

"Oh, no . . ." Han whispered, feeling horror wash over him. "Chewie, something must have gone wrong. She ain't goin' in the right direction. . . ." He checked his instruments again. "She came outta hyperspace within the magnetic field of that neutron star up ahead!"

Rimrunner was still moving, but no longer in a straight path. Instead Salla's ship was within a thousand kilometers of a neutron star, looping up in a high orbit. Han's sensors showed jets of deadly plasma spewing out both sides of the flattened accretion disk that marked the neutron star's location.

"Either the gravity well or the magnetic field must have disrupted her navicomputer, and she came out of the microjump in the wrong place. . . ." Han breathed, feeling as though his chest were being squeezed by a giant, invisible hand. "Oh, Chewie . . . she's a goner. . . ."

Within minutes, Salla's ship would reach apastron, or the highest and slowest point in her orbit around the dying star. Then, scant minutes later, *Rimrunner*'s orbit would pull it looping back around, and Salla's ship would pass through the edge of the plasma jet. The deadly radiation levels there would fry her in moments.

A hundred memories of Salla raced through Han's mind between one heartbeat and the next. Salla, smiling at him in the morning . . . Salla, dressed in a glamorous gown, taking him out for a night in the casinos . . . Salla, her face smudged, fixing a hyperdrive as easily as most people would fix breakfast . . . except that Salla never had learned to cook. . . .

"Chewie . . ." he whispered hoarsely, "we gotta try and save her."

Chewbacca shot him a look, then pointed a hairy finger at the sensors and growled.

"I know, I know, *Rimrunner*'s awfully close to that plasma jet," Han said. "And for us to get close, we risk gettin' our ship knocked out and joinin' *Rimrunner*. But Chewie . . . we gotta try."

The Wookiee's blue eyes narrowed with determination and he roared his agreement. Salla was a friend. They couldn't abandon her.

Han opened a frequency on the *Falcon*'s comm, even as he began frantically ordering his navicomputer to run calculations. "Salla? Salla? This is Han. Honey, you there? We're gonna try and get you . . . but you'll have to do what I tell you. Salla? Come in! Over."

He tried twice more as the navicomputer began spouting possible approach vectors. He knew the magnetic fields, ionized gas, and plasma trails would interfere with communications, but he hoped that the *Falcon*'s powerful sensors and transmitters could punch through.

"Chewie, tell Jarik to get into a vacuum suit and stand by the airlock with the magnetic grapple and the winch. I'm gonna tell her to eject, and we'll match her trajectory and pick her up."

Chewie gave Han a skeptical glance. "Don't look at me like that!" Han snapped. "I know it won't be easy! I've got the navicomputer workin' on an approach vector that will keep us outta the plume's magnetic field. Don't stand there tellin' me all the stuff that can go wrong! Get movin'!"

Chewbacca made a hasty exit.

Han tried the comm unit again. "Salla . . . Salla, this is *Falcon*. Come in." He wondered whether Salla's abrupt reversion to real space had caused her to be flung against the controls. She could be lying there, unconscious . . . or dead.

"Hey, baby, answer me. Come in, Salla. . . ."

He continued to call as he sped toward the apastron coordinates. The neutron star's magnetic field was so powerful that it must have blown out every active system on *Rimrunner* the moment Salla came out of hyperspace. That would almost certainly include *Rimrunner's* sole lifepod, as that system was usually kept "on-line"—ready for an emergency ejection at a moment's notice.

Salla was still moving, coasting at the same speed she had been when she'd first jumped into hyperspace, but now she had no way to brake or alter direction. Most importantly, no power to blast free of the gravity well. She'd be pulled closer and closer in an ever-tighter orbit until her ship encountered the edge of the accretion disk, then . . . boom.

By the time that happened, though, Salla would have been dead for at least five minutes, from passing through that plasma particle jet. . . .

Not if I can help it, Han thought grimly. "Salla? Salla? Can you read me? Come in, Salla!"

Finally, he heard a crackle of static, then a faint reply. ". . . Han . . . *Rimrunner* . . . engines out. Power gone . . . batteries dying . . . can't . . . goner, honey . . . stay away. . . ."

Han swore loudly. "No!" he yelled into the comm. "Salla, listen to me and do exactly what I say! *Rimrunner's* a goner, right, but not you, Salla! You're gonna have to abandon ship, and you've got only a few minutes to do it! Was your lifepod on-line when you got hit?"

". . . affirmative, Han . . . lifepod dead . . . no way to eject. . . ."

It was as he'd thought. Her lifepod was useless, its electronic systems blown.

He wet his lips. "Yes, you *can* eject! We're comin' to get you! Salla, you get your rear down to your aft airlock and stuff yourself into a vacuum suit! Take both suit thrust paks, hear me? When the first runs out, activate the second. Full throttle! I'm gonna try and match your trajectory, but I want you as far away from *Rimrunner* and that plasma jet as possible!"

"Won't work . . . jump?"

"Yeah, dammit, jump!" Han made a course adjustment. "I can be there in eight minutes. I want you blasting away from *Rimrunner* at full throttle on the following coordinates . . ." He glanced at his navicomputer and gave her a string of numbers. "Copy that?"

"But *Rimrunner* . . ." was the faint reply.

"Blast *Rimrunner*!" Han shouted. "It's a ship, you can get another! Now *do* it, Salla! This is gonna be hard enough without you arguing! You've got three minutes to get into that suit! Go!"

He keyed his intercom to Jarik's spacesuit frequency. "Jarik, you standing by with the magnetic grapple and the winch?"

"Affirmative, Han," Jarik said. "Just warn me when I can make visual contact. It's hard to see in this helmet."

"I'll tell ya, kid," Han said tersely. "Here's your coordinates for the grapple." He repeated them. "Timin's gonna be critical here, so don't be slow about it. Any drift, and we'll graze the edge of the magnetic field and then we're in the same fix as *Rimrunner*. Basically, we've got one chance to get in and get out safely. Got that?"

"I copy, Han," Jarik said, tensely.

As Han piloted his ship toward the rescue coordinates, he worried that Salla's thrust paks wouldn't be strong enough to propel her far enough away from her doomed vessel. He didn't want to risk crashing into *Rimrunner*. The *Falcon* was a freighter, not designed for tight, pinpoint maneuvering of this sort. True, Han could make his ship practically stand on her head, but picking up a tiny spacesuited human while trying to stay out of the particle jet's magnetic field was risky enough, without worrying about having *Rimrunner* slamming into them.

Han carefully checked and rechecked his course. He had to do this precisely, on the first try. He had to get her before she got within range of that deadly plasma. He had a brief, hideous vision of what it would be like to bring a radiation-seared corpse aboard, and made himself concentrate on his piloting. This maneuver was probably the trickiest piece of piloting he'd ever tried. . . .

Minutes later, Han, sweating, began entering the course corrections that would bring them to the intersection point. He slowed his ship . . . slowed her again . . . then again. He didn't dare come to a dead halt, for fear that he'd drift into the magnetic field. . . .

He kept his eyes riveted on his sensors. *Rimrunner* was only about fifty kilometers away, now, growing on his screens. "Jarik, I have visual contact with *Rimrunner*. Stand by."

"I read you, Han. Standing by."

Had Salla ejected in time? Han tried calling her. No answer, but there was a good chance that her suit comlink wouldn't be strong enough to reach him through the interference.

The doomed freighter grew on his screens, in his viewport. Han slowed still further, hardly daring to blink. *Where is she? Did she have the courage to jump?*

Salla didn't lack for courage, Han knew that. But jumping into space, with nothing between you and some very hard vacuum was a scary proposition. Han bit his lip, picturing her pushing herself away from *Rimrunner*'s airlock and triggering that first thrust pak. Although he'd spent time in spacesuits himself, he didn't like it, hanging there, with nothing between you and infinity in all directions. And he'd certainly never had to try and cross kilometers of space in nothing but a spacesuit. The Corellian wasn't sure *he'd* have the courage to do what he'd demanded of Salla. . . .

Before she became a smuggler, Salla had spent time as a technician on a corporate transport. He hoped she hadn't lost her spacesuit skills.

Han watched the schematic on his navigation boards. There was the neutron star, with *Rimrunner's* projected downward-spiraling orbit marked out. Salla's ship had reached apastron. The blip that was the *Falcon* was closing rapidly. Thirty klicks. . . .

And there, marked in virulent green, was the deadly plume of the plasma, haloed with the magnetic field in violet.

Han swallowed. *So close . . .*

He was closing on twenty klicks, now. He looked up, and through the viewport made out *Rimrunner's* mynock shape.

Where is she? he wondered, checking the schematic again. *Where is—*

"Got her!" Han suddenly yelled. "Jarik, I see her blip! No visual yet, but stay sharp!" He made a few minor course changes so he'd exactly match Salla's trajectory. She was moving toward him at a pretty good clip, fast enough to stay in a straight line, not fast enough to risk losing control and going into a spin. Han admired her suit expertise.

"Ready, Han," the youth said, then muttered something under his breath . . . a prayer? Han was too busy to inquire.

Han turned on his ship's intercom. "Chewie, you standing by with that med-pak?"

"Hrnnnnnnggggghhh!"

As Han watched her blip, he kept glancing up at the port, and suddenly—

"I got her! Visual contact! Jarik . . . fire magnetic grapple on my order. . . ."

Han counted seconds in his head. *Three . . . two . . . one . . .*

"Fire!"

A tense second . . .

"I got her! Activating winch!"

"Chewie, can you hear her?"

Chewbacca roared. No, he couldn't hear her, but he'd let Han know the moment he could.

"Jarik, Jarik, is she okay?"

"She's waving, Han!" A moment later, the kid said, "Okay, Han, she's inside! Closing the airlock!"

Chewbacca's roar came over the intercom a moment later. "Right!" Han said. "We are getting outta here!"

Han altered course and increased speed, pulling out of the neutron star's gravity well. Checking the schematic, he saw that *Rimrunner* was just passing through the plasma jet and accelerating in its orbit. *That was close!*

"How is she?" Han said over the intercom. "Talk to me, guys!"

A moment later he heard Salla's voice, hoarse but recognizable. "I'm okay, Han. Just a cut on my head. Chewie's fixing me up."

"Jarik, c'mon up here and take the controls," Han said. "I want to see Salla. Chewie, don't forget to check her for radiation exposure. . . ."

"Arrrrnnnnnnnnnnghhhh!" came the exasperated roar.

"That's good!"

"Han," Jarik said, "she's coming up. Stay where you are."

A minute later, the three joined Han in the cockpit.

The Corellian slipped out of the pilot's seat, and Chewie and Jarik took over the pilot's and copilot's seats. Salla sat down in the passenger seat, scowling. There was a bandage on her forehead, half-covered by her wiry mop of black hair. Han bent over her solicitously. "Hey . . . honey . . ."

She pulled away from him, and for a second he thought she was going to swing at him. Her eyes flashed with anger at the universe in general. Taking the hint, Han stepped back. "Han . . . that blip . . ." She pointed. "Is that *Rimrunner*?"

Han turned and looked at the schematic, then the viewport. *Rimrunner* was still in the plasma jet, visible only as an orange glow. "Yeah," he said. "She's really picking up speed. . . ."

Silence reigned in the cockpit as the four watched the blip that was Salla's pride and joy speeding through the last of the plasma, accelerating faster and faster, heading for the accretion disk as the neutron star's gravity pulled the freighter into an ever tighter, closer orbit.

Minutes later, a tiny flare blossomed for a second on the edge of the accretion disk. Salla stood up. "Well, that's that," she said, flatly. "If you gentles will excuse me, I need to use the 'fresher."

Han stood aside as Salla walked back into the *Falcon*'s interior. He thought about how he'd feel if it was *his* ship that had just bought it, and could understand the pent-up anger that she was barely controlling.

Minutes later, he heard muffled thuds and cries coming from the ship's small lounge area. Han glanced at his friends. "I'll check it out."

When he arrived back in the lounge, he found Salla standing with her back to the hologram game board, beating her fists against the *Falcon's* bulkheads and cursing a blue streak.

"Salla . . ." he said.

She whirled to face him, amber eyes blazing. "Han, why didn't you just let me die?"

For a second he thought she was going to punch him, and got ready to duck. But she restrained herself with a visible effort. "*Why,* Han?"

"Salla, you know I couldn't do that," he said, holding up his hands placatingly.

She stamped around the *Falcon's* lounge, obviously on the verge of going nova. "I can't believe I tried that microjump! I can't believe the *Rimrunner* is gone! How could I have been so *stupid*?"

"We'd raced before, Salla," Han said. "This time was just . . . bad luck."

She slammed a fist into a bulkhead, cursed again, then stood cradling her abused hand. "That ship was my life! My living! And now, just . . . gone!" She snapped her unbruised fingers.

"I know," Han said. "I know."

"What am I going to do now? I can't earn a living. I worked so hard to get that ship!"

"You can ride with me and Chewie," Han said. "We can always use extra crew. You're a hot pilot, Salla. You'll find work. Good pilots are always in demand."

"Ride with you?" she scowled. "I don't need charity from you or anyone, Han."

"Hey!" he said, in injured tones, "I am not in the charity business, Salla, you know me! It's just that . . . hey . . . I need the help."

She stared at him. "You . . . *need* . . . me?"

Han shrugged. "Well . . . sure. I couldn't do without you, honey. I don't risk myself—or my ship—for just anybody, you know."

"That's true," she muttered, staring at him intently. Han wondered what was going through her mind, but decided it wasn't a good time to ask. Cautiously, he moved toward her, wondering if she'd push him away again, but she didn't.

He wrapped his arms around her, pulled her wiry form against him, kissed her cheek. "I know how you must be feelin', Salla. I lost a ship not too long ago, too, remember."

"I remember," she whispered. "Hey, Han . . . I forgot to thank you."

"For what?"

"Saving my life, what else?"

He chuckled. "You've saved my hide a time or two in tight spots, Salla, don't forget. Remember that time the Nessies tried to pull a fast one on us? If it hadn't been for you spottin' those bogus datacards, I'd have lost a bundle."

She began to shudder violently. Her teeth chattered. "D-don't buh-beee n-nice ttto mmmeeee, Hhhan," she managed, shivering. "Wh-what's h-happening?"

He stroked her hair. "Adrenaline letdown, Salla. Happens all the time after battles. You get the shakes, and you feel stupid, because by the time it happens, you're safe."

She managed a nod. "I'm ss-such a ff-fool."

"But you're a live fool," Han reminded her. "That's the best kind."

Salla laughed shakily.

Chapter Six:

FAREWELL TO NAR SHADDAA

Salla Zend was very quiet over the next week—so quiet that Han worried about her. He'd never seen her the way she was now. She refused offers to accompany Han and Chewbacca on a couple of Runs, even though Han wasn't kidding when he said he needed her help. Jarik had recently found a girlfriend in the Corellian section of Nar Shaddaa, and was spending all available time with her. The kid had also hired on with Shug because the master mechanic was upgrading the hyperdrives on many of the Desilijic smuggling vessels. It was a big job, and Shug needed all the help he could get.

Salla began hanging out at Shug's spacebarn every day, working on the hyperdrive upgrades, too. But when Han returned home from a run, she was always there to greet him, smiling, with an affectionate kiss. Her behavior toward him was . . . different . . . somehow. She had a way of looking at Han as though she were somehow . . . evaluating . . . him. It made the Corellian uneasy.

The most unnerving thing of all was that Salla asked him to teach her to cook. Having been raised by Dewlanna, Han was a fair cook, though he didn't bother preparing meals just for himself. But, since he and Salla were together almost every night, Han had fallen into the habit of fixing a meal for them.

Suddenly, out of the blue, Salla wanted him to teach her. For some reason Han had a bad feeling about that. He couldn't say why that worried him—after all, it wasn't a big deal, learning to cook, right?—but it did.

He began with easy things . . . breakfast, stews, soups, then graduated to menus such as boiled traladon steaks with tubers on the side, imush-roots chopped and sauteed with hot sauce, Wookiee flat-biscuits with forest-honey glaze.

Salla paid strict attention and approached cooking with all the seriousness she'd have given to tearing down and rebuilding a faulty motivator matrix. She was so *earnest* about it that Han grew more and more troubled.

He considered asking her what was going on, but he didn't want to pry. Salla had just lost her ship. That was reason enough for some eccentric behavior, he told himself.

One night, when she'd served the first meal she'd cooked all by herself, Han finished the last bites of slightly scorched ladnek tail and somewhat rubbery marsh-root soufflé, and smiled at her. "This was tasty, Salla. You'll be a gourmet cook in no time!"

"Really?" she looked pleased.

"Sure," he lied. Truth was, she had a long way to go.

"Han . . . there's something I've been meaning to tell you," she said. "Something really important."

Uh, oh. Here we go, he thought, with a feeling of dread. "What's that?" he asked.

"Well, I've been making some plans. It won't cost nearly what I thought, especially the hall, and I have a little bit saved. With what you've still got from the big sabacc game, we can do it. I've talked to a caterer, and—"

"Salla, what are you talkin' about?" Han broke in, completely confused.

"Our wedding," she said. "I've been thinking about it, how you said you need me, and you're right. We need each other. It's time to go ahead and have a real life together, Han. Like Roa and Lwyll. Remember what a nice wedding they had? We can have something just as nice. I think we owe it to ourselves. All our friends can come."

Han stared at her, too dumbfounded to speak. His first impulse was to shout, "Have you gone *crazy*?" but he counted to ten. Maybe Salla needed medical attention. She *had* suffered a blow to her head. Concerned, he finally managed, "Uh, Salla, I don't think that's in the cards right now."

She chuckled. "I knew you'd say that, Han. Men! They never want to admit how they feel. Don't you remember tellin' me that you kind of envied Roa and Chewie, having a real family?"

Han remembered saying something along that line, but he certainly hadn't meant for it to be interpreted like *this*. He shook his head. "Salla, honey, I think we'd better discuss this. You haven't told anyone about this, have you? Or actually made any concrete plans?"

"Well . . . just a few people," she said. "Shug, and

Mako and Lando, and Jarik. And I put a reservation fee on the hall."

Mako! Han groaned inwardly. His old friend from his Academy days would be having a wonderful time spreading this all over Nar Shaddaa. *Jarik, why didn't you warn me?* he wondered, then he realized that the kid was so head-over-heels for that cute little thing he'd been seeing that he probably hadn't even really listened to Salla.

"Salla," he said, "this isn't like you. We've never made any promises, any commitments. I mean, some-day, maybe . . . but . . ."

She was smiling at him again—that smile that made him feel like a traladon on its way into the slaughter-house. An all-knowing smile that said she wasn't really listening. Desperate to communicate without really hurting her with the truth, Han reached out and took her hand across the table. "Salla, honey . . . we've never even said the word 'love' before. Are you tellin' me that you love me enough to spend the rest of your life with me?"

Her amber eyes shifted, just slightly, then she nod-ded. "I know what I want, Han. You and me together, and an end to risking our lives hauling spice. We'll be like Roa and Lwyll, and go off together to make a new life. An honest life. Maybe we'll have kids someday."

"But do you love me?" he asked, holding her eyes with his own.

"Sure," she said. "Of course I do, Han. You know that."

No, I don't think I do, he thought, cynically. He hadn't missed that slight shift of her eyes. He knew Salla was fond of him, cared for him, and had passion for him. But love?

"Anyway, you'll see, this is the right decision, Han.

We're going to be really happy, and this will be the best wedding ever. We'll have a great party afterward."

Han didn't miss the fact that she hadn't asked him whether he loved her. *She doesn't want to know the answer,* he realized.

For a moment it was on the tip of his tongue to say, "Salla, I don't love you, and I don't want to marry you." But somehow he couldn't quite get the words out. He didn't want to break up with her, and that would certainly do it.

Han silently resolved to talk to Chewie, and maybe Lando about this, since Salla had already shot her mouth off. Maybe one of them would have some idea how to tell her "no" about the marriage, without losing her.

Han didn't want to lose Salla, but he sure wasn't getting married. Especially now, when he was on top of the smuggling heap, with the speedy *Falcon* as his very own! He had places to go, business to do, cargoes to haul, and there was fun to be had—fun that would be totally ruined if he was married. As far as the Corellian was concerned, getting married was tantamount to some unending Imp work detail. Han would hardly have been less dismayed to find himself sentenced to the spice mines of Kessel.

The next day he cornered Chewie in their apartment, and, while ZeeZee trundled back and forth, picking up things and putting them down again in the exact same spot, told him the whole story. His friend growled and moaned, shaking his head. "Whaddaya mean the way Salla's actin' reminds you of Wynni?" Han demanded. "Wynni can't keep her paws off you, tries to seduce you every time we run into her. Salla ain't like that. She just wants to get *married.*"

Chewbacca amplified on his previous statement.

Salla reminded him of Wynni because she wasn't *asking* whether Han wanted her, she was just assuming that he did, and doing what she wanted. Marriage, the Wookiee pointed out, had to be something where both partners had an equal voice. Sometimes one partner might accede to the wishes of the other, but nobody should just *assume* they knew what was best and start making decisions for a couple.

Han's brow furrowed. "Yeah, I see what you mean," he muttered. "Salla ain't askin', she's just takin' it for granted that we're gettin' married." He shook his head sadly. "Today she's out shoppin' for an outfit. She says 'cause I'm Corellian, she wants a traditional Corellian wedding. That means a green dress."

Chewie shook his head and launched into a long peroration on females of any species who regarded males as prizes to be won. He cautioned Han that his sister, Kallabow, had decided in much the same way that she intended to marry Mahraccor. However, Chewie said, Kallabow had been cleverer about it than Salla. She'd merely given Mahraccor plenty of chances to realize that he loved her, Kallabow, until one day he'd done exactly that. They were very happy, Chewie pointed out.

"Well, that ain't what's gonna happen to me, pal," Han said caustically. "You know, I'm startin' to get mad, Chewie. She doesn't care what *I* want—she doesn't even want to know what *I* want. That's no way to make someone fall for you and want to marry you."

Chewie vociferously agreed.

The next night, Han spoke to Lando in a smoky bar at one of the big Nar Shaddaa casinos. The gambler shook his head the moment Han brought the subject up. "Han . . . Han . . . she's dead serious about this, you know. When she told me about it, I started to laugh—'cause I know you, pal!—and Salla just about decked me."

"I *know* she's serious," Han said, morosely. "Blast it, Lando, I don't want to marry her—I don't want to marry *anybody*! Ever, maybe! I like being single, and I like being able to do *what* I want, *when* I want, with *whoever* I want to!"

"Easy, pal," Lando cautioned, and Han realized his voice had scaled up to the point where other patrons of the drinking establishment were looking over at him. He took a hasty gulp of his Alderaanian ale.

"Well, have you tried telling her how you feel?" Lando asked.

"Yeah, a couple of times, now. She just dismisses me. I'll say, 'Salla, this isn't a good idea, I need time to think about this,' or even, 'Salla, I ain't interested in gettin' married now,' but it doesn't do a bit of good."

"What does she say when you say that?"

"She just tosses it off. Says things like, 'don't worry, Han, men always feel like that. It's perfectly normal to have pre-wedding jitters.' "

Lando sighed so gustily that his mustache quivered. "That's tough, pal," he said. "She sounds like she's settled on getting married to you as a good way to fix up her life. She lost her ship, but she's going to gain a husband."

"She wants me to quit the business and leave Nar Shaddaa. Says we can be like Roa and Lwyll, start a new life doing something else. No more smuggling."

Lando shuddered. "Honest work? That's awful!" The gambler was only partly joking.

Han drained his stein of ale and wiped his mouth with the back of his hand. "Lando, what am I gonna do? I ain't gonna marry her, that's for sure. But I can't be mean enough to her to tell her in a way that will make her listen."

Lando frowned. "That's a tough one. Seems to me, the way Salla's acting, she's just asking to be set down. But Han . . . you can't wait. She told me she's setting the wedding for next week."

Han sat bolt upright. "Next *week*? Oh, no . . . Lando, no way!"

Lando nodded. "You've gotta tell her, Han."

"But she won't *listen*!"

"What else can you do?"

Han's features hardened with determination. "I can leave, that's what. I've been meaning to spend some time in the Corporate Sector, look up a master starship tech named Doc. Seems like now is a good time for that trip."

"Corporate Sector's quite a ways away."

"Yeah. And Salla doesn't have a ship, so she can't possibly follow me. Besides, if I just leave, that'll give her the message, clearer than anything I could say. And I'm doin' it right away, Lando. Tomorrow."

"That quick?" Lando was taken aback. "Why so fast?"

"Why stick around?" Han asked. "I'll go see Jabba tomorrow morning, tell him I'm headin' out for a while and don't know when I'll be back. Besides . . ." he sighed, "I care about Salla. I don't want her spendin' her credits on a wedding that ain't gonna happen. So the quicker I go, the more she'll save."

"She's going to be mad," Lando said.

"I know," Han agreed bleakly. "And I wish it didn't have to be like this. She should have some respect for me, not be so hard-headed. If there was another way around this, I'd take it, but I can't think of anything. No matter what I do or say, Salla's gonna get hurt."

"You could knuckle under and marry her," Lando said, cocking an amused eyebrow.

Han shook his head. "Lando, I'd sooner kiss Jabba."

Lando sputtered with laughter until he nearly fell off his barstool.

"I ain't losing my freedom," Han said grimly. "Salla will get over this. Yeah, she'll be mad. Yeah, she'll probably never speak to me again. I'm sorry about that, but not sorry enough to stick around. I'd sooner micro-jump through the Maw."

Lando shrugged, offered his hand. "Going to miss you, pal."

"C'mon along," Han suggested, shaking it. "Chewie and I could use a hand."

"What about Jarik?"

Han made a dismissive gesture. "The kid won't be coming, I'm almost certain. Shug's payin' him more than I can afford to, and he's so hung up on that girl he can't see straight. No way he'd be up for a long trip."

"True," Lando said. "First love . . . isn't it sweet?"

Han rolled his eyes, then the two of them laughed.

"So . . . you comin'?" Han prodded.

"Not me," Lando said. "I've got to put in some time on the spaceship lot. Since Roa left, I've been through one manager after another, and I caught the last one skimming."

"Great," Han shook his head. "Well, I'll miss you, Lando. You watch your back, now, pal."

"You too."

Han spent one last night with Salla, but she was so wrapped up in her plans that she didn't even notice how grimly silent he was.

Just before they turned in, Han looked at her and

said, "Salla . . . I wish you'd asked me before planning all this. I ain't the marrying kind of guy."

She laughed. "All men think that, Han . . . until they get married. Remember Roa? He said all along he'd never do it, then he did, and you never saw anyone happier. That's the way men are."

"Not this guy," Han said, but Salla only laughed.

The next morning, Han went by his place and had ZeeZee pack up his clothes (it didn't take long, Han never had many clothes) into an old backpack. Then he and Chewie went out to the *Millennium Falcon*'s landing pad atop one of the tall buildings of Nar Shaddaa.

Jarik turned up to see them off. Han hadn't told anyone but Lando and the youth that he was going. Jarik held out his hand, and when Han shook it, blurted, "Now I wish I was going! Come back rich, Han! Chewie, you take care of him, okay?"

Han slung an arm around the young man's shoulders, shook him playfully. Chewie gave him a Wookiee head-rub that made the kid yelp. "You take care of yourself, Jarik," Han said. "Don't let ZeeZee drive you crazy. And . . . take my advice, kid. Have fun, but remember: If *I'm* too young to get married, *you* are *definitely* too young!"

Jarik laughed. "I'll remember than, Han!"

"So long, kid. Take it easy."

Minutes later, with Nar Shaddaa behind them, Han keyed his comm system for a holo message. Quickly he gave Salla's name and codes, then instructed Message Central to "hold" the message for two hours. By that time he'd be long gone.

When the message signaled it was ready to "record" Han cleared his throat self-consciously. "Hi, Salla," he said. "I'm sorry it had to be like this, but by the time you get this, Chewie and me will be gone. I tried to talk to you, but you just wouldn't listen."

He hesitated, took a deep breath. "Salla, you're a great lady, but I'm just not ready to get married—to anyone. So try not to take it personally, okay? I think we need a break from each other. I'll be back someday. Try not to be too mad, Salla. I'm just doing what I have to. You take care of yourself, Salla, and say goodbye to Shug and Mako for me."

Chewbacca grunted insistently, and Han said, "Oh, and Chewie says goodbye, too. Stay well, Salla. Be happy."

Reaching out, he hit the "transmit" button, and then slumped back in his seat. "Whew! That was worse than a dozen Runs, pal."

Chewbacca agreed that things of that nature were never easy.

Han nodded. "Okay, pal. And, speakin' of marriage, I think before we light out for the Corporate Sector, you and Mallatobuck deserve a little second honeymoon. So set course for Kashyyyk."

Chewbacca gazed at Han, his blue eyes lighting up. Han grinned at the Wookiee. "Besides, I laid in another cargo of those explosive quarrels that Katarra liked so much. I figure a nice load of Thikkiian brandy might fetch a good price in the Corporate Sector. So is the Corporate Sector by way of Kashyyyk okay by you?"

Chewbacca roared his approval of Han's suggestion so loudly that Han's ears rang.

Minutes later, the *Falcon* was nothing but a rectangular streak traveling through hyperspace on the first leg of her long journey.

Chapter Seven:

HUTT JUSTICE AND
REBEL RETRIBUTION

"Aunt," said Jabba, staring at the screen of his data-pad, "at this rate Desilijic will be bankrupt in forty-four years."

Jabba and Jiliac were in Jiliac's office in her island palace on Nal Hutta. The Desilijic leader had been dangling bright streamers of Askajian silk for her baby to focus on and lurch toward. Of course the baby Hutt could not reach for the vivid streamers—it still did not have arms, though over the past three months, its stubs had grown longer. These days it could spend two or three hours at a time outside its mother's pouch—much to Jabba's irritation. The only time he could gain Jiliac's full attention was while her baby was sleeping in her pouch.

Hearing Jabba's pronouncement, the leader of Desilijic turned from playing with her infant to regard her nephew with mild surprise. "Really?" Jiliac said, and her great forehead furrowed, "that soon? I would not have thought it possible. Still . . . forty-four years, Jabba. We should be able to reverse this trend long before then. What reports are you looking at?"

"All of them, Aunt. I have spent much of the past week doing a complete financial portrait of Desilijic finances."

"Where are the credits going, then?"

"Among other things, I have here the invoice from Shug Ninx's spacebarn," Jabba said, touching a key on the datapad and bringing up the document. "Upgrading all of the sublight and hyperdrive engines on our ships has set us back fifty-five thousand credits."

"That seems a bit excessive," Jiliac said. "Was upgrading all our ships really necessary?"

Jabba sighed so loudly and exasperatedly that flecks of green drool spattered on the floor before him. "Shug Ninx is a rarity among Nar Shaddaa denizens, aunt. The price is fair. And, if you'll recall, we lost three smuggling ships to Imperial patrols over the last six months, and another to privateers. Our ships sublight engines were old and outmoded, and they couldn't elude Imperial tariff ships *or* pirates. And their hyperdrives were so slow that we were getting complaints from customers about their deliveries being delayed! So, yes, the upgrades were completely necessary, to avoid losing more ships."

"Oh, yes, I do recall that now," Jiliac said, vaguely. "Well, if it is necessary, nephew, it is necessary. I trust your judgment."

My judgment is that I should be running things around here in name as well as fact, Jabba thought, grumpily. Aloud he said, "At least the job is done. With any luck, our ships can now haul more spice, faster, and we can begin making back some of our investment. If only Besadii will hold the line this time on its new announced prices for processed spice. This is their third increase in three months."

Jiliac began to laugh, a great, booming sound that echoed in the huge, nearly deserted office. (Ever since she'd had her baby, the leader of Desilijic had dismissed many of her former hangers-on and sycophants, for fear one of them would seek profit by kidnapping her baby and holding it for ransom. These days her opulent throne room held only her most trusted minions, compared to the way it used to be, when Jiliac was a male, childless Hutt. Jabba, of course, still enjoyed being surrounded by raucous crowds, music and dancing girls in his palaces on Nal Hutta and Tatooine.)

When Jiliac stopped laughing she exclaimed, "Nephew, *of course* Besadii will not hold their line! Their strategy lately has been to reduce the amount of spice on the black market, to drive prices up. Simple economics. Highly effective, also."

"I know," Jabba agreed, morosely. "But they have to slither a fine line, Aunt. If they charge much more, they'll be competing with the Imperial spice market. And that might bring them to the unwelcome attention of the Emperor."

By Imperial decree, all spice, especially the ultra-valuable glitterstim, belonged to the Empire. But the prices for the spice sold through legal, Imperial channels was so preposterously high that no one except the fabulously wealthy could afford it. Enter the smugglers and their side deals on Kessel and the other spice-producing worlds.

"We had little choice but to upgrade our ships, Aunt,"

Jabba added. "Our markets were making threats that they were going to begin dealing directly with Besadii."

"Besadii does not have a smuggling fleet that can match ours," Jiliac pointed out, truthfully.

"Not at the moment," Jabba said. "But my sources indicate that Durga has already bought a few ships, and is bargaining for others. He has announced his intention of creating a fleet that will outclass ours. I believe he intends to take over the whole spice trade. We must not allow this, Aunt."

"I agree, Nephew," Jiliac said, waving an aqua streamer. "What shall we do about it?"

"I believe we must redouble our efforts to get more pilots to run our spice, Aunt," Jabba said. "There must be pilots out there who are as good as Solo."

"Is he gone?" she asked, vaguely, stroking her baby's head.

Jabba rolled his bulbous eyes and reached into a bowl for a Carnovian eel-pup, and popped the squirming, squeaking morsel into his mouth. The baby Hutt looked over at him and drooled greenish-brown goo. Jabba hastily averted his gaze and swallowed noisily. "Solo has been gone for several months, Aunt. By all report, he went to the Corporate Sector. His loss is being felt," he waved his datapad. "Solo was the best. I even find myself missing the fellow."

Jiliac turned to regard her nephew in surprise. "Jabba, you are talking about a *human*. And a human *male* at that. Have your tastes changed? I thought you had a penchant for those tiresome scantily clad dancers you fancy. It is hard for me to picture Solo in a dancing costume, cavorting with that great hairy brute of a Wookiee before your throne."

Jabba chuckled at the image. "Ho-ho, Aunt! No, my fondness for Solo comes only from the fact that he makes us money, in an expeditious fashion. *He* would never allow himself to be boarded and his cargo and ship impounded for smuggling. Solo is quite clever and resourceful . . . for a human."

"The Empire is making its presence felt more and more out here in the Rim," Jiliac said. "There was that massacre on that humanoid-inhabited world. . . ."

"Mantooine in the Atrivis Sector," Jabba said. "Since then there has been another, aunt. Two weeks ago citizens of Tyshapahl staged a peaceful demonstration against the Empire and its taxation. The Sector Moff sent ships from the nearby Imperial garrison. The Imperial vessels hovered over the crowd with their ships on repulsors while the commander demanded that they disperse. When they did not, he signaled his ships, and each vessel activated their engines. Most of the crowd was summarily incinerated."

Jiliac shook her massive head. "Palpatine's forces could use a few lessons in subtlety from our people, Nephew. Such a waste of resources! Far better to have landed, then herded them all into ships to be sold as slaves. That way the Empire could have rid themselves of the dissidents, and made a profit at the same time."

"The Emperor should bring you to Imperial Center to advise him, Aunt," Jabba said, half-joking, but it occurred to him that he'd get a lot more done if he didn't have to deal with and around Jiliac each day. The baby Hutt wriggled over in front of him, and he glared at it. The mindless little creature gurgled at him, burped, then spit up.

Revolting! Jabba thought, recoiling from the noxious pool of spreading liquid.

Jiliac summoned a cleaning droid and wiped the infant's mouth. "Don't even suggest such a thing, Jabba," she said, sounding faintly horrified. "You know how Palpatine treats non-humans. His aversion to non-humans is so strong that he does not even recognize Hutts as a superior species!"

"True," Jabba said. "Shortsighted of him. But he is in authority, and we must deal with that. So far we have been able to buy protection from too close scrutiny by the Empire. It is expensive, but worth it."

"Agreed," Jiliac said. "The only reason he left us alone after the battle of Nar Shaddaa was that the Council voted to voluntarily double the amount of taxes we pay to the Empire. Nal Hutta has fifty times the wealth of most planets, and our wealth buys us a certain amount of protection. Not to mention the bribes we pay to the new Moff, and to some of the Imperial Senators and high-ranking officers."

The cleaning droid had finished its efforts, and the floor gleamed again. Hutts kept their floors scrupulously clean and, if they were uncarpeted, highly polished. It was easier to glide around on them that way.

"They say that the renegade Senator, Mon Mothma, has convinced three large resistance groups to ally. They signed a document they're calling the Corellian Treaty," Jabba said. "It is possible that a widespread rebellion may be in the offing. And Aunt," Jabba waved his datapad, "in war, there is profit to be made. We might be able to recoup our losses."

"Those so-called Rebels have no chance against the might of the Empire," Jiliac scoffed. "It would be foolish for us to take sides."

"Oh, I was not suggesting *that*, Aunt," Jabba said hastily, scandalized by the suggestion. "But there are times when profits could be made from aiding one side against the other. No permanent alliance, of course."

"Better to stay out of galactic politics altogether, mark my words, Jabba." Jiliac was holding her baby, bouncing it fondly. *Good way to make it upchuck again,* Jabba thought cynically.

Sure enough, the baby Hutt did just that. Fortunately, the cleaning droid was still within call.

"Aunt . . ." Jabba said, hesitantly, "since times are becoming so . . . complicated, perhaps you might consider sending the baby to the communal nursery for each day? Then it would be easier to concentrate on our business. The child is well able to spend long periods outside your pouch. Besides, they have surrogate pouch-mothers at the nursery."

Jiliac reared up, tail twitching, her expression one of shocked indignation. "Nephew! I am surprised that you would even suggest such a thing! In a year, perhaps, I might consider that, but now, my little one needs me continually."

"It was just a suggestion," Jabba said, in as conciliatory a manner as he could manage. "In order to bring Desilijic's finances back to the level they were before Moff Shild's destructive raid on Nar Shaddaa, a great deal more time and effort will be needed. I am putting in copious amounts of time these days."

"Ho-HO!" Jiliac hooted. "And just yesterday you spent half the afternoon watching that new slave-girl cavort all over your throne room, while your new band of jizz-wailers played for you!"

"How did you—" Jabba began, stung, then he subsided into silence. So what if he'd taken a few hours off to amuse himself? He'd been up at dawn, working with the clerical droids and scribes on Desilijic's financial records, getting them in order so he could prepare a complete report on the implications of the new Besadii price hikes.

"I have my ways, Nephew," Jiliac said. "But of course I don't begrudge you your leisure time. All work and no amusement makes for a dull Hutt indeed. However, in turn, I expect you to respect my need to be with my baby."

"Yes, Aunt. I do. Of course I do," Jabba said, seething inwardly. Hastily, he changed the subject. "I believe Besadii should be called to account for these increases in the cost of their spice. It is possible that we may be able to rouse the other clans against them."

"To what purpose?"

"Possibly official censure and a fine. I have heard enough grumbling among the other clans to suggest that they are suffering from this price increase nearly as much as Desilijic. It is worth a try. Aunt, can you request that the Hutt Grand Council call a meeting of the kajidic leaders?"

Jiliac nodded, evidently wishing to be conciliatory, too. "Very well, Jabba. I will request such a meeting before the end of the week."

Jiliac was as good as her word, and three days later, Jabba, along with the Desilijic bodyguards, undulated into the huge Hutt Grand Council chamber. All representatives or leaders of the Hutt crime syndicates, or kajidics, as they were called, passed through multiple scanning and security devices in order to be allowed to enter, as did their bodyguards. Nothing that could be deemed a weapon was permitted inside. Hutts were not trusting sentients. . . .

Jabba took his place in the location allotted to the Desilijic members, and cautioned the other representatives to allow him to do the talking. As Jiliac's top lieutenant, he had that right, and they readily agreed. Jabba noted that even his parent, Zorba, had sent a representative. The two of them were not close, but it was comforting to know that Desilijic was well-represented, and that all of the Clan families had taken Jiliac's summons seriously.

When the representatives of all the kajidics were present, the Executive Secretary of the Grand Council, a recent appointee named Grejic, called the meeting to order.

"Comrades-in-power, siblings-in-profit, I have convened you today to discuss concerns raised by Desilijic. I ask Jabba, Desilijic's representative, to speak."

Jabba wriggled out in front of Grejic's dais and lifted his arms for quiet. When the other Hutts continued to whisper to each other, he raised his tail and brought it down against the stone floor with a loud WHAP!

Silence ensued.

"Fellow Hutts, I come to you today with some serious allegations of wrongdoing on the part of Besadii kajidic. Over the past year, their actions have grown more and more reprehensible. It all started with the Battle of Nar Shaddaa. All of us suffered because of that attack—*except* Besadii. We lost ships, pilots, cargoes, part of the Moon's shield—not to mention how much trade we lost! And then there was the aftermath of the battle. The loss of part of Nar Shaddaa's shield caused the destruction of several blocks of buildings from the crash of the *Peacekeeper*. Cleanup and reconstruction is still going on. And who has paid for it? Each clan lost property and credits—*except* Besadii. And they alone—they who suffered no loss, who could most afford it—they have paid nothing! We have all suffered and lost—*except* Besadii!"

The other Hutts murmured to each other when Jabba paused. He looked over at the section of floor reserved for Besadii, and saw that Durga had not deigned to appear. Instead he had sent Zier and several lesser members of the kajidic as his representatives.

"And what did Besadii do while Nal Hutta was threatened? They sold slaves to the very Empire that was attacking their homeworld! All of the clans cooperated in paying the credits for the exorbitant bribe of Admiral Greelanx—which proved to be the only thing that saved our world from a devastating embargo. All of the clans, that is . . . *except* Besadii."

The other Hutts murmured muted affirmatives. Jabba was proud of the way his speech was going. He was verging on true eloquence, he thought, and even Jiliac, acknowledged orator that she was, could not have done better. He was actually glad that Jiliac had been too occupied with her baby to appear today. She wasn't as versed in all of this as he was, and things didn't affect her these days the way they used to. . . .

"And in the months since that battle, fellow Hutts, what has Besadii done? Helped us rebuild? Offered to recompense the other clans for their share of the bribe? Sent a single work crew of slaves to help with the rebuilding?" Jabba let his voice scale up to a near-shout. "*No!* Fellow Hutts, what they have done is to raise the prices on their spice to the point where the profits of every kajidic are compromised—at the worst possible time! Some may say this is just good business, just the urge for profit—but I say, *No!* Besadii is trying to take over! To put us all out of business! Besadii wishes that there was no Hutt clan on all of Nal Hutta—*except* Besadii!"

Jabba's voice had risen to a thundering pitch. He slapped his tail for emphasis, hard. The echoes fled around the cavernous hall.

"I demand that Besadii be censured! I demand that the Grand Council take a vote to censure them now, and levy a fine, to be distributed among those they have wronged! I demand this in the name of all Hutts everywhere!!"

The hall erupted into pandemonium. Tails slammed, voices cried out with indignation. Some Hutts turned on the Besadii contingent with threatening tail-waves, shouting insults and curses.

Zier looked around wildly, and saw no friendliness in the hall. He raised his arms and voice, shouting in turn, but his voice was drowned out by the combined fury of the other Hutts.

Finally the furor began to die down. Grejic slapped his tail for quiet, and finally got it.

"By custom, Zier, as the ranking member of Besadii, has the right to answer his accuser. What have you to say to all this, Zier?"

Zier cleared his massive throat, swallowed. "Fellow Hutts, how can you condemn Besadii? Making profit is to be lauded, not denigrated! Jabba and Jiliac lost the most in the attack on Nar Shaddaa, and they are attempting to sway you into siding with them against Besadii. The truth is, Besadii did nothing wrong! We did nothing—"

"You did nothing, all right!" the leader of Trinivii kajidic shouted, breaking in. "Desilijic offered the strategy that saved us. Besadii grabbed profit at all our expense!"

Zier shook his head. "What we did was—"

"We are Hutts!" another leader shouted. "It is our pride to take from other species! It is our pride to make profit! But we do not seek to destroy our own kind! Compete, yes . . . destroy, no!"

Chaos erupted. A cacophony of tail-thumps, shouts, curses, bellows, and raging diatribes filled the air.

Grejic had to tail-thump many times to restore order. "I believe it is time for a vote," he called. "All kajidic representatives in favor of officially censuring and fining Besadii—vote now, yes or no, on the motion."

Each kajidic leader pressed a thumb against the vote tabulator before him.

Moments later, Grejic raised a hand. "The votes are tallied. Forty-seven to one in favor of censuring Besadii."

Cheers rang out.

"Zier of Bes—"

"Wait!" A voice broke in. Jabba recognized that voice, and turned to see Jiliac undulating across the room. "Wait, I did not vote!"

"Jabba voted for your kajidic, Lady Jiliac. Why this interruption? Do you wish us to re-take the vote?" Grejic was respectful, but clearly impatient to get on with the matter at hand.

"Re-take the vote?" Jabba looked at his aunt and their gazes locked. After a moment, she shook her head. "My nephew is my accepted proxy, Lord Grejic. Please proceed."

Jabba let out his breath very slowly. For a moment he'd thought Jiliac was going to question his judgment and his authority in front of everyone. Many of the other Hutts were giving him curious glances, clearly wondering why Jabba had been voting if Jiliac was not going to support his position unreservedly.

Jiliac glided over to lie beside her nephew, but Jabba found himself wishing she'd just stayed away. It was embarrassing to have his judgment questioned in front of his own people. He thought again of what it would be like just to run Desilijic by himself, without interference—and unthinking interference, at that.

"Zier of Besadii," said Grejic, continuing where he'd left off, "it is the will of this Council that you be excused from our ranks until your clan has paid one million credits in damages, to be divided among the other kajidics equally. May I suggest that you endeavor in future not to regard your own people as you would those of other species—as dupes to be exploited."

The Executive Secretary waved to the guards and their ranking officer, who were standing at the entrance. "Guardsmaster, you will escort the Besadii delegation from this hall."

As Zier and the other Besadii undulated along toward the entrance, Jabba saw that they were all trying to look confident and scornful and failing utterly. The soft mutter of the other Hutts swelled into a tumult of hooting laughter, raucous bellows, and shouted insults, jeers and threats.

Jabba smiled inwardly. *Not a bad afternoon's work,* he thought smugly. *Not bad at all. . . .*

Bria Tharen walked briskly down the corridor of her command ship, the light cruiser *Retribution*. She was on her way to review her troops before their planned raid on the slaver vessel *Helot's Shackle*. Inwardly, Bria was excited and eager, but her features were composed and her blue-green eyes were as cold as deep glacial ice.

Mentally she reviewed her battle plan, analyzing it for weaknesses, making sure she'd covered every possible contingency with a backup option. This operation should go down smoothly, but the *Helot's Shackle* was, after all, a heavily-armed Corellian corvette, a formidable vessel in her own right.

Retribution was almost the same size as the *Shackle*, so they should be relatively evenly matched. Bria's vessel was a Republic Sienar Systems *Marauder*-class corvette, sleek and streamlined, capable of both space and atmospheric combat. The Marauders were among the most common capital ships in the Corporate Sector's picket fleet. The Corellian underground had purchased this Marauder second-hand from the Authority, and given it to Bria for her flagship.

The Corellian commander had an operative working on the space station orbiting Ylesia. The operative had tipped Bria off a few days ago that the Ylesian priests were planning on shipping out nearly two hundred Exultation-addicted and malnourished slaves to the mines of Kessel.

For a moment Bria wished she could give in to her own desires and go out with her people in the first boarding wave. The troops aboard those three shuttles would see the maximum amount of combat, make the most kills. And Bria had a personal grudge against this particular slaving vessel. Nearly ten years ago, *Helot's Shackle* had narrowly missed capturing Bria, Han and their two Togorian friends, Muuurgh and Mrrov, as they'd made their escape from Ylesia.

Bria sighed, but she knew that her place during the first wave was aboard her command vessel, coordinating the attack, identifying pockets of heavy resistance in order to best allocate her troops for the second wave.

This was *Retribution*'s fifth mission for the Corellian resistance, and Bria was glad to be back in action. During her eight years with the Corellian underground, she'd done whatever she'd been assigned to do, and done it well. But she had hated the undercover spying projects . . . and hadn't much liked "liaison" work. She'd been glad to leave them behind and get back to real fighting.

It was Mon Mothma who had made it possible for Bria to go back into the real action. The renegade Imperial senator had both the influence and the eloquence to convince individual resistance groups that a Rebel Alliance was a necessity. The Senator was better at it than Bria had ever been, and spent all her time traveling from world to world, meeting with underground leaders. Just a month ago Bria and the rest of the Corellian resistance had celebrated the signing of the Corellian Treaty.

Publicly, Mon Mothma was credited with engineering the Treaty, and there was no doubt that she had helped. But Bria had heard a rumor that Corellia's own Senator Garm bel Iblis had secretly been one of the main architects of the Treaty. In addition to Corellia, the other signatories to the Treaty were Alderaan and Chandrila—Mon Mothma's home planet.

Traveling system to system, world to world, Mon Mothma made contact with resistance groups where they existed, and created new groups where there had been none. The former senator's fame was both help and hindrance; on the one hand it gave her access to important nobles and leaders of industry, but on the other hand, especially in the beginning, some groups had expressed the fear that she might be an Imperial plant, sent by Emperor Palpatine to test their loyalty.

The renegade senator had faced death many times, both from Imperial troops and from suspicious resistance leaders. Bria had met Mon Mothma and conferred with her soon after the senator had fled the Emperor's charge of treason. She'd been impressed— almost awed—by Mon Mothma's quiet dignity, her unswerving resolution and her formidable intelligence.

It had been one of the high points of Bria's life when Mon Mothma had shaken her hand and told her that she, Bria Tharen, had been one of the people who'd been instrumental in getting Bail Organa to change his mind about Alderaan's pacifism. The Viceroy was now committed to the thought of armed revolution against the Empire. He faced considerable resistance from his government, however, and, so far, Alderaan's efforts at arming itself were small and extremely clandestine.

The Corellian Treaty had inaugurated the Rebel Alliance Bria and the other Corellians had been working toward. The individual Rebel groups would retain much of their autonomy, but, in theory at least, strategic command of the Alliance was now vested in Mon Mothma. To date, the fledgling Rebel Alliance had not been tested in battle. Bria was hoping that would soon change.

Bria rounded a corner in *Retribution*'s corridor, and was joined by her medical officer. Daino Hyx would be in charge of handling the slaves once they were rescued. Hyx was a short, bearded man with the brightest blue eyes Bria had ever seen, and a shy smile that most people found irresistible. Hyx had been a scholar at one of Alderaan's top universities. There he'd studied medicine and psychology, and had wound up specializing in the treatment of addictions. Since joining the Corellian resistance six months ago, he'd applied his formidable skills to the problem of the Ylesian Pilgrims.

Bria was convinced that there were many frustrated idealists to be found among the underfed, overworked ranks of the Ylesian Pilgrims. Since her first raid on Ylesia nearly two years ago, sixteen slaves that she'd rescued were currently topnotch fighters or operatives for the Corellian resistance. Another ten had been awarded medals for valor . . . posthumously.

Bria had pointed out to her commanding officers on Corellia that Ylesia, with its thousands of slaves, was a potential goldmine of Rebel recruits—if only they could find a way to overcome the addictive effects of the Exultation. True, Bria herself had overcome addiction to the Exultation to become a valuable addition to the Corellian underground. But it had taken her nearly three years of unrelenting effort to cure herself. She'd tried everything from meditation to drugs—and had only found the strength she needed when she decided to dedicate her life to the eradication of slavery and the Empire that condoned it.

But they didn't have three years to devote to curing the Pilgrims. They had to find a cure that would work in weeks or months, rather than years.

That was where Daino Hyx came in. By thoroughly analyzing the physical, mental and emotional effects of the Exultation (at one point he'd traveled to Nal Hutta to meet a number of t'landa Til males and studied how they produced the effect) Hyx believed he'd found a cure. Hyx's cure involved a mixture of mental, emotional and physical treatments, ranging from anti-addiction drugs to interactive and group therapy.

Today, if all went well, Hyx would get the chance to begin putting his new treatment to the test.

He glanced up at Bria. "Nervous, Commander?"

She smiled faintly. "Does it show?"

"No. Most people wouldn't notice a thing, I'm sure. But I'm not most people. I got to know you pretty well while we were first working on the new therapy. And assessing the mental and emotional states of humanoids is my job, remember."

"That's true," Bria admitted. "Yes, I'm a bit nervous. This is different from capturing a customs patrol ship or raiding some lonely Imp outpost. This time, we're going up against the people who used to *own* me, body and spirit. I'm always just a bit afraid that when I'm exposed to the Pilgrims' addiction that my own will somehow come back."

Hyx nodded. "You have an emotional stake in this

raid, not just a military goal. It's perfectly understand-able that you'd feel anxiety."

Bria gave him a quick glance. "That won't keep me from doing my job, Hyx."

"I know," he said. "Red Hand Squadron is very efficient, I hear. From what I've observed about your people, they'd follow you into a black hole and out the other side."

Bria laughed a little. "I don't know about *that*. If I were crazy enough to mess with black holes, I hope they'd be sane enough to hold back. But my troops would follow me into Palpatine's Imperial Palace, that I know."

"You wouldn't last very long," he said dryly.

She smiled, but no warmth reached her eyes. "But we'd have fun for a while. It would be worth my life to get a shot at Palpatine."

"How soon does the first wave launch?"

She glanced at the tiny chrono-ring she wore. "We're waiting for the signal from my operative on the space station. Then we'll microjump into position. He'll tell us the moment *Helot's Shackle* undocks from the Ylesian space station. We want to catch the slavers before they can leave the system."

"Makes sense."

Bria turned right and entered the turbolift. "I'm going down to do a final check of my troopers who will be going in the boarding shuttles. Want to tag along?"

"Sure."

They took the lift down to the shuttle launch bay. When they stepped out, the launch area was a controlled frenzy of crews making last minute checks of vessels, equipment and weapons. One of the troops, seeing Bria, put two fingers in his mouth and whistled piercingly. "Commander on deck!"

Bria spoke to her lieutenant, Jace Paol, who was overseeing the last pre-battle preparations. "Assemble troops, please."

One quick order later, and the boarding squads were falling in. There would be one squad per shuttle, about ten troops on each. Two waves of three shuttles each, first wave and second wave. First wave would have the responsibility for boarding *Helot's Shackle* and neutralizing the slaver resistance. The second wave would reinforce the first, and help with the mopping up.

Bria walked slowly down the lines of troops, inspecting them, checking their uniforms, their weapons, their expressions. At one point she stopped before a young trooper whose eyes glittered with more than eagerness. Studying his flushed cheeks and reddened nose, she frowned. "Corporal Burrid . . ."

He came to full attention. "Yes, Commander!"

She reached up, touched his cheek, then his forehead. "Fall out, Burrid. You've got at least a degree of fever."

Sk'kot Burrid saluted. "Respectfully, Commander, I feel fine!"

"Right," Bria said. "And I'm the Emperor's Wookiee concubine. Hyx?"

The medical officer took a med-probe out of his belt pouch and touched it to the young man's face. "Two degrees fever, Commander. White cell counts indicate infection, possibly contagious."

"Report to the med droid, Corporal," Bria ordered.

Crestfallen, the young man opened his mouth to protest, then he thought better of it and obeyed. Without a word, his backup from the reserves moved into his place in line.

When Bria had finished her inspection, she paused, then addressed her soldiers. "All right, people. We're waiting now for the signal to make our microjump. The Y-wings will go in first, and make their runs to bring their shields down. Then it will be up to you people. You'll be docking with their airlocks where they have them, and fighting your way in. Where there are no airlocks, we're going to make ones. Special engineering teams will accompany two boarding shuttles. Those squads will cut through the hull just in front of the engineering sections."

She paused. "Remember, there are going to be slaves underfoot, confused, frightened, and probably beginning to suffer from Exultation withdrawal. They may try to attack you. Don't risk yourselves, but make every reasonable effort not to harm them seriously. Use stun beams on those slaves, all right?"

There was a general murmur of agreement. "Are there any questions?"

There weren't. The troops had already been briefed by their squad leaders and platoon leaders, and they'd been through repeated drills.

Bria nodded at the troops. "This is Red Hand's most ambitious undertaking yet, people. If we can pull this off, you can bet we'll be seeing more action. So let's *impress* the Sector Command . . . right?"

Agreement was unanimous.

As Bria turned to confer with her platoon leaders, suddenly her comlink beeped. She activated it. "Yes?"

"Commander, the signal just came through. *Helot's Shackle* has just undocked from the Ylesian station."

Bria nodded, then turned to the platoon leader. "First wave, board your shuttles. Second wave . . . stand by."

The deck reverberated to the pound of running feet as the thirty troopers scrambled into their respective shuttles.

Bria keyed in her personal frequency. "Attention, *Crimson Fury*, this is Red Hand Leader."

"Go ahead, Red Hand."

"Prepare your ships to microjump in three minutes. *Retribution* will be right behind you."

"Copy that, Red Hand Leader. Preparing for microjump."

Quickly Bria and Daino Hyx left the shuttle fighter launch bay, took the turbolift up, then jogged forward until they reached the bridge. The ship's captain looked up as they entered. Bria slipped into a seat behind the tactical schematic. From her station she could also see the viewscreens. "Captain Bjalin," she said. "Ten seconds after the last of the Y-wings has jumped, we will jump."

"Yes, Commander," Bjalin said. Tedris Bjalin was a tall young man whose hairline was receding, despite his youth. He'd joined the Corellian resistance just recently, after his entire family had been murdered during the Imperial massacre on Tyshapahl. Before that time, he'd been an Imperial lieutenant. His Imperial training had served him in good stead, earning him a promotion in the Rebel forces. He was an able officer, a decent man, who'd told Bria that he'd already been thinking of deserting the Imperial Navy when his family had been murdered. That had pushed him over the edge.

Bria watched tensely as the seconds counted down, and, two by two, the six Y-wings jumped into hyperspace. Then the starlines stretched out before them, as *Retribution* jumped, too.

The moment they arrived back in realspace, *Retribution* opened her shuttle bays and the first wave of boarding shuttles launched. They approached *Helot's Shackle* at half speed, behind the Y-wings, which were barreling in at full speed.

Bria watched with satisfaction as the first pair of Y-wings streaked toward the Corellian corvette, firing salvos of two proton torpedoes each, targeting the stern and amidships. Their goal was not to blow a hole in *Helot's Shackle*, but to take down the shields without harming the vessel unduly. Bria intended to take the *Shackle* intact and bring it back to be added into the Rebel fleet. One of the shuttles in the second wave would be carrying a prize crew, consisting of computer techs, engineers, a pilot and damage control and repair teams.

Bria would not have minded catching *Helot's Shackle* unprepared, but she wasn't counting on that, and wasn't surprised to find that the corvette was traveling with its shields up. As the Y-wings hurtled in, the big ship opened fire, but the agile Y-wings easily evaded its blasts. *Retribution* stayed carefully out of range of its fire.

As Bria watched, the four proton torpedoes launched by the Y-wings flashed blue-white, impacted against the shields, and splashed over the slaver's hull without penetrating the defenses. The first pair of Y-wings peeled away and went circling back in case they were needed again.

Helot's Shackle blasted away again, and this time one of its shots grazed one of the Y-wings—a minor hit, but enough to put the fighter out of the action.

Bria was figuring it would take four proton torpedoes to bring down the *Shackle*'s shields. The second pair of Y-wings went streaking in, and the first fired.

This time the blue-white burst spread out, then, suddenly, there was a visible impact against the side of the vessel. A blackened streak marred the armor.

"That's it!" Bria said, and keyed the comm unit, addressed her Y-wing team leader. "*Crimson Fury*, good work! Shields are down! Now let's use those ion cannons of yours to finish 'em! Warn your ships to take evasive! We don't want any more hits!"

"Copy that, Red Hand Leader. Targeting sensor suites and solar fin. Starting our runs now."

The Y-wing pairs began strafing the *Helot's Shackle*, firing their turreted ion cannons at the preassigned targets. The bursts from the ion cannons were designed not to damage the enemy vessel's hull, but to knock out all electrical activity aboard ship—including, of course, the engines, the targeting computers, and the bridge systems. Every electrical system aboard would need to be re-initialized before the *Shackle* would be operational again.

Helot's Shackle fired again and again, but the Y-wings were just too quick and agile for the big ship's weapons to target effectively.

Scant minutes later, the *Shackle* was drifting helpless in space, its electrical systems down. Bria checked her chrono as the first wave of boarding shuttles moved in. *Good. Right on time.* One ship attached itself to the large forward airlock, the one the *Shackle* used to load her cargoes of slaves. The remaining two shuttles grappled against the hull on either side of the slaver's ship and began cutting their way in.

Bria listened as reports flooded in from her squad leaders:

"Red Hand Leader, Squad One reporting from the cargo airlock on the forward hold on Deck 4. We've made it inside, but we're encountering heavy resistance. The crew was getting the slaves out as we came through, but there are still some in here. The Pilgrims have taken shelter, as have we, behind cargo canisters. We've got a brisk firefight ongoing. We're going to push them back, so we can get to the turbolaser access shaft."

"Red Hand Leader, Squad Two reporting in. We've

breached the hull forward of the engines on Deck 4 and set up a portable airlock. My troops are moving in now. . . ."

"Red Hand Leader, the armor plating on this section of the starboard hull is giving us some trouble . . . stand by. . . ." And, a minute later, "Red Hand Leader, we are through!"

Bria watched the progress of the squads through the vessel, weighing when to bring in her second wave. The two squads who'd cut their way in had met with minimal resistance. But the forward squad who'd entered through the airlock was meeting heavy opposition from the slavers as they battled their way to the turbolifts. It was understandable that the slavers would fight to the last. Red Hand's reputation was beginning to spread, and doubtless the crew of the *Shackle* had recognized the symbol of a blood-dripping hand painted on the bows of their attackers' ships.

Bria stood up and addressed the captain of her ship. "Tedris, you're in command of the squadron until I return from the second wave operation. Be prepared to send backup if I contact you, but not until. Have the Y-wings moved out to their patrol stations?"

"Yes, Commander. We'll have at least fifteen minutes warning if anyone decides to join the party. . . . Of course that's just in case the slavers managed to get a distress call out before we jammed their transmissions."

"Good work, Captain."

Bjalin nodded, but did not salute. Discipline in the Rebel forces was far more informal than in the Imperial Navy. It had taken Bria two weeks to break him of the habit of saluting at the drop of a "Sir!"

"Good luck, Commander," he said.

"Thanks. I may need it. My people have pushed them out of that forward hold, but they had lots of time to set up strong defenses. I'm betting they've holed up in the bridge and the access corridors and are working on the electronics. I think I'm going to have to be a little . . . creative."

Bjalin smiled. "You're good at that, Commander."

Ten minutes later, Bria's boarding shuttle had docked with the portable airlock and her reserves were jogging down the corridor of Deck 3 after her, blaster rifles ready.

In the eerie, wan illumination provided by the emergency battery lights, the crippled *Shackle* seemed deserted; Bria knew that was an illusion. Dimly, she could hear the wailing of some of the slaves. Probably they'd been herded to the security hold on Deck 4 and locked in. The commander hoped fervently that none of the slavers had hit upon the bright idea of driving the slaves into Rebel blaster fire in an attempt to delay the invading soldiers while they made their getaway. That had happened once, and Bria still had nightmares about it . . . the pale, shocked faces of the unarmed slaves, the reverberations of the blaster bolts, the screams, the crumpling figures, the meaty sizzle-reek of burning flesh. . . .

Bria led her troops forward, toward the master's cabin in the bow of the ship. It was located directly beneath the bridge, and was the key to her plan.

She keyed her comlink. "Prize crew . . . how's it going?"

"Commander, hull damage appears to be minimal. Our Y-wings targeted well. We have people working on repairs now."

"How about the electrical systems and the computers?"

"That's going to be harder. We can't start up the systems until you've captured the bridge. We don't want to give them any control over the ship."

"They're probably trying to do a restart themselves up there. Can you block that?"

"I think so, Commander."

"Good. Concentrate checking out the systems, then, and the engines. Wait for my signal to re-initialize."

"We copy, Commander."

Bria and her squads met only one pocket of resistance on their way to the master cabin. About ten slavers and one unfortunate slave whom they'd armed and pressed into service were holed up behind a hastily erected barricade in a companionway.

Bria signaled her troops to retreat back around the corridor, then addressed them in a whisper. "All right, people. We're going to lay down a suppressing fire while Larens, here—" she nodded at a short, slight, very agile soldier, "crawls under our fire until he's in range to toss a stun grenade right into the middle of that nest of vermin. Got me?"

"Right, Commander." Larens dropped down, prepared to scuttle forward, the stun grenade held in his teeth.

"On the count of three, then. . . . One . . . two . . . three!"

Bria and the other Rebels dodged into the companionway firing bursts at the barricade, careful to aim high enough not to scorch Larens' rapidly scuttling rear.

Blaster bolts screamed in the confined space. Bria caught a glimpse of an arm with a dagger tattoo, aimed and watched the arm (and its slaver owner, presumably) fall back behind the barricade. She remembered the first time she'd ever shot a blaster, and had a brief, sharp memory of Han that she suppressed. No time for memories . . . time only for the job at hand. . . .

Bare seconds later there was a loud *whump!* and

suddenly the returning fire was gone. Bria motioned her people to follow her. "Remember, the Pilgrim will be wearing a tan robe!"

She ran forward, saw the nest of slavers lying sprawled about. Three were already dead, one of them from having his arm blown off. The Pilgrim was stunned, moving feebly.

Bria stood looking down at the carnage at her feet, and felt hatred surge up in her. Six slavers still alive . . . her finger twitched on the trigger of the blaster rifle she held.

"Commander, shall I set up a guard detail?" Larens looked at her inquiringly. He was new to Red Hand Squadron. Several of the veterans gave him impatient glances.

"They're vermin, Larens," Bria said. "We'll just *insure* that they don't represent a future danger. Mecht, you and Seaan catch up when you've finished here. Drag that Pilgrim into a room so when he wakes up he won't be in the middle of anything."

Mecht nodded. He was a middle-aged man who'd been enslaved himself, though he'd been an Imperial slave, not an Ylesian one. He nodded. "We won't be long, Commander."

Larens started to say something, then obviously changed his mind. Bria motioned to her troops, and they moved on.

Five minutes later, the squad was in the slaver captain's quarters. Bria tried not to look at some of the "toys" the fellow had lying around, evidently for use in amusing himself with some of his slaves. She walked over to the center of the cabin and pointed up at the overhead. "People, the bridge is right up there." She glanced at one of her squad leaders. "Squad One, I want a diversionary attack along the corridors leading to the bridge up on Deck 2."

The squad leader nodded. "Be ready on my signal," Bria said.

"Right, Commander." He took off, his troops following him.

Bria addressed her remaining troops. "Squads Four and Five, you'll attack the bridge with me."

A couple of the newer recruits glanced at each other, obviously puzzled. How were they going to attack the bridge from here?

"Where's Joaa'n?" Bria asked.

A stocky trooper stepped forward, her features almost hidden beneath her helmet. "Here, Commander."

Bria pointed up. "Joaa'n, use your demolition bag of tricks to get us up there."

"Right, Commander." The woman climbed up on a bureau that had been shoved into place, and began using her lasertorch. The new recruits nudged each other and chuckled, as they realized what their Commander was planning.

Three minutes later, the demolitions expert looked down at Bria and gave her a thumbs-up. "Commander, I've rigged a demo charge that will blow us a nice circular hole through the deck."

Bria smiled. "Good." She spoke into her comlink. "Squad Two . . . begin your attack on the bridge."

The Rebels heard the sounds of blaster fire start up again.

"Renna," Bria nodded at another stocky, muscular woman, "you've got a good arm. You stand by with the stun grenades. As soon as it's safe, toss them up through the hole to stun most of those vermin." She looked at the rest of her troops. "People, as soon as Renna's lobbed those grenades through that hole, and the blasts have gone off, we're going up. Remember, people, this is the *bridge* up there. Be careful where you shoot. Too much damage and the prize crew won't speak to any of us for a month. Got it?"

There were chuckles from her squad.

"All right, it's set," Joaa'n said. "Get back and cover your eyes, friends. Thirty seconds."

Hastily, Bria's troops retreated to the cabin's perimeters. A couple of soldiers pulled down their blast goggles, the others just looked away. Bria, Joaa'n and Renna stood back behind a heavy ornamental screen.

Moments later there was a fizzling sound, then a muffled *thud*. Something heavy hit the bureau, slithered off onto the deck. The reek of smoke touched Bria's nostrils. She nodded at Joaa'n. "Good job."

The demo specialist and Renna were already moving, scrambling back up on the bureau. Renna lobbed three stun grenades up through the hole in three different directions. The *ssss-whump!* of the grenades and the resulting cries and thuds told the commander that they were doing their work.

Renna pulled herself up with a boost from Joaa'n, then disappeared. They heard her blaster.

Bria swarmed up the bureau, and was next through the hole as someone grabbed her rear and gave her an undignified, if efficient, boost.

The bridge crew was lying around, mostly stunned, but there were a few slavers scrambling out the door. Bria sighted on one huge Rodian and took him down with a blast between the green-skinned being's shoulders. Another slaver, a Bothan, turned to fire at her, his blaster beginning to stutter with a low charge. Bria ducked, rolled, came up with her sidearm in her hand, and shot him in the face. The vermin was standing in front of the navicomputer, and she didn't want to risk killing him with the blaster rifle's greater power.

Moments later, it was all over. Silence descended, broken only by the moaning of the wounded. Bria took a quick status check . . . six of her people were wounded, and one might not make it. Quickly Bria assigned a special team to rush the wounded back to *Retribution* for treatment.

Minutes later, the prize crew reported that they were ready for the restart. Bria watched tensely, heard a whine, then, suddenly, full illumination replaced the emergency lighting on the bridge. The tactical screens glowed, the navicomputer chirred softly to itself.

Bria left her troops to deal with the vermin and walked out to the turbolift. She keyed her comlink. "Hyx . . . you there?"

"I'm here aboard *Retribution*, Commander," the medical officer reported. "The wounded have been transported over, and everything is looking good. Except for Caronil . . . he didn't make it. Sorry. The medic and I did everything we could. . . ."

Bria swallowed. "I know that. Are you still needed there, Hyx?"

"Not really. The med droids have things under control here. I'm taking the shuttle back to the *Shackle*."

"Good. I'm going to need you soon. Come straight to the Security Hold. That's where the slaves are locked up. I'll meet you there."

Bria took the turbolift down two decks, then started aft. She was nearly to the locked portal when the scuff of a foot behind her made her whirl around, sidearm in hand. Behind her, brandishing a blaster, was one of the slavers who'd somehow escaped capture.

The woman's eyes were glittery, her pupils dilated, her hair a greasy halo around her face. "Stop right there or I'll shoot!" she bellowed, holding the blaster in two trembling hands.

Bria stopped. *Trembling with fear? Maybe . . . but that's not all. . . .*

"Drop your weapon!" the woman howled. "Or I'll kill you!"

"I don't think so," Bria said, calmly, letting her blaster hang down in her hand, muzzle pointed at the deck. "If I'm dead, I'm no use to you as a hostage."

The woman frowned, obviously trying to puzzle out her captive's words. Finally, she elected to ignore them. "I want a shuttle!" she cried. "A shuttle, and some slaves to take with me! You can have the rest! I just want my fair cut, that's all!"

"Not a chance," Bria said, steel underlying her quiet tone. "I'm not a slaver. I'm here to free these people."

The woman appeared completely baffled by this. She cocked her head. "You don't wanna sell 'em?" she asked, skeptically.

"No." Bria said. "I'm here to free them."

"Free 'em?" Bria might as well have been speaking Huttese for all the slaver understood her. "They're worth couple thousand credits apiece, some of 'em."

"I don't care," Bria said.

The slaver's brow furrowed. "Why not?"

"Because slavery is wrong," Bria said. "You're wasting my time, vermin. Kill me or let me go—but you'll get nothing from me."

The woman pondered Bria's words, obviously taken aback by the commander's response. It was plain to Bria that the slaver was under the influence of some powerful stimulant. Carsunum, probably. The woman was shaking all over. The muzzle of the gun was practically vibrating in mid-air. Bria's eyes narrowed as she watched the muzzle of the weapon waver, waver . . .

then drop fractionally as the drugged woman struggled to comprehend a being who cared nothing for personal profit.

Bria's hand moved in a blur as she brought her weapon up, at the same time throwing herself to the side. The slaver fired, but she was shaking so violently that the bolt didn't even singe Bria. The Rebel commander's shot struck the slaver just below her chest. The woman went down with a scream and a gurgle.

Bria walked over to her, kicked away the blaster from the outflung arm and limp fingers, and looked down at the slaver. There was a gaping, charred hole in her abdomen. The woman stared back up at her, panting shallowly. Bria aimed her sidearm at the slaver's forehead. "Want me to?"

The woman shook her head, side to side, then struggled to speak. "N-no . . ." She wheezed in agony. "I—I want . . . to . . . live. . . ."

Bria shrugged. "Fine by me. You've got maybe five minutes, I figure."

With her sidearm in her hand, Bria stepped over the slaver and continued down to the hold.

She had to use her blaster on the lock. Inside, she heard screams of panic. The portal swung open.

The stench hit the Corellian the moment she stepped through the door. Human and alien, the effluvia rolled out, almost visible, it was so thick.

Bria looked over the crowd of wailing, moaning, wretched Pilgrims who were cowering away from her, even as they held out their skinny, talon-like hands, pleading, "Bring a priest! Need the priests! Take us home!"

The commander felt her gorge rise, and it took her a moment to control herself. *That would have been me . . .*

almost ten years ago, now, that's how I would have been . . . if it hadn't been for Han. . . .

A step came from behind her, and Bria whirled, sidearm ready, only to relax when she recognized Daino Hyx. He raised an eyebrow at her. "A little jumpy, Commander?"

Bria smiled sheepishly. "Maybe just a tad."

"That got anything to do with the dead woman out there in the corridor?"

"Not really," Bria holstered her blaster, realizing disgustedly that now *she* was the one doing the shaking. "More to do with *them*." She jerked her head at the agonized Pilgrims. "They're all yours, Hyx. Looks like you've got your work cut out for you."

He nodded, studying them with a healer's kindly detachment. "How soon will the *Shackle* be ready to rendezvous with the transport?"

Bria glanced at her chrono. "I allowed thirty-five minutes to take this ship and get her working again. It's been thirty-nine. I expect to hear—"

Her comlink signaled, and Bria smiled and answered it. "Red Hand Leader here."

"Commander, this is Jace Paol. We have secured the ship, and the prize crew reports we are now hyperspace capable. Proceed to our rendezvous coordinates?"

"Copy that, Jace. I'll advise *Retribution*. Tell Lieutenant Hethar to take her out. *Deliverance* is waiting for us to transship these Pilgrims."

"I copy, Commander."

Bria keyed her comlink. "Captain Bjalin, *Helot's Shackle* is ours, along with her cargo. Prepare to rendezvous with *Deliverance* at our assigned coordinates."

"I copy, Red Hand Leader. We'll meet you there. And . . . Commander?"

"Yes, Tedris?"

"Congratulations on a smoothly run operation."

"Thank you, Tedris."

One month later, Bria Tharen, on a rare visit back to Corellia to meet with her commanding officer, walked quickly into his office. Pianat Torbul, a short, dark-haired man with intense eyes, looked up. "Welcome home," he said. "You're late. I was expecting you two days ago."

"Sorry, sir," she said. "I picked up a last minute call to help the *Pride of the Rim* out with a couple of Imp picket ships. *Retribution* took a hit that damaged sublight engines, and we had to lay up for a day."

"I know," he said, and smiled—his quick, irresistible grin. "I received the report from the *Pride*. Don't be so defensive, Tharen."

She smiled back, then, at his gesture, dropped wearily into a seat. "So, did you get *my* report, sir?"

"I did," he said. "Seems your friend Hyx is reporting great progress in turning those Pilgrims you rescued off the *Helot's Shackle* back into normal citizens. Congratulations. Your faith in him and his new treatment seems to be paying off."

Bria nodded, her eyes lighting up. "It means a lot to me, to be able to give those people back their lives. Their families will be glad to see them. . . . They'll be able to live in dignity, and comfort. . . ."

"Unless, of course, they choose to join up with us," Torbul said. "Which apparently some of them are already talking about doing once they're returned to health. Which may take a couple of months. I gather that malnutrition plays a pretty big part in the brainwashing they undergo on Ylesia."

Bria nodded. "I remember my gums started to bleed

all the time. It took me two months of decent food to overcome most of the effects."

He glanced back down at his datapad. "*Helot's Shackle* is almost finished being refitted for combat. We can really use her, Tharen, thank you for acquiring her for us. With that in mind . . . want the honor of renaming her?"

Bria thought for a moment. "Call her *Emancipator*," she said.

"That's a good one," Torbul said. "*Emancipator* she is."

Torbul clicked off his datapad, leaned his elbows on his desk, and leaned forward. "Bria . . ." he said. "Now that the official stuff is over and done with, I have to tell you that I'm concerned about some aspects of your record."

Her eyes widened in surprise. "But, sir—!!"

"Oh, don't get me wrong, Tharen. You are a good fighter, an able leader. Nobody's gainsaying that. But look at the name those slavers gave you, that your squadron cheerfully adopted. Red Hand—symbol of no quarter. Look at this report on the taking of *Helot's Shackle*. No prisoners. Not a single one."

Bria stiffened. "Sir, they were slavers. They know how the civilized world regards them. They put up a lot of resistance, and not a one offered to surrender. They fought to the last."

"I see. . . ." Torbul said. The two of them exchanged a long look, and it was the ranking officer who looked away first.

An awkward silence ensued until Torbul cleared his throat. "Things are heating up in the Outer Rim," he announced. "The Rebel groups out there are really understaffed. I'd like Red Hand to stay out there for a while, give them some assistance."

"Yes, sir," Bria said. "Sir . . ."

"Yes?"

"I think I may know a way to get more recruits."

"What is that?"

"Well, the best we've ever done curing the Ylesian Pilgrims of addiction before was about fifty percent. Remember?"

He nodded.

"But now, with the new techniques Daino is using to help the Pilgrims we took to Grenna Base, he thinks his success rate will be better than 90 percent."

"That's very encouraging. But what does that have to do with getting more recruits?"

Bria leaned forward, her blue-green eyes holding his dark ones. "Sir . . . there are over *eight thousand* Pilgrims on Ylesia."

He sat back. "What are you suggesting, Tharen?"

"Give me just a little help . . . an old troopship for transport, a couple more cruisers, some more troops, and I can *take* that planet. I can shut down the Ylesian operation for good. We'll take every colony, free every slave there. Hundreds of them are bound to join us, if the percentages we've seen so far are any indication."

"That's a big 'if,' " Torbul said.

"I know, sir. But I think the risk would be worth it."

"We don't have the troops. Not all of the Corellian resistance would be enough to take a whole planet, Tharen!"

"We're getting recruits in from Alderaan every day," Bria pointed out, truthfully. "And there are so many Bothan and Sullustan Pilgrims on Ylesia, those worlds might send us some troops and ships. It's worth asking them. And what about Chandrila? They're part of the new Rebel Alliance—sworn to help us!"

"Recruits . . . it's an incentive, certainly."

She nodded vigorously. "Sir, it could work. We can free those slaves. And while we're at it, we could take the spice to sell on the open market. We're always short of credits. Think of how many turbolasers or proton torpedoes that much spice would buy us! We could bomb the warehouses and factories when we had emptied them. Ylesia and its filthy trade would be a thing of the past."

Bria realized that she had lost her composure, but in her passion, she didn't care. Her hands were shaking; she gripped the edge of Torbul's desk so he wouldn't see the betraying tremor.

"I don't believe the Rebel Alliance would think much of selling drugs as a means of financing the Rebellion," Torbul said.

"Then, with all due respect, sir, *don't tell them where you got the credits!*" Bria's smile was more than a little savage. "You know as well as I do that they won't look a gift traladon in the mouth. They'll take the credits and use them. We need weapons, medical supplies, uniforms, ammo . . . you name it!"

"True," he said. "Fighting a resistance is an expensive proposition."

"Think it over," Bria urged. "I know Red Hand could do it. And without Ylesia siphoning off some of Corellia's best, we'd have more recruits. Think about who's going to Ylesia these days. Young people, dissatisfied with their lives, unable to pay the horrendous taxes, wanting something *more*, a better life. Those are exactly the kind of people we need."

"True," he said again. "But what about the Ylesian atmosphere? Your raid on Colony Three two and a half years ago freed a hundred slaves—but we lost a ship in that blasted atmosphere. That treacherous atmosphere of Ylesia's is one of their best defenses."

Bria's features twisted in remembered anguish. "I warned them, but . . . that wind shear just caught the ship. . . ."

"Tharen . . . it wasn't your fault. But we have to think about that. Command is bound to point that out."

She nodded. "I'm working on that, sir. There's got to be a way to deal with the atmosphere. Better pilots, for one thing. Our people are enthusiastic, sir, but face it . . . most of them haven't had much experience. Our training programs need work. . . ."

"I agree. We're working on ways to make our sims better, and broaden their experience before we turn them loose."

Bria stood up and leaned across the desk. "Sir . . . just promise me you'll think about it. I can do it. I even have some ideas about how to fund the raid. At least consider it, okay?"

He gave her a long, level glance. "All right, Tharen. I promise you I'll think about it."

"Thank you, sir."

Interlude 1: The Corporate Sector

Dressed only in his trousers, barefoot, Han Solo wandered out of the bedroom in Jessa's tiny apartment. Her little flat was located on her father's, Doc's, outlaw tech base, a grim, utilitarian place, but both Doc's and Jessa's personal quarters were surprisingly well-furnished and comfy.

Han yawned and scratched his head, rumpling his hair even further, then threw himself down on the elegant couch with a thud, and signaled on the big vid-unit.

The official news from the Corporate Sector Authority came on, and Han watched it with a cynical grin. The Authority was getting worse every day.

Wouldn't take much to make them as repressive as the Empire....

At least the *Falcon* was now in the best shape of her life. Before his capture and removal to Stars' End prison, Doc had upgraded her hyperdrive until she'd now make point-five past lightspeed. *I oughta be able to outrun just about anything the Imps could throw at me with that,* Han thought smugly. *Or the Authority either.*

Then, in order to induce Han to go after her father and rescue him from Stars' End, Jessa had fixed the Falcon up with an all-new sensor suite and dish, to replace the ones damaged in a fight with an Authority lighter.

Later, following Doc's rescue, the grateful Jessa had recently finished the Falcon's repairs, putting in an all-new guidance system and repairing all of the hull damage the YT-1300 had accrued. Han had even considered giving the ship a coat of paint, so she'd look just like new, but, after some consideration, had rejected the idea. The *Millennium Falcon's* beat-up appearance was one of her strongest assets in catching opponents unaware.

Nobody expected a grubby old freighter to have a military-grade hyperdrive that had been customized and upgraded by the galaxy's master tech, a sophisticated sensor suite, topnotch jamming capability, and all the other improvements Han had bestowed on the love of his life.

Jessa was still asleep in the other room. Han leaned back and propped his feet up on the table, thinking about Jess. She was certainly the best thing to come his way so far in the Corporate Sector. The two of them had had a lot of fun....

Just the other day, they'd flown the *Falcon* to one of the swankiest casinos in a nearby sector, and put on their best bib and tucker for a gambling spree. Jess had gotten her blond curls done in a wild new style, striped bright red, and bought a stunning red gown that was snug in all the right places. Han had been proud to be seen with her, and assured her she was the most beautiful woman in the place.

The news-vid changed from Corporate Sector reports to a brief report from the Empire. Palpatine's forces had stifled yet another uprising on yet another world. Han's mouth twisted. Same old, same old . . . He found himself thinking about Salla, wondering if she'd gotten over being mad yet. He suspected not. It was a good thing she wasn't here to see him with Jessa. Salla was the jealous type. She was one tough lady, but, then, so was Jessa. Han was profoundly grateful that the two of them were unlikely ever to meet.

Thoughts of Salla led naturally to wondering how Lando, Jarik, Shug and Mako were doing. Han even thought of Jabba with something approaching nostalgic affection. He bet the Hutt leader was having a hard time replacing him. If he ever decided to go back to Imperial space, Han suspected Jabba would welcome him with open arms . . . repugnant as that thought was.

Han watched another brief news bite from the Empire. Seemed that the Empire had now declared that the Rebel forces in the Outer Rim had been completely crushed. Sure, he thought. Right. That must mean that they're quite a thorn in the Imps' side. . . .

He wondered whether Bria had anything to do with harassing those Imp forces . . . or was she back to being a spy these days?

Han sighed, realizing that he actually missed Nar Shaddaa. The Corporate Sector was a fun place, lots of adventures to be had and profits to be made, but it wasn't home.

He wondered whether he should just cut his losses

*and head back for Imperial space. At the very least, it
was probably time to head out and look for some action
(translation: profit) here in the Corporate Sector. True,
he'd promised Jessa to help her and Doc in their campaign against the Authority. But that might be risky.
And it wasn't as though he owed Jessa anything. He'd
rescued her father, hadn't he? At great risk to his own
precious hide? A tiny honest corner of his mind reminded him that he'd mostly gone on that rescue mission for Chewie's sake. No way he was letting his pal
languish in an Authority prison. . . .*

*And yet . . . things were very pleasant here for the
moment, though he knew it couldn't last. Right now,
things were going well with Jessa. They were having a
good time. Maybe he'd just postpone leaving for another month . . . or two . . . or three. . . .*

"Han?" came a sleepy murmur from the bedroom.

"I'm here, honey. Just watchin' the news," Han said.
He flicked off the vid and went out to the tiny kitchen.
He'd make Jessa a hot cup of imported stim-tea that
she'd come to be very fond of, and take it to her. . . .

Chapter Eight:

The Queen of Empire

Boba Fett stood in the queue waiting to board the luxury liner *Queen of Empire*, for her voyage to Velga Prime and points in between. The liner was the sister ship to Haj Shipping Lines' *Star of Empire* and was fully as large and opulent.

Boba Fett was boarding the liner from an orbiting space docking platform, but there were nearly a thousand sentients waiting to board, so each line was several hundred beings long. The bounty hunter gauged the slow progress of the line, and figured it would be at least ten minutes before he'd be free to carry his large, heavy traveling case to his cabin.

The line moved forward a few paces, and the bounty hunter shoved his heavy case along with his foot, as he moved with it. For just a moment he indulged himself in imagining what would happen were he suddenly to appear as his real self, as Boba Fett in his Mandalorian armor, instead of as he currently was, disguised as an Anomid.

It was necessary from time to time, he'd discovered, to appear as a being other than himself. Anomids were perfect beings to assume as disguises, since hardly any of their bodies showed in their ordinary street garb. They were willowy humanoids native to the Yablari system, and typically dressed in oversized robes that covered them from their hooded heads to their six-toed feet. They also wore gloves and vocalizer-masks, so hardly any of their translucent, whitish skin showed. Anomids had wispy grayish hair, leaf-shaped ears, and large silvery blue eyes.

Boba Fett of course wore a head-mask beneath his vocalizer-mask, but it was a very good one, custom-made to fit over his own features so that it would move quite naturally on his face. Silver-blue "eyes" were built into the mask, and were specially engineered so he could see nearly as well as he could with his unaided eyes.

Still, he felt somewhat naked without his armor and its extended senses. With his armor on he had a range of visual modes available to him, enhanced audio pickups, and a host of other sensor data displayed on the telltales inside his helmet. With nothing but the Anomid robes, hooded cloak, mask and gloves on, he felt light and vulnerable—too vulnerable.

But it was necessary. If Boba Fett had attempted to book passage on the *Queen* as his true self, panic would have ensued. Each passenger aboard and much of the crew would have been convinced that he, she or it was the bounty hunter's intended quarry.

Citizens, Fett had discovered long ago, all had guilty

consciences. Virtually every sentient in the galaxy had done *something* in his past that he, she or it could flash back on and imagine was a reason for having a bounty placed on their heads. The being who had once been Journeyman Protector Jaster Mereel, and was now Boba Fett, the galaxy's most notorious bounty hunter, had watched the reactions of the citizens around him for years, as he hunted bounties of one sort or another.

He'd seen the face of a young mother clutching her infant change when she'd seen him, seen her clutch her baby to her breast as though he, Boba Fett, were going to snatch the child from her arms and drag both of them away. Several times citizens had panicked when he'd even come into their vicinity, throwing themselves on the floor, babbling out their (mostly imaginary) fatal transgressions and pleading for mercy . . . only to pull themselves up in mingled relief and dawning indignation when they realized that they were *not* Fett's quarry, and had humiliated themselves and spilled their secrets for no reason. . . .

The line moved forward again. Boba Fett automatically surveyed the crowds around him, but he wasn't really expecting to see his quarry. Bria Tharen had boarded the *Queen* on its previous stop, back on Corellia. It was unlikely that she would be coming outside the vessel during its short layover on Gyndine.

The bounty hunter had missed the chance to catch up with the Tharen woman when she'd first boarded the *Queen* because she'd come aboard under an assumed name in the last minutes before the ship undocked. The Haj Shipping Line, while outwardly loyal to the Empire, was known to do favors for the Rebel Alliance when it suited them; the Tharen woman's last-minute booking was doubtless the result of some official string-pulling.

Also, Bria Tharen's assumed identity was not one of the ones she'd used before. This time she was traveling as "Bria Lavval," a minor starlet and cabaret singer who was headed for a booking at one of the large casinos, The Chance Castle, on Nar Shaddaa.

Boba Fett had access to a great many sources of data from many places in the galaxy. Since he hunted bounties from time to time for the Empire, he had access to some of the mid-security level Imperial databases. He also had access to many newswires, and the Guild databases.

Fett had ordered his systems to flag certain "priority" names and physical profiles. When a "Bria Lavval" showed up one morning on his database summaries as a passenger aboard the *Queen* when the liner had departed Corellia that morning, a quick check of the woman's ID and physical description had shown Fett that there was a better than 70% chance that this was actually Bria Tharen—Commander in the Corellian resistance.

Only a visual inspection would assure Fett that she was the right woman, so here he was . . . standing in line to board the huge liner.

The *Queen* was fully two kilometers long, and equipped to carry five thousand passengers. She contained most amenities any sentient could wish . . . indoor pools and spas, casinos, null-gee gliding areas, exercise rooms, as well as upscale shops where a wealthy being could spend a great many credits indeed.

Fett moved forward yet again, nudging his case along with him. It contained, in camouflaged compartments, his Mandalorian armor and several select weapons. The sides of the case were reinforced with durinium, an alloy that would resist sensor scans. And, in the outermost layer of the case, there were microminiature projection devices that would generate false readings about the contents to any scanning device.

Fett finally reached the head of the line, and produced his IDs, ticket and credit vouchers. The ship's official who checked his reservation offered to call for a luggage droid, but Fett politely refused, his harsh voice reverberating through the vocalizer-mask.

Amongst themselves, Anomids did not converse in oral speech, but by an elaborate and very beautiful form of sign language. They were known to be sociable beings, and Boba Fett was hoping there would be no real Anomids on board. If there were, he would have to plead illness and stay in his cabin, for he did not know the Anomid sign-language.

But none of the individuals on the passenger roster had listed Yablari as their world of origin.

When he reached the safety of his cabin, Fett stowed his trunk, first making sure to activate its anti-theft protections. Anyone unfortunate enough to attempt to remove the trunk from Fett's cabin, or to try and open it, would lose digits—at minimum.

The *Queen's* scheduled itinerary called for her to stop at a number of ports of call. Their path would take them through some of the most dangerous areas of Imperial space—including a stop in Hutt space at Nar Hekka . . . hardly a garden spot of the galaxy, but Nar Hekka was head and shoulders above either Nal Hutta or Nar Shaddaa. Fett suspected that Bria Tharen had chosen this liner because it was one of the largest, and thus probably the safest. There had been a lot of pirate activity lately.

Over the next three days, Fett wandered the ship in his Anomid disguise, staying mostly to himself. He made a visual ID of Bria Tharen on the first day, and followed her to find out where her stateroom was. He discovered that she had a suite, and shared it with three men. Two of the men were older, and Fett figured that they, too, were officers in the Corellian resistance. The third man was in his mid-thirties, and, from the way he carried himself, was a seasoned combat veteran who was serving as security and bodyguard for the Corellian officers.

The two officers and the bodyguard, like Bria Tharen, dressed in civilian clothes. The Tharen woman was seldom alone outside of her stateroom. Often, she was surrounded by male admirers, although Fett noticed that she never took anyone back to her cabin with her, merely smiled and flirted casually. She played sabacc, careful neither to lose or win much, and she browsed the shops, but never bought anything of significance.

Fett kept her under observation, and laid his plans carefully. . . .

Lando Calrissian enjoyed traveling aboard cruise ships, and had done a lot of it lately, since losing the *Millennium Falcon* to Han Solo. Now that Han and Vuffi Raa had trained him to be a better-than-average pilot, he could have taken any of the ships on his used spaceship lot for his own, but Lando wasn't that interested in any of them. He was waiting for just the right ship to come along.

His ideal ship would be more luxurious than the utilitarian *Falcon*—but every bit as speedy and capable of defending herself. Lando was on the lookout for a nice yacht he could get for a good price. So far, no bargains had surfaced.

And, besides, private ships didn't have casinos. Lando liked casinos. He'd been spending a lot of time in them for the past year, working to recoup his liquid credit resources. The young gambler had been wiped out by the sabacc tournament, but since then, he'd managed to turn Han Solo's loan of fifteen hundred credits into many thousands. Lando had been able to repay Han the money he'd "borrowed" several months before his friend had taken off for the Corporate Sector.

Queen of Empire, and her sister ship, *Star of Empire,* were two of Lando's favorite ways to get around the galaxy. They weren't as fast as some of the newer ships, but there was no doubt that Haj Shipping Lines knew how to build a luxury vessel. And the *Queen* and the *Star* were *big,* a major advantage these days, with all the pirate activity going on.

This time, he'd chosen the *Queen* for his trip back home. From Nar Hekka, he could easily catch a system shuttle back to Nar Shaddaa. This particular evening, Lando was wearing his newest stylish outfit—red shirt embroidered with black, narrow black trousers, and a red and black short cape that swung from his shoulders with a rakish flare. His dark hair and mustache were impeccably groomed, thanks to a trip to the ship's barber that day. His black softboots shone with the subdued glow of real Numatra snakehide. Calrissian was looking good, and he didn't miss the admiring glances cast at him by some of the female patrons in the club.

Lando was sitting in the *Queen's* swankiest nightclub, the Star Winds Lounge, following a highly successful session at the sabacc tables. His credit pouch was carefully stashed in a secret compartment close to his skin, and was satisfyingly heavy. This trip, he'd make roughly four times what his expensive ticket had set him back. Not a bad profit margin.

While he was gambling—serious business!—Lando was abstemious, rarely partaking of anything alcoholic. But at the moment he was relaxing, sipping a Tarkenian

Nightflower, and munching on a handful of dried, salted jer-weevils. The band in the Star Winds was quite good, doing selections of older hits as well as the modern jizz-tunes, and many patrons were dancing. Lando eyed the unescorted ladies in the lounge, wondering whether he was interested enough in any of them to ask for a dance.

His eyes kept returning to one woman who was sitting at a table with not one, but two male escorts. Human, yes, and stunning. Long reddish hair swept up with jeweled sapphire combs, and a face and figure that just wouldn't quit. Lando couldn't decide whether she was romantically attached to either of her escorts. She sat close beside them, smiling and bending forward to listen as first one, then the other, spoke into her ear. But the more Lando watched her, the more he became convinced that neither of the men was her date. Her smiles were more . . . comradely . . . than romantic. There was no suggestion of a lingering intimacy in the brief contacts of their shoulders as they brushed hers.

Lando finished his drink, and was almost ready to go over and ask the lovely stranger if she'd like to dance, when the excellent Rughja orchestra-band, Umjing Baab and his Swinging Trio, finished their current selection. There were only three members in the band, but, since each Rughja had fifteen flexible limbs, and played at least ten instruments apiece, they sounded like a genuine orchestra. In fact, looking at Umjing Baab and his two band members, it was difficult to discern anything but limbs ending in assorted instruments, though occasionally one of the being's multiple eyes would be visible through the tangle.

The band was very versatile, playing everything from swing-bop to modern jizz selections. The gambler clapped politely as they finished a mellow version of

"Mood and Moons," then settled back in his seat as the bandleader, Umjing Baab, put down his Kloo horn, disengaged from the nalargon, and writhed his way up to the public address system. The Rughja's voice had a mechanical timbre . . . understandable, because it was artificially generated. Rughja were a species whose natural communication was not audible to humanoids. Umjing Baab "spoke," as the spotlight reflected off his glossy, mauve, upper-limbs. "Good evening, gentles. Tonight we have an honored guest with us, a celebrity whom I am hoping we can prevail upon to favor us with a number! Join me in welcoming Lady Bria Lavval!"

Lando clapped politely, but his applause soon became genuine when he realized that the bandmaster was referring to his attractive stranger. Blushing, smiling, she half-rose from her seat to take a bow, but then, urged on by the applause, she picked up the skirts of her long, electric-blue sheath (a color that set off her hair) and walked up the steps to the bandstand.

After conferring briefly with Umjing Baab, she stepped up to the microphone, tapped her jeweled, slippered toe as the percussion started up, and then the band broke into a slowed down version of last year's hit, "Smoky Dreams."

Bria Lavval began to sing. Lando had heard a lot of singers in his time, and she was far from being the best. Her breath control was uneven, and she cut short some of the high notes because of it. But her voice was strong and in key, and her contralto was pleasantly husky. With her figure, face and smile, Lando was willing to forgive her lack of professional technique. Within moments of starting her song, she had all the humanoid males in the palm of her hand.

She sang with passion of lost love, of tender sadness, of misty memories fading with time. . . .

Lando was totally captivated. When she finished the number, he clapped as loudly as the rest of the audience. Smiling and blushing becomingly, she allowed herself to be escorted back to her table by Umjing Baab, who genuflected deeply to her, and then returned to his fellow Rughja band members.

As the Swinging Trio struck up a catchy tune, Lando got unhesitatingly to his feet and walked over to the chanteuse, narrowly beating out a wealthy Alderaanian banker whom Lando had relieved of many of his excess credits earlier that evening.

Reaching Lady Lavval's table, Lando bowed to her, flashing his best, most charming smile. "May I?" he asked, holding out his arm.

She hesitated for a long second, glanced at each of the men sitting with her, then shrugged fractionally. "Thank you," she said, and stood up. Lando escorted her out to the dance floor. She looked around her and frowned slightly in consternation. "Oh, dear. I'm afraid I don't know how to do this one."

Lando was surprised. The margengai-glide had been popular for at least five years. "It's easy," he said, putting his hand on her shoulder, and interlacing his fingers with hers. "I'll show you."

She missed several steps right off, and brought her heeled evening slipper down on his toes once, but after a couple of minutes, and Lando's experienced coaching, Bria began to catch on. Her sense of timing was good, and so were her reflexes. Once she'd memorized the intricate pattern of the steps, she began to enjoy herself, Lando could tell. She was nearly as tall as he was, and as they moved around the dance floor, they began to receive the admiring glances of the onlookers still seated at the tables.

"Good, you've got it," Lando said. "You're a natural."

"I haven't danced in years," she confessed, a little breathless, as the music changed to a fast number. Lando whirled her into a boxnov three-step. She was a little rusty, but it was obvious that the older dance was one she'd done before.

"You're wonderful," he assured her. "I'm the luckiest man on this ship, finding a partner like you."

She gave him a brilliant smile, her cheeks flushed with the exercise and praise. "Flatterer."

Lando put on a mock-hurt expression. "Me? I am under a vow of truth, Lady Bria . . . Bria . . . what a lovely name. You're Corellian, aren't you?"

"Yes," she said, stiffening slightly in his arms, her glance suddenly wary. "Why?"

"I was just thinking that I've only heard that name once before. Is it common on your homeworld?"

"No," she said. "My father made it up from the first syllables of my grandmothers' names. Brusela and Iaphagena. He didn't want to saddle me with either of them, but he wanted to honor both of them."

"Clever," Lando said. "Obviously a man of great diplomacy and tact."

She laughed a little, but there was a sad note underlying her merriment. "That's my father," she agreed. "Lando, I'm surprised to hear you say you've met another Bria. I thought I was the only one."

"You probably are," Lando said. "The other Bria I knew was a ship. My friend Han named his Sorosuub Starmite he leased from me the *Bria*."

She missed a step, recovered quickly. "Han?" she said. "I used to know a Corellian named Han. Is your friend Corellian?"

Lando nodded, and twirled her in a spin. When she was back in his arms again, he said, "Han Solo and I go back a ways. Don't tell me *you* know him?"

She laughed a little. "I do. It has to be the same guy. Brown hair, brownish eyes with a hint of green, a hair taller than you, has a very charming, lopsided smile?"

"Whoa," Lando said, raising an eyebrow. "You *do* know him well, don't you? That guy gets around, doesn't he?"

Her face reddened at his knowing look, and she glanced away and concentrated on the intricate steps for a moment. When she looked back up, her eyes were cool, and a little amused. "He's just part of my past, like a lot of other guys," she said. "There must be a few skeletons in your cargo locker, right?"

Lando, realizing he'd touched a nerve, was happy to let the subject go. "You bet," he said.

They danced several more dances, and Lando enjoyed her company tremendously. He looked over at her table, and realized that her companions had left the lounge. "Who are those fellows who were sitting at your table?"

She shrugged. "Just business associates," she said. "Feldron is my agent, and Renkov is my business manager."

"I see," Lando said, secretly delighted. It was obvious that she was serious that neither of them was any kind of romantic interest. "So . . . do you want to have a drink, perhaps? Somewhere a bit more . . . private?"

She gave him an assessing glance, then nodded and stepped back, out of his arms. "All right. I'd like that. We can talk about . . . mutual acquaintances."

Lando reached for her hand, then raised it to his lips. "Mutual acquaintances it is," he said.

"My stateroom, number 112, in, say, thirty minutes?" she said.

"Thirty minutes," Lando said. "I will be counting them, every one."

She smiled at him, a smile that held rueful amusement as well as pleasure, and turned and left Lando standing on the edge of the dance floor. He watched her walk away, a pleasant occupation. She reached the portal of the lounge, brushed past an Anomid who was loitering there, watching the dancing and listening to the music, then disappeared from sight.

Lando smiled. *Now to find the best bottle of wine in this ship, and some flowers,* he thought, and headed briskly for the bar. *Twenty-nine minutes and counting . . .*

Bria told herself to settle down as she hurried down the corridor toward her stateroom. But she was excited, realizing that she was finally going to get news of Han! Lando Calrissian was obviously more than just a casual friend. Bria was so eager to reach her stateroom that she was almost jogging as she approached the door of 112. *At last! Someone who knows him well, who can tell me how he's doing, what he's been doing . . . where he is!*

Just as Bria reached the door to her cabin, she had the sudden thought that perhaps Han was on Nar Shaddaa, her ultimate destination. Was it possible that in forty-eight hours or so, she'd actually get to *see* him? The thought excited her, even as it filled her with trepidation. After more than nine years, what would it be like to be close to him?

As she unlocked her stateroom door, her hands were shaking. She was so absorbed in memories of Han that she had no warning, no warning at all. One moment the door was opening before her, and the next a powerful thrust propelled her through the portal and into the living room of the suite with such force that she didn't even have breath to cry out.

Her high-heeled slippers skidded on the polished floor, and she tripped, trying to catch herself. Just as she started to fall, Bria felt something sharp sting her back.

She had only an instant to realize that she'd been shot with some kind of knockout drug. As she fell, she managed with the last of her strength to turn slightly, and saw a strange Anomid standing behind her in the doorway. Bria managed a soft, choked cry of warning to her friends before everything around her faded, faded . . .

Faded . . .

And went black.

Boba Fett watched the Tharen woman sag to the floor, then lie there, motionless. Quickly he shut the door to the corridor behind him, and started forward—just as the older men Tharen had been traveling with rushed out of the sleeping cabin on the right.

Boba Fett extended his arm, flexed his hand, and a deadly dart (unlike the soporific one that had felled the woman) shot toward the older of the two Resistance officers and embedded itself in his throat. The man had time for one strangled gasp, and was dead before he hit the floor.

The other man did not hesitate, but came straight in. Boba Fett swept aside the Anomid cape and stood poised as the man, with a wordless yell, attacked.

The Rebel leader might have been a decent officer in planning strategy and attacks, but he was no expert at unarmed combat. Boba Fett blocked his blow with one forearm, then came in with a hard, lethal blow that crushed the Corellian's larynx.

Fett watched dispassionately as the Rebel officer died. It took no more than a minute.

He bent over the dead man, planning to drag him and his fellow off to the corner of the room and throw some sheets over them—more to muffle the stench of voiding from the suddenly deceased bodies than from any sense of decorum.

Boba Fett's peripheral vision was compromised by the mask he was wearing. Without his Mandalorian helmet with its special sensors, the bounty hunter had only an instant's warning of danger. He dodged just as the Rebel bodyguard struck, silent and with the expertise the two older men had lacked.

The bounty hunter whirled away from the younger man, and as he did so, Fett whipped off the Anomid's heavy cloak and flung it into the bodyguard's face. With one smooth movement, his opponent disentangled himself and came in again. He was perhaps in his early thirties, and was bare-chested, barefoot, and wearing only shorts. The man had evidently been asleep in the other room when his officers had made their ill-fated attack.

This fellow, Fett knew instantly, was a combat soldier, trained to use his hands and feet as weapons—and trained also in using the vibroblade he held in one hand. Behind his two masks, Boba Fett smiled slightly, pleased to be challenged, and by someone who plainly knew what he was doing. He had another lethal dart he could have used, but he decided against it. A little exercise would be welcome. It had been a long time since he'd indulged himself in unarmed combat; few foes were worthy of his time.

The man was already dancing in, balanced, his eyes level, vibroblade ready for a disemboweling slash. Boba

Fett let him come, then dodged at the last possible second, pulling himself into an arc like a null-gee dancer, and then spinning around, out of the way. As he moved, his hand moved out and dealt the soldier a stunning clip behind his right ear.

The soldier managed to dodge at the last moment, though, and the blow that had been meant to render him unconscious only dazed him. He staggered a little, shook his head, then came back for more.

Boba Fett was pleased to oblige. They sidestepped around each other in a grim parody of the way Lando Calrissian and Bria Tharen had danced in the Star Winds Lounge only minutes before.

The guard lunged again, and again Boba Fett waited, then evaded the movement at the last possible second. Another blow made the Corellian gasp—this time Fett's instep impacted with the back of his knee. The guard's leg buckled, and, for the first time, Fett saw fear in his eyes. He now knew he was totally outclassed, and yet he conquered his pain and weakness and moved in again. *A man who knows his duty and does not shrink from it,* Fett thought. *Admirable. His reward for his courage shall be a quick and easy death. . . .*

For the first time, Fett went on the attack. His foot lashed out in a precise blow, and impacted with the man's wrist with stunning force. The vibroblade went flying. Fett spun in for the finish. Another sweep behind the other knee, and the man sagged, his legs unable to hold him. But that did not matter. Fett already had him around the neck in a grip as hard and relentless as durasteel. One quick, sideways jerk, and the guard sagged in his arms, dead.

Boba Fett dragged the man over to the corner, and laid him down, then brought the others over, too. He tossed the covers from one of the beds over the bodies.

As he was finishing the task, he saw that the Tharen woman was beginning to stir.

When Bria regained consciousness, she found herself bound so efficiently that she didn't even bother struggling past the first moment. She was alone in the living room, sitting on the lush carpet, propped up against one of the armchairs. Her head was muzzy, and she was terribly thirsty, but she was otherwise unharmed.

Except for the fear. Bria had been in tight situations before, in battle, but she'd never been captured like this. It was the most helpless feeling in the world, to sit there alone, and wonder who had done this to her . . . and why?

It had to have been that Anomid, but Bria had never had any dealings with the aliens before, and she couldn't imagine why any of them would wish her harm. Perhaps the Anomid was a bounty hunter. That was the only explanation that made sense. . . .

She wet her lips, took a deep breath, and prepared to scream a scream that would be heard even outside the closed door of the stateroom. It was then that she noticed two things: the bodies of her companions, covered with bedclothes and stacked efficiently out of sight of anyone at the door—and the sound sponge. The little device was set up on the floor near her and the blinking light showed that it was on. It would effectively muffle any outcry she could make. Bria shut her mouth and her eyes and leaned her head back against the chair. *Great. Whoever that Anomid is, he thought of everything.*

Who could he be? The alien had evidently dealt with Darnov, Feltran and even Treeska (and Bria knew his reputation at unarmed combat) in a matter of minutes.

She could see the wall-chrono, and realized she'd only been out about ten minutes.

As she sat there, struggling to think of something she could do, the Anomid opened the door to the stateroom and entered, carrying a huge, heavy case that he placed on the floor with a thud. Seeing that Bria was awake, he went into the 'fresher and soon returned, carrying a glass of water. He knelt beside her, turned down the sound sponge so she could hear his voice. "That sleeping drug causes great thirst. This is plain water. I have no intention of harming you. The bounty on you is for unharmed delivery."

He held out the water, and Bria leaned toward it, then hesitated. She didn't dare drink it. What if this was an Imperial bounty hunter or agent? What if the water was laced with truth drug? Even though her thirst was now a raging hell in her mouth and throat, she shook her head. "Thank you anyway," she managed. "I'm not thirsty."

"Of course you are," the Anomid said. "I care nothing for your pitiful Resistance secrets." He shoved his vocalizer-mask aside and took a long drink. "The water is safe," he said, holding it back out.

Bria blinked at him, then her thirst won out. She drank deeply as the Anomid helped her. He pushed his vocalizer-mask back into place. As Bria leaned back against the armchair, she said, "You're not an Anomid. They can't speak without their vocalizer-masks. You're obviously a bounty hunter in disguise. Who are you?"

The Anomid regarded her from featureless silver-blue eyes. "Observant, Bria Tharen. I am pleased by your reaction. Hysteria is wearing and useless. As to my identity . . . you would know me perhaps by my adopted name. Boba Fett."

Boba Fett? Bria sagged back against the armchair,

eyes wide, fighting the fear that even the casual mention of that name brought. She found herself praying to childhood gods for the first time in years.

After a moment, she wet her lips. "Boba Fett . . ." she managed. "I do know that name. I didn't think you bothered with dinky Imperial bounties. The one the Imps have on me isn't worth your time."

The bounty hunter nodded. "True. Besadii clan's bounty is a hundred times that."

"Teroenza . . ." Bria whispered. "It has to be. Last I heard, it was fifty thousand, not a hundred."

"Following your capture of *Helot's Shackle*, Besadii doubled that."

Bria tried to smile. "It's so nice to be popular," she managed. "*Helot's Shackle* was a slave ship. I had to stop them. I have no regrets."

"Good," he said. "That should make our short association as pleasant as possible. Would you like more water?"

Bria nodded, and Fett got another glass. This time she took a drink without being asked. Bria was trying to remember her training in what to do if captured. She wasn't in uniform, and thus had no lullaby available to end her suffering. Besides, she was a long way from Nal Hutta or Ylesia . . . a lot could happen between here and there. She decided to bide her time and keep Fett talking, if she could. All her instructions said that the more captors came to regard a prisoner as a real person, the easier captivity became, and the greater the chance that someone would get careless.

Bria was also aware that the chance of Boba Fett slipping up was incredibly unlikely. Still, she had nothing else to do at the moment, did she?

She tried not to look at the sheet-covered bodies in the corner.

"You know," she said, "I've heard a lot about you. Makes me wonder if all the things they say about you are true."

"Such as?"

"That you have your own moral code. You are the consummate hunter, but no bully. You take no pleasure in inflicting pain."

"True," he said. "I am a moral person."

"What do you think of the Empire?" she asked, as he began checking the heavy case he'd lugged into the room. She caught a glimpse of his famous helmet.

"I believe that the Empire, though morally corrupt in some ways, is the lawful government. I obey its laws."

"Morally corrupt?" she asked, cocking her head, "how so?"

"Several ways."

"Name one."

He gave her a glance, and she wondered if he'd tell her to shut up, but after a moment, answered, "Slavery. It is a morally corrupt institution, degrading to all parties."

"Really!" she exclaimed. "Then we have something in common. I don't like slavery much either."

"I know."

"I was a slave," she said. "It was horrible."

"I know."

"You know a lot about me, I guess."

"Yes."

Bria wet her lips. "You know that Teroenza and whoever is running Besadii these days are planning to kill me in some protracted, hideous fashion, right?"

"Yes. Unfortunate for you, profitable for me."

Bria nodded, and fixed him with an appealing gaze. "Since you know so much about me, you know that I have a father, right?"

"Yes."

"Then maybe . . . I know this seems unusual, but under the circumstances . . . perhaps you wouldn't mind . . ." Bria trailed off, fighting for control. It was really sinking in now that she was done for, that she wasn't going to be able to get out of this.

"What?"

She took a deep breath. "I haven't seen my dad in years. We were always close. My mom and brother aren't worth much, but my dad . . ." Bria shrugged. "You get the idea. When I started in with the Resistance, I knew it was too dangerous to see him any more. Too dangerous for both of us. But I've found ways—safe ways—to let him know I'm alive. A couple of times a year, he gets a message through very roundabout channels. Just, 'Bria's okay.' Like that."

"Go on." The bounty hunter's voice was absolutely expressionless.

"Anyway . . . I don't want him to wait and wait for a message from me. Could you . . . let him know I'm dead? He means a lot to me. He's a good man, a decent man. Pays his Imperial taxes, honorable citizen, all that. So . . . if I gave you his name and location, could you just send a message? 'Bria's dead.' That's all."

To Bria's surprise, Boba Fett nodded. "I will do so. What is—"

The bounty hunter broke off as the door chime sounded. Bria jumped, and Boba Fett rose to his feet in one seamless motion, like a hunting animal.

The chime sounded again. Dimly, from outside the cabin, muffled by the sound sponge, Bria heard, "Bria? Hey, it's me, Lando!"

"Calrissian," Boba Fett said quietly. Quickly the bounty hunter turned the sound sponge all the way back up. Going over to the portal, he keyed it open, standing back behind it.

"Lando, no!" Bria shouted. "Go away!" The sound sponge soaked up the noise, absorbing it. Instead of filling the room, her shout was no louder than a whisper.

Clutching his flowers and the bottle of fine wine, Lando stepped eagerly through the door to Bria Lavval's stateroom. "Sorry I'm a few minutes late," he was saying. "The florist was closed, and I had to—"

Calrissian broke off in confusion, his eyes widening as he took in Bria, sitting on the floor by the armchair, her arms bound behind her, and the sheet-covered mound in the corner. He backed up, realizing he'd just made a very bad mistake.

Behind the gambler, the portal shut. "What's going on?" Lando demanded, only to hear his voice emerge in muffled, subdued tones. Seeing the direction of Bria's gaze, the gambler turned and found an Anomid regarding him.

"Nice to see you again, Calrissian," the Anomid said. "You are fortunate that I never mix business and pleasure."

"What—" Lando started, then he caught a glimpse of the big case, lying open on the floor. His dark eyes widened. "Fett . . ." he said.

"Yes," the bounty hunter said. "That had better be the last word I hear out of you, Calrissian. I am not here for you. Cooperate, and I may let you live. You might come in handy."

Lando knew better than to argue. Meekly, he put down the wine and flowers. Moments later, he found himself sitting several meters away from Bria, just as efficiently bound, his back propped against the sofa.

Boba Fett regarded Bria intently. "Tomorrow, when we dock with Nar Hekka's docking platform, you and I are going to leave the *Queen*, walking closely together. I will be armed, but not with any weapon a visual inspection or security scan could discern. You will stay close by my right side at all times, and remain silent. Understood?"

She nodded. "Yes. But what about Lando?" The note of fear in her voice for him made the gambler glance at her appreciatively.

"Calrissian's life depends on you, Bria Tharen. If you give me your word that you won't alert anyone, I will leave him behind, bound and gagged, but alive."

Bria raised her eyebrows. "You would trust my word?"

"Why not?" he asked, with an undertone of mockery. "You value the lives of innocents more than you do your own. I know your type. But just to make sure . . . I plan to wire Calrissian before we leave with a remote control detonator. If we encounter any problems, the cleaning droids will have to scrape his remains off the walls."

Lando swallowed painfully.

Bria glanced at the gambler and gave him a reassuring smile. "You're right about me. I give you my word that I won't cause any trouble."

"Good," Fett responded. "At the moment—"

The bounty hunter broke off as an alarm suddenly shrieked through the *Queen of Empire* with an earsplitting volume. Lando sat bolt upright, his eyes widening. *What the . . .*

Fifteen seconds later the entire *Queen* bounced—there was no other word for it. The huge ship heaved like a buoy on a stormy sea. Lando's stomach lurched, and he fell over on his side. He looked over at Bria, who had managed to remain upright, saw her gagging, struggling not to be sick.

"What's going on?" she gasped. Lando, remembering Boba Fett's order to remain silent, struggled to right himself.

"We came out of hyperspace," Fett said. "The failsafes must have encountered a sudden gravity shadow and reacted automatically."

Lando silently applauded the bounty hunter for his acumen as he managed to roll back over and sit up. It was hard work, with his hands bound behind him.

"What would cause that?" she said. "An engine malfunction?"

"Possible," Fett said. "But more likely an attack. An Imperial Interdictor cruiser could bring a ship out of hyperspace."

"But why would the Imperials attack a cruise ship?" Bria asked.

Lando had been wondering that same thing, and couldn't think of an answer. Bria frowned as she concentrated on the straining vibrations of the ship. "You're right about the attack," she said. "We're caught in a tractor beam."

Grabbing his case, the bounty hunter dragged it behind the ornamental screen that decorated one wall of the luxury suite. Faintly, Lando could hear the swish of robes being doffed.

The gambler managed to catch Bria's eye and mouthed, "Trust me, Lady Bria. Follow my lead if we get an opening." He had to repeat it several times, until she nodded in comprehension and flashed him a shaky smile.

Minutes later the bounty hunter emerged, clad once more in his Mandalorian armor. He carried his blaster rifle, which was his only visible weapon, but Lando knew from experience that the bounty hunter was a walking arsenal of camouflaged weaponry. Walking over to Bria, he removed the restraints from her ankles, and then did the same for Lando. "You two come with me," he said. "And . . . Calrissian . . . remember. You're expendable. Lady Tharen . . . if you try anything, Calrissian dies. Clear?"

"Yes," Bria said.

Lando nodded, then managed to get to his feet unaided, despite his bound arms. Boba Fett, in a parody of gentlemanly behavior, assisted Bria to rise. She wobbled a bit on her high-heeled shoes, flexing her feet and grimacing at the pins-and-needles.

Fett picked up the sound sponge and deactivated it, stowing it in a pocket of his trousers. With the muffling device turned off, Lando could hear the sounds of blaster fire, screams and running feet. A public address system boomed: "All passengers . . . please remain calm and in your cabins. There is an intruder alert, but your crew is working to restore order. We will advise you as matters progress. Please remain calm. All passengers . . ."

Right, Lando thought. *They're going to restore order . . . sure they are. . . .* The gambler glanced at Bria, and she looked at him and shrugged slightly.

They reached the door, and Fett gestured to Lando. "Open it."

The corridor was pure chaos. They had to wait in the doorway until a mob of screaming passengers, most of them dressed only in nightgowns and robes, fled past. Fett glanced at a small, palm-sized device he held. "Turn right," he instructed.

Lando and Bria obeyed. The gambler found it surprisingly difficult to walk with his arms bound behind him. It affected his balance.

Several times they had to step into doorways to allow

shrieking hordes of passengers to run past. The sounds of blaster fire were closer, now, as they neared the boat decks.

They left the passenger cabins behind, and took a series of glidewalks that Fett directed them to. From the sounds, most of the pitched fighting was going on near the docking areas. Sounds of battle grew louder, closer. As they neared the shuttle deck, they saw sprawled bodies littering the corridor, most of them wearing uniforms marking them as the liner's crew. A number of the bodies belonged to passengers, but none wore Imperial uniforms. Bria glanced at Lando as they stumbled along. He was surprised at her composure in the face of carnage—dead bodies made most citizens sick.

Lando strained his eyes for a glimpse of the attackers, but so far they hadn't encountered any. He licked dry lips, knowing that, even with bound arms, he had to try to make some move before the three of them climbed into a shuttle together. In a shuttle, they had no chance. He glanced sideways at his fellow captive, assessing her ability to possibly back him if he tried something.

For a moment it occurred to him to wonder just why this lovely young woman—she couldn't have been much over twenty-five—had *Boba Fett* after her. She must be more than what she seemed, and his observations of her so far backed that up. Most citizens, faced with the most feared bounty hunter in the galaxy, would be reduced to quivering lumps of protoplasm. But Bria was plainly not your ordinary citizen. . . .

They rounded a corner that led to the shuttle deck, only to run smack into a boarding party. Lando froze, Bria beside him, faced with twelve or thirteen unsavory characters dressed in loud, gaudy, mismatched clothes that gravely offended Lando's fashion sense. They were festooned with garish jewelry.

Bria whispered, "Pirates!"

Suddenly things fell into place and Lando realized exactly what had happened to the *Queen*. He'd seen this trick before. These pirates had brought the *Queen* out of hyperspace by towing a good-sized asteroid into the realspace analog of her hyperspace coordinates. Then the gravity "shadow" of the asteroid's gravity well had caused the hyperdrive failsafes to cut in, abruptly reverting the *Queen* to realspace. An audacious and cunning plan—and it took big ships to implement it. Big ships and a daring leader. For the first time, Lando felt a surge of hope. *It's got to be. Nobody else would dare to attack a cruise ship this big. . . .*

"Back the other way!" Boba Fett shouted, and his captives obediently reversed course. Lando and Bria tried to run, but if Lando had thought that walking with bound arms was tough, he'd never imagined that running would be so much worse. At every moment he imagined himself falling down, then being summarily shot by Boba Fett for his clumsiness.

The two captives managed a clumsy jog, and Boba Fett urged them on. But as they approached another curve in the corridor, Lando caught a flash of bright color. More pirates!

"Stop!" Boba Fett barked, his voice sounding doubly harsh because of the mechanical speakers.

Quickly the bounty hunter pushed Bria into a doorway, then yanked Lando over to stand in front of her as a shield. "Don't move, Calrissian," Fett hissed, and moved out until he was in full view.

The pound of running feet approached, and then, more or less at the same time, both groups of pirates converged from opposite sides of the corridor. Boba

Fett, who had been checking his weaponry, tensed, ready to do battle. Against how many pirates? *Twenty-five? Thirty? Maybe more. . . .* Lando guessed.

The two groups drew nearer, then slowed uncertainly. Lando didn't blame them. He wouldn't want to be the first person to fire on Boba Fett, even at these odds. Chances are that the bounty hunter would take quite a few attackers with him.

"What's going on?" a familiar strong alto bellowed from the back of one of the packs. Lando let out a gasp of relief. "Boba Fett, in the name of all the hells of Barab, what are *you* doing here?"

"Collecting a bounty," the hunter replied. "No quarrel with you, Captain Renthal. I'll take my bounty and a shuttle, and go."

Lando filled his lungs, shouted, "Drea! It's me . . . . Lando! Hey, am I glad to see—" Lando's breath went out in a whoosh as the bounty hunter took one fast step backward and the butt of Fett's blaster rifle connected with his solar plexus. The gambler doubled over, wheezing.

Slowly, the ranks of pirates parted, and Drea Renthal, pirate captain and Lando's former girlfriend, emerged. She was a big, squarish woman of about forty-five, with fashionably striped silver and gold hair, a fair complexion, and the coldest gray eyes Lando had ever seen. Renthal wore her typical wild jumble of clothes— red striped stockings, a purple skirt kilted up on one side, a pink silk shirt and armored vest. Her short, spiky hair was half-hidden by an outrageous beret with a long, trailing orange feather.

Lando tried painfully to straighten up. He wanted to wave, but of course his arms were bound. Besides, Boba Fett would probably blast him for his temerity.

Renthal surveyed them, and said, "Lando, you never told me you had a bounty on your head."

Actually, Lando knew of several bounties on his head, in the Centrality, but this was Imperial space. "No bounty, Drea," he called, his voice harsh and breathless. "I was just . . . in the wrong place . . . at the wrong time."

Renthal looked back at the bounty hunter. "Fett, that true? No bounty on Calrissian?"

The hunter hesitated, then responded, "True. I have an old score with Calrissian, but it is . . . personal."

Drea Renthal considered for a long moment. "In that case, Fett, you ought to be willing to let him go. Lando's kind of . . . special . . . to me. I might lose a little sleep if I let you take him. Tell you what . . . let him go, and I'll let you have the shuttle, free and clear."

Boba Fett nodded. "Very well." Without turning his head, he said, "Calrissian . . . go. We will meet again . . . someday."

Lando felt Bria move away from him, giving him room to edge around her and leave. The gambler wanted more than anything to head for safety—Drea and her mob of cutthroats—but instead, he heard his own voice saying, "No. Drea, I can't go without Lady Lavval. You can't let Fett take her."

Boba Fett wasn't often taken aback, but he heard Lando Calrissian's words with surprise—almost astonishment. He'd never figured Calrissian for anything more than a dandified coward. The bounty hunter glanced at the gambler, wondering if Calrissian was just blowing Tibanna gas, making an empty statement, but he could tell from the man's set expression that he meant it—he wouldn't go without Bria.

Fett's gaze returned to Drea Renthal. How much did she care for Calrissian? It was obvious that the gambler was an old lover. But Renthal was a practical woman. One did not rise to the leadership of one of the largest pirate and mercenary fleets without being both pragmatic and ruthless. Perhaps Renthal would just cut Calrissian loose for his foolish stand—and over another woman, yet!

Renthal locked gazes with Calrissian and sighed. "Lando, honey, you're cute and a good dancer, but you're pushing me, here. Why should I give a regnuff's patootie about this floozy? She your current girlfriend?"

"No," Calrissian said. "There's nothing between us, Drea. But Bria here is Han Solo's girlfriend. He risked his life to save your Y-wings and *Renthal's Fist* from being blasted by *Peacekeeper* during the Battle of Nar Shaddaa. Seems to me you owe him."

Again Fett was surprised. Bria Tharen and Han Solo? That was obviously in the far past, since Fett had been monitoring her actions for over a year, and she'd had no contact with Solo.

Renthal blinked. "Bria? Her name is Bria? Like Solo's ship? This is *that* Bria?"

Calrissian nodded. "Yes. She's *that* Bria."

Drea Renthal grimaced and swore. "Lando . . . you just love to make my life complicated, don't you? I'm gonna take this out of your hide, baby? Okay . . . you're right, a debt is a debt." Reaching beneath her armored vest, she pulled out a heavy pouch. "Jewelry and credit vouchers, Fett," she said. "Should be over fifty thousand credits worth in here. Let 'em both go, and you can have your shuttle. I don't want a fight . . . but I'm not letting you leave with them."

Boba Fett surveyed the assembled ranks of pirates, assessing his chances for fighting his way out. There were thirty-two pirates—hardly good odds. Boba Fett's armor would protect him, possibly enough to allow him to escape, but Bria Tharen was wearing a strapless evening gown. She was certain to be hurt, perhaps killed, in any firefight. And her bounty called for a live, unharmed, delivery.

Boba Fett looked at the heavily armed pirates, then at Bria Tharen, and experienced a tiny flare of something that he recognized, with dismay, as relief. Bria Tharen would not die today, or tomorrow, in agony, while the depraved High Priest of Ylesia rubbed his tiny hands and chortled with glee.

Fett took a deep breath. "The bounty on her is one hundred thousand," he said.

"Whoo!" Renthal looked over at Bria. "Honey, what in the name of Kashyyyk's night demons have *you* been doing? All right, Fett, you bloodsucker." Turning to her crew, she opened the pouch and held it out. "C'mon, gentles. I'm collecting fifty percent of my share of the *Queen* right now. Put it here."

It was a measure of Renthal's reputation that there was scarcely any grumbling. Pirates dug into their pockets, their pouches, and soon Renthal's pouch was bulging.

Turning, she tossed it to the bounty hunter. Fett caught it, weighing it, then surrendered to the inevitable. Renthal's ransom for Bria Tharen was indeed a handsome one.

The bounty hunter inclined his head to Lando, and said, "Some other time, Calrissian."

The gambler's teeth flashed in a fierce grin. "I'll look forward to it."

Then Boba Fett nodded to Bria. "Later, my lady."

She drew herself up, and the bounty hunter had to admire her composure. "I hope not. I'll be watching my back."

Boba Fett turned to Renthal, and said, "The shuttle deck is that way."

"Right," the pirate captain said. "Gentles, let's give Master Fett here a nice unobstructed passage to that shuttle deck. We don't want any trouble with him, now do we?"

Respectfully, they parted, leaving the bounty hunter a wide aisle.

With grave dignity, Boba Fett walked between the ranks of pirates. The pirates on the shuttle deck also gave him a wide berth. Selecting a ship, Boba Fett climbed in, checked the controls, signaled for departure and watched the entrance to the ship's docking facility clear. Moments later, the bounty hunter was streaking through the blackness of space.

Alone . . .

Bria's head spun at the sudden turn of events. One moment she was giving herself up for dead, and the next she was safe aboard the pirate queen's flagship, *Renthal's Vigilance*. The *Vigilance* was a huge vessel, twice the size of Bria's Marauder corvette. Drea Renthal had salvaged the Imperial Carrack light cruiser following the Battle of Nar Shaddaa. With her Corellian corvette, *Renthal's Fist*, and her squadrons of Y-wings, the pirate captain's fleet was indeed impressive.

"The minute I knew it was pirates boarding us, I knew it had to be Drea's gang," Lando told her, as several pirates shuttled them over to the flagship while Renthal finished her boarding operation on the *Queen*. "I've seen her pull that trick with the asteroid's gravity shadow before. Only Drea would have had the firepower to tackle something as big as the *Queen*."

Bria looked at the gambler. "Lando, I'm very grateful to you. . . . You stood up for me, and you didn't have to. That took real guts."

Lando smiled charmingly. "What else could I do? You're far too lovely to let Boba Fett have you."

Bria laughed. "It wasn't Boba Fett I was worried about, actually. It was . . . the people who wanted me. They're a nasty bunch. Compared to them, Boba Fett is a gentleman and a scholar."

She sobered, then jerked a thumb back at the *Queen of Empire*'s approximate location. "What will happen to the passengers? Is Renthal . . ." she hesitated, ". . . a slaver?"

Lando shook his head. "Drea? No. She's in it for the quick credits. Slavery is too much work for her. She'll take the valuables, loot the ship, and maybe take a few prisoners for ransom. Once the ransom is paid, she returns them, unharmed. Drea is a businessperson. She's ruthless when the situation warrants, don't get me wrong, but she's not a slaver."

She eyed him, and Lando reached over and took her hand. "Trust me, Lady Bria. I wouldn't lie to you."

Bria nodded, then visibly relaxed. "I do trust you, Lando," she said. "How could I not after you stood up to Boba Fett for me? I couldn't believe you did that."

Lando shook his head, smiling wryly. "Sometimes I surprise even myself."

"And Drea Renthal will take us to Nar Shaddaa?"

"Oh, yes," Lando said. "Your booking's at the Chance Castle, right?"

She hesitated, gave him a sidelong look, then said, "Well . . . actually, that's not what I'm worried about. I'm taking a shuttle from Nar Shaddaa to Nal Hutta. I need to keep a very important appointment."

Lando raised his eyebrows. "What in the galaxy is a lovely lady like you doing going to visit a bunch of smelly gangsters like the Hutts?"

She smiled wryly. "Well . . ."

Lando waited, and when she didn't say any more, prompted, "Bria . . . you really can trust me. I want to be your friend."

She took a deep breath. "I have an appointment to talk to Jiliac the Hutt. It took me a while to get him to agree to see me, but finally he did. I have a . . . business proposition to offer him."

Lando frowned. "Then you'll have to take a shuttle to Nal Hutta. Jiliac became a mommy Hutt last year, and she hasn't been on Nar Shaddaa since, I think."

Bria nodded. "I'll go wherever it takes, talk to whoever I have to." She glanced up at Lando. "I understand that Han lives on Nar Shaddaa?" She couldn't conceal the note of hope in her voice.

Lando shook his head, his gaze sympathetic. "You're too late, I'm afraid. Han lit out for the Corporate Sector nearly a year ago, and hasn't been seen since. I don't know if he'll be back or not."

Bria bit her lip. "Oh." After a second, she looked back up, nodded. "Well, that's the way things go. I'm not sure he'd want to see me anyway."

Lando smiled again. "I can't imagine any man not wanting to see you. He was a fool to let you get away, if you ask me."

Bria chuckled wryly. "Han wouldn't agree with you, I'm sure."

Just then, their shuttle landed in the *Vigilance*'s docking bay. Gathering up her skirts, Bria rose from her seat. Lando gravely offered her his arm to escort her down the gangplank.

"By the way," he said, "how in the galaxy did you manage to get such a bounty placed on your pretty head?"

She shook her head. "Lando, it's a very, very long story."

He nodded. "Doubtless . . . but, since it will take

Drea a couple of hours to finish with the *Queen*, we've got nothing but time. . . ."

"Well, I'm not free to tell you much. . . ." she hesitated.

He smiled. "Why am I not surprised? Tell you what . . . I'll find a bottle, and you can tell me the unclassified parts. Deal?"

She laughed. "Deal."

Interlude 2: Somewhere between the Corporate Sector and the Tion Hegemony

Han Solo awoke slowly, easing gritty eyes open against daylight's painful onslaught. His head pounded like a misfiring thruster, and his mouth tasted like bantha fodder. He groaned and rolled over on his stomach, shielding his eyes from the hideous glare of the sunlight.

Minutes later, he managed to sit up, holding his head and wondering what in the galaxy had induced him to throw that party last night. One in a long series of parties. . . .

He had a dim recollection that it had been fun—lots of fun. Groggily he fumbled for his backpack and found a commercial headache remedy, swallowed it dry. He settled back onto the bed and held still for several minutes, eyes closed, until it began to take effect and the headache eased off.

Opening his eyes fully, he looked around the dimly lit room, seeing clear evidence in the scattered food, bottles and other disorder that it had indeed been a wild party. What was that girl's name? He couldn't remember.

But they'd obviously had a very good time.

Han had been living high for weeks now, off the credits he'd gotten from the Authority Espo ship's purser. Dimly, he realized that his stash of credits was considerably less than it had been several weeks ago, when he'd said goodbye to Fiolla.

He thought about her, wishing she was still with him. But when he'd prepared to leave Corporate Sector space, she'd booked passage home, saying that she had to get back to work—to the promotion she was sure she'd merit, for tracing down that slaver ring.

Since then, Han and Chewie had made planetfall on at least five different worlds. Han looked blearily at the sunlight that showed beneath the curtain in the hotel room. It had a slight orange tint against the white drape. What world is this, anyhow?

For the life of him, he couldn't remember.

Rising, he headed for the 'fresher. His headache was under control now, and he was beginning to feel hungry. Stepping into the shower, he let the hot water pummel him and leaned against the tiled wall. Ahhhhhhh . . .

For a moment he found himself thinking about home, wondering how everyone was doing. Maybe it was time to head back to Nar Shaddaa, while he still had some credits left?

Thoughts of his friends filled his mind. Jarik, Mako . . . and Lando, of course. How was Lando doing these days? Had he ever found a ship to replace the Falcon?

And what about Bria?

Han sighed. Maybe, when he got back to Imperial space, he'd try looking up Bria.

Yeah, right, *he thought.* That should be real easy. Just find the secret HQ of the Corellian Resistance and walk right in, demand to see your old girlfriend . . . probably get a blaster bolt right between your eyes, Solo. . . .

Feeling slightly better, Han shut the water off, and went to get dressed. He decided to get some food, then head back for the Falcon *and Chewie. Time to leave this blasted world . . . whatever world this was. . . .*

Chapter Nine:

Offers and Refusals

Jabba lounged beside his aunt in her private audience chamber on Nal Hutta, watching and listening as Bria Tharen made her appeal to Desilijic. The woman spoke well, he had to admit . . . for a human.

"Almighty Jiliac," Bria spread her hands before her, "just think what an opportunity this is for your clan. If Desilijic will just finance our group in terms of ammunition and fuel, the Corellian Resistance will make sure that Ylesia is no longer a thorn in your side. Wouldn't it be worth it, to see Besadii brought low? And for such a modest outlay! We provide the troops, the weapons, the ships. . . ."

"But you will take the spice stored in the warehouses," Jiliac said, in Huttese. Jabba and Jiliac's protocol droid, K8LR, promptly translated the Hutt leader's words. Jiliac's repulsor sled bobbed slightly as she shifted her weight forward to regard the Rebel commander intently. "All we would gain could only be measured in negative terms. Now if we were to profit from this . . ."

Bria Tharen shook her head. "If we take the risks, we get the spice, Your Excellency. Running a resistance is expensive. We can't just wipe out your enemies for you and gain nothing for ourselves."

Privately Jabba agreed with her. Why was Jiliac being so stubborn?

Jabba spoke up for the first time—in Basic, which he could speak, but rarely chose to. "Let me make sure I understand what you are offering, and what you wish from us, Commander."

Bria turned to him, bowed slightly. "Certainly, Your Excellency."

"One," Jabba began ticking points off on his fingers. "Desilijic will provide you funding to purchase ammunition and fuel for an assault on Ylesia. Two, Desilijic will arrange to eliminate the t'landa Til priests before the attack . . . correct?"

"Yes, Your Excellency," Bria said.

"Why do you need us for that?" Jiliac demanded haughtily. "If your group is such an efficient military force, then you should be able to handle a few puny t'landa Til."

"Because we stand a much better chance of being able to control the Pilgrims if the Priests are already dead," Bria Tharen replied. "It shouldn't be too difficult for a kajidic of your resources to arrange. After all, there aren't more than thirty priests on the whole planet, or so our intelligence indicates. Only about three per Colony, in most cases. Another thing . . . we don't want our troops having to deal with fighting off the t'landa Til's empathic vibes—we want them to be able to concentrate on fighting."

"I understand," Jabba said. "Three . . . in return for our funding and our promise to eliminate the priests, your groups will land and destroy the Besadii enterprise. Blow up the factories, make sure there is nothing left for Besadii to use in rebuilding."

"That's right, Your Excellency," the Rebel commander said. "The risk is ours. Of course, we'll also take the Pilgrims and the warehoused spice."

"I understand," Jabba said. "Your offer merits consideration, Commander. We—"

"No!" Jiliac snorted disgustedly and waved dismissal. "Girl, we have heard enough. Thank you, but—"

"Aunt!" Jabba said loudly, then lowered his voice when Jiliac broke off and turned to regard him in surprise. He continued in Huttese, "May I speak with you privately?"

Jiliac huffed slightly, then nodded. "Very well, Nephew."

When the Tharen woman had been escorted outside the chamber by K8LR and asked to wait for their decision, Jabba said, "Aunt, this is an offer too good to refuse. If we had to hire mercenary forces to eliminate the Ylesian enterprise, it would cost us many times what we'd have to pay to fund these Rebels. It would cost . . ." he ran quick figures in his head, "at least five times as much. We should accept."

Jiliac regarded her nephew with scorn. "Jabba, haven't I taught you better than this? I told you, Desilijic must never support either faction in a war. You want us to join the Resistance? That policy can only lead to disaster!"

Jabba had to take a deep breath and silently recite the Hutt alphabet before he could respond. "Aunt, I am

by no means suggesting that we should ally ourselves
with these Rebels. But we can and should make use of
them to further our own ends! This human female and
her Rebellion are a gift from fate. Bria Tharen is the
perfect leader for this raid."

"Why?" Jiliac blinked at her nephew.

Jabba let out his breath in a quick *huff* of exasperation. "Think, Aunt! Who were the two humans who escaped from Ylesia after killing Zavval all those years
ago? Remember I investigated the matter after Han
Solo came to work for us?"

Jiliac frowned. "No. . . ."

"Well, I did. Han Solo escaped Ylesia in a stolen
ship, with much of Teroenza's treasure in its hold, and
the High Priest's pet slave. Her name was *Bria Tharen*,
Aunt. This same woman! She has a personal grudge
against Ylesia! She will stop at nothing to shut the Besadii slaving world down."

Jiliac was still frowning. "So what if she has a personal score to settle? How can that benefit us,
Nephew?"

"Nothing could suit Desilijic's needs better than the
destruction of those accursed spice factories! Think
of it! Besadii, humbled and impoverished! This is a
bargain!"

Jiliac rocked back and forth on her massive belly,
staring goggle-eyed into space as if trying to picture in
her mind's eye how it would work. "No," she said finally.
"It is a bad plan."

"It is a good plan, Aunt," Jabba insisted, "and, with a
little refinement, can be made to work." After a pause,
he added, "With all due respect, Jiliac, I don't believe
that you have thought the matter through."

"Oh?" Jiliac reared back until she towered over her
relative. "Nephew, your judgment is flawed. I have

been very careful, over the years, not to compare you with your reckless parent, who nearly bankrupted Desilijic with his grand schemes, then was foolish enough to wind up on that mudball prison planet, Kip. However . . ."

Jabba didn't like being reminded of Zorba and his profligate ways. "Aunt, I am nothing like my parent, and you know it! I respectfully submit that you have grown soft and your analysis weak. We must deal with Besadii soon or, most assuredly, we will be ruined. What are your specific objections?"

Jiliac rumbled, and a bit of green phlegm appeared at the corner of her slack mouth. "Too risky, too many uncertainties. Humans are not intelligent enough to be able to accurately predict their behavior. They're just as apt to take our credits, then betray us to Besadii."

"These Rebels are too committed to their cause," Jabba said. "You are right, you don't understand humans, Aunt. Commander Tharen's group is just dedicated enough and stupid enough to risk themselves over those wretched slaves. Humans are like that. Especially *this* human."

"And I suppose *you* understand them?" Jiliac snorted. "Where do these masterful insights of yours spring from, Nephew? From watching them cavort around scantily clothed?"

Jabba was really getting angry now. "I do understand them! And I understand that this offer is not one to toss aside!"

"So you would have us arrange to kill some thirty t'landa Til for the Corellian Resistance," Jiliac said. "What if that was ever discovered here on Nal Hutta? The t'landa Til here would raise such an outcry! They are our cousins, Nephew. Humans are nothing!"

Jabba hadn't thought of that. He remained silent,

mulling her objection over. "I still think it could be arranged," he said. "We've gotten away with multiple assassinations before, after all."

"Besides," Jiliac said, sulkily, "I don't want the Ylesian enterprise destroyed. I want to take it over. What good will it do us to best Besadii if the spice factories are destroyed?"

"We could build other factories," Jabba said. "Anything would be better than having Besadii warehousing that spice and driving the prices up and up!"

Jiliac shook her head. "I am the clan leader, and my decision is no. That is the end of it, Nephew."

Jabba tried to expostulate further, but she waved him to silence, and, with a bellow, summoned K8LR and the Rebel Commander. The droid quickly shepherded the young woman back into the room, solicitously commenting on her bravery the whole time.

Jiliac shot an exasperated glance at Jabba, and harrumphed loudly. "Girl, as I was saying before, when I was interrupted—" she glanced at Jabba meaningfully, "we appreciate your offer, but our answer is no. Desilijic cannot risk allying with the Resistance in this matter."

Bria Tharen's features betrayed her disappointment, Jabba noted. She sighed, then squared her shoulders.

"Very well, Your Excellency." She reached into the pocket of her fatigues and took something out. "If you should ever change your mind, you can reach me—"

Jiliac waved aside the proffered datacard, then glared at her nephew as he reached for it. Jabba gazed at Bria, holding the datacard. "I will keep this," he said. "Farewell, Commander."

"Thank you for the audience, Your Excellencies," she said, and bowed deeply.

Jabba watched her as she walked away, and found himself thinking that she'd look magnificent in a dancing girl's costume. All that reddish hair spilling down over her bare shoulders. Nicely muscled shoulders. This human was fit, exquisitely so, and her height was impressive. What a dancing girl she'd make!

Jabba sighed.

"Jabba," his aunt said, "I did not appreciate the way you appeared to disrespect my decision just now. Never forget that we Desilijic must always present a united front when conducting business with inferior species."

Jabba did not trust himself to speak. He was still bitterly angry over his aunt's refusal to see what a great opportunity Bria Tharen had offered them.

If I were the leader of Desilijic, he thought, *I wouldn't have to listen to her paranoid conservatism. Sometimes you have to take chances to make large gains. Motherhood has made her stupid and weak. . . .*

It was only then that Jabba realized, for the first time, that if Jiliac were out of the picture, that *he*, Jabba Desilijic Tiure, would be Desilijic's next leader. He would have to answer to no one.

Jabba lay there, his tail twitching thoughtfully, then glanced sideways at his aunt. Suddenly her belly rippled, and her baby slithered out. "Mama's precious!" she exclaimed. "Jabba, look! Getting bigger every day!"

She cooed at her baby. Jabba grimaced, belched, and then wriggled rapidly out of the room, unable to stand the sight of either of them for one second longer.

Bria Tharen picked up her glass of wine, sipped it slowly, appreciatively, then smiled at her escort. "That's wonderful. Thank you so much, Lando. You don't know how long it's been since I had an evening where I could just relax."

Lando Calrissian nodded. Bria had returned to Nar

Shaddaa aboard the shuttle from Nal Hutta today, following what she'd said was a "disappointing" interview with the Desilijic leader. To cheer her up, the gambler had promised to take her out for a nerf tenderloin dinner at one of the Smuggler's Moon's finest hotel-casinos, the Chance Castle. Bria was wearing a softly draped gown of turquoise that matched her eyes, and Lando was wearing his black and scarlet outfit, "for old time's sake."

"How long?" Lando asked, twirling his own wine-glass slowly in his fingers. "Well . . . I imagine being a Rebel commando leader is fairly time-consuming. Almost as time-consuming as being the mistress of a Sector Moff."

Her eyes widened, then narrowed. "How did you find that out? I never told you. . . ."

"Nar Shaddaa is the criminal nexus of the galaxy," Lando said. "An information broker owed me a favor, and I called it in. Commander Bria Tharen, right?"

Her lips tightened, and she nodded curtly. "Hey," Lando said, reaching out to touch the back of her hand gently, "didn't I tell you you can trust me? You can. I have no love for the Empire. If I weren't such an arrant coward, I'd join the Rebels myself. I know lots of secrets, and I'm good at keeping them."

She smiled faintly. "Whatever you are, you aren't a coward, Lando. Nobody who stood up to Boba Fett like that could be called cowardly. You should think about joining the Resistance. You're a good pilot, you can think on your feet, and you're smart. You'd be an officer in no time."

She hesitated, then added, more seriously, "And about Moff Sarn Shild . . . all I can say is that appearances can be deceiving. I was on assignment for the Resistance, but I was nothing more than a social hostess and aide for him, though he wanted everyone to think otherwise."

"But you were also spying on him."

" 'Gathering intelligence' is a nicer term."

He chuckled. "So where will you go tomorrow, after you leave Nar Shaddaa?"

"I'll head back to my squadron, and my next assignment . . . whatever that may be. I'm missing two of my senior officers now . . . plus an excellent combat trooper." Her expression darkened. "Fett killed them with no more thought or caring than you or I would step on an insect."

"That's why he's the most feared bounty hunter in the galaxy," Lando pointed out.

"Yes. . . ." She took another sip of wine. "He's like a one-man army. Too bad he's loyal to the Empire. I could certainly use him in combat!"

Lando looked at her. "It means everything to you, doesn't it? Defeating the Empire?"

She nodded. "It's my life," she said, simply. "I would give anything I have—or am—to further that dream."

Lando picked up a piece of flatbread, drizzled Kashyyykian forest honey on it, and took a bite. "But you've already devoted years to that goal. When does Bria Tharen get a chance to have a life of her own? When do you just say, 'enough'? Don't you want to have a home, a family, someday?"

She smiled sadly. "The last person to ask me that question was Han."

"Really? When the two of you were on Ylesia? That was a long time ago."

"Yes," she said. "It's been wonderful to be able to talk to you, find out what he's been doing. Do you know, Lando, in just a few months it will be ten years to the day since we first met. I can hardly believe it . . . where did the time go?"

"Where time always goes," Lando said. "There's a giant black hole in the center of the galaxy, and it just sucks it right up."

She shrugged and smiled wryly. "That explanation works for me. I'll have to remember that."

Lando poured her some more wine. "Anyway, you didn't answer my question. When are you going to have a life for Bria?"

Her blue-green eyes were very intent as they met his across the table. "When the Empire is defeated, and Palpatine is dead, then I'll think about settling down. I would love to have a child . . . someday." She smiled. "I think I still remember how to cook and do domestic things. My mother certainly spent enough time trying to turn me into appropriate 'wife' material, and that included plenty of instruction in 'womanly' duties."

Lando grinned. "I suppose she wouldn't much like your current rebel image. Dressed in combat fatigues, armed to the teeth."

She laughed wryly and rolled her eyes. "Poor mother! It's a good thing she *can't* see me, she'd keel over in utter horror!"

Just then the server brought their steaks, and both dug in with appreciation. "Lando, this is so wonderful," Bria said. "This beats military chow six ways from sundown."

Lando smiled. "Just one more reason I couldn't join the Rebellion," he said. "I have a penchant for fine cuisine. I don't think I could stand a steady diet of rations."

She nodded. "But you'd be surprised what you can get used to . . . with enough practice."

"I don't want to find out," Lando said, lightly. "How could I give all this up?" He waved a hand at the elegant restaurant, and, beyond it, the glittery clamor of the gaming tables.

She nodded. "I have to admit, I have a hard time imagining you in a Rebel uniform."

"At least not without extensive re-tailoring," Lando said, and they both laughed.

"Have you ever been in combat?" she asked him, on a more serious note.

"Oh, sure," Lando said. "I'm a decent gunner as well as a better-than-average pilot these days. I've seen action here and there. And, of course, there was the Battle of Nar Shaddaa. Han, Salla and I were in the thick of it."

"Tell me about that," she said. "It just amazes me that smugglers—as independent and hard-headed as most of the ones I've known are—could band together like that to beat the Imperial fleet."

Always pleased to talk about himself and his escapades to an admiring audience, Lando launched into a fairly detailed narrative of how the smugglers had joined forces with Drea Renthal's pirate fleet to destroy many Imperial fighters and several big capital ships. Bria listened with grave and knowledgeable attention, asking strategic or tactical questions every so often to encourage the gambler in his story.

Finally, when Lando was finished, and they'd ordered dessert, Bria sat back as the server cleared their plates away. "What a story!" she said. "I'm really impressed by the smugglers' daring and expertise. They are all marvelous pilots, aren't they?"

"You have to be good to stay ahead of the Imp customs ships," Lando replied. "Smugglers can handle just about anything—they fly through asteroid fields, play tag with nebulas and space storms, and they can land on anything. Nothing fazes a good smuggler. I've seen them land ships while fighting uneven gravity fields on asteroids barely bigger than their vessels. Gravity shifts, atmospheric turbulence, sandstorms, blizzards, typhoons . . . you name it, they know how to handle it."

Bria was looking at him intently. "Of course. Smugglers would naturally be the most experienced pilots in the galaxy. . . . but they're also good fighters. . . ."

Lando waved a hand. "Oh, they have to be that, too, with the Imps apt to pop out and start blasting at any moment. Of course, during the Battle of Nar Shaddaa they were fighting to protect their homes and property, else most of them would have demanded payment for their services."

She blinked, as though a sudden idea had occurred to her. "You mean . . . you think the smugglers would hire themselves out for a military action?"

Lando shrugged. "Why not? Most smugglers are just like privateers. If there's a decent profit in it, most of them would dare just about anything."

She tapped her bottom lip with a manicured nail as she thought. Lando suddenly looked at her hand intently. "Hey . . ." he said, leaning forward to take her hand in both of his and examine it gently, "what happened, Bria?"

She drew a deep breath. "These old scars? A souvenir of working in the Ylesian spice factories. I usually cover them with cosmetics for social occasions, but I lost everything aboard the *Queen*, remember?"

"Drea promised me you'd get your stuff back," Lando said. "I told her your cabin number." He looked embarrassed. "I feel terrible for mentioning them. I just . . . well, I care about you. It's painful to see them and know how much you were hurt on that world."

She patted his hand. "I know. You're sweet to be concerned, Lando. But I'm not the one you should be concerned about. People are dying every day on Ylesia. Good people. People who deserve better than a life of unending toil, malnutrition, and cruel deception."

He nodded. "Han talked to me about it once. He feels the same way . . . but there's not much we can do about it, is there?"

She gave him a fierce look. "Yes, there is, Lando. And while there's breath in my body, I'm not going to give up on those people. Someday, I'm going to shut that hellworld down for good." Bria grinned suddenly, recklessly, and at that moment, she reminded Lando very much of his absent friend. "As Han would say, 'trust me.' "

Lando chuckled. "I was just thinking that you remind me of him at times."

"Han was an important role model for me," she said. "He taught me so much. How to be strong, and brave and independent. You wouldn't believe what a spineless little crybaby I used to be."

Lando shook his head. "I don't believe it."

She was looking down at her scars. They crisscrossed her hands and forearms in thin, white lines, like glow-spider webs against the tanned skin. "It used to hurt Han to look at them, too . . ." she murmured.

Lando studied her for a long moment. "He's the only one, isn't he?" he said, finally. "You still love him."

She drew a long breath, then looked up at him, her expression very serious. "He's the only one," she said steadily.

Lando's eyes widened slightly. "You mean . . . the *only* one? *Ever?*"

She nodded. "Oh, I've had a couple of offers. But my life is the Resistance. And . . ." she shrugged, "frankly, after Han . . . other men seem sort of . . . bland."

Lando chuckled ruefully, realizing that, despite his

best efforts and his fondest wishes, Bria's heart was with Han—and there it was likely to stay. "Well, at least when he comes back from the Corporate Sector, I won't have earned myself a punch in the nose for stealing you away," he said. "I have to try and look on the bright side, I suppose."

She looked at him and smiled, then lifted her wineglass. "I propose a toast," she said. "To the man I love. Han Solo."

Lando lifted his, clinked it against hers. "To Han," he agreed. "The luckiest guy in the galaxy. . . ."

Interlude 3: Kashyyyk, on the way back from the Corporate Sector . . .

Han Solo stood in the middle of Mallatobuck's living room, in her home on Kashyyyk, watching his best friend tenderly cradle his infant son.

They'd landed on Chewie's homeworld just an hour ago, on their way back from the Corporate Sector. The Falcon was safely docked in the secret wroshyr-limb docking bay. This time, for Han's benefit, the Wookiees provided a series of vine ladders for the Corellian to make the ascent through the wroshyr trees. Knowing now what a quulaar was, the Corellian had flatly refused to climb into one.

The moment that they'd landed, Han had noticed something odd. All of the Wookiees they met kept giving Chewie amused sidelong glances and nudging each other. Chewbacca had seemed oblivious to the byplay, however, so eager was he to see his lovely wife. After all, the Wookiee hadn't seen Malla in nearly a year. . . .

And then, when they'd walked into Malla's house, there she stood, holding a small bundle wrapped in a blanket in her arms. Chewbacca had stood frozen in the doorway, a look of incredulous joy dawning on his furry visage.

Han had slapped his friend on the back with almost Wookiee force. "Hey, congratulations, Chewie! You're a dad!"

After a few minutes to admire the baby (whom even Han had to admit was awfully cute), Han wandered into Malla's kitchen to give Chewie some time alone with his family. He dug around in the refrigeration unit and found some odds and ends of things to munch on, pleased that Malla had told him to make himself at home.

As he sat there, listening to Chewie and Malla discuss names for their son in the next room, Han's thoughts wandered back to the Corporate Sector and the Tion Hegemony, and all the adventures he'd had there. He wasn't coming home rich, that was for sure . . . but he hadn't done too badly, he decided.

And he'd certainly met a host of memorable individuals—some good, most not. Of course there had been the lovely ladies . . . Jessa, Fiolla . . . and Hasti. . . .

Han smiled, remembering.

And then there had been the bad guys. The ones who had tried to stiff him out of credits, or, worse, tried to snuff him like a candle. Quite a host of them . . . Ploovo Two-for-One, Hirken, Zlarb, Magg, Spray . . . and Gallandro. That was one tough fellow, Gallandro. Be fun to watch him in a free-for-all against Boba Fett, weapons being equal. Gallandro could probably outdraw the bounty hunter . . . but Fett's armor would give him some protection. . . .

Han couldn't decide which of them would win. And speculation was moot, after all, since Gallandro had been reduced to a pile of charred meat and bone back on Dellalt, in Xim's "treasure" vaults.

It had been fun running into Roa and Badure. He'd have to remember to tell Mako that Badure had sent his greetings. . . .

Han was surprised to realize that he actually missed Bollux and Blue Max. He'd never realized droids could have so much personality. He hoped that Skynx was treating them both okay. . . .

The Corellian fingered the newly healed knife-wound on his chin. He'd never had time to get it properly treated, and it had healed with a noticeable scar. He wondered whether he should get it removed. . . .

Wasn't it Lando who always insisted that women couldn't resist a rogue? That's why the gambler had grown his mustache, claiming it gave him a rakish, piratical air. Han decided to keep the scar for now. After all, it was a conversation piece . . . or could be. He pictured himself in some of his favorite haunts on Nar Shaddaa, telling the story to some lovely, fascinated lady. . . .

Next stop, Nar Shaddaa, *Han thought*. Wonder if Jabba missed me?

Chapter Ten:
What Goes Around . . .

"**A**way with you!" Durga Besadii Tai rolled his bulbous eyes and motioned the small Ubese chime player to vacate his throne room. "Enough!" The high-pitched, chaotic notes were pleasant, but did nothing to help him work up the fortitude necessary to do what he had to do.

Month after frustrating month, hour after inconclusive hour . . . nothing he had done had brought him any closer to a definitive answer about who had arranged the murder of his beloved parent. Durga had run into a wall as blank as the metal partitions that he now activated to drop from the ceiling and seal off the room from potential eavesdroppers. Tapping his comm unit, Durga grimly activated its privacy field, too. He didn't want anyone to know what he was about to do. Zier . . . Osman, his majordomo . . . no one.

After all his work, all his searching, Durga had been unable to establish even a tenuous link between Aruk's death and either Teroenza or Desilijic; nor was there any evidence to establish collusion between them.

It was time. The sour churning in his gut grew stronger, and he wriggled a bit to ease the pressure. His tail jerked and twitched, the Hutt equivalent of nervous pacing. *I can manage to keep my head out of the noose if I'm just careful enough,* he told himself. *Even so, the price will be very, very dear. But I can stand the uncertainty no longer. . . .*

The privacy field was established, and the walls around him were secure. Durga ran one final security scan, and turned up no possibility of surveillance or a leak. Activating the comm system, the Hutt lord routed the signal through the most secure channel. *Perhaps Xizor will not be there . . .* , he thought, almost hoping.

But it was not to be so simple. The Hutt was routed from one subordinate to another, each more obsequious than the last. Just as Durga was beginning to suspect that this was some kind of run-around, the haze of the transmission coalesced into the translucent figure of the Falleen prince. Xizor's dusky greenish complexion brightened slightly as he recognized his caller. He smiled affably. Was there a hint of smugness in that smile? Durga told himself not to be paranoid. . . .

Now that he'd committed himself to this, the Hutt lord wanted to get on with it. He bobbed his head at the Black Sun leader, and said, "Price Xizor . . . greetings."

Xizor smiled, and his eyes, made even more baleful by the light shining through the image, shifted to contemplate the Hutt. "Ah, Lord Durga, my dear friend.

So many months have passed . . . over a Standard Year. Are you well? I was growing *worried* about you again. To what do I owe the honor of this communication?"

Durga steeled himself. "I am fine, Your Highness. But I still have no definitive proof as to the identity of my father's murderer. I have considered your offer of assistance in discovering my father's killer, and would like to accept it now. I wish for you to use your intelligence networks and operatives to either confirm or lay to rest my suspicions."

"I see . . ." Xizor said. "This is most unexpected, Lord Durga. I thought you were under a family obligation to discover the killer's identity yourself?"

"I have tried," Durga admitted stiffly, hating how Xizor was fencing with him. "Your Highness . . . you offered Black Sun's help once before. Now I would like to accept your offer . . . if the price is right," Durga added.

Xizor nodded and smiled reassuringly. "Lord Durga . . . have no fear, I am at your service."

"I must know who killed Aruk. I will pay your price . . . within limits."

Xizor's smile vanished, and he drew himself up. "Lord Durga, you do me wrong. I want no credits in return, only your friendship."

The Hutt stared at the image, trying to read the real message through the prince's verbal sleight-of-hand. "Forgive me, Your Highness, but I suspect you want more than that."

Xizor sighed. "Ah, my friend, nothing is ever as simple as we would like, is it? Yes, there *is* something I would request of you. A simple act of friendship. As head of Clan Besadii, you are privy to the planetary defenses of Nal Hutta. I would like a complete rundown of the weapons and shields, with exact strengths and locations."

The Faleen prince smiled, and this time there was more than just the suggestion of a sneer.

Durga flinched, then forced himself to control his sudden fear and dismay. *Nal Hutta's defenses? What could he possibly want them for? Black Sun can't be planning an attack . . . or could they?*

Perhaps this was just a test. It seemed unlikely that Xizor was planning something . . . but there was no way to know for sure. Durga envisioned the broad, river-carved expanse outside his palace, silvery Nar Shaddaa a permanent sliver on the distant horizon. Worst case scenario—Nal Hutta was no longer necessary to Besadii; his clan could do without the glorious jewel conquered so long ago. After all, they had the Ylesian system. . . .

And as for the rest of the clan, the non-Besadii citizens of Nal Hutta—well, they were fast becoming his enemies anyhow. There was that little matter of the official censure and that million-credit fine. . . .

Durga glanced at the likeness of portly old Aruk ensconced in its little niche on his dais, then back at the holo-image. "The information is yours," he said, "but I must *know*."

Xizor inclined his head. "As soon as it is received, we shall do everything in our power to assist you, Lord Durga. Farewell. . . ."

Durga inclined his head again, as cordially as he could, then cut the connection. His stomach was in knots. He had a bad feeling about this. . . .

Xizor turned away from his communications console to face Guri, a genuine smile tugging at the corners of his well-shaped mouth. "That was much easier than I thought it would be. The wedge has been driven deep now, and Durga and Besadii will soon split off from the other Hutts. I wonder what it is in Durga's slimy heart that makes him betray his entire species just for a taste of revenge."

Guri gazed at him, serene as always. "My Prince, your patience with these Hutts is finally gaining results. It is fortuitous that Besadii was censured so strongly by the other kajidics."

"Yes," replied the Falleen, steepling his hands and tapping his long fingernails together, "Durga has no love for his fellow Hutts now, if he ever did. His grief and emotional instability will provide us with the key to Hutt space. That, and the Desilijic penchant for simple solutions to complex problems. You have the proof that Durga requires, Guri, do you not?"

The HRD's expression did not change. "Of course, my Prince. Citizen Green was most helpful in acquiring it and sidetracking the pathologists at the Forensic Institute. He is a very competent human."

Xizor nodded, and shook his ponytail off his shoulder. "Wait two hundred standard hours, long enough for it to seem as though we have conducted an investigation, then you will deliver the material to Durga personally," he said. "When Durga sees it, he will wish to move immediately against Desilijic. Go with him, Guri. Assist him, if necessary, in gaining his revenge on Jiliac. But no harm must come to Jabba. Jabba has been useful to me in the past, and I expect him to be useful to me in the future. Teroenza, too, has a part to play in our plans, and should not come to harm. Understood?"

"Understood," said Guri. "It shall be as you wish, my Prince." Moving with lithe, swift strides, she left the room.

Xizor watched her go, admiring her. Nine million credits she had cost him, and worth every decicred.

With Guri at his side, Xizor was ready to challenge the Hutts. . . .

Perhaps, some day, he would even challenge the Emperor himself. . . .

When Han Solo arrived home from the Corporate Sector, he was welcomed back with open arms by all and sundry—except Lando and Salla Zend. Lando, he discovered, had gone off for a romantic getaway with Drea Renthal, and wouldn't be back for several days.

And as for Salla . . . Han hadn't really been expecting to take up their relationship where they'd left off, but he also hadn't expected her to completely snub him. He saw her once or twice, at a distance, in Shug's spacebarn, but the moment she caught sight of him or Chewie, Salla Zend would turn and depart the premises.

When he asked about Salla, his friends all assured him that she'd been fine during his absence, had even been seeing several fellows, though none of the relationships were termed "serious." She'd apparently worked with Lando for a while, though there was no evidence that Salla and Lando were ever anything but business partners.

Jarik had broken up with his girlfriend, and had returned to his normal self, happy to have his friends back. Even ZeeZee seemed pleased to have the rightful owners of the apartment back again.

When Han heard that Lando had returned, he went right over to his friend's flat to see him. They exchanged handshakes, backslaps and a brief hug, then Lando stepped back to regard his friend. "You look good," he said. "Need a haircut."

"I *always* need a haircut," Han said, dryly. "Comes

from spending time with Wookiees. To them, 'scruffy' is a compliment."

Lando laughed. "Same old Han. Hey, let's go down to the Golden Orb. I'm buying!"

Minutes later, when they were seated at a booth, tall mugs before them, Lando said, "So . . . tell me. Where've you been, and how'd you get that scar, buddy?"

Han launched into a shorthand description of his adventures in the Corporate Sector. Even so, they were working on their third round by the time he finished.

Lando shook his head. "Wow, sounds like some of the stuff that happened to me in the Centrality. One bad guy after another. Get a fortune, lose a fortune. So . . . how's my ship?"

Han took a swig of Alderaanian ale, then wiped his mouth on his sleeve. "*Your* ship?" He laughed, enjoying the familiar byplay. "The *Falcon* has never been better, my friend. She'll make point five past lightspeed, now."

Lando's dark eyes widened. "You're kidding!"

"Nope," Han said. "There's an old guy in the Corporate Sector who can make a hyperdrive whirl on its axis and give you two decicreds change. Doc's a master, all right."

"You'll have to take me for a spin," Lando said, impressed.

"So, tell me what's been happening with you," Han said.

Lando fortified himself with a long drink, then said, "Han, there's something I have to tell you. I ran into Bria a couple of weeks ago."

Han sat up straight. "*Bria?* Bria Tharen? How? Why?"

"It's a long story," Lando said, and smiled wickedly.

"So get busy and start tellin' it," Han snapped, his expression darkening.

"Man, that is one lovely armful, that lady," Lando said, and sighed.

In one swift motion, Han lurched forward and grabbed Lando by the collar of his embroidered shirt.

"Whoa!" Lando gasped. "Nothing *happened*! We just danced, that's all!"

"Danced?" Han let go and sat back down, looking sheepish. "Oh."

"C'mon, Han, take it easy," Lando said, "you haven't even seen this woman in how many years?"

"Sorry, pal, guess I got a little carried away," Han said. "I used to care about her a lot."

Lando smiled again, this time cautiously. "Well, she still cares about *you*. A lot."

"Lando . . . the story," Han said. "Tell."

"Okay," Lando said, and launched into a description of his recent adventures aboard the *Queen of Empire*. By the time he'd reached the face-off outside the shuttle bay, Han was leaning forward, hanging on his every word.

When the gambler finished, Han sat back, shaking his head, sipping his ale. "Some story," he said. "Lando, that makes the second time you've stood up to Fett. That took guts, pal."

Lando shrugged, and for once his demeanor was completely serious. "I don't like bounty hunters," he said. "Never have. I wouldn't turn my worst enemy over to one. To me they're on a par with slavers."

Han nodded, then grinned. "Good thing Drea's got a soft spot for you, pal."

"The thing that turned the tide there was reminding her that she owed *you*," Lando pointed out.

"Well, I'll have to let her know that I owe her one, now," Han said. "I just hope you showed her a good time on that little jaunt you took."

"Of course," Lando said. "If it's one thing I know how to do, it's show a lady a good time."

"So . . . when did Bria tell you she cared about me? The whole time you were with Fett, you were ordered to be quiet," Han said, thinking back over Lando's account.

"Oh, I saw her again, here on Nar Shaddaa," Lando said.

Han stared at Lando balefully. "Oh, yeah?"

"Yeah, I did," Lando replied. "Will you *relax*, old buddy? I just took her out to dinner. She got turned down by Jiliac and Jabba over some commando raid on Ylesia she wanted them to finance, and she needed some cheering up." Lando sighed. "She spent the whole time talking about *you*. Really depressing."

Han felt a grin creep over his face. "Yeah?" he said, trying to sound casual. "She did?"

Lando mock-glared at him. "Yes, she did. Xendor alone knows why, but she did."

"I've thought about trying to contact her," Han said. "But after seeing her that time in Sarn Shild's place . . . well, I know now she was on assignment for the Resistance. I guess a good agent does whatever she has to do to get information. . . ."

"I asked her about that," Lando said. "She told me that even though Shild wanted everyone to think she was his mistress, she wasn't. And from what I've heard about that guy, he did indeed have some very odd . . . tastes . . . in partners."

"Huh . . ." Han said, mulling that one over. "You say she talked about me, huh? She still cares?"

"She cares," Lando said. "If you'd been a myrmin on the wall, your head would be even more swelled than it is already." He laughed shortly, and finished off his own drink, "I told you, it was *depressing*, pal."

Han smiled. "Well . . . thanks. I owe you one for saving her, Lando."

"You should look her up, if you can figure how to do it," Lando said.

"I might," Han said, then sobered. "Lando, I'm afraid I got some bad news yesterday."

"What?"

"It's Mako Spince. Seems he got himself into some kind of confrontation out in the Ottega System with some NaQoit bandits. They found him, barely alive, and brought him back here. He's in the rehab-facility in the Corellian section. Shug told me he's crippled. Won't ever walk again."

Lando shook his head, his expression bleak. "Oh . . . hey, that's terrible! I'd rather be dead than crippled, I think."

Han nodded grimly. "Me too. I was thinkin' . . . you want to go see him tomorrow? I ought to. Me and Mako go back a long ways. But . . . I'd rather not go alone, ya know? Between the two of us, maybe we could kinda cheer him up some?"

Lando shrugged. "Sounds like a tall order, considering the circumstances," he said. "But, sure, I'll go with you. Least we can do. Mako's one of us."

"Thanks."

The next day, the two friends went to the rehab-center. Han had only rarely been inside one, and found himself extremely ill-at-ease. After querying the clerical droid at the desk, they were directed to a room. Han and Lando hesitated outside. "Lando . . . I ain't sure I'm up to this," Han confessed, in a whisper. "I'd rather fly a run with Imps on my tail. . . ."

"I feel the same way," Lando agreed. "But I think I'd feel worse if I went home without seeing him."

Han nodded. "Me too." Taking a deep breath, he walked into the room.

Mako Spince was lying in a special treatment bed. There was a whiff of bacta in the air, and the scars on his rugged features were mostly healed, though Han could tell his old friend must have been a mess. The NaQoit bandits weren't known for their kind hearts. . . .

Spince's shoulder-length hair was spread out on the white pillow. Last Han had seen him, it had been black mixed with gray. Now it was the color of iron, dull and lank. Mako's pale, ice-colored eyes were closed, but somehow Han knew he was awake.

The Corellian hesitated, then plunged ahead. "Hey, Mako!" he called out, breezily, "It's me, Han! Back from the Corporate Sector. Lando's here, too."

Mako's pale, cold eyes opened, and he stared at his friends with no expression. He did not speak, though Han knew he could. Mako's right arm was damaged, and he'd lost the use of his legs, but there was nothing wrong with his mind or his voice.

"Hey, Mako," Lando said. "It's good to see you alive. Sorry to hear that things got so rugged out there in the Ottega system . . . uh . . ."

When Lando ran out of words, Han jumped in. Anything was better than the echoing silence. "Yeah, those NaQoit are scum. Uh . . . well, this is a tough break, all right, but, hey . . . don't you worry about a thing. Me and the others, we took up a collection, you know? Plenty there to get you set up with a repulsor chair. Those things scoot right around . . . you'll be up and around in no time, they say."

Han finally ran out of words, and he turned to Lando, questioning with his eyes. Mako still hadn't moved or spoken.

"Uh, yeah," Lando said, trying valiantly to keep up

his end. "Listen, Mako, is there anything you need? You just ask, and we'll get it. Right, Han?"

"Sure," Han said. He struggled for something else to say, but words utterly failed him. "Uh . . . Mako?" he said. "Hey, buddy . . ."

Mako's expressionless face never altered. But slowly, finally, he turned his face away from his friends, and the unspoken message was clear. *Go away.*

Han sighed, shrugged, then looked at Lando.

Quietly, they walked out of the room, leaving Mako Spince alone with his silence.

Han got a *much* better welcome from Jabba the Hutt. He went to see the Desilijic leader in the kajidic's headquarters on Nar Shaddaa. Jiliac's Nar Shaddaa majordomo, a human woman named Dielo, looked up when he walked in, and smiled welcomingly. "Captain Solo! Welcome back! Jabba instructed me to bring you in immediately."

Since Han was used to being kept waiting when he visited Jabba, this was indeed encouraging news.

When Han walked into the huge, bare, audience chamber, he found Jabba alone. The Hutt lord undulated toward him, his stubby arms spread wide. "Han, my boy! It's wonderful to see you! You were gone too long!"

For an awful second, Han thought that Jabba actually intended to hug him. The Corellian stepped back hastily, trying not to wrinkle his nose. He'd have to get used to the smell of Hutts all over again. . . .

"Hey, Jabba, Your Excellency," he said. "Nice to know I've been missed."

"None of that 'Your Excellency,' now, Han!" Jabba boomed, speaking, as usual, in Huttese, which he knew Han understood well. "We're old friends, and no formalities are needed!"

The Desilijic lord was practically oozing camaraderie. Han smothered a smile. *Business must be hurting,* he thought. *Nothing like being needed, I guess. . . .*

"Sure, Jabba," Han said. "So, how's business?"

"Business . . . business has been a bit . . . slow," Jabba said. "Besadii, curse them, is trying to build up a shipping fleet of their own to challenge Desilijic's business. And the Imperials have been, unfortunately, all too active lately. Between the Imperial customs ships and the pirates, the spice business is suffering."

"Besadii's being their typical pain in the butt, eh?"

Jabba's chuckle boomed out in response to Han's witticism, but, even to Han's ears, the laughter sounded a bit hollow. "Han, Besadii must be dealt with. I am not sure exactly how."

Han gazed at the Hutt lord. "I heard the Corellian Resistance wanted Desilijic to back 'em in a raid on Ylesia."

Jabba didn't seem surprised that Han had his own sources for information. The massive head nodded. "We were approached by an acquaintance of yours . . . Bria Tharen."

"I haven't seen her in ten years," Han said. "I understand she's a Rebel leader now."

"She is," Jabba affirmed. "And I was very interested in her proposition. However, since my aunt refused to back the Corellian resistance, I am looking for alternatives to bring down Besadii. We must do *something.* They are stockpiling the best spice, holding it back to drive up prices. Our sources indicate that their warehouses are crammed, and they are building new ones to hold the overflow."

Han shook his head. "That ain't good. And Jiliac? How's she doin'? And the baby?"

Jabba grimaced. "My aunt is well. Her baby is healthy."

"Why the sour expression, then?" Han asked.

"Her attention to motherhood is admirable, I suppose, Han," Jabba said, "but it has meant a greatly increased workload for me. My business interests on Tatooine are being neglected, and it is difficult to keep up with all of Desilijic's concerns." The Hutt lord sighed. "Han, it is getting harder and harder these days to find the time to get everything done."

"Yeah, I know what that's like, Jabba," Han said. He shifted restlessly from foot to foot.

The Hutt, who was in an unusually perceptive mood, noticed the Corellian's restiveness. "What is it, Han?"

Han shrugged. "I'm okay. Sometimes I wish you had a human-style chair in this audience chamber, though. Having a conversation standing up the whole time is hard on my feet." He hesitated. "Mind if I just park my rear on the floor while we chat?"

"Ho-*ho!*" Jabba chuckled. "I have often thought that feet must be inconvenient things to depend on, Han my boy. I can do better than the floor." Turning with far more flexibility than Han would have given him credit for, Jabba curled his tail forward and patted it invitingly. "Here. Sit, lad."

Han, recognizing that Jabba was doing him a great honor, silently told his protesting nose to shut up. He walked over and sat down on the Hutt's tail just as he would have a tree trunk. He smiled, though the reek was awful, this close. "My feet thank you, Jabba," he said.

The Hutt's laughter at such close quarters was

enough to rattle Han's eardrums. "Ho-*ho-ho*! Han, you amuse me almost as much as one of my dancing girls."

"Thanks," Han managed, wondering how soon he could decently get up and leave. Jabba was curled around so he could speak to Han nearly face-to-face.

"So," said Han. "What did you think of Commander Tharen?"

"For a human, she seems quite intelligent and competent," Jabba said. "Jiliac declined her proposition, but I found it of interest."

"As I said, I haven't seen her in years," Han said. "How'd she look?"

Jabba chortled, licking his lips. "I would hire her to dance for me any day, my boy."

Han grimaced, but was careful not to let Jabba see. "Uh, yeah . . . well, she might have somethin' to say about that. You don't get to be a commander just on good looks."

Jabba sobered. "I was impressed with her. I believe her proposition may be feasible."

"What was she proposing, exactly?" Han asked.

Jabba outlined the basics of the Corellian Resistance's plan. Han shrugged. "They'd need some good pilots to get through that atmosphere," he said. "Wonder how Bria's plannin' to handle that?"

"I do not know," Jabba said. "Tell me, Han, approximately how many guards did each Ylesian colony have when you were there?"

"Oh, it ranged from maybe a hundred to a couple hundred per colony, depending on how many slaves they had working the factories," Han said. "Lotta Gamorreans, Jabba. I know you Hutts like 'em because they're strong and they'll take orders, but, let's face it, as a modern fighting force, they're pretty pathetic. Most of the males are too obsessed with using those antique weapons of theirs on each other. Their clan battles spill over into their jobs. The sows are better, smarter, clearer-thinking, but they don't hire out as mercs."

"So you believe that a modern force of Rebels would have no trouble capturing those colonies."

Han shook his head. "It would be a piece of cake, Jabba."

The Hutt lord blinked his bulbous eyes. "Hmmmmm, as usual, Han my boy, you have been valuable to me. I have a load of spice that is ready to ship. Are you and your ship ready to go back to work?"

Han, recognizing the implicit dismissal, stood up. He could feel the oily residue from Jabba's skin on the seat of his pants. *Great, I suppose I'll have to write this pair off,* he thought. *I'll never get the stink out of 'em. . . .*

"Sure we are," he said. "Chewie and me are ready. The *Falcon* is faster than ever."

"Good, good, my boy," Jabba boomed. "I'll have someone contact you about the pickup this evening. Han . . . good to have you back."

Han smiled. "Jabba, it's good to *be* back. . . ."

Kibbick the Hutt stared at his cousin's holo-image in consternation. "What do you mean the t'landa Til have brought their mates here?" he asked. "Nobody told me."

Durga, leader of Besadii clan, glared. "Kibbick, you wouldn't notice if there was a t'landa Til female perched on your *tail*! They covered their tracks well, and it was nearly a week before I found out they were gone! Do you realize what this means?"

Kibbick thought hard. "It means that the t'landa Til priests will be happier, more content?" he ventured, finally.

Durga waved his little arms in frustration and groaned aloud. "Of course they'll be happier!" he shouted. "But what does this mean to *us*? To Besadii? For once in your life, *think*, Kibbick!"

Kibbick ruminated. "This means we'll have to ship more food in for them?" he asked, finally.

"*No!* Kibbick, you *idiot!*" Durga was in such a rage that gobbets of green goo spattered on the holovid pickup, making "holes" appear in his three dimensional image. "It means that we have lost our most important hold over the t'landa Til, my retarded cousin! Now that we no longer have their mates here on Nal Hutta, Teroenza and his Priests could cut all ties to Besadii and Nal Hutta! *That's* what it means!"

Kibbick drew himself up. "Uncle Aruk never spoke to me like that," he said, greatly offended. "He was always polite. He was a better leader than you will ever be, Cousin."

Durga managed to contain himself with an effort. "Forgive my rash words, Cousin," he said, with a palpable effort. "I am a trifle . . . overworked . . . these days. I am waiting for some important news regarding my parent's demise."

"Oh." Kibbick thought about making more of an issue of it, but as long as Durga had stopped yelling, he was so relieved that he didn't. "Well, Cousin, I can see how that would be bad. What shall we do?"

"You'll have to have all the female t'landa Til brought to Colony One and then ship them home to Nal Hutta," Durga said. "See to it personally, Kibbick. I want you to be able to report to me that you watched them get aboard the ship and leave. I want you to use your best, most trusted pilot for the task. Send a contingent of guards, so there will be no trouble from the females on the voyage."

Kibbick thought that one over for a moment. "But . . . Teroenza won't like that," he said. "And neither will the others."

"I *know* that," Durga said. "But the t'landa Til work for us, Kibbick. We are their masters."

"That's true," Kibbick admitted. He'd been brought up ever since he reached the age of Hutt sentience that Hutts were the most superior species in the galaxy. But imagining himself giving Teroenza orders wasn't an attractive proposition. Teroenza was sly and tricky. He was the one who always gave the guards their orders. All Kibbick had to do when he wanted something done was tell Teroenza, and the High Priest would always do it—promptly and efficiently.

But what if he disobeyed, this time? Kibbick could picture him refusing to send his own mate back to Nal Hutta. And then what would he, Kibbick, do?

"But, Cousin . . . what if he says no?" Kibbick asked plaintively.

"Then you will have to call the guards and have them take him away and lock him up until I can deal with him," Durga said. "The guards will obey you, Kibbick . . . won't they?"

"Of course they will," Kibbick said, indignantly, though privately he wondered if all of them would.

"Good. That's more like it," Durga said. "Remember . . . *you* are a Hutt. A natural lord of the universe. Correct?"

"Of course," Kibbick said, his voice a bit stronger this time. He drew himself up. "I am a Hutt just as much as you are."

Durga grimaced. "That's the spirit," he encouraged. "Kibbick, now is the time to take control. If you delay, the situation will only grow worse. It's possible that

Teroenza is actually planning a revolt against Besadii. Has that occurred to you?"

It hadn't. Kibbick blinked. "A revolt? You mean . . . a real one? With troops, and shooting?"

"That's exactly what I mean," Durga said. "And in a revolt, who is the first to go?"

"The leader," Kibbick said, his mind racing.

"Right. Very good. Now do you see why you must take control before Teroenza can make his plans? While you still have the upper hand?"

Kibbick was feeling threatened now, and he didn't like that. He realized that following Durga's advice and taking control back from the High Priest was definitely his best course. "I'll do it," he said, firmly. "I'll tell him what to do, and make sure he obeys me. If he refuses to obey me, I'll have the guards take care of him."

"Now that's the spirit!" Durga said, approvingly. "Good! You sound like a true Besadii now! Call me and tell me as soon as the female t'landa Til are on their way home!"

"I will, Cousin!" Kibbick said, and cut the transmission.

Kibbick promised himself that he'd take care of this matter *right now*. Before he could lose the pumped-up feeling of Hutt superiority. The Hutt lord didn't bother with his repulsor sled, but immediately undulated his way through the Administration Building of Colony One to Teroenza's office. He didn't bother activating the door signal, just barged right in.

Teroenza was in his working sling, at his datapad. He looked up in surprise as the Hutt came undulating his way into his office.

"Kibbick!" he exclaimed. "What is going on?"

"*Lord* Kibbick to you, High Priest!" Kibbick said. "We have to talk! I just spoke with my cousin Durga, and he tells me that you have brought your female t'landa Til here in secret! Durga is most upset!"

"The female t'landa Til?" Teroenza blinked as though he hadn't the faintest notion what Kibbick was talking about. "Where did he get that idea, Your Excellency?"

"Don't try that with me," Kibbick said. "They are here, and Durga knows it. He has instructed me to tell you that they must return to Nal Hutta on the next ship. Summon the guards and have the mates brought here to Colony One for shipment off Ylesia. Do it now."

Teroenza settled back into his sling, his expression thoughtful. Other than that, the High Priest didn't move.

"Did you hear me, Priest?" Kibbick was feeling almost intoxicated with righteous anger. He drew himself up. "Obey, or I shall summon the guards!"

Slowly, the High Priest drew himself out of the sling. Kibbick inwardly drew a breath of relief. But Teroenza made no move toward the intercom. "Hurry up!" the Hutt lord blustered. "Or I shall summon the guards to take you away, and then I shall deal with the females myself!"

"No," Teroenza's voice was flat and quiet.

"No . . . what?" Kibbick was incredulous. No one in his life had ever refused a direct order from a Hutt overlord.

"No. I won't do it," Teroenza said. "I'm tired of taking orders from an *idiot*. Farewell, Kibbick."

"How dare you? I'll have you executed! Farewell?" Kibbick was completely befuddled. "Are you saying you're quitting? Leaving?"

"No, I'm not leaving," Teroenza said, in that quiet tone. "*You* are." His powerful hindquarters twitched, his thin, whip-like tail lashed the air, and suddenly he lowered his head and came at Kibbick with a bellow of rage.

The Hutt lord was so taken aback that he didn't even have time to dodge. Teroenza's horn slammed into his chest. The horn wasn't terribly sharp, but so powerful was the force of the High Priest's charge that it penetrated for nearly its full meter-long length.

The pain was agonizing! Kibbick roared in mingled terror and pain and beat at the t'landa Til with his little arms. He tried to swing his tail around to deal a crushing, killing blow, but the room was too confined.

Dimly, Kibbick felt the t'landa Til's hands shove hard against the solid wall of flesh that was his massive chest, then Teroenza's horn, covered with Hutt blood and ichor, yanked free.

Purposefully, Teroenza began backing away.

Wheezing, choking, Kibbick tried to back up, too, but his back end jammed into the wall. He tried to turn and escape.

Teroenza slammed into his chest again.

And again . . .

And yet again . . .

Kibbick was gushing blood now from his multiple wounds. None were life-threatening in and of themselves. A Hutt's vital organs were buried too deep within their bodies to be easily pierced . . . part of the reason for the old legend that Hutts were immune to blaster fire. They weren't . . . but a blaster bolt that would fry most beings instantly frequently would not hit anything vital on a Hutt, leaving them free to crush their attacker before he, she or it could get off a second shot.

Kibbick tried to shout for help, but all that emerged was a gurgle. One of the blows had punctured a breathing sac. He struggled to pull himself toward the intercom to summon help.

Teroenza rammed him yet again. This time the force

of the t'landa Til's blow, along with Kibbick's growing weakness, caused the Hutt lord to roll over on his side, helpless.

Kibbick's vision was clouding over, but he could still see enough to recognize what Teroenza was withdrawing from a desk drawer. A blaster.

The Hutt lord struggled one more time to rise, to fight back, to summon help, but he was too weak, and the pain too great. Darkness was hovering, closing over his vision. Kibbick struggled against it, but it closed over him like black water at midnight. . . .

With cold precision, Teroenza aimed the blaster and used it to widen and disguise the wounds on the dying Kibbick. He shot again and again, until the massive body was a scorched horror, and the final jerks and convulsions were long over.

Finally he stopped, breathing hard. "Idiot . . ." he muttered, in his own language, and went off to wash his horn.

While he was cleaning himself up, the t'landa Til decided on the best course. A terrorist attack, of course. He'd say it was that Tharen woman and her troops. No one would dare dispute his word. He'd have the guards on duty executed, claiming they'd been bought off and were in on the assassination. . . .

Just the other day he'd closed the deal to purchase a turbolaser. He'd use this as an excuse to set it up in the courtyard. . . .

He knew he'd need more guards, more weaponry. Should he contact Jiliac?

No! Teroenza shook his massive head, drops of water flying from his horn. He had had enough of Hutts—he was through with them! He, Teroenza, was now master of Ylesia! And soon . . . soon . . . everyone would know it. Just a few more weeks to consolidate his power. He'd stop paying Besadii, and use the credits to buy weapons.

Satisfied with his plan, Teroenza, High Priest of Ylesia, left his office and the massive mound of dead Hutt, and went looking for some guards to execute. . . .

Chapter Eleven:

DEATH CHALLENGE

Durga the Hutt stared at the screen of his datapad and rejoiced. At last! Black Sun, in the person of Guri, Xizor's personal assistant, had just provided him with conclusive proof that Jiliac the Hutt, most likely abetted by her nephew, Jabba, had planned Aruk's murder—and Teroenza had carried it out.

Black Sun's evidence was mostly in the form of records of purchases and payments that proved Jiliac's link to the Malkite Poisoners. The Desilijic leader had purchased enough X-1 from them to bankrupt a medium-sized colony. And that X-1 had then been shipped straight to Teroenza. There were also records of items that Jiliac had purchased and sent to the High Priest, valuable items that were now part of the t'landa Til's collection.

So I would not realize he was paid off, Durga thought. *Teroenza thought he could "hide" his pay by taking items for his collection.* The Hutt leader noted that most of those items were not only valuable, but in demand. Should Teroenza ever wish to sell them, he could readily exchange them for many credits on the antiquities black market.

Durga noted with interest that Teroenza had recently done exactly that, and with the proceeds from several of these sales, had purchased a used turbolaser. *He is obviously preparing for a defense of Ylesia,* Durga realized. *Any time now, he is likely to declare his independence. . . .*

Durga's first impulse was to have Teroenza dragged back to Nal Hutta in restraints, but, with an effort, he made himself think out all the ramifications of such an action. The Sacredots, or Under-Priests, would be furious with Besadii on behalf of their leader. Teroenza was popular . . . especially now that he'd managed to have their mates brought to Ylesia.

If Durga had Teroenza dragged way, the Sacredots might refuse to perform the Exultation for the Pilgrims. And without the Priests to give them their daily dose of euphoria, the Pilgrims might refuse to work—they might even revolt! Either way, losing the Priests would be disastrous for production in the spice factories.

Regretfully, Durga realized that before he could have his revenge upon Teroenza, he'd have to make some preparations. Find a new Hutt overlord for Ylesia, and a popular, charismatic t'landa Til to act as High Priest. The new High Priest who would announce bonuses for all the loyal t'landa Til. And, on second thought, perhaps it would be best to leave the t'landa Til's mates on Ylesia . . . at least for the time being.

All of that would probably take a week to accomplish. And until the Besadii ship carrying the new High Priest had landed on Ylesia, Durga couldn't let Teroenza know that he was being replaced. Besadii couldn't take the chance of precipitating a revolt until they had the troops in place to deal with it.

Durga decided to move cautiously . . . keep Teroenza in ignorance until the last moment. Or, if Kibbick had been forced to have the High Priest arrested, they'd have to cover up Teroenza's absence. Perhaps a sudden "illness" on the part of the High Priest would be sufficient?

Could Teroenza's mate, Tilenna, be coerced into acting as the Besadii mouthpiece in her spouse's stead? In exchange for her own life? And a generous settlement?

Durga considered, and decided that she probably could. T'landa Til were a practical people. . . .

It was also possible that Teroenza could still be controlled . . . but it was hard to imagine Kibbick having the wherewithal to do it. Durga would probably have to handle everything himself. Or he might send Zier to attend to it. . . .

Durga wondered how Kibbick had fared in his conversation with Teroenza yesterday. His cousin hadn't called back as he'd promised to, but that didn't mean anything. Kibbick's attention span was short, and he forgot promises.

A flashing light attracted Durga's attention, and he saw that his comm system was signaling an incoming message. The Hutt leader accepted the call, and watched as the image of Teroenza coalesced—almost as if Durga's thinking about him had conjured him up out of thin air.

The High Priest bowed low to his Hutt overlord, but Durga didn't miss the flash of something—something akin to smugness—in his protuberant eyes. "Your Excellency, Lord Durga," the High Priest intoned. "I bring most distressing news. You must brace yourself, my Lord."

Durga glared at the image. "Yes?" he said.

"There was a terrorist attack here early this morning, just after dawn," Teroenza said, wringing his little hands in distress. "It was that Bria Tharen and her band of Corellian Resistance fighters. Red Hand Squadron, they call themselves. They stormed the Administration Building, firing wildly. I regret to tell you that your cousin, Lord Kibbick, was caught in their fire, and killed."

"Kibbick is dead?" Durga was taken aback. He hadn't really expected his cousin to be able to wrest control of Ylesia away from Teroenza, but he'd never expected Kibbick to be killed.

Or, more accurately, murdered.

Durga knew Teroenza's story about Bria Tharen was a lie. His sources had assured him that Red Hand Squadron was clear on the other side of the Outer Rim, and that they'd hit an Imperial outpost just yesterday. No ship in the universe could have reached Ylesia by dawn.

So Teroenza was lying. . . . However, the High Priest had no way of knowing that Durga *knew* he was lying. Durga considered how best he could use this information to his advantage. As he did so, he put a hand up to his eyes, and bowed his head, feigning a grief he didn't feel. Kibbick had been an idiot, and the universe was well-rid of him.

But Teroenza has sealed his own death warrant by this, Durga thought. *As soon as I embark for Ylesia with his successor, he is a dead t'landa Til. . . .*

In a hushed voice, Durga gave Teroenza instructions regarding how he wanted the body to be shipped home.

"It is plain," Durga concluded, "that we must get you better guards there on Ylesia. These Rebels must not be allowed to raid with impunity."

Teroenza bowed again. "I agree, Your Excellency. Thank you for saying you will send us help."

"It is the least I can do, under the circumstances," Durga said, forcing himself to keep sarcasm from permeating his tones. "Can you manage for a few days without a Hutt overlord?"

"I can," Teroenza said. "I shall exert every effort to make sure business runs as smoothly as ever."

"Thank you, Teroenza," Durga said, and cut the transmission.

He then spent several minutes giving Zier instructions on how to find a replacement for Teroenza. Fortunately, Zier was a capable administrator, able to follow orders.

Then, and only then, did Durga turn to the figure who had been standing in his office, patiently waiting, while he attended to business.

"Forgive me, Lady Guri," Durga said, inclining his head to the lovely young human female. "I nearly forgot you were there. Most humans are incapable of waiting so patiently. They fidget."

Guri bowed slightly in turn. "I was specially trained, Your Excellency. Prince Xizor does not like fidgeting in his subordinates."

"Indeed," Durga said. "As you can see, I have reviewed the information you brought, and it confirms my suspicions. Also, as you have seen, my revenge upon Teroenza must wait for a more . . . suitable . . . time. But I intend to confront Jiliac immediately and challenge her to single combat under the Old Law."

"The Old Law?"

"It is seldom invoked these days, but it is an ancient

Hutt custom that, given sufficient provocation, one Hutt clan leader may challenge another to single combat without legal repercussions. The victor is presumed to be in the right."

"I understand, Your Excellency. Prince Xizor informed me that this was likely to be your reaction, as befits an honorable Hutt. He instructed me to accompany you, and to do everything in my power to facilitate your search for justice."

Durga stared at her, wondering what one slightly built human female could expect to accomplish against either Hutts or hordes of Desilijic guards. "You would go as my bodyguard? But . . ."

Guri smiled slightly. "I am Prince Xizor's primary bodyguard, Your Excellency. I assure you that I can protect you from Jiliac's guards."

Durga was tempted to say more, but something about Guri's demeanor stopped him. He knew she was Xizor's primary aide. It made sense that she would also be an accomplished assassin. She must have abilities that weren't readily apparent. Certainly her manner was nothing but confident.

"Very well," Durga said. "Let us go."

They boarded Durga's shuttle, and the trip to the Desilijic enclave took less than an hour by suborbital flight.

They landed on the island that contained Jiliac's Winter Palace, and was the current home of the Desilijic clan. Durga, with Guri at his side, carrying a large box, slithered toward the entrance. "Durga Besadii Tai to see Jiliac Desilijic Tiron. I bring a gift and request a private audience."

The guards scanned both visitors and verified that they were unarmed. After a quick call, they were waved into the palace. The majordomo, a Rodian named

Dorzo, accompanied them to the huge, almost bare, audience chamber, then stepped inside, bowing. "Lord Durga of Clan Besadii," he announced.

Through the portal, Durga could see Jiliac doing some kind of work at a datapad. At the sight of his enemy, rage flooded the young Hutt's body. He quivered with blood lust.

Jiliac deliberately kept them waiting for nearly ten minutes. Durga tried to emulate Guri's stillness. She really was a most *unusual* human, he decided.

Finally, Jiliac nodded at Dorzo, then the Rodian bowed to the visitors and proclaimed, "Her Supreme Excellency Jiliac, Leader of the Clan Desilijic and protector of the Righteous, will see you now."

Durga started forward, with Guri pacing gravely beside him. When they reached Jiliac, the huge Hutt matron did not speak. Since, by custom, Durga could not speak until spoken to, because he was the visitor, again they waited.

Finally Jiliac's massive bulk shifted. "Greetings to Besadii," she said. "You have brought a gift, and that is fitting. You may present it to me."

Durga nodded at Guri, and the human advanced on the Desilijic leader and laid the box before her, as the Desilijic leader hovered on her repulsor sled.

The younger Hutt waved at the box. "A gift for your Exaltedness. A token of Besadii's esteem and our hopes for your future, O Jiliac."

"We shall see. . . ." rumbled Jiliac. She tore at the wrappings, and then drew forth a large, very valuable piece of art. It was a death-mask from the islands of the remote world of Langoona. The natives carved these death-masks and decorated them with semiprecious gems and inlays of silver, gold, platinum and iridescent shell-casings from their warm seas.

Jiliac turned the mask around in her tiny hands, and at first Durga thought she did not recognize its significance. The Besadii leader spared a glance to Guri, and, as they had agreed upon, the woman turned and headed for the exit. She would wait there for him, and make sure he was not disturbed. Durga turned his attention back to Jiliac, ready to enlighten her as to exactly what her gift meant, then he saw her entire huge body begin to tremble.

She glared at Durga. "A death-mask from Langoona!" Jiliac bellowed. "And you call *this* a fitting gift?"

With a powerful swing of her small arm, Jiliac tossed the piece of art into the air, then used her tail to bat it clear across the audience chamber. Striking the wall, it shattered, raining down in pieces.

"I call it entirely fitting, Jiliac," Durga gave no ground. He recited the formal words. "Today I, Durga Besadii Tai, discovered that you killed Aruk, my parent. I challenge you under the Old Law. Prepare to die."

Jiliac bellowed in rage and swung herself off her sled. "*You* are the one who will die, upstart!" she growled, and sent her flexible tail swooping up and around.

Durga dodged, but not quickly enough. The tail slapped his back, bruising him, almost knocking his wind out. With all his strength, Durga launched himself toward Jiliac, butting her as hard as he could with his chest.

Jiliac was nearly twice Durga's size. She was a middle-aged Hutt who was reaching the corpulent stage. Durga had one advantage—his youth gave him speed. But if she caught him with her full weight, even once, the battle would be over, and he knew it.

Bellowing like two prehistoric leviathans, the two Hutts slammed at each other, sometimes hitting, often missing. They hurled themselves against each other's chests, wrestling with their undersized arms, as they sent their tails slamming into everything nearby.

Dorzo had long ago taken to his heels and gotten well out of range.

Kill . . . kill . . . KILLKILLKILL!! Durga's mind shrieked at him. He was consumed with rage. Jiliac slammed him with her tail, nearly sending him rolling over, then launched herself at him with a roar. Durga barely managed to wriggle out of the way before he could be crushed beneath her massive midsection.

The younger Hutt dealt her a hard slap across the side of her head that sent her reeling. She came back at him with a tail-slap that missed, making the entire room shake.

At first, Jiliac howled curses and threats, but within a few minutes, she began panting too heavily, and saved her breath for battle. The Desilijic's sedentary lifestyle was catching up with her. . . .

If I can just outlast her . . . Durga thought, and realized that was a very big *if.* . . .

Han Solo had been going over shipping manifests for the mines on Kessel with Jabba when he, Chewie and Jabba all heard a loud *thud*, followed by a bellow, then another series of thuds and muffled crashing sounds. Human, Wookiee and Hutt looked at each other, startled. "What's that?" Han wondered.

"My aunt must be having one of her temper tantrums," Jabba said.

Nearly a decade ago Han had witnessed one of Jiliac's notorious tantrums, so he had no trouble believing that. He started to go back to work, when *two* bel-

lows reached his ears. One right after another—in two
different voices.

Jabba reared up in alarm. "Come on!"

Han and Chewie jogged beside the Hutt as Jabba led
them toward the sounds. He was amazed at how quickly
Hutts could move when motivated.

When they reached Jiliac's audience chamber, a
beautiful young blond woman was standing in the
doorway. Han looked over her shoulder, and saw Jiliac
locked in mortal combat with a much smaller Hutt. The
newcomer had a disfiguring birthmark that spread over
his eye and down his face. The two creatures were bellowing and straining as they butted their massive chests
together.

As Han, Chewie and Jabba approached, the woman
shook her head and put up a hand to halt their progress.
"No," she said. "Do not interfere. Durga has challenged
Clan Leader to Clan Leader, under the Old Law."

To Han's surprise, Jabba did not bat the woman out
of his way and go to his aunt's aid. Instead he inclined
his head in the Hutt equivalent of a bow. "You must be
Guri," he said.

"Yes, Your Excellency," she replied.

Just then a group of guards came stampeding up the
corridor, force-pikes ready. Jabba whirled to block their
way. The Gamorreans blinked at him in dull surprise.
"My aunt is having one of her temper fits," he said. "You
are not needed."

The leader of the guards looked doubtful, but Jabba
did not move, and he could not see for himself what was
going on. He hesitated, his porcine snout quivering
with the urge to fight.

"I said, *you are dismissed!*" Jabba bellowed, waving
his arms at the guards. They turned, grunting and snort-
ing, and went trotting back down the hall.

Han glanced into the audience chamber and saw Jiliac bring her tail down with stunning force. The smaller Hutt barely managed to dodge out of the way in time. The Corellian looked at Jabba. "You don't want to stop it?"

Chewbacca echoed Han's question.

Jabba blinked at them, his bulbous eyes full of cunning. "Durga is the leader of Besadii clan," he said. "Whichever of them wins, *I* win."

"But . . ." Han stammered, "I . . . I thought you were fond of your aunt."

Jabba looked at him as though he were a retarded Gamorrean child. "I am, Han," he said, gently. "But this is *business*."

Han nodded and glanced at Chewie. He shrugged. "Sure. Business."

"And, Han?"

"Yes, Jabba?"

The Hutt leader waved Han away. "This is no place for a human, lad. Wait for me at my palace. I will join you later."

No place for a human? Han wanted to say, *but what about her?* He glanced at the beautiful woman, and their eyes met. Han stared at her for a long second, and realized that there was something *not right* about this woman Jabba called Guri. She was perfect, but, after looking into her eyes, Han realized that all his instincts were telling him to give her a wide berth. He would no more have put his arms around her than he would have cuddled a deadly viper.

"Uh, yeah," he said. "Later, Jabba. C'mon, Chewie."

Turning, Han and the Wookiee hurried away without looking back.

· · ·

Durga was getting desperate. Despite his best efforts to wear Jiliac down, exhaust her, the older Hutt was still fighting with grim purpose. She was much stronger and heavier than he was, and if just *one* of her blows landed full-on, Durga knew he'd be little more than a grease spot on the floor.

They rammed each other for the umpteenth time, their chests crashing together with such force that Durga cried out. He was bruised over every centimeter of his body—he felt like a piece of dough, pounded and rolled out to make flatbread.

The long fight had taken them clear around the huge chamber, as the smashed furnishings and the holes in the walls testified. Durga suddenly realized they were approaching Jiliac's sled. She must have realized it, too, for suddenly she disengaged, and, wheeling around, she glided toward the repulsor sled at her fastest speed, wheezing and sobbing for breath.

Durga was right behind her, overhauling her. It was obvious to him that Jiliac intended to mount the sled, then use it as a battering ram against him. If she got atop it, he was finished!

He caught up to Jiliac, heading for the controls, only to gasp and dodge as the Desilijic leader swept her tail in a hard arc *under* the sled, aiming for his face.

Durga reacted without conscious thought. Rolling forward onto his chest, bracing himself on his hands, he flipped his tail up over the top of his head. Aiming carefully, he aimed the tip-end of his tail on the way down, sending it slamming into the "Power On" button on the sled, depressing it.

The repulsor sled fell like a stone, straight down onto Jiliac's tail, pinning it firmly.

Jiliac screeched with pain, struggling to yank her tail free. As he rolled back upright, Durga realized that she wasn't going to manage that. Wriggling backward, he positioned himself, then brought his tail down on Jiliac's head with all his strength.

The Desilijic leader screamed.

Durga slammed into her head again. And again . . .

It took five hard blows to drive Jiliac into unconsciousness. *Die!* he thought, walloping sodden flesh. "Die!" he bellowed. "*DIE!*"

He wasn't sure when she died, actually. At some point Durga became aware he was pounding mindlessly on what was now a bloody, crushed ruin of flesh and brain matter. Jiliac's eyes were smashed holes, and her slimy tongue lolled from her mouth.

Durga forced himself to halt, to look around. At the entrance to the room, Guri stood beside Jabba. Somehow Xizor's assassin had prevented the guards—and Jabba—from entering. Whatever the young woman was, she was more than she seemed, Durga decided, his mind dull with exhaustion.

Moving as though he were nine hundred years old, Durga managed to haul himself onto Jiliac's sled and activate it. He was too tired to even wriggle across the room. He barely had the strength and mental wherewithal to guide the sled.

He glided across the audience chamber, leaving the dead Jiliac sprawled in his wake.

When Durga reached the entrance, he paused to confront Jabba. The Besadii figured that at the best of times, he might be evenly matched with Jabba. At the moment . . . there was no way.

Guri stepped forward to bow slightly, respectfully. "Congratulations on the successful outcome of your challenge, Your Excellency."

Durga turned to regard the woman. "Guri. You are Prince Xizor's assassin, correct?"

"I serve the Prince in whatever capacity I may," she said, composedly.

"Could you kill a Hutt?" Durga asked.

"Most certainly," she replied.

"Then . . . kill Jabba," Durga said.

Guri shook her head slightly. "No, Your Excellency. My orders were to help you effect your revenge against Jiliac. That is accomplished. We will leave now."

Durga made an abortive move toward Jabba, only to have Xizor's assistant step between them, her unspoken message very clear. "We will leave now," she repeated.

Jabba moved aside to let them pass as Guri swung herself up nimbly onto Jiliac's repulsor sled. Hearing the pound of running feet, Durga saw guards running toward them, but Jabba stopped them in their tracks with a raised hand.

"I dismissed you earlier!" he said. "Now *leave!*"

The guards obeyed with alacrity.

Jabba looked at Guri. "I did not want to lose them. They are an effective defense against most invaders."

Guri nodded, and sent the sled gliding away. Durga glared balefully at Jabba, but the last of his strength was gone. He could only slump atop the sled, too exhausted even to savor his victory. . . .

Jabba slowly approached his aunt's massive corpse. He could scarcely believe she was dead, and he knew he would miss her. But, as he'd told Han Solo, this was business. For the good of Desilijic as well as his own. . . .

The sight of the ruined, shapeless head actually had the power to turn his stomach. Jabba knew he wouldn't be hungry for a while.

He considered for a moment, wondering what

should be his first actions, now that he was the undisputed leader of Desilijic. He'd likely be summoned to appear before the Hutt Grand Council, but once they'd heard that this was a Clan Leader Challenge under the Old Law, there would be little they could say.

And, if asked, Jabba would tell them Jiliac had indeed caused Aruk to be poisoned. . . .

Without warning, Jiliac *moved*.

Startled, Jabba jerked upright, incredulous. *She's coming back to life! She'll be angry! No!* His hearts thudded wildly in shock. What could be happening? There was no doubt his aunt was dead, no doubt at all—

The massive corpse moved again, and then Jiliac's baby slithered out of her abdominal pouch. Jabba relaxed. *I should have realized,* he thought, embarrassed by his momentary superstitious fear.

The little grub-like creature scooted forward, waving its little stubs, gurgling mindlessly.

Jabba stared at it malevolently. He knew he would be confirmed leader of Desilijic no matter what, but why leave any loose ends?

Slowly, purposefully, he slithered toward his aunt's helpless offspring. . . .

The day after Durga defeated Jiliac, the Besadii leader was so stiff and sore that he could barely move. However, he managed to conceal his pain when Teroenza called him, telling him that Kibbick's body had been shipped home, per Durga's orders.

"Your Excellency," the High Priest said, "I need more guards, and therefore I have taken the liberty of hiring some, at my own expense. It is my hope that Besadii will reimburse me, but I must have additional protection. These Rebel raids cannot be countenanced."

"I understand," Durga said. "I will attempt to get more guards."

"Thank you, Your Excellency."

When he cut the connection, Durga turned to Guri, who had just been taking her leave of him. "He is getting ready to make his move," Durga said. "He is preparing to make his break with Besadii."

Guri nodded. "I believe you are correct, Lord Durga."

"Since the Ylesian troops may well be loyal to Teroenza," Durga said, "I need some way to keep the High Priest in line until I can replace him. Thus I have a request for your master, Prince Xizor."

"Yes, Lord Durga?"

"I ask you to convey to him my request that he grant me some military aid. If he would send troops to Ylesia, that would ease the transition—allow me to get rid of Teroenza, while keeping the Sacredots and Pilgrims content. I know that the prince has extensive resources and several mercenary units at his command. With an effective, modern fighting force on the planet, there is no way that Teroenza's guards would dare mount an armed challenge." He faced her squarely, despite the pain of his bruised body. "Will you ask him for me, Guri? Explain the situation?"

"I will," Guri said. "However, His Highness rarely dispatches troops except to protect his own interests."

"I know that," Durga said dolefully. He didn't like what he was about to say, but better this than to lose everything. "In return for his support, tell your prince that I will offer him a percentage of this year's Ylesian profits."

Guri nodded. "I will convey your proposition, Lord

Durga. You will be hearing from His Highness." She
bowed slightly. "And now . . . I take my leave of you,
Your Excellency."

Durga nodded as well as he could with his aching,
stiff neck. "Farewell, Guri."

"Farewell, Lord Durga."

Bria Tharen was working in her office aboard her
Marauder corvette, *Retribution,* when Jace Paol appeared on the holocomm. "Commander, we have an incoming message for you, your private code, on a *very*
secure channel."

"HQ?" she said.

"No, Commander. This is a civ transmission."

She raised her eyebrows in surprise. "Really?" Not
many outsiders had her private code. A few of the Intelligence operatives—Barid Mesoriaam and others of his
ilk—but they would hardly contact her this directly.
"Well . . . patch it through to me here, please."

Moments later, a small image formed atop her
comm unit.

Bria stared in surprise. *A Hutt?* The only Hutt who
had her private code was Jabba, so this must be he . . .
though Hutts looked alike to her, especially in a fuzzy
holo-message. She spoke to the image. "Jabba? Is that
you, Your Excellency?"

"It is I, Commander Tharen," the Hutt replied.

"Yes . . . well . . . to what do I owe the pleasure of this
call, Your Excellency?"

The Hutt leader inclined his head slightly. "Commander Tharen, I ask that you come to Nal Hutta immediately. I am now the leader of Clan Desilijic, since
my aunt's unfortunate demise. We must talk."

Bria caught her breath. It had been only a month since her interview with Desilijic. And now Jiliac was dead?

She decided she didn't want to know. Bowing her head respectfully, she said, "I will come immediately, Your Excellency. I take it you wish to re-open our negotiation regarding the Ylesian enterprise?"

"Yes," said Jabba. "I have begun placing operatives on Ylesia to take care of the t'landa Til. I am ready to proceed with the Ylesian raid. It is time to put an end to Besadii's economic tyranny."

"I'll be there in two days," Bria promised.

Chapter Twelve:

Ice . . .

Five days after Jiliac's death, Han Solo and Chewbacca visited Han's favorite tavern in the Corellian section of Nar Shaddaa. The Blue Light didn't serve food, only liquor, and it was just a little hole in the wall, but Han liked the place. There were holo-posters on the wall that depicted famous landmarks on Corellia. And the management served Han's favorite brand of Alderaanian ale.

The bartender, Mich Flenn, was an aging Corellian who had been a smuggler until he'd accrued enough credits to buy the bar. Han enjoyed hearing his yarns about the old days, though he had to take everything the old geezer said with a big grain of salt. After all, who ever heard of sentients with strange powers who could leap ten meters into the air and turn somersaults, or project blue lightning from their fingertips?

Han and Chewie stopped by there most evenings. This particular one, they were standing at the bar, side by side, sipping their drinks, listening to another of Mich's tall tales. The Corellian was dimly aware that someone came in during the story and stood beside him, but he did not turn to glance at the newcomer.

Mich's tale was a long one, wilder than ever, about a sentient tree that had once been a powerful sorcerer, and a race of beings who transferred their essence into battle-droids in order to become the perfect fighting force.

Finally Mich ran down, and Han shook his head. "Mich, that was a real doozy. You oughta write all the stories down and sell 'em to the tridee producers. They're always lookin' for crazy stuff like that for their shows."

Chewie voiced an emphatic agreement.

Mich grinned at Han, then began polishing a glass industriously and addressed the newcomer. "And what will you have, pretty lady?"

Han reflexively glanced to his right to see the person Mich was addressing—and froze, startled.

Bria!

At first he told himself he was seeing things, that it was just a chance resemblance, then he heard her speak in that low, slightly husky voice he remembered. "Just some Vishay water, please, Mich."

It's her. Bria. It's really her.

Slowly she turned her head, and their gazes locked. Han's heart was hammering, though he was pretty sure his face was under control. All those sabacc games had taught him something.

She hesitated, then said, "Hi, Han."

He wet his lips. "Hi, Bria." He stared at her, then a sudden movement from Chewie made him remember his partner. "And this is Chewbacca, my partner."

"Greetings, Chewbacca," she said carefully, speaking in almost passable Wookiee—obviously she'd been coached by Ralrracheen. "I am honored to meet you."

The Wookiee voiced an uncertain greeting, obviously wondering what was going on. "Uh," Han said, "long time no see."

She nodded gravely at the ridiculous understatement. "I came to see you," she said. "Could we sit down and talk for a minute?"

Han's emotions were mixed, to say the least. Part of him wanted to take her in his arms and kiss her until she was breathless, another part wanted to shake her while screaming curses and accusations at her. Still another part wanted to just turn around and walk away, prove to her that she meant nothing to him—nothing!

But he found himself nodding. "Sure." As he moved to pick up his mug, Chewie laid a hand on his arm, and growled softly at him.

Han gazed up at his partner, grateful for Chewbacca's sensitivity. He *would* rather talk to Bria by himself. "Okay, pal. I'll see you at home, later on."

Chewie gave Bria a nod, then left the Blue Light. Picking up his mug of ale, Han led the way to a booth in the rear of the dimly lit, nearly empty bar.

Watching Bria approach and then slide in opposite him, he got a good look at her for the first time. She was wearing tan fatigues, military in style, though they bore no insignia or indications of rank. Her hair was pulled up and slicked back in a severe style. Han couldn't decide whether it was cropped short, or just worn in a tight bun.

She wore no jewelry. A well-worn BlasTech DL-18

(Han's own weapon of choice was the heavier BlasTech
DL-44) in a tie-down holster rode her right thigh, low
down, the way he liked to wear his own. Her gunbelt
was studded with extra power paks and bore a vibroblade in a sheath. From the slight bulge in the top of
her boot, Han was willing to bet she had an auxiliary
weapon cached there.

As she sat there, regarding him, Han struggled to
find words, but all he could do was look at her, hardly
able to believe she was actually *there*, that this wasn't
some dream—or nightmare.

She was staring at him, too, her eyes searching his
features. Bria started to speak, stammered, and then
took a deep breath. "I'm sorry," she said. "For startling
you. I should have said something, but my mind went
blank. There didn't seem to be anything I *could* say."

"You came here looking for me?" Han asked.

"Yes. When I saw your friend last month, he said this
was one of your favorite hangouts. I . . . I took a chance
you'd be here tonight."

"You're here on Nar Shaddaa on business?"

"Yes. Staying in those rooms above the Smuggler's
Rest." She smiled wryly. "It's even sleazier than that
place we stayed that night on Coruscant."

Han's dazed brain was slowly beginning to function
again, and his anger was building. He remembered that
sleazy little hotel on Coruscant. That had been their last
night together. He remembered falling asleep . . . and
he remembered waking up alone, abandoned.

Suddenly his hand shot out, and he grabbed her
wrist tightly, feeling the shock of touching her flesh
throughout his body. Her slender bones felt so delicate
in his hand . . . as though he could just snap them. And
he was almost angry enough to try. "*Why?*" he said.

"Why, Bria? You think you can just walk back up to me a decade later? You gotta lot of nerve!"

She stared at him, her eyes narrowing. "Han, let go of me."

"No," he gritted. "I'm not lettin' you go running off and leaving me with no answers this time!"

Han wasn't sure exactly what she did—some unarmed combat trick, but there was a sudden twist, a jab in a nerve, and abruptly her hand was free, and his own was throbbing. He looked down at it, feeling his eyes widen, and then back up at her. "You've changed," he said. "You have really changed." He wasn't sure whether it was a compliment or an accusation.

"I had to change—or die," she said, flatly. "And don't worry, I'm not going to jump up and run away. I need to talk to you, and that's exactly what I'm going to do. If you'll listen."

He nodded, grudgingly. "Okay. I'm listening."

"First of all, let me tell you that I'm sorry for the way I left you. I'm sorry about a lot of things in my life, but that's the one I regret most," she said. "But I had to do it. Otherwise you'd have never made it through the Academy."

"Fat lot of good it did me," Han said, bitterly. "I got cashiered less than a year after getting my commission. Cashiered and blacklisted."

"For rescuing a Wookiee slave," she said, and smiled at him—a smile that made his heart lurch. "I was so proud when I found that out, Han."

Han wanted to smile back, but the anger was still in control, and he found himself saying, "I don't want you to be proud of me. I owe you nothin', sister. I did it all on my own."

He could tell that gibe hurt her. Color stained her cheeks, and her eyes flashed, then, for a moment, it almost seemed as though she were fighting back tears. Then her face was under control again, cold and chiseled. "I know that," she said quietly. "But I was still proud."

"I hear you got a real thing for Wookiees yourself," Han said, and the edge in his voice was sharp enough to draw blood. "Or so Katarra and Ralera told me."

"You were there? On Kashyyyk?" She smiled. "I helped to organize the Resistance group there."

"Yeah, I hear you're some kinda officer in the Corellian Resistance," Han said.

"I'm a commander," she confirmed, quietly.

Han slanted her a look. "Well, now, *that's* impressive, ain't it? For a scared kid who'd never fired a blaster, you've come a long way, Bria."

"I just did what I had to along the way," she said. "Promotions come fast in the Resistance. You should think about joining up, Han."

It was said lightly, but some nuance in her tone told Han she wasn't kidding. "No thanks, sister," he said. "I've seen the Imp forces up close and personal. No way your Rebellion's got a chance against them."

She shrugged. "We have to try. Otherwise the Emperor is going to swallow us all whole. He's evil, Han. I think he engineered that whole business with the Battle of Nar Shaddaa just to get rid of Sarn Shild."

"Oh, yeah," Han said. "Good old Sarn Shild. 'Darling' Shild, wasn't it? You made such a cute couple."

She winced at the sarcasm. "As I explained to Lando, that wasn't what it looked like."

"It *looked* pretty bad, Bria," Han said. "Not one of my better days, you know? To see you there, cooing at him . . ."

Her lips tightened. "I was on assignment. I know how it looked, but Shild wasn't interested in me that

way. I was lucky. But I've done things for the Resistance
I didn't much like . . . and I'll do them again if I have to.
Whatever it takes."

Han was mulling over what she'd said. "You really
think the whole invasion of Hutt space was something
the *Emperor* engineered? But Shild did it! How is that
possible?"

"I was with him, Han, and something very strange
was going on, believe me," Bria said. "Shild changed,
Han. It was scary. Between one month and the next, he
became a different man. Suddenly he was plotting to
take over Hutt space, and started talking about over-
throwing the Emperor."

Han shook his head. "That's crazy."

"I know. I can't account for it, except . . ." she hesitated. "If I tell you, you'll think *I'm* losing it."

"What? Tell me."

She took a deep breath. "They say the Emperor
has . . . abilities. That he can influence people to do
things. Some kind of mental influence."

"Like mind-reading?"

"I don't know," she said. "Maybe. I know it sounds
impossible, but that's the only explanation I can come up
with that makes sense. Shild was popular and ambitious
and corrupt, and he posed a threat to the consolidation
of power. So the Emperor just . . . encouraged . . .
Shild's ambition until he destroyed himself with that assault on Nal Hutta."

Han frowned. "What about Greelanx? How did he
figure into the plan? And who killed him? I kept expecting them to pin it on me, but they just hushed it up. I
never heard anything about it on the news." Han re-
pressed a shudder at the memory of standing in that
locked room next to Greelanx's office and listening

to that loud, uncanny breathing, that heavy, ominous tread. . . .

Bria leaned forward, and, unconsciously, Han did too. Her voice dropped to a whisper, a bare thread of sound. "They say it was . . . Vader."

Han was whispering too. "Vader? You mean Darth Vader?"

She nodded. "Darth Vader. He's the Emperor's . . ." She hesitated, searching for a term. ". . . enforcer."

Han sat back. He'd heard of the guy, but he'd never encountered him. "Huh," he said. "Well, I'm just glad they didn't try and finger yours truly."

Bria nodded. "Rebel intelligence later discovered that Admiral Greelanx was under Imperial orders to make the attack fail. The Hutt bribe was incidental. My guess is that it was all a set-up from the beginning, part of an Imperial plan to discredit and eliminate Shild. And to hurt Desilijic and the smugglers. You'll notice that Besadii, who supplies the Empire with slaves, wasn't affected."

Han thought it over. "It still sounds crazy, but you do hear things about the Emperor. Spooky things. I always just dismissed them as people bein' hysterical." He laughed shortly and took a swig of his ale. "Pretty scary . . . *if* it's true."

She shrugged. "Neither of us will probably ever know. But this is ancient history, now. Not what I came to talk to you about. Han, I—"

Bria's low-voiced conversation broke off as a couple of smugglers slid into the booth opposite theirs. Han looked around. "Place is filling up," he said. "Want to get outta here?"

She nodded. Han followed her out onto the street, and they walked briskly, without talking, until they were on a quieter side street. The glidewalk was broken, and there were few sentients around. Han looked at her. "You were saying?"

She looked over at him. "Han, I need your help."

He recalled what Jabba had told him. "With the assault on Ylesia?"

She nodded and smiled. "Quick as ever. Yes. Jabba's bankrolling us. We're going to take the whole planet, Han."

Now it was Han's turn to shrug. "Not my problem, sister. I've changed, too. I ain't in the charity business. I only play for profit, these days. I don't stick my neck out for anyone."

She nodded. "So I hear. I'm not asking for charity. It's profit I'm talking about. More credits than you'd make on a hundred smuggling runs."

"What do you want from me, then?" Han realized that his anger at her was building, though he wasn't quite sure why. It was almost as though he'd have been happier if she *had* asked him to help her for old times' sake, or something. But that didn't make any sense.

"The Rebel Alliance is still very new, Han," she said. "Our people have guts and loyalty, but most of them aren't seasoned fighters. My own Red Hand Squadron has experience, but we can't handle this job all by ourselves."

Han stared at her in surprise and more than a little unease. "Red Hand Squadron? *You* command Red Hand Squadron?"

She nodded. "It's a good group. We've seen some action."

"I've heard of it," Han said. "I've heard you give no quarter to slavers."

She shrugged and didn't answer. "Anyway, as I was saying, the Resistance needs help to get us down through the Ylesian atmosphere. Experienced pilots to guide our ships in. Maybe some help with the fighting, but, let's face it, you've seen the Ylesian defenses. A bunch of Gamorreans and other losers who sleep on duty. It's not the ground assault I'm worried about, it's their blasted atmosphere. The Corellian Resistance has already lost one ship there."

Han nodded. He was mad clear through, but he was hiding it well. He wanted to hear the whole thing before he let her have it. "That atmosphere is tricky, all right. But the average smuggler pilot has dealt with worse. So . . . you need pilots to guide your ships in, maybe provide some armed backup. In return for what?"

"Spice, Han. You know that Besadii has been stockpiling it. Choice andris, ryll, carsunum, and, of course, glitterstim. They've been trying to drive the prices way up, and there are warehouses stuffed full of it. We'll split the take with the smugglers."

Han nodded at her. "Go on. . . ."

She looked at him. "And for you and me . . . there will be Teroenza's treasure room. Picture how much he's added over ten years. Hundreds of thousands of credits worth of antiquities. He's bound to have maybe a million credits worth of stuff . . . maybe two. Think about it."

"How many troops do you have?"

"I'm not sure yet. I have to report back to our command ship for this sector. We've asked for aid from any Resistance group that wants to help, particularly the Bothans and the Sullustans—there are a lot of Sullustans and Bothans on Ylesia. We figure they may want to be part of the rescue."

"And you're going to free the slaves."

"We'll take them along with our share of the spice. And before we leave, we'll reduce those factories to slag, along with everything else. We're going to shut that hellhole planet down for good."

Han considered. "What about the priests? The Exultation could be a powerful weapon. I've seen it knock people on their butts who weren't expecting it."

She nodded. "Jabba's taking care of them. They'll be assassinated before we ever land."

Han looked at her, and felt cold rage wash through him. *How dare she? Come back and ask me to get involved with her little revenge scheme?* "You'd better get your timing down pat."

"Yes," she agreed. "This will be the biggest military operation the new Alliance has ever tried. We hope to get recruits from it, as well as the spice. Financing a revolution is an expensive proposition."

"Ambitious," Han said, dryly. "Why not just attack Coruscant if you want to commit suicide?"

"It's doable," she insisted. "Ylesia isn't that heavily guarded. Han, you were there. Remember? Oh, I'm sure we'll encounter some resistance, but my people can deal with that. Your friends can stay out of the shooting until we secure the place. The combat experience will be good for our troops. If we can pull this off, it will be an example to inspire other planets to join the Alliance. Our only hope of defeating the Empire is if we unite."

Han looked at her. "And this is why you came to me. To get me to contact the smugglers for you, encourage 'em to join up with the Resistance for this little mission."

"Lando told me that you and Mako Spince are people they'll listen to. I knew you. I don't know Spince."

Han finally let his impassive mask drop, and glared at her. "So what you're sayin' is that you dump me ten years ago, ignore me that whole time, and then you come back thinkin' I'll *help* you put my friends' lives in danger. I don't trust you, Bria. I've heard about Red Hand Squadron, all right. You ain't the woman I used to know, and that's plain."

"I have changed," she said, her eyes holding his. "I admit it. So have you."

"Lando told me you still cared about me," Han said, coldly. "I think you were lyin' to him, plannin' even then to *use* me. You don't give a hoot about me—about anything we used to have. You only care about your revolution, and you don't care who you walk over to reach your goal." He snorted. "And all that bilge about Sarn Shild . . . sure. Right. You expect me to *believe* a man like that would keep you around if you weren't—weren't—a—" Han finished with a word in Rodian used for the lowest class of streetwalker.

Bria's mouth dropped open and her hand found the grip of her blaster. Han tensed, ready to go for his own, but her eyes suddenly flooded with tears . . . and he knew then she wouldn't draw. "How *dare* you?"

"I dare a lot these days, sister," Han said. "And I say what I think. I dare to think you're a real lowlife comin' back here this way. You can forget sucking me in again with your pretty face. I've changed, all right. I've gotten *smart*—smart enough to see right through you."

"Fine," she said, blinking back the tears. "You just turn your back on both me and a fortune. I don't call that smart, Han. I call it stupid. And the idea that a *drug runner* is putting on moral airs is really laughable, you know?"

"I'm a smuggler," Han shouted. "We have our own code!"

"Yeah, running drugs for Hutts!" she was yelling too. "You and Jabba! Birds of a feather!"

The idea that she would class him with the Hutts

was the last straw. Han spun around and started to walk away.

"Fine!" she cried. "I'll go see Mako Spince, that's what I'll do. He can't be as dumb as you!"

Her unwitting pun made Han laugh nastily. "Fine," he snarled, not turning around. "Have fun gettin' him to talk. Goodbye, Bria."

He strode away from her, his bootheels clicking against the permacrete, his head high. It felt good to leave her standing there, looking after him.

It felt *real* good. . . .

Durga faced Prince Xizor's image on his comm unit. "Guri has explained your difficulty," the prince said. "I will dispatch two companies of mercenaries under the capable command of Willum Kamaran to Ylesia. Commander Kamaran's Nova Force will help you keep Teroenza in line until he can be dealt with. Which should be speedily, my friend."

"Thank you, Your Highness," Durga said. "As Guri may have told you, I will share the profits from Ylesia with you this year, to recompense you for your help. Fifteen percent."

The Faleen prince's mouth curved down, and he shook his head sadly. "Durga, Durga . . . I thought you had some respect for me. Thirty percent for the next two years."

Durga batted his bulbous eyes in disbelief. *Worse than I ever imagined!* He drew himself up. "Your Highness, if I granted you that, I would be deposed as leader of Besadii."

"But if you do not have my troops in place, and soon, you will lose Ylesia altogether," the prince pointed out, truthfully.

"Twenty percent, one year," Durga said, feeling actual pain as he spoke the words. "They will not have to be there long, remember."

"Thirty percent, two years," the head of Black Sun said. "I do not negotiate."

Durga drew a deep breath, feeling the ghosts of bruises and injuries from his battle with Jiliac awaken. "Very well," he said, sullenly.

Xizor smiled pleasantly. "Fine. The mercenaries will embark as soon as possible for Ylesia. It is a pleasure doing business with you, my friend."

It took every bit of willpower Durga could summon to say, "Very well, Your Highness. Thank you."

He cut the connection and slumped in despair, imagining what Aruk would say to all of this. *I'm trapped,* he thought. *Trapped. All I can do is try to make the best of it. . . .*

Han did not sleep well that night. Thoughts of Bria and her proposition raced through his mind like an asteroid on a collision course. *I can't trust her . . . can I? I don't want to see her . . . do I?*

He dozed, and dreamed of mounds of glitterstim, which mutated without warning into piles of credits. He leaped into those piles, rolled around in them, shouting joyfully, and suddenly Bria was there with him, and he was holding her, rolling over with her, kissing her in the midst of piles and piles and piles of credits . . . more wealth than he'd ever imagined. . . .

He jerked awake with a gasp, and then lay there, his arms behind his head, staring into the darkness.

Maybe I ought to do it, he thought. *This might be my big chance to make that big stake. I could get out . . . make a bundle, and retire. Find myself a nice little place in the Corporate Sector and just let the Empire go to blazes all by itself. . . .*

He lay there, tossing and turning, punching his pillows in frustration, until he could stand it no longer. Swinging out of bed, he headed into the 'fresher, then dragged on clean clothes. He also combed his hair, reflecting ruefully that the haircut had gone beyond the realm of "should get one" to "want to be mistaken for Chewie's cousin?"

Then, carrying his boots, he tiptoed out through the dark, silent apartment, not wanting to wake Chewie, or Jarik, who was sleeping on the couch. He was almost at the door when he stubbed his toe on something unyielding and heard a plaintive electronic bleat.

ZeeZee! Han dropped his boots, swore aloud, then snarled at the antiquated droid, who was babbling apologies in its twittering, querulous voice.

"Shut up!" Han snarled, and slammed out the door. He was back a second later to collect his boots, and then gone again.

The Smuggler's Rest was on the border of the Corellian section. Han arrived there before the place was even open, and had to buzz for the night-clerk. It suddenly occurred to him that he didn't know what name Bria had registered under, but he'd barely begun to describe her, when the bored clerk brightened. "Oh *her*," he said, licking his lips. "She expecting you, buddy?"

"Let's just say she'll be glad to see me," Han said, sliding a credit piece across the counter.

"Okay, sure. Room 7A."

Han went up in the ancient turbolift, and then walked down the dark, noisome hallway. He tapped on the door. Moments later, he heard her voice, sounding wide-awake. "Who's there?"

"It's me, Bria. Han," he said.

There was a long pause, then the locks clicked and the door swung open into the darkness. "Come in with your hands up," Bria's voice said.

Han walked in as directed, and only when the door was closed behind him did the lights come on. He turned to find Bria wearing a nightshirt that was too short for her, her blaster in her hand. "What do you want?" Her voice was anything but friendly.

Han found it hard not to look at her long, shapely legs. "Uh . . . just wanted to talk to you. I've . . . I'm . . . reconsidering your proposition."

"You are, eh?" She still didn't look friendly, but at least she lowered the gun. "Okay, give me a minute."

Grabbing her clothes, she disappeared into the 'fresher, and came out again a minute later, fully clothed, down to her boots.

Han nodded down at her right leg. "What's in the boot?"

"Hold-out blaster," she said, with a small, feral smile. "A nice little ladies' model."

"I see," Han said. He sat down on the edge of the rumpled bed, feeling her warmth still amid the covers. Bria sprawled in the room's single chair. "You go lookin' for Mako after we . . . parted?"

"I made some inquiries," she said, and her mouth twisted. "Found out why you were laughing when you walked away."

"Yeah," Han said. "Tough break for Mako. I don't know what he'll do now." He cleared his throat. "Anyhow, I didn't come here to talk about Mako. I've been thinking about your offer. Maybe I was too hasty. Let's face it . . . I was sore about the way you dumped me. I had to get that outta my system, maybe."

He hesitated, and she stared at him. Her hair was hanging in wisps around her face, and Han was glad to realize that it wasn't all chopped off. She must have had it up in a tight bun earlier. She waved at him. "Go on."

"So, uh . . . yeah. Maybe I shot my mouth off a little, earlier," Han admitted. "Wouldn't be the first time."

She widened her eyes. "No! You can't mean it!"

Han resolutely ignored the sarcasm. "Anyhow . . . it won't happen again. So . . . I want in. I'll give my friends your proposition, and help train your pilots how to deal with the Ylesian atmosphere. I'll bet some of the privateers would also want in. I'll talk to 'em in return for what you promised me. Fifty percent of Teroenza's treasure room, or seventy-five thousand credits worth of the spice, whichever is more."

She considered. "And you'll be civil?"

"Yeah," Han said. "I'm always civil to business partners. And that's all this is. Just . . . business."

Bria nodded. "It's a deal." She leaned forward and offered her hand. "Just business."

Han took it, reflecting that she had a grip many men would envy. "Okay."

Chapter Thirteen:

. . . AND FIRE

Durga activated his comm system, and keyed in the codes his parent had given him years ago. He wondered if they'd still be the correct ones. This was a very important call. . . .

The connection took several minutes to establish, and it was not a good one. His party must be a long way from the Outer Rim. . . .

Finally, the picture coalesced. The holo-image of the most famous bounty hunter in the galaxy appeared . . . wavering, all the edges fuzzy. But Durga could hear Fett's mechanically filtered tones clearly.

"Boba Fett, it is I, Durga, Lord of Besadii," the Hutt said. "Greetings."

"Lord Durga," the flat voice conveyed nothing . . .

not interest, surprise or eagerness. Nothing. "I am a long way from the Outer Rim. What is it?"

"I wish you to take on a Priority bounty," Durga said. "The situation is very delicate, potentially volatile. That is why I need you. I know that you perform exactly as you specify you will. There can be no mistakes in this case. I need the best."

Boba Fett inclined his head. "You are willing to pay the extra for a Priority bounty? I must be adequately recompensed for turning my attention away from other assignments and concentrating solely on yours."

"Yes, yes, I am," Durga said. "The bounty is on the High Priest of Ylesia, Teroenza. I am willing to pay the sum of two hundred thousand credits."

"Not enough. Three hundred thousand," Boba Fett said. "And I will head back for the Outer Rim immediately."

Durga hesitated, then nodded, "Very well. The timing here is crucial. I wish to have you bring me Teroenza's horn as proof of his death. But you must wait to make the kill until I have left Nal Hutta and am within five hours of landing on Ylesia. You must kill Teroenza in such a way that none of the other t'landa Til will know of his death for some hours. Otherwise, if the other priests discover that their leader has been killed, they may try to stage a revolt. Understood?"

"Affirmative. Contact you and confirm the timing before making the kill. Make sure no other t'landa Til realize that he is dead."

"Correct." Durga than recited his ship ID codes, and Fett assured him that he had them.

"I would like to remind you of the terms regarding a Priority bounty," Fett said. "I will concentrate on reaching the target you have specified, and will take no other bounties until I have delivered the High Priest's horn to you. And the Priority bounty for Teroenza is three hundred thousand."

"Correct," Durga confirmed.

"Fett out."

The fuzzy holo-image of the armor-clad bounty hunter rippled, then vanished.

Durga then activated his comm for local frequencies, so he could check in with Zier. His Hutt lieutenant had assured him that he had narrowed the search for Teroenza's successor down to three t'landa Til. Durga would go to interview them personally, and select the new High Priest of Ylesia.

Durga ruminated about how pleasant it would be to have the bloody horn of the High Priest in his two dainty hands. Perhaps he'd have it mounted, and hang it on his wall. . . .

Over the next two days, Bria Tharen and Han Solo traveled around Nar Shaddaa together, recruiting smugglers and privateers to serve as pilot guides and—in the case of the privateers—potential backup for her Ylesian operation. They stressed the easy pickings to be had on Ylesia, the wealth of spice stockpiled by Besadii.

Both were careful to stick by their "just business" agreement, but Bria sensed a growing tension in Han, and knew that it reflected her own feelings.

He told her about what he'd been doing for the past ten years, and she told him a little about her life with the Resistance. She explained to him that after leaving him on Coruscant, she'd wandered from world to world, constantly fighting her craving for the Exultation. "Two times I actually bought a ticket and stood in line to board a ship back to Ylesia," she said. "And both times when it came down to it, I just couldn't. I stepped out of line and went off and collapsed."

Finally, she'd found a group on Corellia that had helped her deal with her addiction, helped her realize why she felt so empty, so driven. "It took me months of hard digging into myself," she said. "Months to figure out why I wanted to hurt myself. I finally got it through my head that just because my mother hated and despised me for not being what she wanted me to be, I didn't have to hate myself. I didn't have to destroy myself in some twisted attempt to please her."

Han, remembering Bria's mother, gave her a sympathetic glance. "I used to feel cheated that I'll never know who my parents were. That is . . . until I met your mom, Bria," he said. "There are worse things than being an orphan."

She gave a shaky laugh. "You are right, Han."

Many smugglers and privateers were very intrigued by Bria's proposition, and they signed up droves of them. It didn't hurt that Jabba was backing the enterprise and urging those who piloted for him to go. Many of the pilots who'd worked for him in some capacity were agreeing to be pilot guides.

All the while, the Rebel Alliance was assembling ships out in space so the captains and ground commanders could be drilled on the battle plan. After Bria and Han had recruited enough smuggler captains so they'd have at least one smuggler per group of Rebel assault ships, they took the *Millennium Falcon* to rendezvous at the Rebel deep space coordinates—a spot well off the regular shipping lanes, but within one easy hyperspace jump of Ylesia.

Bria was fascinated by the *Falcon* and suitably impressed by her speed and armament. Han enjoyed showing her around his ship, pointing out all his special modifications. In preparation for this ground assault, he'd finally gotten around to getting Shug and Chewie to help him install that belly gun he'd wanted for so long. Since this was a ground assault, there was a good chance that it would come in handy.

When the *Falcon* was on an approach vector to dock with the *Retribution*, Bria smiled at Han. "You showed me yours . . . now let me show you mine," she said.

Han laughed, and it was the most relaxed moment they'd had since they'd met. "Beautiful ship," he said, admiring the Marauder corvette's clean, streamlined silhouette against the starfield.

They were greeted when they disembarked by the captain of the *Retribution*, Tedris Bjalin. Han regarded him in astonishment. "Tedris!" he exclaimed, staring at the tall, balding man in the Rebel uniform. "How in the galaxy did *you* get here?"

Bria looked from one to the other. "You know each other?"

"We sure do," Han said, pumping Tedris's hand, and exchanging backslaps. "Tedris and I graduated in the same class in the Academy."

"It's a long story," Bjalin said. "After what you said to me that time aboard the *Destiny*, I couldn't help thinking more and more about how the service was getting as corrupt as the Empire. And then . . ." his bony features twisted. "Han, I'm from Tyshapahl, remember?"

Han had forgotten. He stared at his old friend, realization slowly dawning. "Oh . . . Tedris . . . I'm sorry. Your family?" The Corellian had met Tedris's family, during graduation.

"Killed during the massacre," Tedris confirmed. "After that, I couldn't stay. I knew I had to fight them, any way I could."

Han nodded.

Bria took Han on a tour of her ship. He was seeing yet another side of her, and, as an ex-military man himself, was impressed by the discipline and alertness of her troops. The sentients of Red Hand Squadron obviously revered their commander. Han discovered that many of them were ex-slaves, people willing to give their lives to the mission of freeing those in bondage.

Bria took Han to meet with other Rebel Commanders, and they attended several planning sessions for the raid. The Bothans were providing security, and the Sullustans had sent ten ships and nearly two hundred troops. In the years since Han and Bria had left Ylesia, Sullust had lost many citizens who had gone to Ylesia to become Pilgrims.

In addition to many ships from the Corellian Resistance, there were troops from Alderaan (though much of the Alderaanian support was in the form of medical personnel, transport pilots, and other non-combatants) and Chandrila. "It was hard to convince the Alliance that this could be done," Bria confided to Han. "But it's become brutally apparent that our troops need combat experience. I was able to convince HQ that this raid would help the troops gain the confidence to start going up against the Imperials."

All of the Rebel ships from the Outer Rim had been detailed to the raid. Han surveyed the gathering fleet, and conceded that maybe they did have a chance. He wound up giving a number of briefings to the Rebel pilots who'd be flying the Rebel assault landing shuttles into the Ylesian atmosphere.

During his first such briefing, Han ran into yet another old friend. "Jalus!" he exclaimed, as the small, droopy-jowled Sullustan trooped into the *Retribution*'s briefing area. "What the heck are *you* doin' here?"

Jalus Nebl pointed to his ragtag Rebel uniform.

"What does it look like?" he squeaked. "The *Ylesian Dream* is now *Dream of Freedom*, and she's served the Rebellion well for several years now."

Han introduced Bria to the Sullustan, and she was pleased to at last meet the brave pilot who had saved them from *Helot's Shackle*. The three reminisced about the past, and their daring escape from the slave planet. Both Jalus Nebl and Han were impressed to hear that Bria's group had taken *Helot's Shackle*, now renamed *Retribution*.

The reconditioned *Retribution* would be flying with the Resistance on this raid, carrying assault shuttles and backup troops under the command of another Rebel Commander.

As Bria watched Han interact with the Rebel Commanders and other mission personnel, she realized that she had never been happier. Han seemed to enjoy the chance to return to the old military lifestyle, eating meals in the galley, joking and talking with her troops. They were respectful of his knowledge and his military background as an Imperial officer—especially after Tedris Bjalin recounted some of "Slick's" wilder escapades during their Academy days.

She found herself hoping that Han would realize that the Resistance was where he belonged—with the Resistance, and with her. Every moment they were together was like coming home, she thought—though she was careful to keep her "just business" distance.

All the while, she wondered what Han was thinking about her. . . .

At the end of their second day with the gathering Rebel fleet in their deep-space rendezvous, Bria received a message that she was needed to meet with some potential allies from the Resistance on Ord Mantell. Han offered to take her there in the *Falcon*, proud of the chance to show off his ship's speed—though the first time he tried to jump into hyperspace, the cranky *Falcon* refused to cooperate. When two elbow-whacks failed to work, Han had to spend several sweaty and embarrassed minutes with a hydrospanner to get his ship to cooperate.

Once they were in hyperspace, Bria sat in the co-pilot's seat, watching Han handle his ship, admiring his sureness. "She's a wonderful ship, Han," she said. "I watched you win her, you know."

Han turned to her, surprised. "What? You were there?"

Bria explained about her trip to Bespin during the big sabacc tournament. "I was rooting for you," she said. "When you won, I wanted to—" she recalled herself, blushed, and fell silent.

"Wanted to what?" Han asked, his eyes very intent.

"Oh . . . I just wished I could break cover and congratulate you," she said. "By the way, whatever did you do to that Barabel to make her so mad?"

Han looked at her, then his mouth twitched and he burst out laughing. "You met Shallamar?"

"Not formally," Bria said, dryly, "but I wound up standing beside her during some of the play after she'd been eliminated. That was one cranky reptiloid, let me tell you."

Han chuckled, then explained about how he and Shallamar had had a run-in back on Devaron five years ago. "She told me she was going to bite my head off," Han said. "And she'd have done it, too, if it hadn't been for Chewie."

"Devaron? Oh, yes, I remember—" Bria said, and then, at Han's look, fell silent again.

She bit her lip before the intensity of his gaze. "So it *was* you that day at the Ylesian revival," Han said. "I thought I was seein' things. I swore off drinkin' for months after that day."

Bria nodded. "Yes, that was me, Han. But I couldn't let you blow my cover. I was in that crowd for a mission."

"What was that mission?"

She met his eyes steadily. "To assassinate Veratil, the t'landa Til. You fouled it up, though. Far as I know, Veratil is still alive. Though probably not for long."

Han regarded her for a long moment. "You really have done just about anything for the Resistance, haven't you?"

Bria was distressed by his stare. "Don't look at me like that, Han!" she cried. "They're evil! They deserve to be killed!"

He nodded slowly. "Yeah, I guess they do," he said. "But . . . it's kinda unnerving, you know?"

She gave him a shaky smile. "Sometimes I unnerve myself."

When they reached Ord Mantell, Bria met with the Resistance leaders there to explain the mission and its importance. She was elated that, after their meeting, the Resistance promised to dispatch three ships and a hundred troops, plus appropriate support and medical personnel, immediately.

As Han and Bria were preparing to board the *Falcon* for the trip back to the Rebel deep-space rendezvous, one of the junior officers came up to her with a message flimsy. She scanned it, then looked up at Han. She gave him a tight smile. "HQ just got a message from Togoria. There's a small contingent of Togorians who have volunteered to come along. They want us to pick them up on our way back."

Han smiled slowly. "Muuurgh and Mrrov?" he guessed.

"It doesn't say. But it's a good bet they're part of the group," Bria said. "Can we?"

"Sure," he said, not meeting her eyes. "Togoria's a pretty world. I wouldn't mind seeing it again."

Bria looked away, too. It was on a Togorian beach that she and Han had first become close. It was a beautiful world, fraught with memories for both of them.

They didn't talk much during the trip. Bria found herself so nervous that her stomach was in knots. She wondered how Han felt. . . .

Han eased the *Falcon* down onto the landing field bordering Caross, the largest city on Togoria. After completing his post-flight checks and updating his log, he and Bria headed for the landing ramp. A group of Togorians were already heading out to the field, and Han thought he recognized one huge black male with white chest hair and whiskers. And there was a smaller, orange and white female with him.

Bria smiled excitedly. "Muuurgh and Mrrov!"

The humans jogged down the ramp, and reached the ground just in time to be seized and hugged so violently their feet left the ground. "Muuurgh!" Han shouted, so glad to see his old friend that he wound up thumping the huge felinoid on the chest with his fists while his feet dangled. "How are ya, buddy?"

"Han . . ." Muuurgh was nearly choked with emotion. Togorians were an emotional people, especially the males. "Han Solo . . . Muuurgh very happy see Han Solo again. Too long it has been!"

He obviously hasn't been practicing his Basic, Han thought, amused. Muuurgh's Basic had always been rather fractured, but after all this time, it was worse than ever.

"Hey, Muuurgh! Mrrov! It's great to see you both!"

After their greetings were over, Mrrov explained that there was a contingent of Togorians who'd had run-ins with Ylesia over the years who wanted to be part of the assault. "Six of our people were either enslaved or close to those enslaved there, Han," Mrrov said. "We wish to have a part in making sure that no other Togorians will ever again be trapped by that terrible place."

Han nodded. "Well, we can get started any time you wish," he said.

Muuurgh shook his head. "Not possible until tomorrow, Han. Sarrah's mosgoth was attacked mid-flight by big liphon. Broke its wing. Sarrah has borrowed mosgoth, sent us message, will be here tomorrow. Tonight Han and Bria our honored guests, yes?"

Han looked at Bria and shrugged. "Uh, sure," he said.

She didn't meet his eyes. "Fine. . . ."

They spent the afternoon catching up with their friends on ten years' of history. Muuurgh and Mrrov seemed a very happy couple—even though, in true Togorian tradition, they spent only a month out of each year together. They had two cubs, both female, and Han and Bria met them. One was barely more than a kit, and she was extraordinarily cute. Bria and Han spent a couple of hours playing with them in the beautiful gardens.

That evening, the humans were wined and dined with the best of Togorian food and drink. Togorian storytellers regaled them with tales of their own escapades from ten years ago, when they'd escaped from Ylesia. Han barely recognized himself—the accounts had obviously been "enhanced" over the years, until he emerged as such a heroic figure it was almost laughable.

Han was careful with the strong Togorian liquor, and noticed that Bria drank only water. "I can't drink," she said, when asked. "I'm scared I'll get to like it too much.

I have to be careful . . . once addicted, you can get addicted again, to other things."

Han admired her restraint, and said so.

After the festivities were over, Muuurgh and Mrrov conducted their guests to the finest of their guest apartments, then bade them goodnight.

Han and Bria stood on opposite sides of the living room and regarded each other in silence for a long, uncomfortable moment. Han glanced at the door leading to the one bedroom. "Uh . . . guess Muuurgh and Mrrov still think we're an item," he said.

"Guess so," she agreed, unable to meet his eyes.

"Well, I guess it's the pallet out here for me," Han said.

"Hey," Bria remonstrated, "I'm a soldier. I've slept in mudholes before, with no blanket. No need to treat me like a lady, Han." She smiled and took out a decicred piece. "Tell you what . . . I'll flip you for the bed."

Han grinned at her, his most charming smile. "Okay, babe. Fine by me."

Bria looked at him, and their eyes locked. "Oh, dear." She sounded as though she'd just run four or five klicks.

Han was feeling a bit breathless himself. " 'Oh dear' what?" he said, taking a step toward her.

Bria smiled shakily. "The galaxy is no longer safe for humanoid females," she said. "You've learned what you can do with that lopsided smile, haven't you?"

As a matter of fact, Han did have some idea . . . and so did a number of women he could name. He took another two slow steps in her direction, and chuckled, genuinely amused. "Hey . . ." he said. "There are times when it works better than my blaster."

Bria was so tense he wondered if she were going to bolt, but she didn't move as he took another step toward her. Looking down, Han saw that her hand was shaking. "Aren't you going to flip that thing?" he asked softly.

She nodded and took a deep breath, and her hand steadied a bit. "Sure. Call it."

"You sure it's not a trick coin?" Han asked, taking another step.

"Hey!" she protested. "It's a real decicred!" With mock indignation, Bria showed him the disk, twirling it to demonstrate that it was indeed a regular coin. On the obverse was the head of the Emperor, on the reverse was stamped the symbol of the Empire.

Han took another step, and now he could have reached out and touched her shoulder. "Okay . . . I pick . . . heads," he said, quietly.

Bria swallowed and flipped the coin, but she missed catching it, because she was shaking again. Han, however, did not miss. He caught the coin, held it without looking. "Heads we share the bed. . . ." he said softly. "Tails . . . we share the floor."

"But . . . we agreed . . ." she was stammering and trembling all over now. "Just . . . business . . ."

Han tossed the coin over his shoulder, and in one lunge he pulled Bria into his arms. He kissed her with all the pent-up passion of the past days . . . and all those lost years. Kissed her mouth, her forehead, her hair, her ears . . . and then returned to her mouth. Finally, when he raised his head, he breathed, "I say . . . the heck with business . . . right?"

"Right . . ." she murmured, and then it was her turn to kiss him. She wound her arms around his neck, holding him as tightly as he held her.

Behind them, forgotten, the decicred piece lay on the woven matting covering the floor, shining faintly in the dimness. . . .

• • •

The next morning, Han woke up smiling. He got up and went out to stand on the little balcony overlooking the beautiful Togorian garden. He breathed deeply, hearing the twittering of the tiny flying lizards and remembered one alighting on Bria's finger all those years ago, that first time on the beach.

He wished they had time to go back to that beach. . . .

Hey, he thought, *when this Ylesian thing is over, we'll have all the time in the world . . . and all the credits we could want. We'll come back here. Then maybe we'll head for the Corporate Sector, do some business. With the* Falcon, *we can go anywhere, do anything. . . .*

He wondered whether Bria would actually leave the Resistance for him. After what they'd shared last night, he didn't see how she couldn't. They were good together, so good there was no way they'd be apart from now on. . . .

Han heard a step behind him, but didn't turn, only stood staring out at the garden, inhaling the spicy scent of the Togorian tree-flowers. Arms slid around his waist, and he felt her hair against his back as she leaned against him. "Hey . . ." she said quietly. "Good morning."

"It's good all right," he said quietly. "The best in a long time. Ten years, I think."

"Did I tell you last night that I love you?" she murmured, kissing the back of his neck. "You need a haircut. . . ."

"Several times," he replied. "But you can say it again if you want."

"I love you. . . ."

"Sounds good," he said. "I think you need more practice, though. Try it again. . . ."

She laughed. "You're getting a swelled head, Han."

He chuckled, and turned to hold her. "You know, the *Falcon* is going to be so full of huge Togorians all the way back to the rendezvous coordinates, that you just might have to sit on my lap."

"I could manage that," she said.

Sarrah proved to be extremely short for a Togorian, only about two meters tall. But he was in excellent condition, his muscles sliding beneath his sleek black fur like oiled cords.

On their way back to the deep-space rendezvous, Han swung by Nar Shaddaa to pick up Jarik and Chewbacca. He'd been wondering how Chewie and Muuurgh would get along. When he introduced the Wookiee and the giant Togorian, Han was treated to the unusual sight of Chewie actually looking *up* at another being. Muuurgh regarded the Wookiee assessingly, then said, "Greetings to Han Solo's friend. He tells me you are his brother-in-fur."

Chewie roared softly, and Han translated. "Chewbacca sends greetings in return to Muuurgh," he said. "He is honored to meet a brother-in-fur from the past, the hunter Muuurgh."

Solemnly, the two huge creatures regarded each other, then both turned to Han. He looked up at them, and could tell that they liked each other. "You guys," he said, "have got a lot in common."

Indeed, said Chewie. They had Han.

"Any friend of Han Solo's is a friend of Muuurgh's," the Togorian announced.

Han heard the door signal to his apartment buzz, and opened it to find Lando standing there. For once the gambler wasn't dressed in the height of fashion, but in military style rough fatigues, and he wore heavy boots. He was armed with a blaster and a blaster rifle. "Hey!" Han said. "What's up? You goin' to a war?"

"I just heard about your little jaunt to Ylesia," Lando said. "I want in. Can I ride along on the *Falcon*?"

Han regarded his friend in surprise. "Pal, this ain't your kind of thing," he said. "We ain't expectin' much in the way of resistance from those Gamorrean guards on Ylesia, but there's bound to be some shootin'."

Lando nodded. "I'm a good shot," he said. "Han, I've almost got enough credits saved to buy a new ship, a real beauty of a sleek little yacht I've had my eye on. I figure for a share of that spice in the warehouses, this is worth a little risk to my precious hide. Another ten thousand credits, and that little beauty is mine. . . ."

Han shrugged. "Okay by me," he said. "You're welcome to join the party."

Thus, it was a *very* crowded—but thankfully short—flight back to the Rebel rendezvous coordinates.

The Rebel fleet was mostly gathered by now, along with most of the smuggler vessels. Bria and the other Rebel commanders conducted final briefings so that each smuggler and each Rebel assault group knew exactly what part they would play in the attack. Each group of Rebel assault shuttles had at least three or four smuggler ships to guide them down through the atmosphere. There were nine colonies now on Ylesia, and there were nine attack forces, each commanded by a Rebel commander like Bria.

She'd chosen the toughest objective for herself—Colony One. It boasted the largest warehouses, the most Pilgrims and the best defenses. But Bria was sure that Red Hand Squadron could handle it.

Especially with Han flying beside her. By now, Han was familiar with Jace Paol, Daino Hyx, and her other officers. He wondered if any of them realized that he and their commander were now a couple.

The assassinations would be starting any time on Ylesia, and the main attack was set for tomorrow morning (ships' standard time, which had nothing to do with day or night on Ylesia) when the Pilgrims would be desperate for the Exultation, and amenable to taking orders from anyone who promised it to them. . . .

As Han and Bria ate supper that night in *Retribution*'s galley, Han's attention was suddenly drawn to the external monitoring unit that showed the masses of gathering ships. A familiar shape—one he'd known from childhood—was moving into view.

He stopped chewing, then swallowed hastily, and pointed. "Bria! That big old *Liberator*-class transport! Where'd you get it?"

She looked at him and grinned. "Looks a bit familiar, doesn't it?"

Han nodded. "I'd swear that's *Trader's Luck*! The ship I grew up on!"

She nodded. "It is. I was saving it for a surprise. The Corellian Resistance bought it a couple of years ago at scrap prices, and we've converted it into a troop carrier. We named it the *Liberator*."

Han had heard that the vintage ship had been abandoned following Garris Shrike's death. He looked at the old vessel, feeling his throat tighten. He was glad to know that the *Liberator* now had a new life. "You're going to use her to get the Pilgrims shipped to safety, right?"

"Many of them," she agreed. "Your old home will take them to a new life, Han."

He nodded, and finished his meal, his eyes seldom leaving the huge, antique vessel. Memories flooded him . . . memories of Dewlanna, mostly. . . .

Since the *Falcon* boasted only a few sleeping bunks, Han decided to stay the night in Bria's cabin. They held each other close, each of them acutely aware that tomorrow they would be going into battle.

And in battles . . . people died.

"After tomorrow," Han whispered to her in the darkness, "we'll always be together. Promise me."

"I promise," she said. "Together."

He sighed and relaxed. "Okay," he said. "And . . . Bria?"

"Yes?"

"You watch your back tomorrow, sweetheart."

He could tell she was smiling, from the way her voice sounded. "I will. You too, okay?"

"Sure."

Hours later, Bria was awakened from a troubled doze by the soft chime of her cabin intercom. She came instantly alert, and, pulling on a robe, went into her adjoining office. The communication officer on duty told her she had an incoming message. "Send it through to me here," she said, pushing her hair back from her face.

Moments later, Bria was facing her commanding officer, Pianat Torbul. She stiffened to attention. "Sir?"

"Bria . . . just wanted to wish you luck tomorrow," he said. "And to tell you . . ." he hesitated.

"Yes? Tell me what?" she prompted.

"I can't be specific. But our intelligence reports that the Empire has something *big* underway. Really big. Something that could crush the entire Rebel Alliance in one or two engagements."

Bria stared at him, in shock. "Some kind of secret fleet?" she asked.

"I can't tell you," he reminded her. "But bigger than that."

Bria couldn't imagine what he was talking about, but she'd grown used to the "need to know" system long ago. "Okay, so what does that have to do with this raid tomorrow?"

"It's going to take everything we have, every resource we can muster, every credit we can scrape together, to deal with this," Torbul said. "Your mission was important before this . . . now it's critical. Take everything you can get, Bria. Weapons, spice . . . everything."

"Sir . . . that's my objective," she said, her heart beginning to thud.

"I know that. I just . . . thought you should know. We're dispatching several intelligence teams to Ralltiir to try and find out more. They'll need credits for bribes, surveillance equipment . . . you know the drill."

"Of course," Bria said. "Sir, I won't fail you."

"I know you won't," Torbul said. "I shouldn't have contacted you, perhaps . . . you're under enough pressure. But I thought you should know."

"I appreciate your telling me, sir. Thank you."

Torbul gave her a quick salute and broke the connection. Bria sat there in her office, wondering if she should go back to bed, or just start the day early.

She heard Han's voice, a little rough with sleep, from the other room. "Bria? Everything okay?"

"Everything's fine, Han," she called. "I'll be there shortly."

Rising, she paced slowly back and forth, remembering what he'd said to her earlier. They'd be together . . . always. *Yes, we will,* she thought. *We'll be together. We'll guard each other's backs, and together we'll fight and we'll prevail against the Empire. And if we have to sacrifice to achieve that . . . we will.*

She knew that Han would understand about the treasure and the credits. He pretended to be such a mercenary, but at heart, he wasn't, she knew that. . . .

Her mind once more at rest, her resolve firm, Bria went back to bed. . . .

Sunset at Ylesian Colony Five. The ruddy rays of the low sun, breaking through a hundred gaps in the massed clouds, were projected as pastel spikes across the sky. By the choppy waters of the Sea of Hope, the robe-clad Pilgrims assembled on the beach cast long shadows across the sand.

Pohtarza, Head Sacredot of the colony, raised his ugly t'landa Til head and surveyed the crowd, his horn sweeping slowly back and forth as he did so. His bulbous eyes shone like blood as they bulged from his grayish, wrinkled flesh. After a moment, he brought up his diminutive arms, and the ceremony began.

"The One is All," he intoned in the rumbling, nasal-heavy language of the t'landa Til.

Five hundred voices echoed the phrase back. . . . *The One is All.*

At that very moment, at Colony Four on the other side of the planet, it was just after midnight. Dark clouds drifted across the moonless night sky, extinguishing stars, making the night even blacker. On the wall of the Priests' Quarters, there was a soft, chitinous scratching. Ylesian vermin frantically darted away in all directions.

Noy Waglla, small and bug-like herself, scuttled up the smooth permacrete and, barely pausing to chew a hole in the grating, through the window. She crouched, poised, on the sill.

Below her, in the darkness, she could hear the sleeping noises of the Priests she had come to kill. Jabba would pay well for this, enough that she might someday be able to return to her own species. The great creatures in their sleeping harnesses filled the small room, made it stink of musk. The Hyallp crawled up the nearest rough-textured harness, and paused below the enormous head. The t'landa Til shifted slightly, and she backed away, alarmed, but, after a moment, the Priest's snoring resumed. Waglla advanced even closer.

This is going to be easy. . . . Waglla seized the large vial strapped to her back in her formidable mandibles, pulled out the stopper with her palps. Jabba had tested the substance himself. A drop of the poison called *srejptan*, placed on the Sacredot's lower lip, would kill even the largest t'landa Til in seconds, silently and without struggle. Retracting several of her legs, Waglla climbed toward the Priest's mouth.

"The All is One," intoned Pohtarza.
The All is One.

Aiaks Fwa, Whiphid assassin and bounty hunter, waited in the corridor leading to the underground mud baths of Colony Seven. It had been a tedious few weeks, living as Pilgrim, trying to blend in, when all his instincts called for getting it over with, hunting the ugly *muphrida* down and escaping. But the Bloated One had specified tonight as the time, and Fwa wanted to collect his full fee.

The sound of t'landa Til voices echoed up from the dimness below, and Fwa heard their characteristic shuffling gait. The assassin checked the two small hold-out blasters he had smuggled into the compound. Fully charged, of course.

He tensed, thinking that the credits he was about to become entitled to were not so much the prize of a hunt, so much as a gift. Security here in Colony Seven was lax beyond belief.

Fwa could see them coming now, and he pressed himself into a hollow in the uneven wall. As he'd expected, it was his targets—the three male Sacredots. He could smell them, and his sensitive nostrils recognized the reek of the males.

They were close now, coming closer, closer. . . .

Fwa leaped out with a ferocious roar, blasters raised. *Aim for their eyes!* he thought, as he fired his first salvo.

"In service to the All, every One is Exulted."
. . . every One is Exulted.

Tuga SalPivo, down-on-his luck Corellian space-tramp and jack-of-all-trades, paused for a moment at the edge of the Ylesian jungle and looked back. Colony Eight was a gray smudge in the very first light of dawn. Sunrise was still an hour away. SalPivo grinned and wiped the sweat off his face with a back-and-forth motion, catching a whiff of the vinegary vomm powder residue on his hand. He couldn't wait to see the explosion. . . .

It was so quiet. Even the scraping and peeping of the Ylesian jungle was gone. There was no wind at all.

SalPivo forced himself not to blink as he waited. When the brilliant orange flame flowered from the t'landa Til's sleeping chamber, there was a moment before the sound reached him, and he thought, *It doesn't seem real. . . .*

Then the crack and boom rolled over him, almost knocking him down, followed by the cries and wails of the remaining inhabitants. *Job well done,* he said to himself, chuckling. *I'll be back on Poytta before the fire's put out. . . .*

"We sacrifice to achieve the All. We serve the One."
. . . *serve the One.*

The Rodian named Sniquux sniffed the air thoughtfully, his aqua snout wiggling. Mid-afternoon sun slanted down into the wide courtyard, and dust seemed to hang in the hot, thick air. With infinite care, he secured the last strand of monofilament fiber across the opening of the passageway to the factory compound. Colony Nine was not yet finished, but the main buildings and dormitories were close enough to completion to start up operation. Nearly three hundred Pilgrims were resident, most of them employed on the construction gang. Sniquux had come in with the last bunch, his experience as a permacrete artisan coming in handy.

Here they come! The Rodian stepped back from the invisible wire, then ducked under it, making sure he came nowhere near the deadly stuff. Once in the corridor, he made his way up to the first level balcony, which overlooked the courtyard. The six t'landa Til, three males and three females, were returning from their post-siesta walkabout, ambling toward the dinner hall and their supper. A cadre of Gamorrean guards surrounded them, their axe heads glinting in the sun. Sniquux pulled the sound projector remote control from his little pouch, hefting the device and feeling the smoothness of its contours.

I don't even have to get near them, he thought, delightedly. *I love this assignment. I don't have to risk my delicate little neck.* His ears twitched expectantly as he turned the dial to its maximum position and engaged the trigger.

Suddenly, from the other side of the courtyard, a hideous, shrill wailing began, a sound so high it made Sniquux shiver. It was an ancient recording of the savage thota, the principal predator of the t'landa Til on their long-lost homeworld of Varl.

The t'landa Til froze for a second, their protuberant eyes swinging in every direction as they tried to locate the source of the cry. The head Sacredot, Tarrz by name, reared up onto his hind limbs and spun about, calling to the others, but it was no use. The huge creatures stampeded mindlessly in all directions, trampling Gamorreans as they headed for the openings in the courtyard wall that Sniquux had booby-trapped. Finally even Tarrz panicked and dashed for the nearest exit.

The Rodian, who had a taste for bloodshed, smacked his prehensile lips as the Priests came apart, monofilament slicing them more cleanly then any blade. Tarrz got halfway through the opening before his upper torso peeled back, revealing the dark maroon interior, internal organs laid out side by side, blood pooling and spilling as he fell to complete the gash. In a trice, they were all dead, big pools of wine-red blood slowly spreading around the quartered corpses, and only a few dazed Gamorreans were left to try to figure out what had happened.

Maybe this'll mean a promotion, Sniquux told himself. *Jabba seems to like me already . . . all I have to do is stick with him. . . .*

"Prepare for the blessing of Exultation!" Pohtarza took a step forward and sensed the Priests on either side of him doing the same. The Pilgrims broke ranks, pressing forward, falling over one another, uttering little whimpers of anticipation. Pohtarza began to inflate his neck pouch, scanning the expectant faces, when something caught his eye. There was a humanoid Pilgrim pushing toward them, nothing unusual about that. However, instead of a Pilgrim's cap, there was a dark hood thrown over his head.

Pohtarza stared in fascination. The hood was *empty*. The thing was quite close now—he was sure of it. Suddenly the hood fell back and the headless thing pulled a weapon out of its robe. Nameless dread gnawed at the t'landa Til; he took a few steps back, bumped into one of his brothers. The robe fell to the ground, and the Sacredot looked straight into the muzzle of a blaster, seemingly floating in the air. His thinking seemed fuzzy and oh-so-slow, but one thought came with crystal clarity. *Oh. An Aar'aa. Just an Aar'aa . . .*

Then brightness fell from the air. . . .

At Colony One, the oldest and largest of the Ylesian facilities, only a few moments later, it was nearing mid-day. Teroenza sat in the shallow, squishy mud like a beached whaladon, hardly moving, eyes closed. The developments of the last day were discouraging beyond belief.

Durga, curse him, had called his bluff. Teroenza opened his eyes and took in the depressing sight: beyond Veratil and Tilenna and the other t'landa Til soaking in the mud, sleek Nova Force ships littered the landing field, and small teams of heavily armed sentients wearing the uniform of the mercenary unit were everywhere.

How could Durga have known what he planned? Maybe the young Hutt was smarter than he'd thought. Now that he reflected on it, Teroenza decided that it had probably been a bad idea to kill Kibbick so brazenly.

But the worst of it was that Teroenza still couldn't

know for sure how much Durga knew. Perhaps the Nova Force troops were Durga's response to the High Priest's disingenuous requests to beef up the Ylesian defenses. Maybe he *didn't* suspect foul play in Kibbick's death.

Teroenza liked that idea. If true, the t'landa Til would just have to wait, and hope that this situation was temporary, and that, after a while, Besadii would grow weary of paying Nova Force to stay here. *Wait. I can wait a little longer. In any event, that's all I can do.* . . .

The Nova Force commandant, a squat, heavy-gravity world human named Willum Kamaran, was approaching the edge of the flat, treading gingerly, not wanting to soil his shining black boots. Finally, he gave Teroenza a disgusted look and motioned for the t'landa Til to come to meet him. The High Priest decided that he'd at least pretend to cooperate until he found out more. Hoisting himself to his feet, Teroenza started in the man's direction.

Without warning a lash of energy sizzled into the mud in front of him, spattering him with ejecta. The High Priest halted in confusion. *What?*

Teroenza turned to see three beings in camo uniforms come racing out of the jungle, blaster rifles blazing. The Gamorreans who had been guarding them were already dead.

Ptchoo. Ptchoo. Ptchoo.

The sound of blaster fire was all around him. Teroenza tried to run, tried to change direction, but slipped in the mud, falling to his knees.

Is this Nova Force? Has Durga ordered them to execute us now? Teroenza thought, hysteria nearly getting the better of him. At the edge of his vision, he saw that Kamaran was also shooting now. But not at him. At the intruders. Other Nova Force soldiers were coming up behind him, blasting away. *By Varl, they're trying to protect us!*

There was no place to run. Teroenza froze in panic. Veratil, he could see, lay motionless, a smoking hole where an eye used to be. Tilenna had run deeper into the mud, but was unable to submerge herself, and was flailing back and forth in complete terror. Teroenza realized suddenly that it was only a matter of time. Taking a deep breath to still the fear erupting in his heart, he let himself fall, then lay still, playing dead.

The blaster fire abruptly stopped, and Teroenza opened his eyes. *It worked!* The intruders lay dead. The High Priest dared to raise himself and survey the scene. *Tilenna!*

She was half covered by mud and water, and her head was under. *She can't breathe. . . .* Before he had reached the body, Teroenza knew the truth. He cradled the massive head as best he could in his weak arms, trying to find a spark of life in his mate, but she was gone.

Kamaran had taken a hit in the arm, and his tan uniform was covered with dark brown smears. And there was Ganar Tos, Teroenza's majordomo, making his way through the milling soldiers, pausing for a moment at the mud's fringe, then plunging right in.

"My Lord Teroenza," he cried, his weak old human's voice barely more than a croak. "It's terrible. All over the planet, assassins are killing our Priests! We've had reports from Colonies Two, Three, Five, and Nine. Offworld communication has been cut. Oh, sir! Lord Veratil . . . and Tilenna! Sir, what can we do?" He wrung his hands distractedly. "Sir, this is the end. There can be no more Exultations. What shall we do?"

Teroenza snorted heavily, trying to think. Was this Durga's work? No, it couldn't be; the Besadii enterprise depended on the t'landa Til. Who was responsible for this? And what should he do now?

Chapter Fourteen:

THE BATTLE FOR YLESIA

Jalus Nebl entered the Ylesian atmosphere with great care, watching for storm cells, and staying in constant touch with the Rebel assault shuttles that were following him. He was a lead ship, and well aware of his responsibility. "Shuttle Three," he said into his comm unit, in his squeaky Basic, "watch yourself. You're drifting too far to port. Storm cell 311 is headed in your direction. The ionization from those lightning storms will mess up your instrumentation. Increase speed and close up."

"This is Shuttle Three, we copy, *Dream of Freedom*."

They were flying through thick clouds now, and the *Dream* was buffeted by high winds. Darkness surrounded them. They were flying toward the sun, but they would not reach daylight before they landed.

The Sullustan checked his instruments. "Tighten formation," he ordered. "All ships, tighten formation."

He saw the running lights of his starboard wingman for a moment, then the clouds blotted them out. They were being slammed by gusts, and the clouds were so thick that Nebl didn't even bother to glance at his viewscreen. Instruments-only flying. Rain and hail and electrical storms raged nearby, lighting the inky clouds in actinic flashes. Nebl followed the progress of his formation on his tactical sensors.

It had been ten years since Nebl had flown through the Ylesian atmosphere, but he was surprised how it all came back to him. He was leading half the Rebel ships assigned to Colony One in, and Han Solo was leading the other half in the *Millennium Falcon*. Han had taken his Sullustan friend for a brief tour of his ship yesterday, and the two pilots had caught up on old times while Nebl enjoyed watching Han show off his pride and joy.

Nebl spotted another storm cell, pointed it out to his formation, and then sent his ship swooping down, automatically checking his landing vector. His assigned landing spot was directly in the middle of the Colony One compound. He was carrying a squad of troops, and their assignment was to secure the andris factory.

As he flew, Nebl could hear the Assault Commander aboard the transport *Liberator*, reporting on the fleet's progress. The Rebel forces had taken the Ylesian space station, having met heavier resistance than expected, but they were now reporting in that it was secured.

Nebl stayed in close touch as he led his formation down, down. He was tracking the storm cells so the more inexperienced pilots wouldn't have to. In theory at least, if they followed Nebl's lead, they'd be able to concentrate on their piloting as opposed to their navigation.

They were almost down below the heaviest cloud

layer now. Colony One was still in darkness, though dawn would arrive in about an hour. Nebl noticed that his rightmost shuttle was falling behind, and quickly established contact.

"Assault Shuttle Six, you're falling behind. What's happening?"

"Having trouble with a stabilizer," the young pilot's voice was strained. "I've got my copilot working on it."

"Formation, reduce speed. We don't want to lose Shuttle Six," Nebl ordered.

Obediently, they reduced speed. The next voice Nebl heard over the comm was Han Solo's. "Hey, Nebl, what gives? You're slowing."

The Sullustan explained the problem. "Well, I don't want to go in ahead of you, so I'll drop back, too," Han said. The *Falcon* and her ships slowed, falling back, leaving Nebl, as planned, still in the lead.

Both groups were still in good formation when they dropped below the cloud cover, and saw the nighttime lights of Colony One. Nebl was in the lead, and he'd repositioned Shuttle Six so it was now beside him, so he could nursemaid the Rebel pilot down. Nebl's other ships were flying half a ship's length behind the *Dream* and Six as they swooped toward their assigned landing coordinates.

Nebl had almost no warning. One second he was heading for his landing coordinates, everything fine, and the next his sensors suddenly blatted out a warning. Glancing down, Jalus Nebl saw that he'd been targeted—by a heavy turbolaser!

What? he thought blankly. *Where—*

The explosion was so massive, so all-consuming, that poor Nebl never even had time to realize he'd been hit.

• • •

Han Solo watched with horror as *Dream of Freedom* and Assault Shuttle Six were simply *eradicated* by two blasts from a ground-mounted heavy turbolaser. The turbolaser blasted again, and two other shuttles performed frantic evasive maneuvers that caused them to run straight into a treacherous wind-shear. Their stubby wings impacted, and then, flaming, they hurtled down toward the jungle. Fireballs painted the darkness with crimson, marking the crash sites.

Han was frozen with shock for a half-second. *A turbolaser! Where'd that come from?* Then he checked his position, and those of the ships in formation with him, and began his own evasive. At the same time he activated his comm, shouting, "Formations One and Two—veer off! Bria, order your ships to their alternate landing sites! Veer off! They got a heavy turbolaser down there! Nebl bought it!"

Without waiting for a response, Han swooped the *Falcon* up on her side and changed his approach vector—and not a moment too soon. A wash of fatal green energy streaked toward his ship, narrowly missing her belly. Han saw a damage control warning light up on his board, and realized the shot had knocked out the extension and retraction controls on his new retractable blaster. The close brush had also managed to fry the terrain-following sensors. He swore, even as Chewie howled. Han heard shouts from Jarik, who was in the ventral gun turret and must've gotten a spectacular—and terrifying—view of the blast.

Too close for comfort!

He peeled away, accelerating to get well out of the range of the turbolaser. None of the other ships was hit, thankfully.

The alternate landing sites were on the beach, more than two kilometers from the center of Colony One.

Han brought the *Falcon* in for a landing, setting her down on the hard-packed sand, not far from the breakers. He sat there for a second, just breathing hard, enveloped by the Ylesian darkness. He kept his lights on, so none of the other pilots would be tempted to land on top of him.

To his right as he sat in the cockpit, were the dunes, and, beyond them, the mudflats and Colony One. To his left was the Zoma Gawonga, which, in Huttese, meant "Western Ocean." Behind and before him stretched the beach, and already other ships were settling into place.

Leaving Chewie to finish up their post-landing checks, Han keyed his comm. "Shuttle One, this is the *Falcon*. Bria, this is Han. Come in, Shuttle One."

A crackle of static, then her voice. Han let out a sigh of relief. He'd lost track of formation a bit back there, and, while he *thought* Shuttle One wasn't one of the ships hit, he hadn't been positive until now.

"Han, I read you. Shuttle One landing now, alternate site. I'm going to deploy my troops for the ground attack. We'll go in over the dunes. My squad will head through the jungle for the compound."

"I'm coming with you," Han said. "Don't go without me."

"Copy, *Falcon*." She hesitated. "Han, we need to secure the Admin Building. Can you take care of dispatching the Togorian squad?"

Han knew she was thinking about the Treasure Room. The plan all along had been for Muuurgh, who knew the layout and the jungle, to lead his squad of Togorians in there. But now they'd have to go a lot farther. . . .

"Right," he said. "I'll do that."

Han went back to the lounge, where the Togorians were unstrapping, checking the charges in their weapons, and commenting to each other about rough rides. They wanted to know why all the stomach-churning aerial acrobatics. Han spent a minute explaining, then went on to tell Muuurgh, Mrrov, Sarrah and the other Togorians that they'd landed much farther from their target than anticipated. "This will be tougher than we originally planned," Han said. "You're going to have to make about a two-kilometer hike through the jungle."

Muuurgh stood up, careful not to whack his head in the cramped surroundings of the *Falcon's* lounge. "Do not worry, Han," he said. "Muuurgh will lead the way through the jungle to the Administration Building. Muuurgh hunted all around Colony One, and Muuurgh remembers terrain well."

Han pulled on his infrared goggles and his light helmet, picked up his weapons, then he and Chewbacca followed the Togorian squad down the ramp. Han watched their bright yellow images make their way up the beach. He pushed up his goggles, and was instantly engulfed in complete darkness. The Togorians had vanished like shadows into the surrounding blackness. The Corellian took a deep breath of the late-night air, and the smell of the Ylesian ocean brought back a rush of memories.

"Chewie," he said, "stay sharp. This world can be a real pit. Good thing it ain't rainin', for once." He tapped his goggles. "You need a pair of these, pal?"

Chewie shook his head, affirming that Wookiee night-sight was far superior to human vision. He could see fine and didn't need goggles.

When Han turned to go up the landing ramp, Lando and Jarik came trooping down it. Like Han, they were carrying heavy blaster rifles and wearing helmets with infrared goggles. They stood together at the bottom, watching the Rebel soldiers assembling from the shuttles. Most of the landing vehicles were down now.

"So . . . where do you guys think you're goin'?" Han asked.

"To find some action," Jarik said. "I ain't missing this!" The youth clutched his blaster rifle, bouncing on his toes, obviously excited at the chance to take part in his first ground assault.

Han had always figured he'd let Jarik stay in the ship. Safer that way. "Wait a minute," he said. "The Togorians are gone to capture the Admin Building. Me and Chewie are headin' out with Bria. If you guys go lookin' for action, then who's gonna guard the *Falcon*?"

"Lock it and activate the security systems," Jarik said. "Nobody's gonna get inside unless you let 'em, Han."

Lando gestured at the beach. The last Rebel and smuggler ships were coming in for a landing. "Won't Bria post a rear guard to watch the ships?"

Han glared at the gambler. Lando suddenly realized he was being a bit dense, and shut up.

Smugglers were pouring out of their vessels now, and several of the captains were plainly not happy. Han braced himself as Kaj Nedmak and Arly Bron stormed up to him, along with several other smugglers and privateers he didn't know. "Solo, what do you think you're doing, leading us straight into a turbolaser?" Bron demanded. "I nearly lost my engines!"

Han shrugged and spread his hands. "Hey, it's not my fault! I didn't know! I almost got fried myself!"

Just then, Bria approached, with Jace Paol, her second-in-command. "It's not Han's fault," she said to the unhappy crowd. "I am going to have a word with the Bothans, though. They were supposed to have done the recon necessary for this mission. Unless that turbolaser was just installed, they should have pinpointed it before now."

More grumbling from the assembled captains. Bria held up her hand for quiet. "Don't worry, you'll get what's coming to you," she said, her voice and eyes hard and full of authority. "Just stay here on the beach until we have the compound secured. Or . . . anyone who enjoys a fight is welcome to tag along."

Most of the smuggler and privateer captains shook their heads and walked away, but one or two decided to go in with the Rebels—probably to make sure they got to earmark the best spice in the warehouse for themselves. Han looked at Bria. "Chewie and me are goin' with you," he said.

Jace Paol spoke up, "Commander, request permission to take my squad in and knock out that turbolaser. We're going to need to land more shuttles later on, and we can't, with that thing blasting ships out of the sky."

Bria nodded. "Permission granted, Lieutenant. Take a demo team with you. Take out the laser, and if it can't be salvaged, destroy it."

"Right, Commander."

"Jarik Solo here. I'd like to go," Jarik spoke up to Paol. "That laser nearly singed my rear. I'd like a chance to be in on taking it down."

Paol nodded at the young man. "Glad to have you."

Han caught Lando's eye and jerked his head at Jarik. Lando sighed, then stepped forward. "Count me in, too, Lieutenant. I'm Lando Calrissian."

"Glad to have you, Calrissian."

Han waved at his friends as they started off down the beach with Paol's squadron. He watched as Bria gave final orders to the troops who would remain behind as rear guard for the ships on the beach.

Then he and Chewie started up the beach with Bria

and her troops. Her comlink chirped, and she turned it up so she could hear. Han listened to the voice of the Assault Commander, Blevon, up on the *Liberator*. "Rainbow One to all stations, we have multiple reports of heavy resistance. Be on the alert."

Bria glanced at Han, then at her chrono. "All forces have landed. We're running behind." She muted the comlink so it was just a distant mutter of commanders reporting in, then broke into a jog. Han and the squads ran after her.

The infrared goggles took some getting used to. Han nearly tripped over beach drift, and once he got tangled in a bunch of thorny sand-grass and got thoroughly scratched. Chewie obligingly lifted him up bodily, freeing him. His skin stinging, Han warned the others behind him.

Been a long time, he reflected, scrambling behind Bria up the dune, clutching the heavy A280 rifle. Sand sifted and fell around him, and the footing was treacherous. The last time he'd done something like this was not a pleasant memory. . . .

Bria was the first to reach the top. She flattened herself, waving caution with a hand-signal to her followers. Han wasn't expecting any fire—after all, they were not even in sight of the compound—but caution in battle was always a good thing. He dropped to his belly and wriggled up beside her, with Chewie right behind him. Sand sifted down his open collar, making him itch. He couldn't spare the time to scratch, though.

Together, Han, the Wookiee and Bria eased up the last half-meter and peered over the top of the dune—

—and nearly got the tops of their heads blown off. Repeating blaster fire hammered them, turning some of the sand to glass instantly, spraying them with minuscule hot particles that stung like insects.

Chewie howled as he, Han and Bria threw themselves flat, covering, until the fire ceased. The Rebel commander took a sensor reading and looked at Han, her face a yellowish blur with white lips against the varied greens of the infrared. He could see her frown beneath the masking goggles. "Han . . . I'm detecting at least twenty energy signatures out there, waiting for us. Whoever these guys are, they're not a bunch of Gamorreans."

Han stared at her. "That and the turbolaser . . ."

"Yeah." She thumbed her comlink to transmit. "Rainbow One, this is Red One. We took turbolaser fire as we landed and changed to our alternate landing site. We're on the ground with moderate casualties. Four ships lost—three shuttles, one friend." "Friend" Han knew, was the agreed-upon code for a smuggler or privateer ship. "Encountering heavy resistance, but continuing our assault."

The voice of Assault Command came back. "Rainbow One copies, Red One. Do you need White One?"

Blevon was asking whether Bria needed reserves from the *Liberator*.

She keyed her link. "Negative, Rainbow One. The reserves can't land while that turbolaser is still up. We're working on it. Red One out."

"Rainbow One," Blevon acknowledged her, and then was quiet.

Bria switched frequencies to her inter-squad channel. "Jace, this is Bria. Have you sneaked a look over those dunes yet?"

"I did," Paol's voice was grim. "Who *are* those guys?"

"I don't know," Bria said. "But they're obviously professionals. You circle around through the jungle and come down the mudflats from the north. I'll go through

the jungle and come up from the south. We'll catch
them in a crossfire."

"Copy," Paol said. "You *would* make *me* crawl through
the mud."

Bria laughed grimly, and broke the connection.

It took Han and Bria's team nearly ten minutes to
make their way far enough down the beach so they
could be sure to be shielded by the jungle. They went
up and over the dunes, then down again, into the jungle.
Han followed Chewie's lead as they slogged through
rotting vegetation. His nose wrinkled at the smell, and
Chewbacca whined protestingly. Wookiees had a much
more acute sense of smell than humans. Sweating and
slipping through the muck underfoot, Han wished he'd
worn boots with more traction.

Finally, they reached the edge of the cleared area.
Bria's sensors confirmed that their targets were just
ahead. They crouched in the jungle and her comlink
chirped softly. She turned the volume up. ". . . receiving
multiple reports of heavy resistance. Green One reports
confirmation that some professionals for a merc outfit
calling itself Nova Force, have been captured. Rainbow
One out."

"Nova Force? Mercenaries?" Han looked at Bria.
"Oh, great! How'd *they* get here?"

She shrugged.

Han scowled. "And I told the smugglers and privateers this was going to be a piece of cake!"

Han listened tensely as she checked in with Jace
Paol. Everything was in place. . . .

Han's pulse was racing. He swallowed, and his saliva
tasted metallic. "You ready, pal?" he whispered to
Chewie, who was checking the charge in his bowcaster.

"Hrrrrnnnnnn!"

Han checked the charge in his blaster rifle, even though he *knew* it was full.

Finally Bria nodded, and together, the squad wriggled out of the jungle, crawling along cropped vegetation, their hands and knees digging into the muck. It had rained recently, of course . . . this was Ylesia. Han's fingers encountered permacrete. A landing field or road . . . it hadn't been there ten years ago.

Bria counted down seconds with Paol, then—

"Fire!"

Han rose to his knees, sighted with his goggles, and saw a dim shape wearing an unfamiliar helmet, yellow marking body heat. He fired.

The waning night exploded into blaster fire, choked-off screams and battle cries. Still firing, Han and Chewbacca moved forward with Bria's troops. The soldier to his left went down. He glanced at her, saw a black hole where her face had been, whiffed charred meat, and kept going.

Moments later, as the enemy fire stuttered out and died, Bria yelled for cease-fire. Han and Chewie approached, seeing the scattered bodies before them. Bria nudged one with her toe as Jace Paol, as smeared with mud as a t'landa Til after a wallow, approached. "Look at that emblem on the sleeve," she said. "An exploding star. And look at their armor and equipment. Professionals, all right." She counted bodies. "Twenty. There are probably more manning the turbolaser."

She and Han looked across the compound. In the pre-dawn darkness, they could make out the tower with the turbolaser atop it. "Good thing they can't swing that thing down to hit targets on the ground," Han said. "Or we'd be cooked."

Jarik and Lando came up and the four friends stood off to the side as Bria ordered a few members of her squads to assist the wounded back to the ships, and to salvage the Nova Force weapons. "Remember, people," she said, "we are taking it all. If it can be re-used, salvage it."

They nodded.

Han looked at Lando and Jarik, crusted with mud, and shook his head. "Lando, if Drea Renthal could see you now . . ."

Chewie began laughing.

"Shut up, Han. You too, Chewbacca," the gambler said, flicking fastidiously at his ruined clothes. Luckily for him, he'd donned rough clothing in preparation for the night's work. "I don't want to hear it. I haven't been this dirty since . . . well, it's a long story."

Han chuckled, and looked at Jarik. "So . . . how'd you do, kid?"

Jarik nodded. "Pretty good, I think, Han. I got at least two of 'em."

Han clapped him on the shoulder. "Great. We'll make a warrior out of you, yet."

Jarik's teeth flashed white in his mud-blackened face.

As soon as the wounded were taken away by medics, Bria keyed her comlink, then ordered her waiting troops to advance on the double. "Let's take that compound! Advance in squads! Demo teams, be ready!"

She turned up the volume on the comlink, and they heard: "Rainbow One, this is Green Two. I'm assuming command here. Green One is down."

"Rainbow One copies, Green Two. What's your status?"

"Almost done here. Just mopping up. Expect to have the target secure in five minutes."

Bria made a face. "We're running behind." She clicked on. "Rainbow One, this is Red One. Front line

resistance has been dealt with. Bringing up reinforce-
ments, and advancing into the compound."

"Red One, status on that turbolaser?"

"Rainbow One, I have two squads preparing to deal
with that now. Red One out."

"Rainbow One . . . out."

Han and Chewie watched Paol's group as they
headed off through the jungle to come at the turbolaser
crew from the east. Then they were busy, advancing
with Bria's troops into the compound. They met scattered resistance from Ylesian guards, which, for the
most part, they dealt with easily . . . as they'd expected
to. The night was no longer silent, even when the guns
were quiet. The moans and pleas of the wounded, yells
for assistance, plus assorted shouted alien words. . . .

As they advanced, Bria's squads kept reporting in:

"Red Hand Leader, Squad Three reporting. Andris
Factory secured. Demo teams are moving in."

"Red Hand Leader, Squad Six reporting. Welcome
Center secured. Demo team has been summoned."

"Red Hand Leader, Squad Seven, we are moving in
on the dormitory. It is under guard by the mercs . . . but
there are only about six of them. Not expecting any
trouble. . . ."

"Red Hand Leader, Squad Two reporting. We're
moving into position to take that turbolaser. Estimate
attack will commence in . . . five minutes."

Han and Chewie stayed close by Bria's side, as the
three guarded each other's backs. Bursts of blaster fire
echoed through the compound, mixed with screams,
Gamorrean grunts and squeals, and alien wails.

Han figured that there were probably a platoon's
worth of mercenaries—thirty to forty troopers, all told.
The Nova Force soldiers were truly professional. They
fought bravely and well until it was obvious that defeat

was inevitable, then they surrendered. They were fighting for credits, not a cause, and it made sense to live and fight another day.

Once a crazed Pilgrim toting a scavenged blaster pistol came leaping out of the shadows and nearly winged Bria. Han shot the female Bothan down, killing her—he was rushed, and had no time to aim for a disabling shot. Bria stared down at the Pilgrim in horror, and for a moment Han thought he saw tears in her eyes. "Honey . . ." he said. "There was nothing else I could do. . . ."

"I know," she gave him a wan smile. "It's hard, though, having them attack you when you're trying to *help* them."

Han patted her shoulder consolingly. She took out her comlink in response to a chirp from Assault Command and heard the ID: "Rainbow One."

A minute crawled by. Bria motioned her squad to fall in behind her. Then the AC channel spoke again, an outwardly calm voice that carried an undercurrent of strain: "Rainbow One, this is Blue One. I need some help here!"

Blevon's voice was flat: "Blue One, say your status."

"Thirty percent casualties, and they've got us pinned down with repeating blasters, at least two of them. One in the warehouse, the other in the dormitory. I need White One."

"Blue One, this is White One. I can drop two platoons in three minutes. Where do you want them?"

"Why don't you take the warehouse? Put one platoon north, just on the south side of Hill Three-One. Land the other in the jungle to the east, and hit them from the side. I'll take the dormitory."

"Sounds good to me, Blue One. White One out."

"Blue One out."

Bria looked over at the turbolaser. The first flush of

dawn was brightening the sky. "Jace should be moving in any moment. . . ."

As if her words had been a signal, the area around the turbolaser erupted with blaster fire, shouts, screams and the sounds of at least two grenades launching. Explosions filled the air.

Bria waited a few tense seconds, then activated her link. "Squad Two, report! Are you in? Have you got it?"

No reply. Han and Chewie looked at each other tensely as they sheltered beside the glitterstim factory. One of Bria's troops came trotting around from the rear of the building. "We're all secured, Commander. I've called for a demo team."

She nodded distractedly. "Good work, Sk'kot. Squad Two, this is Red Hand Leader. Report, please. What's happening?"

Silence for ten endless heartbeats, then suddenly they heard the channel click. "Red Hand Leader, Squad Two." It was Jace Paol's voice. The troops around Han and Chewie grinned and gave a low cheer. "We've got it, but we have people down. Send the medics. Out."

Bria hastily called in backup for Squad Two, then summoned in the medics' shuttle, telling them it was safe to fly into the compound.

She called into her comlink. "Squad Eight, how are you Togorians doing?"

A voice came over the comlink, speaking accented but understandable Basic. "Mrrov here. The building is almost secured, Bria. We are going to have to search the jungle for snipers, though. Some of the guards managed to get away. There are some ships landed up here, mostly small shuttles, but one big one. We have the ships under guard. It's possible some of the guards may try to escape."

Bria addressed the comlink. "Great going, Mrrov.

I bet you people made short work out of those Gamorreans."

Mrrov growled an amused laugh.

Bria switched channels, just in time to hear: "Red One, this is Rainbow One. Say your status."

Bria had just opened her mouth to reply when blaster fire erupted from the center of the compound, aimed at them. Bria, Han, Chewie and the other squad members, dropped, covering against the wall. Han spat out a mouthful of mud, and wished he could rinse his mouth out with the water from the flask on his hip. But he didn't want to chance moving.

"Cover me, people!" Bria yelled over her shoulder, then she began worming her way forward. Han and Chewie were right behind her. Blaster fire began whanging past, over their heads.

She turned, glanced back, saw him. "Stay back!" she hissed. "I can handle this."

"I know you can," Han yelled. "I just want to watch!"

For the first time ever, he heard her swear. She took careful aim with her blaster rifle, then, when the target came up from behind a vehicle, squeezed off a round.

The guard went down and lay motionless.

"Good shooting!" Han applauded.

Together, they ran back into cover with the troops. Bria spotted the comlink she'd dropped, picked it up.

"Red One, this is Rainbow One; say your status," Blevon's voice was still calm.

Bria was calm, but a little winded. "This is Red One. The turbolaser has been knocked out, and we hold most of the factories. We're attacking the warehouse and dormitory right now. Should be done in ten minutes."

"Understood, Red One. Will you need White One?"

"I don't think so, Rainbow One. We're beating them."

"Rainbow One copies."

They waited, listening tensely. Then . . . "Rainbow One, this is Gold One. Objective secure."

"Rainbow One . . . copy that."

A minute later, they heard, "Rainbow One, this is Orange One. Target is secured."

"Rainbow One. Copy that."

The other commanders from all the colonies except Colony Three reported in, one by one. By that time, Bria had checked in with all her people. "Rainbow One," she said. "This is Red One. Report target is secure here."

"Rainbow One, copy that."

"We still haven't heard from Colony Three," Bria said, worriedly. "They're the ones who needed backup. Hope everything's okay. . . ."

As if in answer to her concern, a different voice spoke up. "Rainbow One, this is White One, reporting from Colony Three. Target is secure."

Blevon said, "Acknowledged, White One. Where's Blue One?"

The new voice was bleak. "She's dead."

Bria looked up. "Well, that's it. Ylesia is ours, gentles, except for mopping up. Let's call in those ships."

Han turned to Chewbacca and pulled the Wookiee aside. "Chewie, I need you to do something right now," he said.

"Arhnnnn?"

"We've got this area secured, but it sounds like Mrrov and Muuurgh could use some help up in the Admin Building. *Where the Treasure Room is.* I want you to check on 'em, make sure they've got it secured, give 'em a hand if they need it. Your night vision is about as good as a Torgorian's, and if they're chasin' some of those guards through the jungle, you could be a big help, and you know it."

"Hrrrrrhhhhh!" Chewbacca, as usual, took a dim view of being separated from his partner.

"Come on!" Han said. "I'm worried that some of those guards might break in and start stealin' Teroenza's collection! That's *our* stuff, remember?"

Chewie grumbled, but his resistance was weakening.

"Listen up, furball," Han snapped, "I don't have time to argue. I trust Muuurgh and Mrrov, but I don't know those other Togorians. And all it would take is one busy guard who managed to break in. So you help Muuurgh and Mrrov secure the place, make sure the Treasure Room is still locked up, and come straight back. Shouldn't take you half an hour. You remember the location of the Treasure Room on that plan I sketched for you?"

"Hrrrrrrnnnnnnnnn . . ."

"Good. Get your furry butt in gear."

Chewbacca was not happy, but the Wookiee departed without further argument.

By now, ships were dropping from the pink-tinged sky like metal rain, landing in the center of the compound.

Han was just taking a swig of water from his flask when a dark figure ran toward him. Han pushed up his goggles, squinted in the wan pre-dawn light, and realized it was Lando. Even before he saw the gambler's face, Han knew something was wrong. He hurried toward his friend.

"Han . . . it's Jarik. Kid took a hit. . . . He isn't going to make it. He's calling for you."

"Blast!" Together, they ran.

Lando led him over to the temporary aid station the medics had set up, then pointed to a stretcher. Han walked over, looked down, and recognized Jarik's unruly hair—and that was practically all. The young man's face was a scorched, reddened horror. At first Han thought he was dead, then he saw that Jarik was still breathing. He looked up hopefully at the nearest medic. The Alderaanian shook her head grimly, mouthed, "Sorry."

"Hey . . . Jarik . . . can you hear me?" Han took the grimy hand in his, grasped it firmly. "Kid . . . it's Han. . . ."

Jarik no longer had much in the way of eyelids, and Han knew he must be blind. But he turned his head slightly, and his mouth moved. "Han . . ."

"Don't try to talk . . . you're gonna be fine. They'll pop you in a bacta tank, and you'll be chasin' girls and shootin' Imps in no time."

A faint thread of expelled air, and Han recognized it as the ghost of a laugh. "Liar. . . . Han . . . got . . . to . . . tell you."

Han swallowed. "Yeah? I'm listenin' . . ."

"Name . . . my name . . . it ain't . . . Solo. Lied to you."

Han cleared his throat. "Yeah, I know, kid. That's okay. I give it to you. Far as I'm concerned, you earned it long ago."

"You . . . knew?"

"Sure. I've known from the beginning, Jarik."

The lax fingers tightened once, and then released. Han leaned over, checked for a pulse, then gently released his grip and stood up. His eyes were stinging, and it took him a second to regain control. The medic bustled by, and Han grabbed her sleeve. "He's gone. Where's his ID?"

She handed him a com-chip. Han took it, then keyed in, "Jarik Solo," under the "name of deceased" field.

The medic called for help, and two labor-droids

trundled forward. Han watched as they efficiently wrapped the dead youth in the sheet, then carried him over to the row of bodies laid out neatly on the ground.

Before he could turn away, they were putting another wounded Rebel onto the stretcher. "Water . . ." the woman croaked. Han took out his flask. "You're gonna be okay," he said, as he helped her to drink. "Don't worry."

The woman drank thirstily. "Thanks. . . ." she slumped back onto the stretcher.

"That's okay," Han said. "What's your name?"

"Lyndelah Jenwald. . . ." she muttered, and winced. "My arm hurts. . . ."

"We'll get you some help," Han promised, and went in search of a medic.

Satisfied that Jenwald was getting the attention she needed, he left the aid station and joined Lando, who looked at him sadly. "Han, I'm sorry. I tried to look after him, but they launched a grenade and I had to hit dirt, and the next thing I knew . . ." the gambler broke off, shaking his head.

Han nodded. "I know what it's like. There wasn't anything you coulda done, Lando. Don't beat yourself up." Han took a deep breath. "He was a good kid."

"Yeah—" Lando broke off as both humans heard a familiar roar. Han hastily waved at Lando and went running away from the aid station toward Chewbacca.

The Wookiee, seeing that Han was still unharmed, grabbed Han's shoulder and ruffled his hair in a Wookiee greeting. Han took a deep breath. "Chewie, pal," he said, "brace yourself. Jarik bought it."

The Wookiee stared at him for a moment, then threw back his head and voiced a roar of mingled rage and grief. Han silently echoed his friend's distress.

Chewbacca pulled Han out of the way, began gesturing and growling emphatically. "Mrrov?" Han said. "Wounded? She gonna make it?"

Chewie wasn't sure, but he thought so.

"I gotta go find Muuurgh," Han said. "Tell you what, Chewie, you go get the *Falcon*, fly her over to that apron by the Admin Building. Then we'll be ready to load 'er up."

Chewie nodded and loped away. In moments his tall form was lost to view amid the hurrying troops, dodging between the parked shuttles and tramp freighters.

Han looked back for Lando, but his friend was gone. He went back to the aid station, asked where the Togorians were being cared for. The medic he questioned didn't know. It took three tries for Han to find out.

Finally, he was directed to another auxiliary aid station, where most of the non-humanoids were being treated. Han saw Muuurgh's huge black shape crouching beside a pallet, and hurried over.

"Hey, Muuurgh!"

The Togorian turned at the sound his voice, then leaped up and grabbed Han in a fierce hug. "Muuurgh is glad to see Han Solo. They are taking us up now, and Muuurgh did not wish to go without saying farewell."

Han looked down at Mrrov. A bandage covered half her head. "What happened?"

"Muuurgh and Mrrov were on guard at the landing field, and three Gamorreans rushed us. She took two hits from a force-pike before Muuurgh tore her attacker's throat out."

"Oh, hey, pal . . . I'm so sorry. . . ." Han said. "She's gonna be okay, isn't she?"

"She has lost the eye," Muuurgh said. "And medic says perhaps her hand must come off. He does not know. But she will live. And she will take pride in knowing that the slaves are free, the Priests are dead."

Han nodded, and couldn't think of anything to say. The medics approached with an anti-grav pallet, and loaded the wounded Togorian female onto it. Han walked with Muuurgh to the medical shuttle, watched as Mrrov was loaded in, and gave Muuurgh a last, silent hug goodbye.

After watching the shuttle lift off, Han turned back toward the big spice warehouse, figuring that was where he'd find Bria. Seeing Jace Paol hurrying by, Han asked the lieutenant where she was. Paol jerked a thumb back at the Pilgrims' dormitory. Han jogged over that way, then paused, midway between the warehouse and the dormitory.

Rebel troops were herding Pilgrims out of the dorm, and the dazed, frightened slaves were plainly on the verge of panic. Bria stood before them, a microphone in her hand, and addressed them. "Listen to me!" she called. "The Priests are all dead! You are free now, and we've come to help you!"

"They killed the Priests!" one old man shouted, and began to sob. Wails and moans filled the air.

"Just get on these shuttles quickly!" Bria said. "We have medics and medications to help you feel better. We can cure you!"

The crowd grew increasingly restive. *Another moment and there will be a riot,* Han thought, uneasily. It was obvious that Bria wasn't getting through to them at all.

"We want Exultation!" one shouted, and the next moment, they were all chanting and waving their fists in the air. *"We want Exultation!"*

Bria waved at the shuttles. "Just get on the shuttles! We'll help you!"

"We want Exultation!"

The crowd surged forward, and Bria, with a disgusted air, signaled her troops. They opened fire with stun beams, and Pilgrims began collapsing in droves.

Having been stunned a few times himself, Han's body ached in sympathy for the Pilgrims, and he was a bit shocked by Bria's ruthlessness in ordering her troops to simply shoot the slaves.

But there wasn't much point in saying anything about it, he decided. As he stood there hesitating, watching the labor droids begin loading limp Pilgrims into the shuttles, Bria turned away and saw him.

Han waved, and she ran toward him. He grabbed her, hugged her fiercely, so relieved that they'd both made it through alive. "Jarik?" she asked.

Han shook his head. "No," he said. "He didn't make it."

"Oh, Han . . . I'm so sorry!"

Wrapping his arms around Bria, Han held her close, kissed her, and felt her kiss him back. They stood wrapped together in the midst of chaos.

Finally, she pulled away, and said, "It's time to head for the Admin Building. We've got to see to the Treasure Room."

Han nodded. "Chewie's got the *Falcon* up there by now, ready to load her up," he said, looking around. The sun was up by now, and the scene before him was organized chaos with Rebel troops everywhere. Bria tugged at him, but Han didn't move. "Where's Lando?" he asked. "He was here a few minutes ago. Did he go to pick up his share of the spice?"

"Come on!" she urged.

Han looked over at the warehouse, figuring that Lando would probably be right there, waiting to get his share. He spotted him, and took a step toward the warehouse, only to have Bria pull him back. "No! Come on, we have to go!"

Han's eyes narrowed. "There's something funny going on in there," he said. He could see Lando, and Arly Bron and Kaj Nedmak and about six other smuggler captains standing there, near the open doorway of the warehouse. Just . . . standing there. Not moving. Han looked at Lando, and Lando looked back, but the gambler didn't move.

"Come *on*!"

Han started toward the warehouse, then stopped in surprise and dismay. Now he could see what was resting beside the door, covering the smugglers. A heavy repeating blaster on its tripod, with a Rebel soldier standing behind it. And posted at intervals, three additional Rebel guards—all with their weapons trained on the smugglers.

"What in blazes is going on?" Han demanded, swinging around to confront Bria. "What are you *doing*?"

She bit her lip. "I hoped you wouldn't find out," she said. "It would have been easier. Han, I got my orders last night. There's something really big going on, and we need every credit we can scrape up. Everyone is going to have to make sacrifices. The smuggler captains are being held hostage for a little while. Their crews are being allowed to pick up the unprocessed spice . . . but we have to take the prime stuff. We need it, Han. I'm sorry, but I don't have any choice."

Han's mouth dropped open, and he glanced back over his shoulder to see other smugglers glaring at him. *Oh, blast!* he thought. *They think I was in on this from the beginning!*

What was he to do now? Give up his own share in the Treasure Room, to side with the smugglers? Most of them wouldn't lift a finger to help him out, if their positions were reversed, Han knew that. Besides . . . he didn't know any of them that well.

Except Lando . . .

Han shook his head and looked at Bria. "Honey, why didn't you *tell* me what you were planning?"

"Because you would never have gone along with it," she said.

"But Lando is my friend." Han shrugged. "The rest of 'em . . . I barely know. But Lando . . ."

"Come on," she said. "Your share of the Treasure Room is yours to do with as you please. If you feel bad, give Lando his share later."

Han thought that over, and then sighed. *I'll make it up to you, Lando,* he thought. The Corellian shrugged mentally as he walked away with Bria, leaving the smugglers behind. *I don't like this . . . but what else can I do?*

He reflected that it was a good thing that Chewie wasn't here. The Wookiee had an overactive conscience. . . .

When Han and Bria reached the Admin Building, they found Chewie waiting for them, and the *Falcon* on the apron. Chewie demanded to know where Lando was, and Han hesitated. "He's going back with Arly," he said, after a second.

Fortunately, Chewie was too taken up with the Treasure Room to notice Han's discomfiture.

Han had picked up a small thermal detonator from the Rebel arsenal, and it was the work of a moment to blow the door.

He stepped inside, and stood there in shock. Most of the shelves were already stripped bare. "Wha—"

"Teroenza must've been getting ready to clear out!" Bria exclaimed, pointing. "Look, it's already boxed up for us!"

The big rear cargo door of the Treasure Room stood ajar, as though some of the treasure had already been loaded—but Han didn't see a ship out there. He figured that Teroenza had summoned a ship, only to fall prey to the assassins yesterday. "All right!" he shouted, and swung Bria around. "Thank you, Teroenza!"

He gave her a short but passionate kiss, then turned back to regard the boxes of booty. "Okay, we'll need a repulsor-lift dolly," he said. "There's one aboard the *Falcon*. Chewie, you—"

"Don't move, Solo," came a voice from the past. Han froze as Teroenza crawled out from where he'd been concealed behind the white jade fountain. The High Priest had a blaster rifle in his hand, and his eyes held a mad glitter that told Han there was no way to talk his way out of this one.

"Hands raised," the Priest directed. Han, Chewie and Bria all put their hands up. Han glanced at the others, trying frantically to think of a way to get out of this. But Teroenza had the drop on them but good. . . .

"I shall enjoy this, Bria Tharen and Han Solo," Teroenza said. "I have summoned a pilot, and he is coming to collect me from Colony Four. I shall be free of this wretched world . . . and I shall have my treasure. I shall miss my mate, but, on the whole, not a bad bargain. Perhaps Desilijic can use my services. . . ."

"Hey," Han said, "Jabba's a friend of mine. You kill me, he won't take it kindly."

Teroenza laughed wheezily. "Hutts do not have friends," he said. "Farewell, Solo."

Pointing the blaster at Han, Teroenza's small, stubby finger began to tighten on the trigger.

Han shut his eyes. He heard the sound of the blaster's whine—

—and he felt nothing. No pain. No searing heat.

After a prolonged moment, Han heard the sound of a body fall with a loud *thud*.

He shot Bria instead of me! he thought, and opened his eyes.

But the body on the floor belonged to Teroenza. There was a huge, gaping hole where the Priest's bulbous left eye had been.

Han stared wildly, wondering if he'd gone mad and was imagining all this. *What's going on?*

Beside him, Bria gasped.

Han watched as Boba Fett stepped out of a dim corner of the room, his blaster rifle held in his arms.

Oh, great! he thought. *Now Fett will just kill us all!*

The bounty hunter kept them all covered as he walked to Teroenza's huge form, and then knelt on one knee. Keeping them covered with the blaster rifle with one hand, Fett used a vibro-saw with the other. The little instrument whirred, slicing easily through flesh and bone as Fett carefully cut off Teroenza's horn.

Han's head was whirling with shock.

Finally the bounty hunter rose to his feet again, and then began backing slowly away, the grisly trophy tucked under his arm.

Han couldn't help it. "You're *leaving*?" he blurted.

Did Boba Fett's mechanical voice hold a slight undercurrent of amusement? Han couldn't decide if he was imagining it. "That's right," the bounty hunter said. "The Priest is a Priority bounty. I'm not here for you."

And, having reached the opening in the wall, Boba Fett backed through it and vanished as suddenly as he'd appeared.

Han's mouth dropped open, and he felt light-headed with relief. "Bria!" he yelled, and grabbed her again.

The three shouted and celebrated for a long moment, in the deserted Treasure Room.

Han headed off to the *Falcon* to get the repulsor

dolly. When he returned, they spent several minutes organizing the boxes for efficient loading.

Suddenly a Rebel assault shuttle settled down on the permacrete beside the *Falcon*. Han stared at it in surprise as Jace Paol and a squad of Rebels disembarked. "Bria . . ." he said, "hey, what's going on? This is *our* treasure. We're taking it, and we're going away in the *Falcon* . . . right? Together . . . right?"

He looked at her, and she stared back at him. She bit her lip and didn't answer. Han felt a cold knot settle into his stomach. "Bria . . . honey . . . remember, you promised? We'd be together, right? Always?" He swallowed. "*Bria . . .*"

Chewie roared with anger and frustration, and suddenly Bria's blaster was there, in her hand, covering them both.

"Han," she said quietly, "we need to talk."

Chapter Fifteen:
The Last Kessel Run

Han stared at Bria's drawn blaster, poleaxed. "Honey, what are you *doing*?"

"I need it all, Han," she said. "Not for me, but for the Resistance." She waved to the Rebels and they came in, took Han's repulsor-lift dolly, and began stacking boxes on it.

Han stared in disbelief as the first load of treasure went out the door. "Bria . . ." he said hoarsely, "you can't do this. This ain't happening. You're . . . you're just tryin' to kid me, right?"

"I'm sorry, Han," she said. "I have to take it all. Everything my teams could salvage off this wretched world. All the processed spice, all the weapons, all the treasure. I know it's not fair, but I can't help that."

"Did the other Rebel commanders do this, Bria?" Han asked.

"Not as far as I know," she said. "But I was the one that got the communication last night, Han. Intelligence has discovered that the Empire has some kind of big project underway. *Really* big. So big that the fate of entire worlds could depend upon it. We have to find out what they're up to, and that will take credits . . . lots of them. For bribes, surveillance, troops . . . you name it. I just hope what we've gotten here on Ylesia will be enough."

Han wet his lips. "I thought you loved me. You said you did."

Another load went out the door. Han stared at it, wanting to moan aloud. Chewie *did* moan aloud.

Bria sighed and shook her head. "Yes, I love you," she said, softly. "I want us to always be together. Come with me, Han. You can't go back to Nar Shaddaa now. Come with me and we'll fight the Empire together. You, me and Chewie. We'll make a great team. We all have to make sacrifices, and we'll have made ours in giving up the treasure. You don't think I'm keeping any of this for *myself*, do you?"

Han shook his head, and his voice was very bitter. "No, I don't think that, Bria. Not for a moment." He took a deep, ragged breath. "Bria . . . I loved you."

Her face twisted in anguish at his use of the past tense. "Han, I love you! I *do*! But I can't let how I feel about you jeopardize the Rebel Alliance! This raid was a test, and we passed it! The other Resistance groups are going to see that we can get things done! Han . . . we took a whole *planet*. This raid is going to go down in Rebellion history, I just know it!"

"Yeah, as the raid where Bria Tharen stuck it to people who trusted her. Including the guy she said she loved."

Tears welled in her eyes, broke and ran. She stepped out of the way as her soldiers maneuvered yet another load of treasure out the door. "Han . . . please, please . . . come with me. You're a born leader. You don't need to live like a criminal. In the Rebel Alliance you could be an officer, and they do pay us! Not much, but a little, enough to live on! Please, Han!"

He stared at her coldly. She was crying so hard now that Jace Paol stepped over and took the blaster out of her hand. "We're loading the last bunch of boxes now, Commander."

She nodded, then tried to pull herself back together, wiping her eyes on her sleeve.

"Please, Han. If you're too mad now, I understand. Just . . . send me a message. Jabba knows how to reach me. Please, Han."

"I'll send you a message," Han said. "Remember everything I said to you that night at the Blue Light? Well, it was all true, and I was a fool for ever trustin' you." He dug in an inside pocket, and took out a small pouch. Inside was a piece of flimsy. "Recognize this, huh?"

She looked at it, came closer, and then backed away, nodding, her face very pale and set. "Yes . . ."

"Well, I'm such a fool that I carried it around with me all these years," Han snarled. "But as of today, I am no woman's fool, sister. No woman is ever gettin' to me again. *Ever.*"

With slow, deliberate movements, he ripped the flimsy into tiny pieces, then let them slip through his fingers and scatter to the floor. "You'd better get in your ship and get outta here while the getting is good, Bria.

If I ever see you again in this life, I'll shoot you on sight."

She stared at him in shock, until Jace Paol took her arm and said, "Commander . . . we've finished loading."

"I understand," she said, in a small, shaking voice. "Han . . . I am sorry. I will always love you. Always. There has never been anyone but you, and there never will be. I'm sorry. . . ."

Paol encircled her shoulders with his arm, and said to Han. "I left you one box and your dolly, Solo. I'd advise you not to waste time here. The charges are set to go off in thirty minutes."

Slowly, Paol backed out the door, keeping his blaster trained on Han and Chewie. The Rebels beside the shuttle kept the Corellian and the Wookiee covered.

Han stood there in silence as the Rebel shuttle took off.

When it was gone, he drew a deep, ragged breath, and it hurt. Another, and it hurt, too. His eyes stung, but he bit his lip until the pain allowed him to gain control. "Chewie," he said, "this has been a great day, you know that?"

Chewie made a sympathetic, mournful sound.

"Well, we have to get moving," Han said. "Tell you what, keep an eye on the time, and trot through the compound. Maybe they dropped some vials of glitterstim or something. I'll scour Teroenza's living quarters. I think he had some valuables in there. Meet me back here in seventeen minutes, pal."

"Hrrrrrrmnnnnnggggggghhhh!"

The Wookiee took off.

Han scoured the treasure room and Teroenza's apartment, finding a few odds and ends, and a sobbing Ganar Tos. Han looked at the old humanoid coldly. "You are lucky you never married her," he said. "Get outta here, Tos. This building is gonna blow in fifteen minutes."

The ancient Zisian scuttled out the door like a bug. Han snorted in disgust and ransacked the apartment.

When he carried a sack of minor collectibles out to the *Falcon*, Han looked around for Chewie. *Hurry up, furball*, he thought.

He went inside the ship to warm her up, and then heard Chewie's roar, demanding that Han come out and see what he'd found!

Han's heart leaped. *A box of glitterstim vials!*

He raced out of the ship, only to stop short in confusion. Chewbacca stood there with a group of big-eyed, ragged children, hollow-cheeked and scared. He held the littlest tyke in his arms. The other eight looked to be between the ages of four and twelve.

Han stared. "What? Where in blazes did *they* come from?"

Chewbacca explained that he'd been scavenging amid the deserted buildings, when he'd heard sobbing down in a cellar at the back of the dorms. These children had apparently been born to some of the Pilgrims, and forgotten by their Exultation-addicted parents in the aftermath of the raid.

All the children were human, and Han guessed they were Corellian. He groaned aloud. "Chewie! You were supposed to find somethin' *valuable*!"

Chewbacca indignantly pointed out that children *were* valuable. "Only if we sell the little darlings as slaves," Han snarled.

Chewie's upper lip drew back, and he snarled, too.

Han raised his hands. "Okay, okay, I was just kidding! You know I'd never deal in slaves! But what are we gonna do with them?"

Chewbacca pointed out that since the buildings were

going to blow up in less than five minutes, now was not a good time to argue about the best course of action.

Han scowled. "Okay, kids. Get on board. C'mon, c'mon. I can rustle up some emergency rations I suppose. . . ."

Two minutes later, the *Falcon* took off, and Han circled once around the Colony. Below him, the buildings blossomed one by one into giant fireballs. After a few hours, there would be nothing left but charred, slagged remains to be re-conquered by the jungle. . . .

Durga, Lord of Besadii, stared down at the Ylesian nightside through the viewport of his yacht in disbelief. Infernoes blossomed, clearly visible from space. The former sites of the colonies were marked by massive forest fires, whipped by the ever-present winds.

There were survivors, Durga knew that. The Nova Force troopers who'd surrendered . . . old Ganar Tos. They'd contacted Durga aboard his yacht from a few portable comm units they'd salvaged. The moment the Hutt yacht achieved orbit, there they were, yammering to be rescued. But of the factories and warehouses . . . nothing was left except burning rubble.

Gone . . . Durga couldn't believe it. Between one day and the next—in a matter of *hours*. . . .

Gone. All gone.

Durga drew a deep breath and thought about the call he'd received only minutes ago from Prince Xizor. A pleasant, reassuring call, reminding Durga that he still owed Black Sun credits, but that in the wake of this disaster, Xizor would be happy to work out payment arrangements. The Black Sun leader had hinted that he'd be pleased to help Besadii rebuild the Ylesian enterprise.

No, thought Durga. *Not again . . .*

For one thing, the Rebels had carried away thousands of Pilgrims, and Xizor's intelligence indicated that they seemed to have found a "cure" for the Exultation addiction. With that many Pilgrims telling the truth about Ylesia, it would be hard to gain new recruits.

And the t'landa Til High Priest whom Zier had recruited had taken one horrified look at the planet, and flatly refused to have anything to do with the whole scheme.

No, Durga thought. *I'll try something else next time.*

And there would be a next time, of course. He'd find another way to make Besadii richer than ever. And if he, Durga, had to serve Prince Xizor, well, then, he would rise to the top of Black Sun.

His immediate goal was to become a Vigo. And after that . . . perhaps he'd challenge Xizor himself. Or even the Emperor. Durga knew he was clever, and he figured he was just as capable of ruling Imperial space as anyone. . . .

Durga glanced down at his one souvenir from this disastrous day. A long, blood-smeared horn. *At least Aruk has been avenged,* he thought. *May he rest in peace. . . .*

The Hutt lord keyed his intercom and his pilot responded immediately. "Arrange for pickup of those mercenary troops," Durga instructed. "And set course for Nal Hutta. I'm done here. Take us home."

"Yes, Your Excellency," the pilot responded.

Durga settled back and sighed. Picking up Teroenza's horn, he stroked it thoughtfully, and began planning for the future. . . .

Han Solo and Chewbacca were still arguing about what to do with the Corellian orphans when they came out of hyperspace six hours later, and their comm system began to beep, signaling an incoming message.

Chewie insisted that they must take the children back to Corellia, so they could be cared for by family. Han protested the waste of fuel and time. "Dump 'em in a spaceport on any civilized world, and someone'll take care of 'em," he argued.

Chewbacca commented that as a father himself, he felt their only course was to take the children back to Corellia.

Han glared at the Wookiee as he activated the comm to receive the incoming message. Jabba the Hutt's image materialized atop the control panel. "Han, my boy!"

"Hello, Jabba," Han said. "What's happening?"

Jabba frowned slightly at the Corellian's lackluster greeting, then the Hutt lord forgot his displeasure. "Han, congratulations to you! The raid was a complete success! I am very pleased!"

"Great," said Han, grimly. "Is that why you made an interstellar call?"

"Oh . . . no, Han," Jabba chuckled. "I have a load of spice I want you to pick up from Moruth Doole on Kessel. Bring it to me immediately on Tatooine, understand? The deal is arranged, the spice is paid for."

"Okay, Jabba," Han said. "My usual cut?"

"Certainly, certainly," Jabba boomed. "And perhaps a nice bonus for quick delivery."

"I'm on my way, Jabba."

"Fine, Han my boy." Jabba peered at the Corellian thoughtfully. "And, Han . . . get some rest afterward. You look a bit haggard, if you don't mind my saying so."

"Right, Jabba," Han said. "Will do."

He broke the connection and scowled. "Great. A load of whiny kids, and I gotta take 'em with me on a

Run. Maybe I oughta consider gettin' out of the smuggling business, Chewie."

Chewbacca's only comment was that while they were on Kessel, they needed to pick up some traladon milk and flatbread for sandwiches.

Han groaned aloud. . . .

Twelve hours later, with the load of spice safely secured in the below-decks smuggling compartments, Han eased the *Falcon* up from Kessel. Leaving Chewie to pass out food to the children, Han headed toward the Maw, checking his course. Suddenly a light flashed on his control board, and he realized that an Imperial customs ship was bearing down on him! "Chewie! Get up here!" he shouted, and began pouring on speed.

Moments later, the Wookiee was in the cockpit. "Strap those blasted kids in!" Han shouted. "Then get up here! We've got two Imps on our tail, and it's gonna be a rough ride!"

"Hrrrrrnnnnn!"

Han sent the *Falcon* hurtling along, faster even than the day he'd raced Salla. As Chewie slipped into the co-pilot's seat, Han heard a muffled squeak behind him, and 'anced back to see a wide-eyed urchin staring at the M...w. "What are *you* doing up here?" Han snapped. *Great, just what I need! A snivelin' kid!*

"Watching," the little boy said.

"Aren't you scared?" Han grunted, flipping the *Falcon* up on her side to avoid a wash of ionized gas from one of the black hole clusters. The Imp vessel shot at him, but it was a clean miss.

Great! Gettin' shot at with these kids here!

"No, sir!" the kid chirped. "This is *neat*! Can you go *faster*?"

"Glad you like it," muttered Han. "Kid, I'm sure gonna try. . . ."

He poured on the speed, skimming past the first of the black hole clusters. Their velocity made everything blur, almost as though they were going into hyperspace. Han had never gone so fast in the *Falcon*. "Whooooo!" he shouted, as they narrowly missed being pulled in by a black hole's gravity well.

"Whooooo!" echoed the kid behind him.

Han began laughing like a maniac as they hurtled along. "Like that, eh, kid? Watch me outrun these Imperial slugs!"

"Go!" yelled the child. "Faster, Captain Solo!"

"What's your name, kid?" Han asked as they came around the last curve of the Maw's terrible gravity wells, sheering so close that the engines strained in protest.

"Kryss P'teska, sir."

"And you like to go fast, eh?"

"Yeah!"

"Okay . . ."

Han threaded his way into the Pit, zipping along, and avoiding the hurtling asteroids by the seat of his pants. He realized that he was gaining on the Imp. The customs ship was barely visible now. . . .

If I can get just a little farther ahead . . .

Sweat gathered on Han's forehead and ran down to sting his eyes, but he never eased up on his speed. The Imperial ship was far behind him now. Han ducked and dodged asteroids, and realized he was nearing the edge of the Pit.

"Great," he grunted. "All we gotta do is get outta here, and then make the jump to lightspeed. . . ."

Chewie suddenly started whining and gesturing frantically at the board. Han looked at his instruments and groaned aloud. "Oh, *blast*! Three Imps out there on the perimeter of the Pit! What else could they be doin' but waitin' for us! And one of 'em is a big sucker!"

Han's mind raced. "Chewie, we ain't gonna be able to outrun these Imps," Han said. "And we're outgunned. But we've lost that guy on our tail, at least for the moment. I think if we can get far enough ahead, we should go ahead and dump the load just inside the Pit—the way you did that time with Colonel Quirt on that other Run. After they've searched the *Falcon* to their hearts content, we come back and retrieve the cargo. Whaddaya say?"

Chewie was in full agreement. "Okay, take over. We gotta do this real fast," Han said. "Here's the coordinates."

"Hrrrrrrnnnnnnnhh!"

Leaving the Wookiee to head for the coordinates he'd selected, Han raced back to the passageway with the secret compartments, with Kryss in hot pursuit. "You kids, give me a hand here," he said, getting out coils of wire. Several of the children assembled and stood there, staring at him. "What're your names?" Han said.

"Cathea, sir," said a young girl of perhaps twelve or thirteen, with a long blond braid of hair. "I'll help."

"I'm Tym," said a small boy.

"I'm Aeron," said a dark-haired child. "I'll help!"

"Good," Han grunted, heaving up the deckplates. "Help me get these barrels carried into the starboard airlock, and we'll wire 'em together."

Within two minutes, the spice was ready to be jettisoned. Han shooed the kids out of the airlock, then closed it firmly behind them. He ignored the standard depressurization procedures, and, using the manual override, forced the outer doors to slide wide apart—blowing the spice barrels out into the void.

"Chewie!" he yelled. "Jettisoned! Log these coordinates!"

With luck, Han should be able to track the spice's progress and find it again after a little searching. The barrels themselves were made of an alloy that would show up on his sensors if he got close enough.

It was the best he could do, under the circumstances.

Han ran back up to the cockpit, and raced back along his course, so he'd emerge from the Pit approximately where they'd be expecting him to. As he headed out of the Pit, the Imp customs ship came hurtling up from behind him. Han looked at Chewie. "That was close."

Han's comm unit began signaling, and he activated it. "Unidentified ship, prepare to be boarded," an angry voice said, just as Han felt the *Falcon* seized by a tractor beam. "This is the Imperial light cruiser *Assessor*. Offer no resistance and you will not be harmed."

Han sat there, with the kids clustering around him in the cockpit, watching as the *Falcon* was drawn toward the big Imperial ship. "Kids, let me do the talkin'," he said.

Moments after docking, the Imperials were at the *Falcon*'s airlock, demanding to be admitted. Han sighed and got up to let them in, with a trail of children tagging along behind him.

The Imperial captain himself was part of the heavily armed boarding party. "Captain Tybert Capucot," the balding man with the supercilious air said, looking at Han as though he were a particularly unappetizing sight. "Captain Solo, you stand in suspicion of smuggling spice from Kessel. I am authorized to search your ship."

Han waved at the interior. "Search away," he said. "I got nothin' to hide."

Capucot sniffed and managed to stare down his nose

at Han—even though the Imperial officer was several centimeters shorter than the Corellian.

The captain beckoned a scanning crew into the ship. "Search every millimeter," he ordered. "I want that spice."

Han shrugged and stepped aside.

The Imperials searched . . . and searched . . . and searched some more. Han and Chewie winced as they heard crashes from the lounge and the aft cargo compartment. "Hey!" Han protested, "I'm just an honest trader! I'm an Imperial citizen, you can't trash my ship like this!"

"Honest trader," Capucot sneered. "If you weren't running spice, then what were you doing?"

Han thought fast. "I was . . . uh . . . well, I was takin' these kids back to Corellia," he said. "You see, there was this big rescue operation on a slave world, and . . . uh . . . well, these kids got left behind. So I brought 'em with me."

The captain glared at Han. "Corellia is *that* way," he said, icily, pointing aft.

Han shrugged. "I had to stop off and buy food. Didn't I, kids?"

"Yes!" lisped little Tym. "We was hungry! Captain Solo saved us!"

"Captain Solo risked his life for us," said Cathea, twirling her long braid. "He's a hero."

"He saved us," Aeron said. "We was gonna get blowed up."

Little Kryss came over and took Han's hand, stood looking up at the Imperial Captain. "Captain Solo is the best pilot in the whole galaxy. He sure can outrun those Imperial sl—"

Han managed to put his hand over the boy's mouth just in time. "Heh," he chuckled, grinning weakly.

"Kids. They say the craziest things. You a family man, Captain?"

Capucot was *not* amused.

Finally the scanning crew returned, not looking pleased. "Sir, we found nothing. We made a thorough search, Captain."

Tybert Capucot's face reddened. He stood there, searching for words, then met Han's gaze. "Very well," he said. "Our brave hero Captain Solo claims that he was taking these children to Corellia. Such a noble act deserves an Imperial escort. Set your course for Corellia, Captain. We will escort you there."

Han opened his mouth, then closed it again. With an effort, he nodded. "Sure. Let's go."

It took him the best part of a day to reach his homeworld. Han raged at the delay in collecting his spice. He knew that if anything happened to it, that Jabba would not be lenient. Business was business, and Hutts did not know the meaning of mercy. . . .

When he reached Corellia, he found that the Imps had broadcast his arrival ahead of them, and there was a media blitz waiting for them. Han and Chewie were congratulated, hailed as heroes, and only the fact that Han had already won the Corellian bloodstripe kept the grateful government of his homeworld from awarding him one.

Han was in a panic to get back to the Pit and his dropped load of spice. Finally he was able to say goodbye to the children—who actually were pretty good kids, he was forced to concede—and head back out, a free citizen.

The Corellian made best possible speed back to the Pit, and to the coordinates where he'd dropped the load of raw glitterstim. He spent the next four hours combing the outer edge of the asteroid field, becoming more and more frantic. "It's *got* to be here!" he exclaimed to Chewie.

But it wasn't.

Han searched for another two hours, using the auxiliary sensor units in the lounge to augment the ones in the cockpit. Suddenly he was interrupted by a roar from Chewbacca in the cockpit. "I'm comin'!" he yelled, racing forward.

Chewie pointed to the sensors showing two blips converging on them rapidly. Han checked the ship IDs and then swore bitterly, smacking his forehead with his hand. "Great! More Imps! That's all I need! Why *me*?"

He dropped into the pilot's seat and reversed course, heading back into the Pit. Chewbacca growled an inquiry, wanting to know why they were running when they had no spice on board anyway.

"Don't you get it?" Han snarled as he increased speed until the asteroids zipped past them in a blur. "They must've found the spice we dumped, and they know what we were searchin' for! You know Capucot didn't believe us . . . he's behind this! These slugs will arrest us on suspicion of smuggling and impound the *Falcon*! We'll never get her back!" He made a hard turn to port to avoid an asteroid the size of an Imp destroyer.

"Besides . . ." he added, "I don't want 'em trashin' the ship again searching her. We just got done cleanin' up the mess Capucot and his boys made."

Together, Han and Chewie sent the *Falcon* streaking back through the Pit, toward the Maw. His pursuers were two Imperial tariff ships, and they followed him with reckless determination.

Han's hands moved over his controls like a man possessed as they skimmed and flipped their way through the treacherous asteroid field. Chewie was howling aloud with terror at the chances his partner was taking. "Shut *up*, fuzzface!" Han yelled. "I gotta concentrate!"

Chewie's howls dropped to moans . . . possibly prayers. Han was too busy to listen.

They were nearing the end of the Pit, heading straight for the Maw. "Chewie, I'm gonna have to shave the belly armor right off the *Falcon*, and hope those Imps won't want to mess with these black holes," Han said, tightly. "Those slugs are *not* givin' up!"

Chewbacca arrrrhhhhhhnnnnned in despair. "I can't help it! They're not getting the *Falcon*!"

The two Imperial ships stuck to the smuggler vessel as though they were hooked by tractor beams. Han and Chewie worked frantically over the *Falcon*'s control board, adjusting their course, speed, direction, shielding. . . .

In desperation, Han sent the *Falcon* closer to the black hole clusters than any sane person would ever go. Only the ship's breakneck speed might save them.

The *Millennium Falcon* skimmed so close to the black holes in the Maw that only her terrible velocity kept her from being captured and sucked in. The watching eyes of the accretion disks seemed to widen and narrow as the *Falcon* soared and swooped in and around the treacherous gravity wells. The Imperial ships hurtled after him at top velocity.

Han did an impossible spin, flip and swoop as he came around toward the last of the Maw. Studying his instruments, Han saw that one of the pursuing Imperial ships, the smaller of the two, hadn't been able to duplicate his maneuver—the ship vanished into the embrace of the black hole's accretion disk with a tiny, ignoble flare.

"Yes!" he said, fiercely. "You're not gettin' me! Not today, not *ever*!"

Now the last Imperial ship was falling behind . . . and the *Falcon* was nearly out of the Maw. "Yes, Chewie! We did it!"

"Arrrrrhhhhhhhhnnn!"

Han sent the *Falcon* hurtling past Kessel, and then, suddenly they were free of the gravity wells. Han hastily bent over the navicomputer, then a moment later, shouted, "Course laid in! Punch it, Chewie!"

Moments later they were safe in hyperspace. Han slumped back in his seat. "That was too close," he muttered, hoarsely.

Chewie agreed.

As he sagged in his seat, Han noticed something. "Hey, Chewie. Look!" He pointed at the instruments. "We set a record!"

Chewie commented bitterly that their speed record had come at the expense of his nerves. Han's eyes narrowed. "Hey, this is weird," he said. "It says we actually shortened the *distance* we traveled, not just the time. Less than twelve parsecs!"

Chewie growled skeptically and rapped on the distance gauge with hairy knuckles, commenting that Han's wild piloting must have caused a short and the gauge was off.

Han argued, but when Chewbacca, short-tempered, snarled at him, he gave up. "Okay, okay, I'm too tired to argue," he said, throwing up his hands.

But I did do it in under twelve parsecs . . . , he thought stubbornly.

But now he had more pressing problems to consider than speed or distance records. What in the universe was he going to tell Jabba?

Chapter Sixteen:

TOPRAWA ... AND MOS EISLEY

Han faced the craggy, scarred holo-image of Bidlo Kwerve, Jabba the Hutt's Corellian majordomo. Behind Kwerve he could see the sand-colored walls of the Hutt Lord's desert palace on Tatooine. "Hey, Kwerve," Han said, "let me speak to the boss, please."

The ugly Corellian thug had jet-black hair with a vivid white stripe running through it, and vivid green eyes. Kwerve smiled, a small and nasty smile. "Hey, it's Solo," he said. "Jabba's been callin' you. Where you been, Solo?"

"Here and there," Han said, shortly. He didn't like being played with. "Ran into a bit of trouble with the Imps."

"Well, that's too bad," Kwerve said. "Let me see if I can get Jabba to talk to you. Last time I knew, he was pretty ticked 'cause you're overdue with that cargo. He's got some plans for that spice."

Han stared stonily into the comm. "Just patch me through, Kwerve, and stuff the jokes."

"Oho, who said I was jokin', Solo?"

The Corellian majordomo's scarred visage disappeared in a wash of static, and for a moment Han thought he'd cut the transmission. He reached out to break the connection himself, when the static was suddenly gone, replaced by Jabba's massive holo-image. "Jabba!" Han blurted, in mingled relief and trepidation. "Hey, listen . . . I got a little problem."

Jabba did not look happy. He was smoking some brown substance that roiled around in the combination hookah and snackquarium he'd inherited from the dead Jiliac, and his huge pupils were dilated from the drug.

Great, Han thought. *I had to call when he was spiced. . . .*

"Uh, hey, Jabba," he said. "It's me, Han."

Jabba blinked several times and finally managed to focus. "Han!" boomed the leader of Desilijic. "Where have you *been*? I was expecting you here last week!"

"Uh, well, Jabba, that's what I called to tell you about," Han said. "Listen . . . it's not my fault. . . ."

Jabba blinked muzzily. "Han, my boy . . . what are you saying? Where is my load of glitterstim?"

The Corellian swallowed. "Uh, yeah, about that load, Jabba. Well, you see . . . it was almost like they'd set a trap for me! The Imps were waitin' and they—"

"The customs officials have my spice?" Jabba roared, so loudly and suddenly that Han couldn't help flinching back. "How *could* you, Solo?"

"No! No, no, Jabba!" Han cried. "They didn't get it! Honest, they've got nothin' on you, nothin'! But . . . in order to keep the customs guys from finding it, I had to dump it. I marked it, but they wouldn't let me go right away. And when I went back for it . . . it was gone, Jabba."

"My spice is gone," Jabba said, staring blearily at Han, his voice ominously quiet.

"Uh . . . yeah. But, hey, Jabba, don't worry. I'll make it up to you, I promise. Me and Chewie will work it off, we'll pay you the value, don't worry. You know we're good for it. And honest, Jabba, I got a feelin' I was set up, you know? How many people besides you and Moruth Doole knew I was goin' on a Run?"

Jabba ignored Han's question. His bulbous eyes blinked rapidly as he took several puffs on the hookah. Then, reaching out, he grabbed a wriggler from the liquid-filled globe and stuffed the squirming thing into his mouth.

"Han . . . Han, my boy, you know I love you like a son," he said slowly, portentously. "But business is business, and you've broken my primary rule. I can't make exceptions just because I am fond of you. That load cost me twelve thousand four hundred credits. Deliver the spice or the credits to me within ten days, or face the consequences."

Han wet his lips. "Ten days . . . but, Jabba—"

The connection was abruptly broken. Han sagged back in his pilot's seat, wrung out. *What am I gonna do?*

Six days later, having tried and failed to scrape up the credits from some of the sentients who owed him money, Han went back to Nar Shaddaa. He hated to do it, but he was going to have to borrow the credits from friends.

He discovered that someone involved in that nightmare Run . . . some Imp officer, or trooper . . . had evidently talked about what had happened. His fellow smugglers regarded him with a mixture of awe and trepidation.

Awe because he'd set a new record for the Run, trepidation because the news was out—Jabba was displeased, most displeased, with his former favorite pilot.

Shug was off-planet, and Han cursed when he discovered that the master tech was gone. He knew Shug was good for that much, though it would strain his resources.

Han made the rounds, managed to pick up a couple of thousand credits by calling in some old favors. But news of what had happened to some of the captains on Ylesia had spread, and several people simply looked the other way when Han approached.

Han finally went to Lando's place. He didn't want to, but he was out of options.

He knocked on the door, and heard the gambler's sleepy voice from inside. "Who is it?"

"Lando, it's me," he called. "Han."

The Corellian heard steps, then suddenly Lando jerked the door open. Before Han could utter a single word, the gambler's fist lashed out in a vicious suckerpunch, catching Han in the jaw and sending him flying back across the hallway. The Corellian slammed into the wall, then slid down, landing on his rear.

Han grabbed his jaw, spots dancing before his eyes, struggling to speak. Lando loomed over him. "You have got to have the most colossal nerve in the entire galaxy, coming here after what you pulled on Ylesia!" he yelled. "You're lucky I don't just shoot you, you lousy, lowlife, double-crosser!"

"Lando . . ." Han managed to croak, "I swear, I didn't know what she was plannin'. I swear. . . ."

"Right," Lando sneered. "*Sure* you didn't!"

"Would I have come here like this if I wasn't innocent?" Han mumbled. His jaw wasn't working very well. He could feel it swelling. "Lando . . . she did it to me, too. I didn't get nothin' from that trip. Nothin'!"

"I don't believe you," Lando said, coldly. "But if I did, I'd say, 'good!' You two deserve each other!"

"Lando," Han said, "I lost a load of spice I was carryin' for Jabba. I'm desperate, buddy. I need to borrow—"

"*What?*" Lando grabbed Han's jacket in both hands and yanked the pilot to his feet. He slammed the Corellian against the wall. The gambler's dark face was barely a handsbreadth from Han's. "You came here to ask me for a *loan?*"

Han managed to nod. "I'm good for it . . . honest. . . ."

"Get this through your head, Solo," Lando snarled. "We've been friends in the past, so I'm not going to do what you so richly deserve and blow your head off. But don't *ever* come near me again!"

Slamming Han against the wall one more time, Lando let the Corellian go. Han slid down the wall again, as Lando stormed back into his flat. The door banged shut, and Han heard the lock click.

Slowly, painfully, Han got to his feet. His jaw was throbbing, and he tasted blood.

Well, that's that, he thought, staring at the closed door. *Now what?*

"We're not going to get out of here, are we?"

Commander Bria Tharen ignored the barely audible question as she ducked down behind the pile of rubble and ejected the spent power pak from her blaster. Or tried to. The pak was jammed. Looking at her weapon, she saw that the constant firing from the past few minutes of battle had fused the power connectors together, making it impossible to remove the empty pak.

She swore under her breath, and crawled over to the body next to her. Jace Paol's features were frozen into an expression of tight, concentrated anger. He'd died fighting, the way he would have wanted to go. Grabbing his weapon, she eased it out from beneath his body, but before she had it all the way out, she saw the barrel was fused. It was as useless as her own.

Glancing over at the pitiful remains of Red Hand Squadron, Bria said, "Anyone who can, give me cover. I've got to scrounge me up something to shoot with."

Joaa'n nodded and gave her a thumbs-up. "Ready, Commander. I don't see anything moving out there at the moment."

"Okay," Bria said. Tossing the useless weapon aside, the Rebel commander peered carefully over the rubble, then stealthily slid around to the side, out from behind her cover. She didn't bother getting to her feet, not sure that her wounded leg would support her. Instead, she scuttled forward on hands and knees, keeping low, through the ragged hole in the outside wall of the half-destroyed Imperial comm center where they were making their last stand.

A few meters away, an Imperial trooper lay, a hole still smoldering in his breastplate.

Quickly, Bria crawled over and stripped the dead man of his weapon and spare power paks, noting wryly that the trooper must have used all his grenades before he'd been shot. *Too bad . . . I could have made good use of a couple of grenades. . . .*

Bria thought about taking the man's body armor, but it hadn't done him any good, had it?

Here, outside the remains of the Imperial comm center on the restricted world of Toprawa, she could hear better. And breathe better, too. The stench of battle was replaced by a cool night breeze. Bria crouched behind a fallen block of permacrete, daring to pull off her helmet for a second, then wipe her grimy face. She sighed with pleasure as the gentle breeze cooled her sweaty hair. The last time she'd felt a cool, pleasant breeze like that had been on Togoria. . . .

Where are you, Han? she wondered, as she often did. *What are you doing right now?*

She wondered if Han would ever know what had become of her. Would he care if he did? Did he hate her now? She hoped not, but she would never know. . . .

Bria thought about that day on Ylesia, and wished things could have been different. Yet . . . if she'd had it to do over again, would she have done things any differently?

She smiled sadly. *Probably not. . . .*

The credits she'd raised had come in handy, and had led directly to this assignment. Torbul and the other Rebel leaders had sent intelligence units to infiltrate Ralltiir, and they'd discovered that the Empire was shipping vital plans for its new secret weapon to its records center on Toprawa.

Torbul had been straight with her when he'd discussed the mission, using terms like, "recovery iffy," and "expendable."

Bria had known what she was getting into, but she'd volunteered Red Hand Squadron anyway. She knew they needed the best for this job, and she was confident her people could deliver.

And they had. . . .

This was the biggest anti-Imperial offensive of the Resistance so far, a coordinated offensive assigned to transmit the plans for the latest Imperial secret weapon. Bria didn't know all the details, but her assignment had been to seize this Imperial comm center on Toprawa and hold it, while the comm techs transmitted the stolen plans to a Rebel courier ship . . . a Corellian corvette that would "accidentally" pass through this highly restricted star system.

When Torbul told Bria that the Rebel Alliance needed volunteers to accompany the intelligence team to Toprawa, to hold off the Imps while the comm techs did their job, Bria hadn't hesitated before volunteering. "Red Hand will go, sir," she said. "We can handle it."

She looked out across the plaza, seeing the carnage of war reflected dimly in the streetlights. Bodies, over-turned ground-cars, wrecked speeders . . . the place was a mess.

Bria thought about Ylesia, reflecting that place had been an even bigger mess . . . and she was proud that she had some responsibility for that. Glancing up at the sky, she thought about *Retribution*. They'd lost contact with her, and Bria feared the worst.

Time to get back to work, she thought, and crawled back into the wrecked comm center.

Hearing the deep thrum of heavy repulsorlift units behind her, Bria sheltered behind the wall and peered out. Looking up, she saw the faint glint of light from the armor of a massive rectangular object floating above the permacrete of the ruined plaza. The Imperial heavy armor, one of the "Floating Fortress" class units, settled down into a covered position behind the remains of the communications and sensor tower, obviously getting ready for yet another assault on Red Hand Squadron . . . or what was left of it.

Bria scrambled backward, crawling quickly, to pass the word to her remaining troops.

"Listen up, people," she said, to the survivors—so few!—who were sheltering behind the barricade. She began passing out the power paks, dividing them up equally. "They're coming again. We've got to look sharp, hold them off as long as possible."

They didn't talk, just nodded, and prepared to go to work. Bria was proud of them. Professionals. Dedicated professionals.

It won't be long now, she thought, finding a good spot for herself behind the barricade. "People . . ." she said aloud, "has everyone got their lullaby?"

Murmured assents. Bria checked her own. She'd stuck the tiny pill to the collar of her fatigues, so that all she had to do was turn her head and stick her tongue out to get it. You never knew if your arms would be working, after all.

Come on, she thought to the Imperials. *It's rude to keep us waiting.*

What the Imps didn't know was that they were already too late. Red Hand had managed to hold the Imperial reaction force at the outer perimeter while the Rebel comm techs transmitted the plans to the courier vessel. It had been close; the Imps had chopped the comm/sensor tower in half just seconds after the transmission had ended—but Bria had seen the acknowledgment from *Tantive IV* with her own eyes. "Transmission complete."

Bria had also seen, before the sensors were cut off, the image of an Imperial Star Destroyer closing in on the Rebel Blockade Runner. Had that courier gotten away? She'd never know. . . .

Bria wondered exactly what they'd been transmitting, but knew she'd never know that, either. As it was, she and her people knew too much . . . that's why they couldn't risk being taken alive.

Not that the Imperials seem inclined to take prisoners anyway today, she thought.

As she bent down to check the bandage around her thigh, the trooper next to her voiced the same quiet question she'd refused to answer earlier. "We're not going to get out of here . . . are we?"

Bria looked at him, pale under his battered helmet, his eyes wide and staring. Sk'kot was a good trooper, loyal to her, loyal to their cause. But he was so young. . . .

Still, he deserved a straight answer.

"No, we're not, Sk'kot," Bria replied. "You know that. The Imps have destroyed our ships. No retrieval. And even if we didn't have orders to hold this comm center for as long as possible, there's nowhere for us to go on this world. Even if we could get past the troopers . . . we've got no transport." She gave him a wry grin, and gestured at her wounded leg. "I'd look really silly trying to hop out of here, wouldn't I?"

He nodded, and his face twisted with anguish.

She looked at him closely. "Sk'kot . . . we can't be captured. You understand that, right?"

He nodded again, then took out his lullaby and stuck it to his collar, the way Bria had. "Yeah, Commander. I understand." His voice was shaking, but his hands on his weapon were steady.

He leaned closer to her, not wanting the others to hear. "Commander . . . I . . . I don't want to die." His admission seemed to drain him, and he trembled.

"Help me with this bandage, would you, Sk'kot?" she said, motioning for him to tighten the medpac tighter on her leg. The kid's hands steadied a bit as he pulled on the straps binding it to her wound. "Tighter!" she told him, and he leaned back, putting his weight into it. A jolt of pain got though to Bria, past the painkillers that let her move about despite her injury.

"There, that's got it."

Young Burrid sagged down next to her. Bria put her

arm around him, as she would a brother she loved, and leaned close to him.

"I don't want to die either, Sk'kot. But I sure as blazes don't want the Empire to win. I don't want good people massacred, or taken as slaves, or taxed until they can't feed their families or live a decent life. Or just murdered by some Imperial Moff who woke up cranky that morning."

Sk'kot smiled slightly at her turn of phrase. "So it's okay that we're not going to get out of here, right, Sk'kot? It's okay that we're going to go down doing our jobs, because they—" she jerked her chin at their dead comrades, "did theirs. We can't let them down, right?"

"Right, Commander," Sk'kot said. Bria hugged him tight, with a small, sad smile, and he returned it. He'd stopped shaking.

Just then, Joaa'n, keeping lookout, called, "They're moving out there."

Bria rolled aside, pushing Sk'kot toward his position. She looked quickly between two pieces of rubble, and without taking her eyes off the opening, issued orders. "Joaa'n, you stay down at first and get your launcher ready. After the rest of us open up, try to duck out and nail that Floating Fortress. Got that?"

"Yes, Commander!"

"People, remember to change positions after shooting, or they'll zero in on you with the repeating blasters. Everyone ready?"

Murmured affirmatives answered her. Picking up her borrowed blaster carbine, Bria checked the charge. Sighting down the barrel, she thought, *Goodbye, Han. . . .*

Something moved in the breached wall. Bria took a deep breath. "Open fire!"

• • •

Tatooine is such a dump, Han thought, as he and Chewie made their way along the night-dark back streets. *Jalus Nebl was so right. . . .*

The two smugglers had arrived just hours ago. Han had decided that the only way to approach Jabba for more time to pay off the dumped load of spice was to talk to him in person. But things weren't looking too promising. So far he'd been unable to reach Jabba on the comm to request an audience. And back in Docking Bay 94 where the *Falcon* was berthed, he'd encountered that dumb Rodian, Greedo, nosing around. The fool had tried to shake Han down for a payoff, implying that Jabba had taken a bounty out on the Corellian.

As if echoing Han's thoughts, Chewbacca observed quietly that word was out on the streets that the Rodian kid, Greedo, was hanging around in the company of a has-been bounty hunter, one Warhog Goa.

Han snorted. "Chewie, you know as well as I do that Jabba's just sendin' us a little message, hirin' that dumb thug, Greedo. If Jabba really wanted me dead, he'd hire somebody competent to do the job. Greedo's so stupid he couldn't find his behind with both hands and laser-torch."

"Hrrrrrrrnnnnnn . . ." Chewbacca also had a low opinion of the Rodian.

Han had a few spare credits, and he'd decided to check out the local games of chance. Maybe he could win enough credits to make a substantial downpayment that would satisfy Jabba for the moment, then he could concentrate on scraping up the rest of the credits. . . .

They walked into The Krayt Dragon Lounge, and stood looking around. Over in the corner, sure enough, there was a sabacc game in progress.

As Han and Chewie approached, the Corellian looked more closely at one of the players, a slender man with red hair and regular features. "Hey!" Han exclaimed. "Small universe! How are you, Dash?"

Dash Rendar looked up, gave the Corellian a wary smile. "Hey, Solo! Hey, Chewbacca! Long time no see. What's this I hear about some caper on Ylesia?"

Han groaned aloud. Dash Rendar gestured to empty seats, and Han and Chewie took them. "Deal me in, gentles," Han said, digging out a handful of credits. "Chewie, you wanna play?"

The Wookiee shook his head, and wandered off to the bar in search of liquid refreshment. Han glanced at Rendar. "Hey, Dash, where'd you hear about the Ylesian raid?" After the way people had treated him on Nar Shaddaa, it felt good to run into someone he knew who was still speaking to him.

"Oh, I ran into Zeen Afit and Katya M'Buele last week, and they told me," Rendar said, dealing cardchips. "They said their group of Rebels treated them square, but the ones you had thrown in with stiffed everyone. That true?"

Han nodded. "Yep. True. They stiffed *me*, too, but nobody will believe me." He scowled. "But I ain't lyin' when I say it. Jabba's on the verge of takin' out a real bounty on me, 'cause I can't pay him what I owe."

Rendar shrugged. "Tough luck," he said. "Personally, I make it a policy never to get mixed up with those Rebel groups."

"Well, that's always been my policy, too," Han said. "But this seemed like such a sweet deal. . . ."

"Yeah, Katya and Zeen were real happy, throwing credits around like they were bantha fodder," Rendar said.

They'd only been playing for a few minutes, and Han

was losing, when he felt a tug on his sleeve. He looked down to see a little Chadra-Fan standing there. "Huh?"

She squeaked at him, and Han frowned. He wasn't too good with her language.

"Kabe says there's someone outside wants to see you," Rendar translated.

Jabba! Jabba finally got my messages and wants to see me, Han thought. *He's sent someone to bring me to him. Now I can talk to him, smooth things over. . . .*

Han tossed in his card-chips and stood up, motioning to Chewie to finish off his drink. "Okay, deal me out on this hand. I might be back later."

With one hand on the grip of his blaster, Han and the Wookiee followed the street urchin out the back door, into the alley. They stood there for a second, looking around, but saw no one.

Suddenly Chewie whirled. "Rrrrrhhhhh!"

It's a trap! Han realized at the same moment.

The Corellian's hand dropped to his weapon, but before he could draw, he heard an all-too-familiar voice. "Freeze, Solo. Drop the blaster. And tell the Wook that if he moves, you're both dead meat. I'd like another Wook scalp for my collection."

"Chewie!" Han spoke sharply to the snarling Wookiee. "Don't move!" Slowly, Han drew his blaster, let it drop from his fingers into the dusty alley.

"Both of you turn around. Slowly."

The Corellian and the Wookiee obeyed.

Boba Fett stood there, in the dim recesses of the backstreet. Han knew that he was a dead man. Jabba must've decided to hire a *real* bounty hunter to make sure the job got done right. Han tensed, but Fett didn't fire. Instead his artificially filtered voice reached the Corellian. "Relax, Solo. I'm not here for a bounty."

Han didn't relax, only watched in wonderment as

Fett tossed Kabe a credit. The urchin scampered forward and caught it, then vanished into the dimness, chittering happily.

"You're not here for a bounty?" Han said.

"Hhhhhuuuhhhh?" echoed Chewie, as amazed as his partner.

"Jabba told Greedo there was a bounty on you," Fett said. "But he's just using that idiot to keep you on your toes. A reminder that he's serious about you paying up. If Jabba really wanted you dead, you know who he'd hire."

"Yeah," Han said. "You got a point." He hesitated. "So . . . why *are* you here?"

"I landed an hour ago," Fett said. "I made someone a promise, and I always keep my word."

Han frowned. "What are you talking about, Fett?"

"She's dead," Boba Fett said. "I promised her a while back that if she died, I'd tell her father, so he wouldn't spend his life wondering what had happened to her. But she never got around to telling me his name. So I decided to tell you, so you can send Tharen a message."

"Dead?" Han whispered, through stiff lips. "Bria?"

"Yes."

Han felt as though he'd been gut-punched. Chewie made a soft sound of sympathy, and put a hairy hand on his friend's shoulder. Han stood there for a long moment, trying to deal with all the conflicting emotions. Grief was uppermost in his mind. Grief and regret. . . .

"Dead," he repeated, dully. "How did you find out?"

"I have access to Imperial datanets. Bria Tharen died thirty-six hours ago. The Imperials have a confirmed ID on her body. Her squadron was playing rear guard during some intelligence operation."

Han swallowed. *Don't tell me she died for nothing!* "Did they attain their objective?"

"I don't know," the mechanical voice said. "Someone has to tell her father, Solo. I gave her my word . . . and I always keep my word."

Han nodded dully. "I'll do it," he said. "Renn Tharen knows me." *This is gonna hit him hard.* . . . He swallowed, and it hurt his chest. Chewie whined softly.

"Good," Fett said, and the bounty hunter took a step back into the shadows. A moment later, Han and Chewie were alone. Slowly, the Corellian reached down and retrieved his blaster. Memories of Bria assailed him. . . .

Did you think of me, honey? he wondered. *I hope it was quick and painless.* . . .

Han's steps came slowly as he and Chewbacca turned and walked to the mouth of the alley, and then turned onto the street. He had to find someone who'd let him use a comm unit . . . he had a very important message to send. . . .

Epilogue

The next day, Han made his way through the baking streets of Mos Eisley spaceport, wishing he'd worn a short-sleeved shirt instead of his grimy white one with his battered old black pilot's vest. Within ten minutes of being out on the street, he had three different sentients come up to him, each with a warning that Greedo was out looking for him.

Han nodded, thanked each of the informants, flipped each of them a decicred. It never hurt to have good contacts. . . .

The midday glare was painful to human eyes, and Han squinted as he walked. *There are a lot of Imp stormtroopers out,* he thought, watching several squads trot by. *Wonder why?*

The sight of the blaster rifles they carried made him

think of Fett and last night. After leaving the bounty hunter, Han had found a bar owner who'd allowed the Corellian to use his comm unit, in return for a couple of credits.

The Corellian had carefully recorded a message to Renn Tharen. It had been hard to know what to say. In the end, he'd settled for: "Sir, this is Han Solo. I know you remember me. I have some bad news for you, sir. Bria is dead. She died bravely, though. You can be proud of her. She didn't want you to always wonder, so she asked someone to give you the message. Sir, I'm sorry. . . . I know she loved you. Han Solo out. . . ."

Han took a deep breath, and said his own, silent, farewell to Bria Tharen. *Rest in peace, Bria,* he thought. *Goodbye, babe. . . .*

He reminded himself that Bria was part of the past. There was no use dwelling on painful memories. *I have to concentrate on the present. . . .*

Today he needed to see Jabba, that was for sure. And he had to find some work. Any work. . . .

He knew that Chewie was probably over at Chalmun's Cantina. Chalmun was some kind of distant relative of Chewie's, along with half of Kashyyyk. . . .

Han headed over to Chalmun's. Even at this midday hour, Chalmun's was bound to be jumping. Han could hear the jizz band tootling away as he approached the entrance.

Inside, it was dim, and comparatively cool. Han took a deep breath, scenting intoxicants from a dozen worlds. He walked down the steps, nodding at Wuher, the sour, ugly bartender. Wuher jerked his head to his right, and Han reflexively looked over that way. Chewbacca was heading purposefully toward him.

The Wookiee was plainly excited and pleased about

something. He stopped Han by the entrance and conferred with his partner in low-voiced grunts and moans.

Han tilted his head sideways, and peered past the Wookiee at two humans who were standing at the bar. "A charter?" he said. "Well, hey, that's better than nothing! Good work, Chewie! Is that them? That old guy in the Jawa robe, and that kid in the moisture farmer's outfit?"

Chewie nodded, commenting that even though the old man looked harmless, he'd dealt effectively with Doctor Evazan and Ponda Baba just moments before—and used a most unusual weapon to do it.

Han frowned, impressed. "Pulled a lightsaber, you say? Huh. I didn't know anyone still had them. Okay, I'll work out the details with the old guy and the kid. You take 'em over to that empty booth and I'll join you in a second."

Han paused for a moment to check out Chalmun's as Chewbacca ushered their prospective customers over to the corner table. *Good. No sign of Greedo. . . .*

Then he started across the crowded cantina, where Chewie, the old man, and the boy sat waiting. . . .

THE BEGINNING . . .

ABOUT THE AUTHOR

Ann C. Crispin is the bestselling author of more than sixteen books, including four *Star Trek* novels and her original *StarBridge* science fiction series.

Her first appearance in the *Star Wars* universe came when her friend Kevin Anderson asked her to write two short stories for the *Star Wars* anthologies, *Tales from the Mos Eisley Cantina* and *Tales from Jabba's Palace*.

Ann has been a full-time writer since 1983 and currently serves as Eastern Regional Director of the Science Fiction and Fantasy Writers of America. She is a frequent guest at science fiction conventions, where she often teaches writing workshops.

She lives in Maryland with her son, Jason, five cats, a German shepherd, two Appaloosas, and Michael Capobianco, a writer of hard sf. In her spare time (what's that?) she enjoys horseback riding, sailing, camping, and reading books she didn't write.